FOR REASONS UNKNOWN

Michael Wood is a freelance journalist and proofreader living in Sheffield. As a journalist he has covered many crime stories throughout Sheffield, gaining first-hand knowledge of police procedure. He also reviews books for CrimeSquad, a website dedicated to crime fiction.

MICHAEL WOOD

For Reasons Unknown

KILLER
READS

an imprint of HarperCollins*Publishers*
www.harpercollins.co.uk

Killer Reads
An imprint of HarperCollins*Publishers*
1 London Bridge Street
London SE1 9GF

www.harpercollins.co.uk

This paperback edition 2015

First published in Great Britain by
HarperCollins*Publishers* 2015

A catalogue record for this book is
available from the British Library

ISBN: 978 0 00 815867 5

Set in Minion by Born Group using Atomik ePublisher from Easypress
Printed and bound by CPI Group (UK) Ltd, Croydon, CR0 4YY

MIX
Paper from
responsible sources
FSC™ C007454

To Mum
Thank you. For everything, thank you.

Prologue

It could have been any sitting room in any house throughout the country but it wasn't. It was a room in the middle of South Yorkshire Police HQ, designed to give a relaxed, homely atmosphere. From the outside, it looked friendly and inviting, but if walls could talk they would tell a different story. Here, parentless children were comforted; victims of rape and sexual abuse were given tea and sympathy; and elderly victims of brutal crimes were consoled by fresh-faced WPCs with soothing tones and a never-ending supply of tissues.

Sitting on the floor was a blond, blue-eyed eleven-year-old boy dressed in a grey tracksuit that didn't belong to him. He was surrounded by blank sheets of paper and an array of wax crayons, coloured pencils, and felt-tip pens. Squatting next to him was a young PC, who, against orders from his superiors, had not changed out of uniform.

The door opened and in walked Dr Sally McCartney. Unlike the PC, she had softened her appearance. Gone were the severe ponytail and conservative jacket. She had removed her glasses and suffered the anxiety of touching her eyes to put in contact lenses. She shot the PC a look of indignation. He could have at least taken off his uniform jacket.

'Hello Jonathan,' she said. The young boy didn't look up from his drawings. 'My name is Sally. I've come to have a chat with you if that's all right?'

He continued to scribble on the paper. Sally McCartney knelt down to his level and looked over his shoulder. He had drawn a house and was colouring in a large tree next to it.

'Is this your house?'

Jonathan nodded.

'It's very nice. That's a lovely tree too. Do you climb it?' No reply. 'Which room is yours?'

He pointed to the top right window with the blue curtains, then went back to colouring in the tree.

'Is the room next to yours your brother's?'

He nodded again.

'Jonathan, we've been looking for your brother but we can't seem to find him. Do you know where he might be?'

Jonathan stopped drawing and looked up as if in thought. He looked across to Dr McCartney and fixed her with an expressionless stare, then returned his attention back to his drawing.

'Jonathan, we need to find your brother. It's very important. Do you know any of his friends?'

The door opened and Detective Sergeant Pat Campbell popped her head into the room. She looked haggard, having been on duty for more than twenty hours. She signalled for Dr McCartney to join her in the corridor.

'Why didn't that PC change out of his bloody uniform as I told him to?' Sally asked before the DS could speak.

'I don't know. He should have done.' The DS sighed and looked to the ceiling. 'Has the boy said anything?'

'Not yet.'

'It is paramount we find his brother.'

'I heard that his mother was still alive. How is she?'

'I don't know where you heard that from. Both parents were pronounced dead at the scene. They were hacked to death.'

'Jesus. Well he doesn't need to know any of that. Not now at any rate.'

'We've managed to locate a relative in Newcastle. She's coming straight down, but it'll be a few hours before she gets here. Look, whatever happened in that house, he saw it, or at least heard it, and I need to know.'

'I'm aware of that.'

Pat Campbell looked over the doctor's shoulder, through the narrow glass window in the door, and into the room at the young boy drawing as if nothing extraordinary had happened. 'How does he seem?'

'He's in a complete shutdown, which isn't uncommon. When it comes to anything traumatic sometimes our brain takes time to come to terms with it and until it does, it shuts down. It's a self-preservation thing.'

'So he'll soon come out of . . . whatever this is, and be able to tell us what happened?'

'In theory, yes.'

'Why only in theory?'

'Depending on what he saw his brain may not want him to remember.'

'Bloody hell,' Campbell said, leaning back against the wall for support. 'What's with the drawings?'

'It's a way of helping young children process what they've witnessed. Whatever they draw is usually an indication of what's going on in their heads. Hopefully it will help to understand what went on in that house, and then we can take our therapy from there.'

'And what's he drawn so far?'

'He's drawn his house with a tree next to it.'

'Does that tell you anything significant?'

'Not yet,' she half smiled. 'It's early days. He's clearly looking at what happened from the outside. If his next drawing is also a house, I'll ask him about the inside and see what he draws when I talk about the rooms in the house.'

Pat shook her head. 'My God, the mind is a powerful thing isn't it? I don't envy your job.'

There was nothing the doctor could say to that. There were times she didn't envy her job either. 'Is there any chance of getting him in some of his own clothes? That sodding tracksuit stinks.'

'I'll get something brought over from the house.'

'And how about a glass of milk and some chocolate?'

'Whatever you want.'

'Thank you.'

She turned and went back into the room. Jonathan had drawn two adults, a child, and was currently on a second child: his family. Dr McCartney bent down next to him and watched him draw in the details: the hair, the clothes, the eyes, the smiles. He then picked up a red felt-tip and with a forceful action that caused the doctor and PC to jump, he scribbled all over the picture. He didn't stop until his mother, father, and brother were completely covered in blood.

4

Chapter 1

Twenty years later

Matilda Darke had been looking forward to this day for nine months. In that time she had been through a painful miasma of emotions; from a deep depression where she wanted to spend the rest of her life under the duvet, to mild hysteria where tears would flow like a swollen river for no apparent reason. Now, after a long course of Cognitive Behavioural Therapy, weekly sessions with a psychologist, and popping antidepressants as if they were about to be rationed, she was back to her fighting best, she told herself.

It was the first Monday in December. She'd woken two hours before the alarm, to a freezing cold house. The central heating had failed to switch on, and, according to the digital thermometer on her windowsill, it was minus four degrees outside. It wasn't much warmer inside.

She showered longer than usual, until the blood in her veins thawed and was flowing around her body once more, then forced down a breakfast of black coffee and two slices of granary toast. Chewing was a chore. Part of her was excited to return to work, hold her head up high and show the world she was still a force to be reckoned with. Another part of her was crying inside and longing for the security of her duvet.

Her three-year-old Ford Focus stuttered in the cold but didn't take too long to warm up. It was as if it knew she wanted a smooth ride with no trouble on her first day back.

The twenty-minute journey went without a hitch, and she was soon turning into the familiar car park. She took a deep breath, allowed herself a little smile, and turned left to her usual parking space.

Matilda quickly slammed on the brakes and gripped the steering wheel tightly. Her heart beat rapidly in her chest and the prickly sensation of an oncoming panic attack rose up the back of her neck.

'Walpole, Compton, Pelham, Newcastle, Devonshire,' she whispered under her breath.

She looked ahead at the brand-new black Audi in her parking space. Who did it belong to? Had the owner not been informed of her return? She had a lump in her throat that was hard to swallow. Suddenly she didn't think coming back was such a good idea.

Fifteen minutes later, after finding an empty parking space at the back of the building, she was sitting on an uncomfortable chair, the padding in the seat dangling out, waiting to be called into her boss's office.

She looked around the small anteroom at the cheap framed prints on the walls. There was a tall vase of plastic flowers in the corner; each fake petal had a thick layer of dust, dulling the lively colours to a pathetic grey. There was a sharp smell of pine disinfectant in the air, which itched at the back of her throat.

The light above the door turned from red to green.

'Shit,' she said to herself. 'Here we go.'

She stood up and straightened her new navy trouser suit. It was the first item of clothing she'd bought in over a year, and it had been an unwelcome surprise to find she'd gone up a dress size. She ran her fingers through her dark blonde hair, neatly trimmed only last week. Matilda was forty-one years old, and felt like she was about to enter the head teacher's office to be told off for cheating on her maths test.

Before pushing down the door handle she looked at her hands; they were shaking. This was not a good sign.

'Oh my goodness, look at you.' Every word was said as if a sentence of its own. It was highly unprofessional, but Assistant Chief Constable Valerie Masterson leapt up from behind her over-sized desk and took Matilda in a tight embrace. 'Sit yourself down. I have a pot of coffee just made.'

They sat at opposite sides of the desk, which dwarfed the slight frame of the ACC. They examined each other in silence for a long minute.

To Matilda, Valerie looked much older than her fifty-three years. She was thinner than the last time they'd met, and she had more wrinkles, as if she had a slow puncture. Matilda briefly wondered if Valerie was thinking similar negative remarks about her; *Can she tell I've put on weight. Is my hair a mess? Have I aged much?*

'You're looking very well,' Valerie lied convincingly.

'Thank you. I feel well,' Matilda lied back.

Valerie Masterson, a caffeine addict, did not like the black goo that came out of the vending machines dotted around the police station, so had her own personal Gaggia in her office. She poured them both a medium-sized cup, white with one sugar for herself and, remembering, black for Matilda.

'So, your first day back. Are you ready for this?'

'I really am. I want to put this past year behind me and get back to normal as quickly as possible.'

'I'm sure you do. Unfortunately, I can't return you to active duty just yet.'

The painted-on smile suddenly fell from Matilda's face. 'Why not? We discussed on the phone last week . . . '

'What I mean is that I have to adhere to the conditions laid out in your psychiatric report.'

'My what?'

Valerie leaned forward and pulled a brown folder from deep within her in tray. She took out the five-page report and began skimming through it.

Matilda was itching to lean across the desk, snatch the report from her, and find out what that belittling therapist had been saying about her.

'Now there's no need to worry. I don't know any of the details of your sessions with Dr Warminster. Those, as you know, are private. However, Dr Warminster was asked to submit a report before you returned to work; giving her opinion on your readiness and the level of workload you would be able to cope with.'

'She's not happy with me returning to full-time duty?' Beneath the desk Matilda screwed her hands into tight fists, her fingernails digging hard into her palms. Her knuckles were white. The pain ran up her arms and she could almost feel the instant relief.

'Not at all. She has written a glowing report. She admires your courage and your recovery.' The ACC smiled.

Was that a genuine smile or was it forced? There was no wrinkling around the eyes to express a sincere smile, but then there wasn't much room on her face for more wrinkles. Matilda chastised herself for letting her mind wander. 'But . . . '

'She just doesn't think you should be running a major department straightaway. She recommends you be eased back into work slowly, and I tend to agree.'

'Is this a cosy way of telling me I'm being demoted?' Throughout her nine months away, one of the main issues on Matilda's mind was being stripped of the Detective Chief Inspector title she had worked so hard to achieve.

'You are not being demoted Matilda. You are one of South Yorkshire's leading DCIs. You're well known for your work and dedication. But I can't have you handling a major investigation until all parties concerned know you are ready to do so.'

'All parties?'

'You, me, Dr Warminster, the Chief Constable. We are all behind you one hundred per cent.'

Newcastle, Bute, Grenville, Rockingham, Pitt the Elder, she said to herself. Why was the mere mention of her therapist's name causing her such anxiety? She managed to control her stress by reciting the names of British Prime Ministers; a technique suggested by Dr Warminster in the first place.

Matilda knew that the support of her superiors was a hollow promise. Yes, she had made a mistake. Yes, she had suffered for it. 'Look, there's no denying I've changed in the past year, but I am still a DCI. I'm still capable of doing my job. If I didn't believe that, I wouldn't be here now. I know I can do this.' She wondered who she was trying to convince.

Valerie reached into her top drawer and pulled out a thick file. The folder had seen better days and was covered in coffee-mug rings and splashes. 'Do you remember the Harkness killings?' she asked, interlocking her fingers and resting her hands on top of the file.

Matilda knew where this was going. 'You're giving me a cold case aren't you?'

'I just want you to look at it. A month, six weeks at the most.'

'Is there any new evidence?'

Valerie looked down at the file. 'Not as such.'

'What does that mean?' Matilda folded her arms. She could feel the prickling heat in the back of her neck.

'Do you know the case?'

'Everybody does. It's part of Sheffield folklore.'

'The house is being demolished tomorrow.'

'About time.'

'I had a reporter on the phone from *The Star* last week asking if the case was up for review.'

'I'm guessing that it is now.'

'Due to budget cuts we no longer have an active review board looking at resting cases. The house being demolished isn't only going to have local interest but national too. It was a big story. I don't want them thinking people can get away with murder in South Yorkshire.'

'So it's a PR exercise?'

9

'Matilda, I believe this case can be solved. It may have been a long time ago but the killer is within these files. I know it. If anyone can find the killer of Stefan and Miranda Harkness, it's you.'

Matilda knew she was being placated. With the botched Carl Meagan kidnapping still fresh in the minds of the Sheffield people it would not look good if a DCI with a heavy cloud over her head was leading a major investigation. If, on the other hand, she could solve a well-known cold case there would be smiles all round. She reached forward for the file, but pulled her hand back quickly.

Grafton, North, Wentworth, Petty, North and Fox.

'I'll need a DC.'

'I'll assign one to you.'

'And an office to work in.'

'Not a problem.'

'Where's all the evidence?'

'On its way from storage. You'll have access to everything pertaining to the Harkness case and carte blanche on interviews.'

Matilda rolled her eyes. The files were on their way. The decision had already been made. She began to wonder if this was the beginning of the end for her. Did anyone want to work with her any more? 'What if I can't solve it?'

'I have faith in you.'

'That's not what I asked.'

'Then it remains a cold case.'

'Will I be able to return to the murder team when all this is over?'

'That will be reviewed at the time.'

She could feel a tension headache coming on. The impulse to throw her ID on the table and resign was bubbling up inside her, almost at eruption level.

'Are you still seeing Dr Warminster?' Valerie asked when she saw the DCI chewing her bottom lip.

'I have no choice in the matter. A bit like the situation here.'

'Matilda, a great deal has changed in this past year. Work on this case, keep seeing Dr Warminster, and everyone will be happy.'

'Everyone except me.'

'Did you honestly think you'd be able to return to front-line duty as if nothing had happened?'

'Yes I did. A review panel cleared me of any wrongdoing. I should be able to pick up where I left off.'

'And you will. This is the final hurdle. Look, South Yorkshire Police isn't exactly going through the best of times at the moment; the Hillsborough Inquiry and the child abuse scandal in Rotherham are just two major headaches I have to contend with. I cannot be seen to have you return to front-line work as if nothing's happened.'

Grudgingly, Matilda picked up the file. She feared that the second her fingers gripped the folder there would be no going back.

'There's one more stipulation . . .' Valerie began.

Of course there is.

'Dr Warminster has recommended reduced working hours.'

Matilda didn't say anything. She was already being stripped of her powers, her role within the force taken away from her, segregated from her colleagues; anything else they added was out of her control and not worth fighting over. This was a battle she was not going to win.

'You're not to start work before 9 a.m. and you're to be out of the station by 4 p.m. Is that understood?'

Matilda rose from her seat clutching the cold-case file firmly to her chest. 'That's fine,' she said through gritted teeth. 'I'll be able to get home in time for my game shows.'

She turned on her heels and swiftly left the room. She wanted to slam the door, but would wait until she arrived home, and, at the top of her voice, would scream into a pillow from the pit of her lungs – another stress-relieving exercise from the two-faced harpy Dr Warminster.

Chapter 2

The detached five-bedroom house in Whirlow sat in its own grounds. It was set back from a main road, and a boundary of neatly trimmed evergreens sheltered it from view. A gravel driveway forked off; one way leading to a double front door, the other to a detached garage, which sat proudly next to the house. Made of classic red brick in the Victorian era, it also included two impressive chimney stacks, and large windows.

A house and grounds of this age needed regular attention to remain looking grand. Unfortunately, nothing had been tended in over twenty years. The evergreens had been left to wild abandon, the branches drooped lifelessly, and the once brilliant green was now dull.

The garden was overgrown, the driveway almost hidden under weeds and brown leaves. The house itself was dead. Windows had been smashed and boarded up with cheap plywood. One chimney had collapsed, and the lead stolen from the roof, which had very few tiles remaining. The garage door was covered in graffiti.

A strong wooden fence surrounded the entire plot. Crudely attached stickers informed passers-by that the house was due for demolition. The once grand building was now an eyesore to everyone in the neighbourhood, and had a knock-on effect to selling prices of nearby properties.

Towards the back of the plot there was a gap between the last fence panel and the evergreens. It was a tight squeeze, but just manageable for someone thin enough to wriggle through without being seen from the main road.

Once through, the man dressed in black dusted himself off and stood up to look at the house. It was pathetic and sad to see such a wonderful building fall into a state of decay.

There wasn't much to see; the downstairs windows were all boarded up. The padlock on the sheet of plywood covering the back door was rusted and didn't take much striking from a rock to break it. He pushed open the door and entered.

The back door led straight into the kitchen, once the heart of the family home. It was dark and had the bitter smell of death. Cobwebs hung from the walls and light fittings, and a thick film of dust covered every surface. The kitchen had all the mod cons a wealthy family could wish for, though everything was now dated. The food processor was the size of a microwave oven. A yellowed salad spinner sat on the work surface next to the cooker. Did people still use salad spinners?

The man went through the kitchen into the large hallway. A sweeping staircase with ornate wood panelling led up to the first floor. The stairs looked warped. He wasn't sure if he should risk climbing them.

He went through to the living room and was surprised to find the furniture still there. He could understand burglars not taking the relic kitchen implements, but he thought someone would have made use of the corner suite and even the bulky television set. He smiled at the memories the room brought back and sat down on the seat he had graced as a child. It was closest to the television so he could watch his favourite programmes without being disturbed by someone passing the screen and blocking his view.

The dining room was a sad sight. The unit that housed the best crockery had been pulled off the wall, all the plates smashed on the floor. He bent down and picked up a jagged piece. He wiped the dust from it and smiled at the pink flowery pattern. His mum had loved this dinner service. It was only to be used on special occasions; Christmas, birthdays, and big family dinners. Probably kids had broken in and smashed it, not caring about the sentimental value.

From the hallway he looked up the stairs. He was tempted to ascend, despite how unstable they looked, but was frightened about what he would see. If the kitchen had been left in the state it was on the final night someone was living here, what would the bedrooms be like? Did the police clean up after a crime or would the walls be covered in dried blood, carpet matted with the leaked insides of its occupants, and bodily fluids allowed to dry and disintegrate into the very soul of the house?

The memory of what happened on the first floor angered him. It all came flooding back. He no longer wanted to go upstairs. He wanted to leave this place. He should never have come back.

He quickly left, slamming the back door behind him and securing the plywood back into position. Nobody would care that a padlock had been broken. He looked at his shaking hands, they were covered in dust. It was in his hair, up his nose, and in his mouth. He could taste the decay, the mould and the decomposition, not only of the building but of the people who had once lived inside.

Chapter 3

Everything had already been set out for Matilda; a room allocated and the dusty Harkness files brought out of storage.

The office was no bigger than one of the holding cells in the bowels of the police station. Behind the door was an old mop and metal bucket, long since abandoned. The room had a pungent smell of damp. The only window was covered with a yellowed venetian blind, each metal slat caked in dust.

Matilda walked around the desk, briefly glancing down at the files, and pulled at the cord. It was brittle and snapped in her hands; the blind was staying shut. There would be no natural light in here. The only light came from the bare sixty watt bulb dangling from the ceiling. If there was ever a room to tip a depressive DCI over the edge, this was definitely it.

Matilda turned her back on the window and surveyed the room that would be her place of work for the next four to six weeks.

'Welcome back Matilda,' she said to herself, 'we've really missed you.'

She looked at the faded labels on the folders neatly placed on what was her new desk; witness statements, forensic reports, crime-scene photos, police reports – it was all here: everything she needed to know about the Harkness case. She reached out for one, but her hand stopped short of picking it up. What was this mental block she had all of a sudden?

There was a box file on the corner of her desk. She leaned forward and quickly flung back the lid. It was practically empty apart from a thick paperback book. Frowning, she lifted it out and studied it. The pages had yellowed with age and it had obviously been well thumbed before being archived. The cover, although faded, was an image of a crime scene: the slumped body of a naked woman lying face down on a crumpled bed surrounded by splashes of blood. Matilda knew straight away what this was: *A Christmas Killing* by Charlie Johnson was the 'definitive true account of Britain's most brutal unsolved crime', according to the blurb.

She briefly remembered the book being released in the late 1990s but had never read it. She tried to avoid true-crime books wherever possible.

According to the first page, Charlie Johnson was one of Britain's leading crime writers, having worked on several national newspapers in a career spanning two decades. Apparently he had covered many of Britain's shocking crimes for national and international media. Matilda wondered if Charlie Johnson had actually written his biography himself. There was no author photograph, but she pictured him having small piggy eyes and a permanent smug smile that could only be removed by a sharp slap.

INTRODUCTION

The British police force is one of the finest, and most respected, in the world boasting an array of dedicated detectives who will stop at nothing until they find their culprit. Unfortunately, there are times when a case can go cold, the killer goes to ground, and justice for the victim is trapped in a state of limbo.

One crime which shook the nation in the 1990s was the case of the Harkness killings at Christmastime. A hard-working husband and wife were brutally slain while their youngest child was forced to look on in horror. What happened on that fateful night has never been fully revealed . . . until now. Featuring lengthy interviews with witnesses, family, friends, and neighbours, *A Christmas Killing* will throw a new light on the case and . . .

Matilda's reading was interrupted by her mobile phone ringing. She was thankful of the interruption. The introduction, written like he was a fly on the wall at the time of the killings, was vomit-inducing.

'Good morning DCI Darke. How does it feel to be back in the saddle?' The cheery caller was Adele Kean, the duty pathologist and Matilda's best friend.

Adele's breezy tone was infectious and Matilda found herself smiling for the first time. 'I'm not back in the saddle unfortunately. You could say I'm in the side car.'

'What are you talking about?'

Matilda leaned back carefully in her wooden chair, hoping it wasn't as brittle as the blind. 'Apparently I'm not to be trusted. I have to prove myself again before I'm allowed to play with the big boys.'

'Oh Matilda. I'm so sorry. We did wonder whether this would happen didn't we? I suppose it's not come as too great a shock.'

'No, I suppose not. I'm not even allowed to sit with the big boys. I've been given a grotty little office no bigger than a cupboard under the stairs.'

'Well if it's anything like the cupboard under my stairs the cat usually puts her finds there. Be on the lookout for dead sparrows.'

'Judging by the smell I think there may be a dead albatross in here somewhere.'

'Is everyone pleased to have you back?'

'I've not seen anyone. It's like they're keeping out of my way. I don't know what they think I'm going to do to them. I've had a meeting with the ACC. She's given me a project to keep me out of trouble.'

'What?'

'Apparently I have to pass a test before I can move on to the next level. I've been given a cold case to solve,' she said, lifting up the cover of the first file and taking a look at the top sheet.

'Well, you do enjoy a puzzle.'

'A puzzle I can solve. This isn't a cold case, it's frozen solid. It's its own little ice age.'

'What's the case?'

'The Harkness murders.'

'Bloody hell. Well, anything you want to run by me give me a holler. I don't mind playing Jessica Fletcher.'

'I'll remember that when I'm tearing my hair out. Did you know the house is being demolished tomorrow?'

'Is it? Well I'm not surprised. It's stood empty for years, even Dracula would apply for rehousing if he lived in there.'

Matilda laughed and felt herself relaxing.

'It's good to hear you laugh, Mat. Fancy meeting for lunch? Panini on me.'

'Yes OK. I'd like that. I'm not sure what time I'll be free though.'

'That's OK. I'm off today. Give me a call.'

Matilda promised that she would, said goodbye, and hung up. She realized she was still smiling and had an air of confidence about her. This always happened in Adele's company. Her positivity was as infectious as a baby's giggle. Adele should be bottled and issued on the NHS to people with depression.

A knock on the door brought Matilda back to reality. She looked around at the drab office and felt her stomach somersault. How was it possible her mood could leap up and down so rapidly? She made a mental note to bring her antidepressants tomorrow.

She called for her visitor to enter, but her mouth was dry. She cleared her throat a couple of times and tried again.

The door opened a small amount, the hinges creaking loudly. A head peered around the door. It was DS Sian Mills.

'Hello, I heard you were back,' her voice was soft, almost timid, as if talking to a patient who had just woken from major surgery.

Matilda was not sure she had the strength for this. All the old familiar faces she had seen, known, and worked with would hunt her out one by one to have the same welcome-back conversation. Some would be genuine, Sian in particular, others would be more perverse. They would want to see the state she was in, and get the gory details of her absence. Matilda suddenly realized she was the human equivalent of a car crash.

She took a deep breath. 'Sian, good to see you. Come on in.'

'Welcome back Mats. You've been missed. You really have.'

'Thank you. I like your hair.'

'Thanks. I wasn't sure at first. I thought it made me look like a twelve-year-old boy. Stuart likes it though.' She ran her hand around the back of her neck. 'You're looking . . . well,' she said for want of a better word. She tried not to stare too much at the woman who was, in effect, still her boss. It was difficult, however, not to notice such a drastic change in her appearance.

'Thanks. I feel well.' Would the lies this morning never stop?

'I didn't realize you were coming back today. If I'd known I'd have made some muffins or got you a card.'

'That's really sweet but I don't want a fuss.'

'No. Of course not. You're right. Start as you mean to go on and all that,' she half laughed.

'Something like that.' She gave a weak smile and glanced at the Harkness files.

'You'll have to come up to the Murder Room, see us all, have a coffee.'

'I will. Maybe a bit later.' Another lie.

'How about lunch? We can catch up. Did I tell you Stuart's father died? He's only left us his boat. Can you believe that? What are we supposed to do with a boat in Sheffield?'

'Some other time perhaps. I've got plans this lunchtime.'

'Oh. OK. No problem. I understand. Well, let me know when.'

'Will do.'

'Well I'd better be going.' She made her way to the doorway. 'It really is great to have you back.'

Matilda offered a painful smile as a farewell. Any words would have choked her.

As soon as Sian left the room, closing the door behind her, Matilda felt her body begin to relax once more. She had been tense throughout the conversation. Why should she feel on edge around Sian? She had known her for years, worked with her on many investigations, cried and ranted at the state of the judicial system when a killer went free, and had a few too many Martinis together at Christmas parties. If she couldn't relax around a friend, how was she going to react around others she considered to be mere colleagues?

Pitt the Younger, Addington, Pitt the Elder, Grenville, Cavendish-Bentinck.

Maybe she had returned to work too early, but then how much longer could she keep putting it off? Surely nine months was more than enough.

She shook her head as if dispelling the dark thoughts, and busied herself with the evidence boxes scattered around the room. She lifted one up, expecting it to be heavy, but was surprised by how light it was, and placed it on her desk. She removed the lid tentatively and peered inside. There was only one item in it: sealed in an evidence bag was the neatly folded white shirt belonging to a small boy. Standing out against the pure white cotton material, pools of dried blood covered the front.

Matilda reached in and lifted it out. She held it firmly in both hands. Searching back in her memory twenty years, she briefly remembered eleven-year-old Jonathan Harkness being found alone at the crime scene. How long had he been there? Had he been present in the room as his parents were butchered in front of him? If so, why hadn't the killer turned on him too? Respectfully, she gently placed the shirt back in the box and returned the lid.

Another knock at the door brought her back from her reverie. She sniffled and realized she was on the brink of tears, clearly from the effects of the bloodied shirt belonging to an innocent child mixed with her already fragile emotional state. Maybe she would feel better once she started on the case properly.

'Come in.'

This time the door breezed open and in bounded DC Rory Fleming like Tigger on Ecstasy.

'Rory, good to see you. What can I do for you?' She tried to sound jolly but it came out rather laboured.

'I've been assigned to you ma'am, for the Harkness case.'

'Oh right. Well come on in. Have a seat, if you can find room.'

He shut the door and sat on the hard wooden seat on the opposite side of the desk. They eyed each other up in painful silence.

'So, are you pleased to be back?'

'Right,' she began, slapping her hands on the desk, 'let's get things settled before we begin. Firstly, you don't need to treat me like I'm made of glass. I'm not going to break. Secondly, you don't have to be careful about what you say. There's bound to be some mention of missing children or kidnapping at some point, and while it will bring back memories, they're my memories and not yours, so don't worry. Thirdly, the length of time I was off was due to personal reasons, which have no effect on my work, so you don't need to know about them. Is that all right?'

Rory looked taken aback by the speech. He nodded as if summing it up. 'That's fine by me,' he gave a pained smile.

'Good. So, how are things with you?'

'No offence but that's a personal matter, which has no effect on my work, so you don't need to know about that.'

Matilda threw her head back and gave out a natural laugh straight from the pit of her stomach. Yes, she definitely had made the right decision to return to work.

21

Chapter 4

DC Rory Fleming was a good-looking young man in his late twenties. He had the clean-cut look of a fresh-faced Premiership footballer with brawn to match. He took care of his appearance; always wore well-fitted, clean suits, which hung on him like they did on the shop dummy, and he seemed to have a new tie every day. Now, trapped in an office the size of a prison cell, with a mountain of paperwork to wade through and with no natural ventilation, his skin was dry, his hair ruffled, and his once crisp white shirt creased, with the sleeves rolled up.

He had just finished reading a section of Charlie Johnson's 'definitive book' on the Harkness killings. Twenty years ago Fleming was still an infant, overly excited about the upcoming visit from Father Christmas, and stealing chocolates from the back of the Christmas tree.

DC Fleming was Sheffield born and bred. He knew of the Harkness case, having heard the story many times from various relatives, and colleagues on the job, but he wasn't familiar with the gory details. The killings were frenzied. From the crime-scene photographs, Stefan Harkness had been killed at his desk. It appeared the killer had come from behind and caught him unawares. All it took was a single stab wound in the back of his neck to render him immobile. He had been unable to fend off his attacker, and died where he sat.

The killing of his wife, however, was one of unadulterated rage. The bed was covered in blood and the sheets disturbed. From the height and direction of the blood sprays she had been knifed in the chest and tried to flee her attacker. She stumbled onto the bed and managed to get to the other side before being struck again. Once on the floor the violent attack continued with the knife raining down on her back. The wounds were deep. Whoever committed this crime had the power to plunge the knife deeply and be physically able to rip it out again.

'Where are you up to?' Matilda asked, interrupting his reading.

'The bit where Jonathan was found by a neighbour.'

'What do you think?'

'Of the book? It's a bit . . .'

'Shit?' Matilda completed the thought for him.

'I wasn't going to say that. It's a bit . . . I don't know . . . voyeuristic. It goes into a lot of detail. How did this Charlie Johnson get all this stuff?'

'Your guess is as good as mine.'

Extract from *A Christmas Killing* by Charlie Johnson

CHAPTER ONE: A DARK AND DEADLY NIGHT

Wednesday December 21, 1994

It had been dark for most of the day. A grey sky heavy with snow loomed over Sheffield and the temperature hadn't risen above zero all day. A biting wind from the north made it feel colder and whenever a gust blew it felt like needles against bare skin. Work had to be done, and school had to be attended, but when darkness fell the best place to be was indoors, wrapped up warm and in front of a roaring fire.

Wednesday night marked the first in a series of Christmas events at St Augustine's Church at Brocco Bank. The first night was a carol concert in which local school children would spend forty-five minutes delighting the congregation with their unique rendition of popular Christmas songs. The Harkness family was not a religious one but Stefan and Miranda were well known within the community; Stefan, a Professor of Medical Oncology at the University of Sheffield and Miranda, a GP. Their attendance was expected. Stefan had recently acquired a grant to set up the Lung Cancer Clinical Trials Group. In the New Year he would begin creating synthetic cancerous cells to be injected into laboratory mice. It was a highly controversial study but the growth of the cells and their effect on the body in stimulated climates could yield a better understanding of lung cancer. If successful, further tests involving other cancers could be carried out. Miranda had recently been made a partner in the Whirlow Medical Centre. She was keen to work more in family planning and was in the early stages of setting up a clinic to provide confidential advice to sexually active teenagers. This project had received negative press and many locals saw it as glorifying teenage promiscuity. In January, Miranda, and the other partners at Whirlow, would send a letter to all patients and the neighbouring community to allay any doubts they may have in the programme. Making up the Harkness household were the two children, Matthew aged fifteen and eleven-year-old Jonathan. The brothers were chalk and cheese. They didn't get on and rarely spent time together. The parents were not worried. They assumed their age difference played a large part in why they didn't interact and allowed them both free rein to be their own person. Matthew, a typical surly teenager, was excused from attending the concert. Straight from school he went to best friend Philip Clayton's house, where he stayed for dinner and played in a bedroom on the family computer. He stayed later than usual and at nine o'clock used his friend's mountain bike to cycle the ten-minute journey home. Judith Clayton, Philip's mother, waved him off and watched as Matthew cycled down the road and turned left. Once he was out of sight she went back indoors.

The concert started at eight o'clock, and from seven, Miranda was busy getting dressed. In the main bedroom, a half-dressed Stefan was working on a speech he was to give at a departmental Christmas dinner he was attending on December 29th. His speech was to congratulate the team on obtaining the grant which would see them continue their work for the next two years. He wanted to show them how proud he was and he needed the right words. He had already spent several sleepless nights poring over his notepad yet he was still unhappy with the tone. The youngest son, Jonathan, had been left to his own devices and was getting changed in his bedroom. However, he still wasn't dressed with only fifteen minutes before they had to leave. His mother harshly chastised him to stop playing with his Lego and get dressed.

The Harkness family never made it to the carol concert. Their absence was noticed by many.

After the children had finished singing, a reading was given and the vicar spent ten minutes congratulating everyone involved for such a splendid evening. He then went on to read out the events due to take place over the next few days culminating in midnight Mass on Christmas Eve followed by a very special service on Christmas morning. In the hall at the back of the church, a buffet had been laid on by the Women's Guild. Once everyone had aired their views on the angelic singing and choice of carols, the conversation turned to the absence of Stefan and Miranda Harkness.

On her way home from the concert, family friend Aoife Quinn drove to the Harkness's house in Whirlow to see why they hadn't attended. When she arrived the house was in darkness apart from one room at the back of the house, Jonathan's bedroom. Ms Quinn knocked on the front door several times without any reply before going to the back of the house and knocking on the kitchen door. Again, she received no answer. She looked up at the window, seeing the light seeping through the gap in the curtains; she knew something was wrong. She tried the handle but the door was locked. She could not leave and go home without finding out what, if anything, had happened. Aoife crossed the road to neighbour Andrea Bickerstaff, and asked if she had a spare key. She did but they decided to phone the house first rather than just walk in. Andrea admitted she had not seen any member of the Harkness family leave the house since Miranda had come home earlier in the afternoon. She telephoned and waited as it rang continuously. The answering machine was not turned on; something Miranda always did when they left the house. It was obvious something was amiss. By now it was almost ten o'clock. Andrea Bickerstaff joined Aoife Quinn and together they went back across the road. Andrea only had a key to the back door. As she put the key in the lock she found there was an obstruction. She forced the key hard and a clang was heard on the other side. A key was already in the lock and Andrea had pushed it out. Andrea went in first and made her way through the ground floor of the house, first calling out for Miranda and then for Stefan. Aoife followed and stopped at the bottom of the stairs. Sitting on the top step was eleven-year-old Jonathan. He was pale and cold and in a state of undress. Aoife called Andrea over and they both looked up at the boy. He was unresponsive to their calls. Aoife walked up the stairs slowly and tried to get the boy's attention. She asked if he was all right and where his parents were, but he did not reply. Eventually, she was close enough to see the dried blood on his hands. Fearing the worst, she instructed Andrea to take Jonathan downstairs but not to touch anything or allow him to wash his hands. Tentatively, she placed a comforting arm around his bony shoulders and eased him up. She almost had to carry him down the stairs. Once they were out of sight, Aoife continued her climb. She had been in the house many times before and knew her way around. At the top of the stairs she turned left and entered the main bedroom where Stefan and Miranda slept. She was stopped in her tracks by the sight of horror which opened out before her. Stefan was slumped over his desk. He was dressed in a white shirt, black socks and black boxer shorts. His back was covered in blood. He had been stabbed once in the back of the neck. A pool of blood surrounded him on the floor.

Aoife steadied herself by putting a hand on the door frame. After a moment to compose herself she walked further into the room. Her eyes were drawn to the high blood sprays on the wall and ceiling above the bed. As she made her way around the bed she saw Miranda on the floor. She was dressed in a conservative floor-length ivy-coloured dress. It was soaked in her blood and torn where the knife had cut through to slash at her body. She had been stabbed eight times in the chest and fourteen times in the back. Aoife was brought back to reality from her state of shock by Andrea calling from the bottom of the stairs. She wanted to know what was happening. Aoife quickly ran out of the room and said they needed to call the police.

A murder investigation was launched and Jonathan was taken to hospital. He had no physical injuries but he was unrespon-sive. He did not react to any test by doctors and did not blink when a light was shone in his eyes. He was in a catatonic state. He was placed in a private room at Sheffield's Children's

Hospital and guarded by a police officer who stayed with him all night. A missing person investigation was simultaneously launched to seek the whereabouts of fifteen-year-old Matthew Harkness. Neighbours saw him leave the house that morning to go to school but nobody remembered him coming home. In the days that followed, police investigated the lives of the Harkness family both personal and professional. Media interest was high and the story had the whole country gripped. Stefan's sister Clara came down from Newcastle to look after Jonathan, who, after three days, had not uttered a word. Matthew was still missing.

'I don't like this,' Rory said, putting the book down.

'What? Is it badly written?'

'Not just this book, the whole true crime thing. I find it gruesome. It's so detailed and graphic. And another thing, how did Charlie Johnson know all the little details, like Jonathan's mum shouting at him for playing Lego? Who told him that?'

'I thought the same thing. Maybe he's just using creative licence. Have you noticed what's missing out of all of these files?'

'No. What?'

'A statement from Jonathan.'

'Well, he went mute didn't he?'

'Yes, but for how long? Surely he started speaking again at some point. There's a psychiatric report on him suffering from shock but that's it. From the file's point of view his aunt took him back with her to Newcastle and that's it. I'm beginning to see why this case was never solved.'

Rory went back to reading the book, his lips moving slightly over each word. 'Do you have those photographs of Jonathan taken at the scene?'

Matilda had been reading the post-mortem reports. She lifted a folder and then another, eventually finding the pack of pictures he wanted.

28

Rory rifled through them. He was unfazed by the blood-stained bed, the saturated carpet, and blood-spattered ceiling. Towards the back of the pack he found the pictures of Jonathan he was looking for.

Jonathan had been dressed like his father: white shirt, underwear but no trousers. They were caught by their attacker unawares. The pictures of the eleven-year-old showed him with a blank expression on his face. His hands were red with drying blood.

'What do you make of this?' He held up one of the photographs and waited while Matilda marked her place in the report with a Post-it note. She took the picture from him and studied it carefully.

'What am I looking at?'

'His hands.'

'OK. Go on.'

'Why are his hands covered in blood?'

'Put yourself in his position, Rory; he's just found his parents dead, he's frightened. What does any small boy want when he's frightened? His mum. He'll have run over to her and tried to rouse her in some way. Of course his hands are going to be covered in their blood.'

'Yes, fair enough. It wasn't long after Stefan was killed before Miranda was killed. If Jonathan had gone into the bedroom then surely the killer was still in there too. Why didn't the killer murder Jonathan as well as his parents?'

Matilda frowned. 'Maybe the killer's gripe wasn't with Jonathan. Maybe it was all about the parents.'

'But Jonathan must have seen the killer if he'd gone into the room.'

'Well, according to Jonathan's aunt, his mother came up the stairs and saw Jonathan on the landing with blood on him. He'd obviously gone into the bedroom and come back out again.' She thought for a moment and then continued. 'Remember back to when you were a kid and you wanted your parents' attention? You don't just walk into the room and wait until you're allowed to speak; you call for them on your way to the room don't you?'

'I suppose.'

'So the killer heard him coming and hid in the en suite until he left. There's a big difference between killing an adult and killing a child. The majority of convicted killers are appalled by crimes against children.'

'Yes. That's true. I suppose that's why paedophiles are kept apart from everyone else in prison,' he said. 'Hang on a minute, Jonathan's aunt said his mother came up the stairs and found Jonathan with blood on him?'

'Yes. So?'

'Where did you get that from?'

Once again Matilda rifled through the mess of paperwork on her desk before she found the two-page document she was looking for. 'A statement by Clara Harkness given in May 1995.'

'That's what, six months after the killings? Jonathan was living in Newcastle by then. So he was obviously talking.'

'Obviously.'

'Yet there's still no statement from Jonathan Harkness. Why not?'

Matilda had to admit that she had no idea why Jonathan was never interviewed. On the other hand, maybe he had given a statement and it had somehow disappeared from the archive over the years. As she looked around the room at the opened boxes of evidence, the stacks of files and packs of photographs, she wondered if she had really been given all the information the ACC had promised. Already the case was throwing up more questions than answers. She was surprised to find DC Fleming so articulate. Where had this sudden intelligence come from?

Rory coughed. Matilda looked up and saw he was studying his watch. She turned back to her post-mortem report and was interrupted by a louder cough. Rory was still staring at his watch.

'Is something the matter?'

'Well, it's just that . . .' he seemed nervous and unable to make eye contact with his boss. 'The thing is . . . the time.'

Matilda looked at her own watch. It was just after 4.15. 'What about the . . . oh. You've been told about my curfew?'

'Yes, sorry.'

'Don't apologize; it's not your fault. Thank you for reminding me. I'd hate to get a detention on my first day back at school.'

They both laughed, but it wasn't genuine.

'Shall I continue reading up on the case?'

'No. Why should you have to stay behind and I go home? Have an early finish. Go home to that girlfriend of yours.'

'Oh. We're engaged now, actually,' he said, his cheeks reddening slightly in embarrassment.

'Really? Congratulations. When's the big day?'

'We've not decided yet. Amelia is aiming for promotion so wants to get that out of the way before having to plan a wedding.'

'What does she do?'

'She's a junior solicitor. She wants to specialize in criminal law.'

Matilda was tempted to say something about the potential for a conflict of interest in any of his cases going to court in the years to come, but the sweet smile that lit up his face was full of the innocence of youth. She didn't want to spoil it for him. She found herself relaxing in Rory's company. Before her nine month enforced sabbatical she saw Rory as just an annoyingly loud, over-eager DC who would need a serious change of personality if he expected promotion. However, cooped up in the broom cupboard and working on a one-to-one basis she was seeing him in a different light. He was warm and approachable.

'So what have the others in the Murder Room been up to in my time away?' The question surprised even Matilda. She had never engaged in gossip before, and although the personal lives of her team were important for her to know in order to find out how they were going to approach particular cases, she kept the majority at arm's length.

'Well Sian's been bitten by the *Great British Bake Off* bug. She's been trying out her skills on us, bringing in muffins and cakes. She's actually quite good. She's also just inherited a boat which she's been harping on about for months.'

'Yes, she mentioned that this morning. It was one of the first things she said.' Matilda smiled.

'We think Aaron may be going through a mid-life crisis. Ever since he turned thirty-four he's gotten all moody. I think there might be trouble at home. I know his wife wants a baby. I'm guessing he's not playing with a full load.'

'Blimey Rory, you're worse than a bunch of women at a school gate.' She didn't tell him to stop though.

'Oh, big news about Scott. You know we all thought he was gay? Well he went out with the blonde one from the press office for a couple of weeks but it didn't last. Still, I won a fiver off Aaron so I wasn't complaining.'

'What's the new girl like? Faith is it?'

He rolled his eyes. 'She's a bit of an enigma. She seems to think she's been hand-picked to join the team, like she has something special to offer. She's not even trying to fit in with us and she got Sian's back up straight away by helping herself to the chocolate drawer and replacing what she took with nut bars and packets of seeds.'

'How's her work?'

'She's good at what she does; she's just not much of a team player.'

'Maybe she's nervous.' Matilda found herself sympathizing with a woman she didn't even know. She could certainly understand what it was like entering an already established team. Even though she'd been with the Murder Investigation Team from day one, she found herself feeling like an outsider again.

She didn't want to dwell on this for too long; her mood was beginning to sink again. 'Look, you get off. I'll tidy up in here. Tomorrow is the demolition of the Harkness house. We'll meet there at nine o'clock; watch the house being torn down, then plan what we're going to do next in the pub. OK?'

'Fine by me. I'll see you tomorrow.'

As soon as he had gone Matilda closed her eyes and took several deep breaths. The stale air in the room was not helping. She put the post-mortem report, a pack of crime-scene photographs, and witness statements in her bag. She may not be allowed to be in the station past four o'clock, but nobody had said anything about working from home.

Chapter 5

Jonathan Harkness was a timid, frail figure of a man. Standing at six foot tall and weighing a little under ten stone, he looked almost emaciated. His icy blue eyes were sunken and his cheekbones prominent to the point of bursting out of his skin. His thin lips were red and dry. His skin was pale and lacked life, as did his unruly hair.

He held himself rigid and constantly looked about him, as if frightened of the world he lived in. His body language was cold and unapproachable and his shoulders were permanently hunched. He never allowed himself to relax, not even for a second. He was always on his guard.

Jonathan hadn't been a confident child and preferred his own company to that of his contemporaries. Twenty years ago, when he was eleven years old, his entire world was torn apart by the brutal murder of his parents. Everything that happened to him after that night, every decision he made, was born from the fragile mind of a young man who was unable to break free of that night in December 1994 when he had stood in the doorway of his parents' bedroom and seen the nightmare unfold before him.

He was grateful for Aunt Clara, who took him away from Sheffield, but once the residents and local press in Newcastle realized who he was, the gossip began, the phone calls began, and they were all after his version of the events.

Eventually it died down and Jonathan could grow up in the shadows, just like he wanted. Now, with the stiff cream envelope in his post box and the logo of the company he knew all too well, his nightmare was about to return. He had been expecting this day to come and now that it had he was surprised by how sanguine he was about it all. It was only a letter after all. What damage could a letter do?

Richards and Rigby Publishing
3rd Floor Muse House
Swansea Avenue
London
EC1 2BF
December 3, 2014

Dear Jonathan,
I hope this letter finds you in the best of health. As I am sure you are aware your childhood home is due to be demolished in the coming days. I have already had many journalists contact me asking if I will be willing to write a feature on the demolition and a review of the murder of your parents.

Coincidentally, next summer I will be releasing a new book titled *Britain's Unsolved Murders* and will be revisiting some of the crimes I have covered in the past. Naturally I would like the Harkness killings to be at the heart of the book.

I have spent time looking online and chatting to journalists and I see you have never told your story. You must realize that yours is a story worth telling and the whole country would certainly still be interested in reading it.

For your own convenience I can be up in Sheffield in just a couple of hours and we can discuss your story and fees in

person. Please contact me as soon as possible so we can get
the ball rolling.

    Kind regards,

    Charlie Johnson

Bloody Charlie Johnson! Would he ever be free from this man? And
how the hell did he know Jonathan had moved back to Sheffield?

Jonathan took Charlie's letter into the kitchen and set fire to it over
the sink. He dropped the burning sheet and watched as the paper
curled and the yellow flames destroyed the neatly printed letter. He
turned on the cold-water tap and flushed the scorched scraps of paper
down the plughole. He knew more letters would come.

He looked at the calendar on the kitchen wall and saw the red
ring he'd drawn around tomorrow's date. He took a deep breath
as he felt a tightness in his chest. He wasn't sure if he was strong
enough to get through this.

Tomorrow was a big day. The house he had been brought up
in was being demolished. It was the end of an era and, hopefully,
a chance to put the ghosts to rest.

He intended to visit the house in Whirlow and watch as it was
razed to the ground. He was unsure how he would feel about it.
He was never one for showing his emotions, not even in private.
He doubted he would cry. There was one worry he had about
tomorrow which he could not seem to come to terms with; would
his brother Matthew attend the demolition? He hoped not. He
was absolutely certain he couldn't cope with seeing him again.

Chapter 6

Matilda Darke tried to make it out of the station without anyone seeing her. She wasn't bothered about being accosted and forced into a hug and asked how she was feeling; she just didn't want anyone to notice the files sticking out of the top of her bag.

As she made her way to the car park she sent a quick text to Adele apologizing for missing lunch and wondering if she was still free for a chat over coffee. The reply came almost instantly: COSTA ON DIVISION STREET. TEN MINUTES. YOU'RE BUYING. Matilda smiled to herself as she left the building. The smile dropped as she passed the Audi still in her parking space.

Costa on Division Street was in Sheffield's City Centre, on the cusp of the student district. It was a large coffee shop with friendly baristas and comfortable seats. Adele was already waiting outside for her.

Adele Kean was the same age as Matilda, forty-one. She was a single mother with a son in his early twenties. Her short, sensible hair, and her eyes, were dark brown.

As soon as she saw Matilda she stepped forward and opened out her arms, scooping up her best friend and gripping her tight.

'First day over with,' she said quietly in her ear. 'I knew you could do it.'

Matilda looked at her with a tear in each eye. 'You knew more than me then. I've lost count of the amount of times I've wanted to cry today.'

'And did you?'

'Not once.'

'Good girl.' Adele took a step back and held Matilda at arm's length. 'You look different, brighter, more relaxed.'

'Well I don't feel it. I actually feel physically drained. I'm shattered.'

'No. You look years younger. There's a sparkle in your eyes I haven't seen in ages. Come on, let's get those coffees and you can fill me in.'

Adele took the lead, linking arms, and heading into the warmth of the coffee shop. She went to find a seat while Matilda ordered; a large latte each, a mozzarella and tomato panini for Adele and a meatball one for herself. She slowly made her way with the drinks through the maze of armchairs to the back of the shop. Adele had already shrugged herself out of her knee-length cream duffel coat and was rubbing her hands together to warm up.

'It's a shame they don't do a latte large enough to swim in,' she said, taking the two-handled mug from the tray and cupping her hands around it.

'I don't know how you can drink as much caffeine as you do. I'd be bouncing off the walls.'

'Unfortunately, I'm not allowed to drink vodka at work so I have to make do with caffeine. I need something to give me a kick when I'm elbow deep in dead bodies.'

Matilda shrugged herself out of her winter coat and hung it over the back of her chair.

'That's new,' Adele said, commenting on her outfit.

'Well I had to make a good impression for the first day back. Do you like it?'

'It's very professional.'

'That's a no then.'

'Well it's not what I would've chosen, but you look good in it.'

38

'I've gone up a dress size.' Matilda leaned forward and lowered her voice.

'We all put on a bit of padding in the winter. It keeps us warm when the government runs out of gas.'

'Well it'll be coming off when the spring hits. Nothing in my wardrobe fits any more.'

'Come spinning with me; you'll love it.'

'I seem to remember you saying that about Pilates and I hated it.'

'That was just a fad; nobody does Pilates any more. So come on, let's have all the gossip from your first day.'

'There's nothing to tell.'

'There must be. Is everyone pleased to see you?'

'The ones I've seen are. I'm guessing the ones who aren't have stayed out of my way. I think Ben Hales has been avoiding me.'

'He seems to have done a good job while you've been away.'

'That's not really what I want to hear Adele.'

'I'm not saying he's better than you but you can't deny he's good at his job. He's not got the people skills you have. I was speaking to Sian a couple of weeks ago when that body was fished out of the River Don. She was telling me how the atmosphere changes when he enters the room. He just can't chat to people.'

'He's never been able to. He can't make eye contact. I heard he only made DI because of who he's married to.'

'Who is he married to?'

'Sara Monroe as was. Her father used to be Chief Constable down in Southampton.'

'Bloody arse-licker. Have you seen the car he drives?'

'It's not an Audi is it?'

'A bloody great big Audi.'

'I thought so. It's been in my parking space all day.'

'Paid for by Chief Constable Father-in-law no doubt.'

Their gossiping was interrupted by a young barista bringing over their food. He looked like a student who was working part-time. As he turned to walk away Adele admired his bum.

'Adele! He's young enough to be your son.'

'So I can't even look now?'

They both laughed. It almost felt like old times – before Matilda's life fell apart.

'I was trawling the Internet this afternoon and did a bit of digging about the Harkness killings,' Adele said between bites. 'There wasn't a shortage of suspects.'

'I know. The Harkness case really was a mammoth task. Stefan was a researcher doing something with testing on animals. He'd received death threats from animal rights groups and I've got a file of over thirty interviews to go through. Miranda was a GP and was setting up a clinic to help teenagers know all about safe sex. That didn't go down too well in the local community. If I was Poirot and I wanted to gather all my suspects I'd have to hire the Crucible Theatre.'

'I don't envy your task.'

'Neither do I. The problem is I feel like I have to solve this to prove myself once again. It's like an initiation.'

'Did Masterson actually say that?'

'Not in so many words. What with the house being demolished tomorrow it's back in the press and it doesn't look good for South Yorkshire Police to have a famous unsolved case on its hands. I just don't think I can solve it.'

'Come on, Mat, less of the negativity. Look at yourself; you're back at work. You've made it. Show them what they've been missing out on while you've been away.'

Matilda threw down the remnants of her panini. Suddenly the weight of the task was back on her shoulders. She felt the room closing in on her, the lights seemed to dim, and the background noise of a hissing coffee machine and chatting customers all mingled into white noise. She closed her eyes and took in a slow deep breath.

Adele had been through many of these panic attacks with Matilda over the past nine months. She knew the drill. She leaned

40

across the table and put her warm hand on top of Matilda's ice-cold one.

'Let's start at the 1900s. Arthur Balfour,' Adele encouraged.

Matilda didn't say anything. She screwed her eyes tighter and took a deeper breath. Everything went dark. The background noise of coffee drinkers chatting and the machines spitting out steam grew louder and mingled into one undefinable squeal.

'Clear your mind Matty. Come on, Arthur Balfour.'

'Arthur Balfour . . .' she said slowly.

'You can do this, come on. Concentrate. Arthur Balfour.'

'Arthur Balfour, Sir Henry Campbell-Bannerman, Herbert Henry Asquith, David Lloyd George.' Matilda's breathing began to steady.

'Two more.'

'Andrew Bonar Law and Stanley Baldwin.' She took a deep breath, in through the nose, out through the mouth. Did someone have their hands around her throat, squeezing the breath out of her?

'Another two more. Keep breathing.'

'Ramsey Macdonald and Neville Chamberlain.'

'Are you all right?'

Matilda took a final deep breath and felt her body relax. She slowly opened her eyes. 'Yes I'm fine. Thank you.'

'Don't mention it. That therapist of yours might be a bit of a cow but she knows her stuff. Who would have thought the Prime Ministers of this country would have such an impact on mental health?'

'It didn't have to be Prime Ministers. It could have been anything; kings and queens, American states, anything.'

'Doctor Who actors?'

'I think I'd soon run out of those.'

'How about James Bond actors?' Her face almost lit up. 'Though as soon as I got Sean Connery in my head I'd stop right there.'

Matilda was looking past Adele and out of the window. How could she function as a member of the police force if every time a sliver of doubt entered her head she fell into a maelstrom of panic?

This wasn't even an active case; it was a cold case that nobody expected her to solve. How would she cope under the pressure of a murder investigation in the here and now?

'What are you thinking about?' Adele asked.

'I'm just beating myself up. I'm really not ready for this.'

'Yes you are. You're worth ten of Ben Hales. This is who you are. You're going to get better and I'm going to help you.'

Matilda shrugged. 'You've got your own life. You've got Chris.'

'Chris can take care of himself. He's a big boy.'

'Yes and I'm a big girl . . . '

'Who's suffered a great loss,' she interrupted. 'There's no shame in accepting help. Now, I will help you and not just with your panic attacks,' she said, lowering her voice so she wouldn't be overheard. 'I'll help with the Harkness case too. We'll be like Cagney and Lacey.'

'Which one are you?'

'I could never remember which was which. I'll be the good-looking one. Kean and Darke Investigators Extraordinaire.'

Matilda smiled, but not with her eyes. 'You've got your own work. I can't ask you to help me all the time.'

'You're not asking. Look, what is actually bothering you in all this; is it Ben Hales?'

'No. I'm worried that I'll screw up again.'

'You didn't screw up before.'

'Didn't I? Adele, I killed a child, for crying out loud.'

Chapter 7

The winter months meant dark evenings, dark nights, and dark mornings. Usually the only daylight Jonathan Harkness saw was when he looked through the window of the bookshop he worked in. Any other time he was surrounded by darkness, and he loved it.

When he was away from work he was still surrounded by books. His flat was full of them. He lived on the ground floor of a small apartment block. There were two bedrooms, a large living/dining room and kitchen and bathroom. There were books in almost every room, taking up every available space.

Aunt Clara had told him the ability to read and write was important. While hiding from the agony of the murder of his parents he lost himself in fiction. While hiding from the neighbour children and the bullies at school he sought solace in fiction. Eventually books became an obsession and he spent every waking moment reading.

His biggest passion was crime fiction. In his living room, the large back wall was lined from top to bottom with purpose-built shelves, all of them bursting with books. Hardback and paperbacks of all sizes. They were in alphabetical order and then categorized in the order they were written. He lived in his own little library.

It wasn't long after he had moved into the flat that he ran out of space for his collection and he turned the box room into a reading room. He built shelves and bought an expensive leather wing chair. He blacked out the window to make sure no natural light would fade the colours on the spines of the book covers. This room was his haven. Every night when he finished work he would have a bite to eat, usually a sandwich, then go into his reading room – closing the door behind him, locking himself away from the outside world – and absorb himself in fantasy.

Reading the exploits of detectives such as Wexford, Jordan, Thorne, Banks, Dalziel and Pascoe, Dalgliesh, Frost, Grace, Rebus, Stanhope, Cooper and Fry, Serrailler, and Morse he was able to leave behind his own life and troubles and be somebody else.

He would read until his eyes stung with fatigue before retiring to bed and falling asleep, hopefully dreaming of his favourite detectives and not of the horror that haunted his real life.

Jonathan was a Luddite. He did not own a television or a computer. He didn't have a mobile phone and had no interest in the Internet. He didn't own any CDs and the only music he listened to was whatever the radio station was playing when he was woken up in the morning. His life revolved around books.

By the time Jonathan arrived home it was pitch-black and the temperature was well below freezing. He was wrapped up in a knee-length black reefer coat, had a black scarf swathed around his neck several times, and black leather gloves. He held himself rigid, his body language closed and stiff.

He carried two plastic bags. One contained the bare essentials from the corner shop: butter, milk, coffee, cheese, bread; and the other held three paperbacks from the bookshop. Even when he had the day off, he couldn't stay away from the place.

He opened the main door leading into the well-lit communal hallway. His neighbour directly above him, Maun Barrington, was at her post box. Her eyes lit up when she saw him and she smiled.

'Hello Jonathan, you're home late,' she said.

'I've not worked today, had a few things to do.' He pulled the scarf down from around his mouth. He didn't make eye contact and kept his head bowed. He had learned to judge who was around him without looking up and actually seeing.

Her smile dropped. 'It's not like you to take time off work.' She waited, expecting him to elaborate but he didn't. 'It's a cold one today isn't it?' she asked, desperate to keep the conversation going.

'It certainly is,' he said, unlocking his post box and taking out the single item of junk mail. He looked at the envelope, saw it was a circular offering him cheap broadband, and immediately tore it in half; placing it in the bin under the table.

'I bet we're in for a long winter, don't you?' Maun said looking outside into the darkness. 'So depressing.'

Jonathan was just opening the interior door taking him to the corridor where the two ground-floor apartments were when she stopped him.

'Jonathan, I don't mean to intrude but . . . '

'Yes?'

'Well, I know tomorrow is the day of the demolition. It can't be an easy time for you.'

'No it's not. Not much I can do about it though. It's not my house.'

'Are you going?'

He thought about it even though his mind was already made up. 'Yes, just for a while.'

'Would you like me to come with you?'

He gave her a feeble smile. 'That's nice of you to offer but no thanks.'

'I don't mind.'

I bet you don't. 'No, honestly, it's fine. I'm going into work straight afterwards. I just want to see it get started. I'll only be there about ten minutes.'

'Are you sure?'

'Positive.' He edged further into the corridor.

'Well, you know where I am if you change your mind.'

He smiled at her once again and walked quickly away. Conversation over.

Maun Barrington was in her early sixties. She was a widow and had been for almost twenty years. She and Jonathan were very alike; neither had any family and no friends to speak of. The only difference was Maun wanted people around her whereas Jonathan didn't. She liked Jonathan. She was happy to have him in her life. Nobody else in the building acknowledged her and she looked forward to her conversations with him. She wished he would stay for longer chats, or accept more of the invitations to dinner in her flat that she offered.

As Jonathan left she went upstairs into her own home and closed the front door behind her. The layout to her flat was identical to Jonathan's. She stood in the hallway in silence and listened intently. She heard footsteps coming from below. Jonathan was moving into the kitchen. She went into her kitchen. She heard the sound of running water; he was probably washing his hands. She washed her hands.

From the kitchen, Jonathan made his way into the living room and turned on the fire. He then went into every room and closed the curtains. Upstairs, Maun copied his movements.

Chapter 8

It was a strange sensation arriving home to a cold, empty house but it was something Matilda would have to get used to.

She switched on the lights in the living room and kitchen and poured herself a large glass of vodka from the freezer. Next to the kettle were her tablets. She popped two antidepressants from their blister pack and swallowed them with a mouthful of alcohol. She followed that with two herbal mood lifters she'd bought. Neither seemed to be working. She went into the living room and flopped onto the sofa. She was living in a four-bedroom house all on her own. It was far too big, but her husband had bought this place for them to grow old in. He designed the interior, drew up the plans for the attic conversion and the conservatory. Everything had his mark, his personality on it. She couldn't leave here.

Without putting the glass down she struggled to pull the files and photographs out of her bag and slapped them onto the coffee table. She would read through them and make notes until she couldn't keep her eyes open, then force herself to go to bed. At least she wouldn't be thinking of James and the heartache of losing him.

On the mantelpiece was a silver-framed photograph of her and James on their wedding day. He looked very handsome in his dark grey suit. A radiant smile lit up his face and he had the warm blue eyes of a young Paul Newman. He had a few laughter lines but they added character. He was gorgeous. There was no other word for it. Next to him was the grinning Matilda in a floor-length white dress. It was a simple yet elegant design. She held onto her husband and beamed into the camera. She was happy. They were both happy.

Now the life had gone out of Matilda. Her skin was grey and her hair lifeless. She couldn't remember the last time she had smiled like that. She looked up at the photograph and her whole body ached. She missed him so much.

Her body was lethargic but she had work to do. She lifted herself up The files and photographs she'd taken out of her bag were mingled together into a confused mess on the coffee table. How apt, she thought. The whole case was a mess, her head was a mess.

Pushing aside the files, she found Charlie Johnson's book and opened it at random. She leaned back on the sofa and read aloud. As long as she couldn't hear the sound of the ticking clock she wouldn't feel quite so alone.

'*Chapter Six: Brotherly Love?*' She looked at her wedding photo once again as if she was reading to her dead husband. '*The age gap between Matthew and Jonathan was obviously problematic. According to neighbours, the brothers rarely interacted and were never seen together. The Harkness parents were busy with their successful careers, and, although they had a nanny when Matthew was growing up, there wasn't one for Jonathan.*

'*Jonathan was often left with neighbours after school if his parents were working late or was enrolled in several after-school clubs. During the school holidays he was anywhere but at home. Just how much input did Stefan and Miranda have in Jonathan's upbringing?*

'*Neighbour Aoife Quinn, although a close friend of the Harkness family, did not leap to the defence of Stefan and Miranda when the subject of their parenting skills was brought up. "They were a brilliant couple, hardworking and totally dedicated to their careers. However, I think having Jonathan was a mistake. Miranda never said as much, but reading between the lines, he was an accident, and an abortion would not have looked good for her career."*

'I wonder if Jonathan has read this,' Matilda asked aloud. 'I bloody hope not. Imagine reading that you were a mistake. Poor sod.'

She poured herself another glass of vodka and downed the double shot in one gulp. She wiped her mouth with the back of her hand and sniffled. She was crying. She wasn't crying for her husband though, she was crying for Jonathan Harkness; a man she was yet to meet, yet a man she had a great deal of sadness for.

Despite never wanting children, for a split second, as she looked into her husband's beaming face, she wondered what they would have been like as parents. She had never considered herself maternal, but if she had known James was going to die after five years of marriage she would have spent her whole married life pregnant, making sure she had something of him to cherish.

Bloody hell! Was everything going to bring her back to James and her sad pathetic excuse for a life? She flicked through the paperback and stopped at a different section.

'*Chapter Eight: Alternative Theories,*' she began again. '*Despite Stefan Harkness being a leading authority in cancer drug trials in the western world his work often came under close scrutiny and caused a great deal of controversy. By the time he was thirty he had already been before three government select committees to justify his work.*

'*At the time of his death in December 1994, news of his current work was well known in the scientific field and by interested parties. The fact he was testing on animals was no secret and he had received threats to halt his work or "suffer the consequences of your deplorable actions" as one rather prosaic letter written in pig's blood said.*

'*In the weeks leading up to his death Stefan Harkness had received abusive phone calls, anonymous letters, and a box containing the rotting corpses of three dozen mice was delivered to the house addressed to the Harkness children. Despite extensive investigations by South Yorkshire Police none of the activists, who eventually held up their hands to sending the hateful mail, were considered credible suspects for the double murder.*'

Matilda put the book face down on the sofa next to her and looked up at the wedding photo. 'Well we knew that didn't we James? This Charlie Johnson bloke certainly seems to be a font of knowledge. I wonder who his source was.'

Should she read on or have another drink of vodka? She looked from the bottle to the book and back again. The alcohol won.

Jonathan Harkness sat in his reading room. He was rereading *On Beulah Height* by Reginald Hill for the third time.

Next to him on the small table was a large mug of tea – milk with one sugar – and two digestive biscuits on a square of kitchen roll. He had been reading for over two hours.

The door to the room was closed and the only light came from the thin standard lamp, which was behind the wing chair and loomed over him.

When he came to the end of the chapter he looked up at the mass of books that surrounded him. He was content here. He was safe in this room. In reality his mind was diseased, and forever tortured him with paranoia and depressive thoughts, but in this room he was safe. He could live the life of the characters, interact with them, help Dalziel and Pascoe solve the crime. His lips spread into a smile and then he returned to the paperback and continued reading.

Directly above, Maun Barrington was rereading a story in the local newspaper. It had arrived at lunchtime. She was shocked by the amount of space the paper had given to the story, surely it didn't warrant a whole page – it was just a house being demolished.

She went over the conversation she'd had with Jonathan in the foyer a couple of hours ago. He couldn't wait to get away from her. Why? She shrugged off her pointless reverie. He was bound to have a lot on his mind with tomorrow's events. She was still puzzled as to why he didn't want her going with him. He always sought her advice.

She decided to attend anyway, keep out of sight so Jonathan didn't see her. She wanted to be there. She wanted to see his emotions; the agony, the relief, the heartache and the horror so she could be there for him later when he came home from work. She had a strange unsettled feeling in the pit of her stomach that something was going to happen. Change was coming. Whatever it was, she hoped she wouldn't lose Jonathan because of it. She couldn't cope with losing anyone else.

Chapter 9

Overnight the temperature had plunged to a perishing minus five degrees. By 6 a.m. everything was covered in an icy white glaze. Pavements were slippery underfoot; frost crunched under the weight of tyres; and the dead, frozen body of a man was discovered behind an industrial bin in Sheffield City Centre.

A man on his way to work, taking a short cut to the tram stop on West Street, stumbled across the body next to an 80s themed nightclub on Holly Lane. He dialled 999 then waited impatiently for uniformed officers to arrive. By the time they did, not only was the witness hopping from foot to foot to keep warm but he was thoroughly pissed off at being late for work on employee evaluation day.

A tall constable tentatively made his way to the steel bin. A pair of legs was sticking out from behind but nothing more. The closer he went more of the body was revealed. When he reached the face he quickly clamped a leather gloved hand over his mouth. It looked as if the victim's head had exploded.

The call came through to the MIT and was answered by DS Sian Mills. When she relayed the news to Acting DCI Hales he almost punched the air with excitement.

'Grab your coat and a DC and let's go,' he said to Sian. He was out of the door before he'd finished talking.

At fifty, Ben Hales had never quite reached his full potential and he didn't know why. He was a well-built man with plenty of padding around the middle and dark salt-and-pepper hair cut short. His personality was prickly, and, if you didn't know him, could be mistaken for severe. Nobody in work knew him. A fact that he didn't care about.

'Blimey, what's got into him?' Faith Easter said. She'd nearly been sent flying by a departing Ben Hales as she entered the room.

'Don't bother taking your coat off. Uniform have found a body. Come on.'

It wasn't far from South Yorkshire Police HQ to the murder site and there was no great rush, but Hales had his foot firmly pressed on the accelerator all the way there. Sian was in the passenger seat sending a text to DS Aaron Connolly letting him know where they all were, while Faith was in the back seat holding on tight to the door strap.

Hales pulled the Audi up at a dodgy angle and jumped out of the car. The two uniformed officers had been joined by a further five who were busy securing the area with blue and white police tape. A small crowd of perverse onlookers had already gathered.

This was exactly what Hales had been hoping for; an active murder investigation he could get his teeth into and show his bosses who had the ability to lead the Murder Investigation Team. He clapped his hands together as he approached the uniformed officers.

'Right then, who was first on the scene?'

'We were, sir. I'm PC Ashcroft and this is PC Rutherford.'

'What have we got?'

'A dead man behind the industrial bin. He's been very badly beaten.'

'Who found him?'

'A passer-by on his way to work.' He looked at his notebook. 'Jason Patterson. I've got his address and contact details.'

'Doctor?'

'On his way, sir.'

'Forensics?'

'On their way, sir.'

'Excellent. I want you to keep a record of everyone who comes onto the scene and don't let anyone in who shouldn't be. That's anyone from the press and anyone who isn't anything to do with analysing a dead body. Do you understand?'

'Yes sir,' he replied through chattering teeth.

'Good lad. Also, tape off this entire area, not just the alleyway, and get the crowd moved further back.'

'Yes sir,' he repeated.

Hales turned to Sian and Faith, a smile on his face. 'Let's take a look at him then.' The women exchanged a puzzled glance.

Holly Lane was a small alleyway behind the City Hall. It was mostly used as a cut-through for people to get to the tram stop or the amenities on West Street. There was a spacious car park to the left and a nightclub to the right.

The body was undisturbed. Hales had no intention of disturbing him either, not until the doctor and forensics had been. If he wanted to impress the ACC he needed to do everything by the book. Now was not the time for cutting corners or making mistakes.

Hales bent down to get a good look at the victim. He screwed his face up at the state of him; his features were broken, eyes swollen shut, nose smashed, jaw shattered. His hair was matted with frozen blood. Whoever had killed him had been relentless in their attack. This was a vicious crime and Hales could not be more pleased.

'Faith, find out who runs the nightclub. I want CCTV footage and I want to know what time they were open until last night and whether they had any trouble. Also, there's a car park across the road, I want CCTV from that too and check with the City Hall. I want to know what show was on and the time it finished and, again, CCTV from the front and back of the building. Get uniform to help you.'

'Yes sir.' She turned quickly almost hitting Sian in the face with her ponytail.

'This shouldn't be too difficult,' Hales said to Sian. He smiled. 'We're slap bang in the middle of the city centre surrounded by nightclubs and a big concert venue. CCTV should solve this before lunch if we're lucky. A badly beaten-up male outside a nightclub; no prizes for guessing where he'd come from.'

Sian had her arms wrapped around her and held herself rigid with the cold. She frowned at her boss.

'We'll wait until forensics have been, run his prints and if he's not on the system I want you to have a look through missing persons. Also, give the station a call; ask if anyone has reported anyone missing in the last day or so.'

'It's a bit early for that isn't it?' Sian asked, teeth chattering.

'Time is of the essence Sian. By the way, I'd invest in a decent winter coat if I was you.'

Sian turned away. An energetic Acting DCI Hales was unsettling to watch. He was usually monosyllabic and rigid. Where had his sudden animation come from?

A deep red Vauxhall Astra pulled up and out stepped the pathologist, Dr Adele Kean. They made eye contact straight away.

'Morning Sian, bloody freezing isn't it?' she said, quickly taking off her coat and opening the boot to find a blue protective suit.

'On days like these you just want to wrap yourself in the duvet and forget about work.'

Adele smiled. 'What have you got for me then?'

'A dead male, beaten to death by the looks of him. I hope you've not had a fry-up for breakfast as you'll be bringing it straight back up.'

'I'm a good girl; Greek yogurt and blueberries for me.'

'Really?'

'No chance. It's two coffees and a slice of toast. I'm never in the mood to eat first thing but I have to choke something down. I can't leave the house on an empty stomach.'

55

'My husband's the same. He'd throw up in the car if he didn't have breakfast.'

'Who's in charge?'

'Acting DCI Hales,' Sian said with the emphasis on acting.

'Did you see Matilda yesterday?'

'Yes briefly. It's good to have her back. Pity she's not back in charge of the murder team. It would have been nice to see her take this on.'

'Well, it's not for long. You'll have her back with you soon.'

'I hope so.'

'Not a fan of your current leader?' she asked as she was struggling into a blue forensics suit and a pair of plastic overshoes.

'I don't know what's got into him this morning but he's bouncing around like a five-year-old.'

'Oh great that's all we need.'

Adele grabbed her case from the boot and went over to Hales, who was still standing at the edge of the alleyway looking down at the body.

'Good morning,' she said in her usual cheerful manner.

He was startled from his thoughts and quickly turned around. 'Oh, good morning Adele. You were quick.'

'The call came through while I was on my way in so I detoured.'

'Well prepare yourself for a nasty one. All I can tell you is that he's male. I can't give you an age range or a description, he's been roughed up pretty badly.'

'If you want to come with me you'll need to suit up. Sian,' she called over to the waiting, and shivering DS, 'can you bring some footplates from the back of my car?'

'I'm guessing whoever designed these suits were the same people who created maternity clothing,' Sian said as she approached the pathologist and handed over the aluminium footplates.

Adele dotted them around the alleyway, finishing directly in front of the victim.

'Stick to the plates, please,' she said as Hales, now suited up, entered the mouth of the alley.

She then stepped forward, surveying the surrounding area before looking down at the victim. She took a deep breath and then pulled the mask up over her mouth and nose. Hales was not kidding; he looked like he'd been through a blender.

'I think it's safe to say he was killed here,' she said, pointing at the frozen globules of blood on the walls. She lifted up the left hand and had a good look at the fingernails. 'They're nice and neat so he took care of himself. There are some good pieces of skin under here too, whether they belong to him or the attacker I don't know but we'll definitely be able to get a match from them.'

'Excellent,' Hales said to himself. 'Time of death?'

'That's not going to be easy seeing as it was bloody cold last night. I don't think it got above freezing all day. He could have been here since ten o'clock last night or just an hour.'

'Can't you be more accurate?'

'Not right now. Rigor mortis has been given a helping hand by the weather. I'll take temperature readings but he's stone cold.' She shivered. The thin plastic suit she had over her clothes was not designed to withstand such cold temperatures. She couldn't wait to get into her office and turn on the heater. 'I've got my assistant coming. She'll take some photographs, we'll get him bagged, then back to the lab and we'll take some samples. Give me a couple of hours and come by for the PM.'

'Thank you, Adele.'

Hales turned his back on the crime scene and headed for the Audi. He tried to suppress his grin but this could not have worked out better. Last night he had hardly slept. Lying next to his snoring wife his mind had been a whirl of what was going to happen to him and his career now Matilda Darke was back. He'd had the creeping feeling he'd get a phone call over breakfast from the ACC telling him to return to the CID incident room, but now he could relax, for the time being. This was a fresh murder scene, and, judging by the gossip that had been doing the rounds at the station yesterday, Matilda was in no fit state to lead one. This would be his. All his. And, fingers crossed, so would every other suspicious death that happened within the South Yorkshire boundary.

Chapter 10

Matilda woke with a vodka-induced headache and had to force herself out of bed. It was only her second day back at work but it felt like she'd never been away, and not in a good way. As she dragged herself to the shower she wished she had never gone back.

The force of the hot water stung her aching body. She was tender and every muscle seemed to be screaming out in pain. She ignored the cries to return to bed and allowed the water to cascade down her body. To continue the torture she quickly turned the temperature from hot to as cold as it could go and the needles became sharper. She soon woke up and once again her brain was alert and ready.

Like yesterday she had to force down her breakfast of an extremely strong coffee and a slice of toast before dressing and leaving the house. She had sent a text to DC Fleming the night before, saying she would pick him up and they would go straight to the Harkness house in Whirlow to watch the demolition. It was pointless going into the station first. Or did she just want to avoid seeing her replacement, Acting DCI Ben Hales?

When she reached Rory's terraced house in Woodseats she pulled up and beeped for him. Within a minute the front door was pulled open and he bounded out of the house like a puppy going for his morning walk. She heard him shout a cheerful goodbye behind him and head towards the car. He had a silly grin on his face. She tried to remember a time when she was as happy about her job as he seemed to be, but the memory didn't appear to exist.

'You're looking chirpy this morning,' she said, indicating she was about to pull out into traffic, before Rory had secured his seatbelt.

'Well for the first time in I can't remember how long I had an early finish yesterday. I cooked a lovely meal, then we curled up on the sofa and watched a DVD together.'

She glanced at him and noticed his smile was even wider. She could guess the lovely evening had continued into the bedroom. She would also bet they didn't get to the end of the DVD.

Underneath his Jonathan Creek duffel coat Rory was dressed smartly in a navy blue suit, white shirt, and light blue tie. Matilda was wearing the same navy suit as yesterday; the trousers were creased, and there was a stain on a lapel she couldn't remember getting. Compared to her subordinate she felt like a bag lady.

'Another cold one this morning,' Rory said, making conversation after a silence of a couple of minutes. 'Forecast said there could be some snow by the weekend.'

Matilda didn't reply. She didn't feel as if she had anything to add to the pointless dialogue.

'What's the plan for today then, after the demolition I mean?'

'Well I thought we'd track down Jonathan Harkness. He's the only relative living in the area. We'll tell him we're having another look at the case and see what he has to tell us.'

'And if he doesn't have anything new to tell us?'

'Then we work the file. There has to be something in there that someone's missed.'

'Do you think he'll remember something new twenty years down the line?'

'I've absolutely no idea. The brain is a complicated organ. It can block things out to protect a person from whatever horrors they've experienced or it can torture them by repeating it over and over.'

'Fingers crossed for the last option then. Let's just hope it hasn't screwed him up too much.'

'Well I'm expecting him to be a complete basket case. Anything different will be a bonus.'

By the time they arrived at the scene in Whirlow a huge hydraulic excavator was being slowly driven off a low-loader. There was a team of more than a dozen workers in HI-Vis safety gear milling about preparing to begin.

The house had been surrounded by large plywood sheets to stop potential thieves or squatters gaining access and this was now being taken down. Two members of the team donned hard hats and entered the property via the back door. They were to give the house a final sweep just to make sure a homeless person wasn't taking shelter, before the house was pulled down.

Matilda pulled up a few hundred yards away from the house. From the back seat she lifted a pile of papers: the reports she had taken home and Charlie Johnson's book, which she was almost halfway through, and began flicking through them.

'I was talking to my fiancée about the Harkness case last night and she had a look on the Internet about it while I was in the shower. She thinks Matthew may have a part to play in the murders.'

'Does she?' Matilda replied, not paying much attention.

'It makes sense if you think about it. He wasn't in the house at the time and he went missing soon afterwards. It was days before he was found and he had no alibi.'

'He had no motive either.'

'All kids have a motive for killing their parents, no matter how tenuous.'

She wondered whether that was his opinion or that of his fiancée's. She didn't say anything.

'Maybe they'd had an argument; maybe he was jealous of the attention his parents paid towards his younger brother.'

'The attack was frenzied. Whoever killed them had nothing but hatred for them. It would have had to have been a pretty big argument for him to do that. Besides, if he was jealous of his brother, why not kill him too?'

Rory shrugged.

'Read chapter ten,' Matilda said, handing Rory the paperback. 'Apparently, Jonathan was an accident. His parents rarely had time for him. There was no reason for Matthew to be jealous.'

Extract from *A Christmas Killing* by Charlie Johnson.

CHAPTER THREE: WHERE'S MATTHEW?

The police arrived quickly on the scene and Jonathan was escorted off the premises under the cover of a large blanket to shield him from the horror of seeing his parents in such a state. He was taken to Sheffield's Children's Hospital where he was assessed for injuries. At this point, he had not spoken a single word to anyone and police believed him to be in shock.

There was someone missing from this scene though; fifteen-year-old Matthew Harkness. He had not returned home from school but gone straight to the home of best friend, Philip Clayton, to play a computer game. He left later than usual and used Philip's mountain bike to cycle home. The journey should have only taken ten minutes but he didn't make it, and there was no sign of a bike. After interviewing neighbours, police launched a manhunt to locate Matthew. Nobody had seen Matthew since he left for school earlier that day. The back gardens of all the houses in the road, along with nearby parks, were searched immediately. However, it was dark and little could be seen. A full-scale search was to begin the following morning as soon as it was light enough. Fears were growing among police that Matthew could have been kidnapped by the killer(s), though this was never made public. A sharp frost overnight and freezing temperatures hampered the search for Matthew. Police turned out to search back gardens once again and the local community helped out however they could. Police spent the whole day searching the dense Ecclesall Woods before moving on to Ran Woods. Nothing was found. The search then moved to nearby parks including Abbeydale Park, Millhouses Park and Abbeydale Golf Course. Again, there was no sign of the missing teenager, or the red and black mountain bike belonging to his friend. By the time darkness fell on the first full day of the investigation Matthew was still listed as a missing person and no ransom demands had been made. All day the temperature had not risen above freezing. Police feared for Matthew's safety. Wherever he was, he was obviously in danger from either his kidnappers or the severe cold weather.

'I just find it odd that he went missing,' Rory said. 'I mean, you wouldn't do that unless you had something to hide.'

'According to Matthew, when he was eventually found,' she began, casting her eye down his statement, 'he had come home and saw the police cars with flashing lights outside the house. He thought his parents had called them as he was late coming home and he just panicked and continued cycling.'

'But his parents weren't thick; they'd have just called the parents of the friend he was staying with. They wouldn't call the police.'

'His parents weren't thick but maybe he was.'

'I'm sorry but I don't buy it. He was missing for three days before just turning up out of the blue. If he was worried about getting into trouble for being late home he would have stayed away just the one night, not for three, not in the middle of winter.'

'Unfortunately,' Matilda began, flicking through the three-page statement, 'it doesn't go into a great deal of detail. It doesn't even say where he was hiding, for crying out loud. All it says is that he was hiding in the woods. Sheffield is one of the greenest cities in the country; it's surrounded by bloody woods.'

'Is Matthew still in Sheffield?'

'No. He moved away as soon as his education was finished. I've no idea where he is now. We'll have to try and track him down. These case notes are pitiful.'

She closed the file in frustration and looked up as the roaring sound of the hydraulic excavator slowly moved onto the plot of the Harkness house. It was demolition time.

A few nosy neighbours had congregated. They were dressed appropriately in long coats, hats, and scarves. They had their hands firmly in their pockets to keep warm or their arms wrapped tightly around their bodies. Some people didn't care about the cold; they just wanted to be witness to an event that would go down in local history.

From a nearby Mondeo a young man in his early thirties wearing an open-necked shirt, faded blue trousers, and scuffed black shoes climbed out from behind the steering wheel. From the passenger seat, a gruff-looking man close to retirement hoisted himself out with a large camera around his neck.

'Bloody press,' Matilda said under her breath.

'Are we getting out?' Rory asked.

'No I don't . . .' she stopped when her eyes fell on something of interest. She quickly scanned through the reports in front of her once again and found what she was looking for: a photograph. She looked up through the windscreen then down at the picture again.

'Do you reckon that's Jonathan Harkness?' She showed Rory the photo of an eleven-year-old Jonathan in school uniform. He was looking directly into the camera lens and had a forced smile on his face. It was obviously a school photograph and he didn't seem too pleased to be having it taken.

Rory looked at the picture then up at the young man in the black coat who was standing away from the crowd on his own. 'It looks like him. Same build, same hair.'

'Come on then.' She whipped off her seatbelt and jumped out of the car.

Shortly after arriving at his childhood home, Jonathan saw the journalist and photographer climbing out of their car. He hoped they wouldn't recognize him and lifted up his coat collar. He was standing alone, away from the crowd of ghoulish onlookers, but wondered if this might draw attention to the reporter so he slowly edged back to join them.

As soon as the large hydraulic excavator made its way onto the overgrown garden where he used to play, his attention was firmly aimed at the home he was born in.

His heart was beating loudly in his ears and he took a deep breath. He was dressed for the weather, wrapped up in scarf and gloves, but he was shivering underneath his thick winter coat. His mouth was dry and he swallowed painfully a few times. He watched as the arm was slowly raised a little higher than the roof. The bucket was angled and just as it made contact with the house he closed his eyes tight. The crunching sound caused him to jump. He opened his eyes and saw the large hole in what used to be his bedroom.

A large section of the front of the house was soon torn down and for the first time in more than twenty years, daylight penetrated the rooms. He looked up at the damaged building and saw the blue and white striped wallpaper that adorned the walls of his sanctuary.

He hadn't realized how much this was going to affect him. As soon as he saw the wallpaper he could feel a lump in his throat and tears gathering in his eyes. He was hoping for a cathartic experience, closure maybe, but he couldn't cope with this. It was killing him. The crowd of gawkers around him gossiped among themselves; their voices fighting with the noise from the demolition site.

'That used to be such a beautiful house. What a waste.'

'That place always gave me the creeps. It should have been torn down years ago.'

'Can you imagine what went on in there?'

'I wonder what those poor kids are up to these days.'

'I used to have that wallpaper in my back bedroom.'

As Jonathan walked away he was stopped by a tired-looking woman and a sharply dressed young man behind her. He wondered if they were more reporters. Bloody vultures.

'Are you Jonathan Harkness?' Matilda asked.

'Who?' His voice was gruff, his throat still dry.

'You are aren't you? Don't worry; I'm not from the newspapers.' She fished her ID from her inside pocket. 'I'm Detective Chief Inspector Matilda Darke, this is Detective Constable Rory Fleming. We're from the Murder Investigation Team at South Yorkshire Police. Would it be possible to have a few words?'

Jonathan looked from Matilda to Rory then back again. 'I'm sorry but I'm about to go to work.'

The sound of a wall collapsing behind them broke their concentration. Both Matilda and Rory looked in the direction of the house while Jonathan closed his eyes. The agony of grief and terror was etched on his face.

'I understand this is a very difficult day for you Mr Harkness but we'd just like a brief chat.'

'I don't have anything to say.'

He looked sad. His face was pale and his blue eyes dull. He had the look of someone on the brink of tears.

'We're having another look at the case.'

'What?' Now Matilda had his full attention. He looked genuinely shocked. 'Why?'

'We review cold cases every so often, and with the demolition we've decided to take another look.'

'Is there new evidence?'

'We don't know yet.'

'Look, between the book and your archives you pretty much have all the information there is.'

'You're right, there is plenty of information, but there's one thing missing: your statement.'

Jonathan looked up from the ground and into Matilda's eyes. 'My statement?'

'I know you went mute after everything that happened, it's hardly surprising, but your statement is vital to finding out the truth.'

'I really don't think . . . '

'Mr Harkness,' Matilda's voice took on an edgier tone. 'This is an official police investigation. We need your statement. Would you like to come down to the station now?'

The look on Jonathan's face at the mention of going to the police station was one of horror. His eyes widened, his mouth opened a little and his bottom lip quivered. He took a deep breath as if to steady his nerves.

'If you don't feel comfortable at the station we can do it at your home. Your choice.'

Behind him the side of the house collapsed and exposed the living room. Jonathan turned to look at the wreckage and quickly screwed his eyes shut again.

'We'll go back to my flat.'

The crowd of onlookers had grown, some were even filming it on their mobile phones. One member in particular stood out from the rest as she was the only person not interested in the demolition. She took a step back and looked at Jonathan talking to a good-looking young man with shiny hair and a dishevelled woman who could win first prize in a Vera Stanhope lookalike competition. She had enough experience of police officers in her time to recognize who they were. What were they doing here? Surely a house being demolished didn't warrant police interest, especially officers in plain clothes. The conversation between the three of them seemed very tense. She was itching to know what they were saying but didn't dare risk getting closer in case she was noticed. Maun waited until they had disappeared around the corner before following.

Chapter 11

The journey from Whirlow to Jonathan's apartment was a short car drive away, conducted in silence. When they arrived at the building Matilda was shocked to find he had moved so close to the house where his parents had been brutally murdered. He'd obviously not laid his demons to rest even after twenty years. Would she still be living in anguish at the loss of her husband two decades from now?

Jonathan pointed out the living room to his guests then hurried into the kitchen to prepare coffee for them all.

'He doesn't have a TV,' Rory said straightaway in hushed tones.

'Trust you to notice that,' she replied, and she smiled.

'Look at all these books.'

Both Matilda and Rory were agog at the collection. They were even more surprised by the neatness of the display.

'Do you think he's read them all?'

'I doubt they're there for ornamental purposes.'

'I've never seen so many outside of a branch of Waterstones.'

'Come off it Rory, when was the last time you stepped foot into a bookshop?'

A blank expression swept across his smooth face as he tried to think. Matilda thought she detected the smell of burning as the cogs turned in his pretty little head.

'I bought the Guinness Book of Records last Christmas.'

'Hardly a Booker winner.'

'A what?'

Jonathan entered carrying a tray with three mismatched cups and a cafetière full of black coffee. He made for the middle of the room then turned away, setting the tray down on a small table in the corner. He looked down at the carpet and unconsciously put a hand to his neck. Matilda followed his gaze and noticed four indentations where a piece of furniture used to stand; probably an old coffee table.

'We were just admiring your collection.' Matilda pointed to the bookcases as if they needed pointing out. They dominated the whole room.

'Thank you.'

'Have you read them all?' Rory asked, still bewildered by the display.

'Of course,' Jonathan replied harshly.

'Where's your TV?'

'I don't have one.'

'Why not?'

'There's nothing of interest I want to watch. I believe that if you're not a fan of soap operas or reality shows you're not catered for.'

'I have to agree with you there,' Matilda said. 'I pay my TV licence and a subscription to Sky but I certainly don't get my money's worth.'

'I expect being a detective takes up a lot of your time too.'

'You tell me,' Matilda said. She nodded towards the crime fiction collection with a smile.

'Would you like to take a seat?' Jonathan smiled back at Matilda.

Matilda and Rory both unbuttoned their coats as they sat on the leather sofa. Jonathan remained ready to leave the house; coat buttoned, scarf wrapped around his neck.

With slightly shaking hands, he poured them both a cup of coffee. He told them to help themselves to milk and sugar while he drank his black. Rory looked disappointed at the small plate with half a dozen boring digestive biscuits; he'd been hoping for something chocolatey, a Hobnob or a Bourbon. Jonathan sat on a matching armchair next to a small wooden table that held about twenty paperback novels.

'Why aren't those on the shelves?' Rory asked.

'Because I haven't read them yet.'

'Where do you work?' Matilda asked, taking a lingering sniff of the coffee.

'Waterstones in Orchard Square.'

'Really?' Rory laughed.

'Yes,' Jonathan frowned.

'Would you mind if I recorded this conversation?' Matilda asked. She took a digital recorder from her pocket. Jonathan shook his head, so she pressed a couple of buttons then set it down on the small table between the two of them. 'I'd like you to tell us your story.'

Jonathan sighed. 'Why?'

'As I said, we're having another look at the case and I've been through the statements, reports, and paperwork and there doesn't seem to be a statement from you. Did you ever make one?'

Jonathan closed his eyes and took a deep breath. Subconsciously he was tapping each of the four fingers on his left hand against his thumb. After tapping twice with each finger, eight taps, he stopped for a second before starting again.

Matilda recognized the signs of anxiety; she should do, anxiety was a permanent house guest for her. She looked across at Rory but he was still staring at the books. She wondered if her traits were as obvious.

'After it happened,' he began. His voice broke. 'After it happened I was in a state of shock. I didn't speak for a very long time. The police came to see me many times. They kept bringing different kinds of specialists, all of them trying to get me to talk in their own unique way but it didn't work. I seem to remember one woman using hand puppets.' He gave a nervous smile at the memory.

70

'How long was it before you talked again?'

'About eighteen months.'

'And you'd left Sheffield by then?'

'Yes. I was living with my aunt up in Newcastle.'

'When did you move back to Sheffield?'

'About five years ago I think.'

'Why did you decide to come back?'

Jonathan lowered his head. 'My aunt died, and as much as I enjoyed living in Newcastle it was always her home, not mine. Sheffield is all I know.'

Matilda nodded then changed the subject. 'On the night your parents died . . . '

'They were killed,' Jonathan interrupted with a solid, almost stern voice. 'They didn't die; they were killed.'

'Sorry. On the night they were killed, you were all getting ready to attend a carol concert, weren't you?'

Jonathan rolled his eyes. 'Do I really need to go through all this again? I'm sure with all your reports and Charlie Johnson's book you can piece it all together.'

'Have you read Charlie Johnson's book?'

'Yes. My aunt bought a copy. She wanted to know how accurate it was.'

'How accurate is it?'

'In places it's so spot on it's like he was there making notes.'

'Did you talk to Mr Johnson at the time of him writing it?'

'No. He tracked me down to Newcastle and wrote to us and phoned us a few times. He even sent a signed blank cheque in the post asking us to name our price.'

'Did you?'

'No. Aunt Clara tore it up and posted the pieces back to him.' Jonathan smiled at the memory. 'I received a letter from him a few days ago actually. He's working on an updated version and wants to interview me. How he found out I'm back in Sheffield is beyond me.'

71

'Did you reply?'

'Why would I do that?'

Matilda took another sip of her coffee, it was delicious. 'Getting back to the night of the murders, where were you in the house at the time?'

'I was in my bedroom,' he replied, taking a deep breath, preparing himself to relive the horror.

'And what happened to make you leave your bedroom?'

'Nothing. I was getting ready and my dad was going to tie my bow tie. I went across the landing and into their bedroom and just found him slumped over the desk.'

'Was he dead?'

'I think so.'

'What did you do then?'

'I'm not sure. The next thing I remember is my mum coming up the stairs having a go at me for not being dressed. Somehow I'd got blood on my hands. She looked at them and asked if I'd cut myself but I didn't answer. She looked at me and I guess she could tell by the look on my face that something must have happened. She sent me back to my room.'

'Did you go?'

'Of course. She told me to go to my room, close the door behind me, and not to come back until she came for me.'

'What happened then?'

'In my bedroom there was a closet with a chest of drawers in it. I used to hide behind it from my brother. I closed the bedroom door and hid in the closet and waited for my mum to come back for me.'

'How long were you there?'

'I've no idea. I came out because I was cold.'

'Did you hear anything?'

'No.'

'Anything from your parents' room?'

'No.'

'I've seen the crime-scene photographs and judging by them your mum must have put up quite a fight against her attacker. She must have screamed or shouted. Did you not hear anything?'

'No. Nothing at all.' Jonathan's replies were cold and lacked emotion.

Matilda and Rory exchanged a glance.

'OK. What happened when you came out of your bedroom?' Matilda asked.

Jonathan took another deep breath. It was as if he was preparing himself to walk along the landing all over again, dreading what nightmare waited for him in his parents' bedroom. 'To be honest I can't remember much after that. I know I was taken to the hospital but I don't know how long I stayed there. My aunt came down to see me but, again, I don't know how long it was between what happened and her arriving.'

'Now, on the night of the killings, where was Matthew? Where was your brother?'

The very mention of his brother's name hit Jonathan like a slap in the face. He looked up quickly from the floor where his gaze was fixed during his reverie. The expression on his face was one of sadness. He had a slight furrowed brow and his eyes were filled with tears.

'He was at a friend's house,' he said eventually, his voice falling in volume slightly.

'Can you remember which friend?'

'No,' he said, not giving it any thought. 'I didn't know any of his friends.'

'Why not?'

'There's four years between me and my brother. We didn't mix.'

'According to his statement, when he arrived home, later than he was supposed to, he saw the police cars and assumed your parents had called them to report him missing. Is that something they would have done if he was only an hour or so late?'

'I'm not sure. My brother couldn't do anything wrong in their eyes. They'd have called out the coast guard, army, and MI5 to look for him if they couldn't find him.'

'Your brother went missing for three days. Why would he do that?'

'I really don't know. You'd have to ask him.'

'Do you see him much now?'

'Not at all.'

'When was the last time you saw him?'

'I've no idea. I can't remember.'

'When you left Sheffield you were split up weren't you? Why was that? Why didn't Matthew go with you to live in Newcastle?'

He shuddered at the mention of Matthew's name, which caused Matilda and Rory to exchange bewildered looks. What had happened between the siblings to cause such a reaction?

'Well, my brother was at a critical stage with his schoolwork. It would have been silly to disrupt him. Whereas I had just started secondary school; it didn't matter much to move me. Also, we didn't get on, and my aunt didn't want me upset any more than I already was.'

'But surely it's more important to keep two brothers together after losing their parents.'

'I suppose it depends on the brothers,' Jonathan said looking deep into Matilda's eyes for the first time.

'Where did Matthew go to live?'

'With the friend he was with on the night of the killings; the family took him in.'

'That was very generous of them. Did you see much of Matthew once you'd moved away?'

'Not much. We met up once around Christmas a couple of years after but we didn't get on. There was an atmosphere.'

'So you just lost touch.'

'Yes.'

'Do you know what happened to him?'

'Well my aunt kept in contact with the family, and they kept her up to date on his life and education. He did well at school and college and moved to Manchester to go to university.'

'And after university?'

'I've absolutely no idea. He could still be in Manchester for all I know.'

'Why didn't you get on? Surely it wasn't just the age thing. You're blood relatives; you must have had something in common.'

'My brother wasn't a very nice person. He was a bully. We were poles apart.'

'In what way?'

'He was confident, outgoing, very popular and I . . . well I'm not any of those things am I? You see it at school don't you, all the good-looking, popular, confident boys picking on the weak. I was a very easy target.'

Matilda noticed he was scratching his left hand vigorously. It was red and it wouldn't be long before he broke the skin. 'Did your parents know what was going on?'

Jonathan scoffed. 'It would have been hard for them not to. He did get into trouble once. He pushed me down the stairs and I broke my left arm.'

'What happened?'

'My dad actually saw him do it. There was no way he could allow him to go unpunished. He was grounded for a weekend while I spent the whole summer struggling to wash with my arm in a plastic bag.'

'Why did he push you down the stairs?' Rory asked. The first time he had spoken since the questioning began.

'Because I was there,' he replied as if it was obvious.

'What else did he do?'

'How long have you got?' Jonathan adjusted himself in his armchair. He was clearly uncomfortable with these questions regarding his brother. 'Actually, no offence, but I thought you wanted to talk about my parents?'

75

'We're trying to establish a motive for the murders. Having read the reports and witness statements nobody stands out as having a reason to kill your parents.'

'So you're looking at my brother?' he frowned.

'Do you think it's possible?'

'I don't know. He bullied me but does that make him a killer?'

'You tell me,' Matilda said with a hint of a smile. 'You read a lot of crime fiction. Do bullies usually go on to murder people, especially if they think they can get away with it?'

'I suppose it depends on the kind of bullying.'

'And what kind of bully was your brother?'

'It was both physical and mental. After the broken arm incident he made sure my parents never saw the bruises. He became more inventive, sneaky.'

'What did he do?'

'He used to spit in my breakfast and make me eat it. He'd steal things from around the house and hide them in my room so when they were found I'd get into trouble. One time I woke up in the middle of the night to find him standing next to my bed and urinating all over me.'

'Oh my God. Surely that constitutes abuse?' Rory asked.

'Well I thought so.'

'Did you ever tell your parents?'

'What was the point? They always took his side. I wasn't wanted. My mother didn't find out she was pregnant with me until it was too late to do anything about it. Even if she had known she could hardly have had an abortion. How would it look for a GP who specialized in family planning to kill her own unborn baby?'

Matilda leaned forward. 'Jonathan,' she said, using his first name for the first time. 'Do you think your brother killed your parents?'

'I've no idea,' he said eventually after a long silence.

'You must have thought about it once or twice in twenty years.'

'What would his motive have been? They doted on him. They gave him everything he wanted and more. Why would he ruin all that? If he was the murdering type surely he would have killed me; got me out of the way so he could have our parents all to himself?'

'Does Matthew know you're back in Sheffield?'

'I very much doubt it.'

'Do you know how to contact him?'

'No.'

'Did you think he would have attended the demolition?'

'To be honest I was petrified of going myself in case I saw him. I'm not sure I want to see him again.'

'But he's your brother.'

'In blood only. Look, I don't mean to be rude but is there anything else? I should have been at work by now.'

'No. I think we've covered most things. We may need to talk to you again if that's all right?'

'I'm not going anywhere.'

Matilda turned off the recorder and slipped it carefully into her inside pocket. She stood up. 'May I use your toilet before we go?'

'Sure. It's the next door on the left.'

'Thank you.'

Matilda locked the bathroom door behind her but had no intention of using the facilities. She opened the bathroom cabinet. Among the usual items of toothpaste, face wash, and indigestion remedies, of which he seemed to have an abundance, Matilda wasn't entirely surprised to find a prescription of antidepressants. He was taking the same type she was on, Venlafaxine. However, where she took just 25 mg twice a day, morning and evening, Jonathan was taking a total of 300 mg every day. Surely his dark past and his abusive brother two decades ago didn't warrant such a heavy dosage? Realistically the only person she knew who she could ask about depression and the medicinal cures was her therapist Dr Warminster, but she would rather not involve her in her working life any more than she had to. She wondered if Adele had any knowledge of prescription drugs.

She pulled the flush on the toilet and washed her hands before leaving the bathroom. She had plenty of work to be getting on with but, for some reason, she didn't want to leave Jonathan alone with his thoughts. Her visit had obviously opened a Pandora's Box of memories and she dreaded to think of the fallout when he was cocooned in his self-imposed isolation.

Chapter 12

Matilda and Rory didn't exchange a single word when they left Jonathan's apartment. They both felt shattered, exhausted, and physically drained. They made their way to the car and Matilda climbed in behind the wheel. Closing the door, putting on the seatbelt, and starting the engine seemed to occur in slow motion. She sat in silence with her hands gripping the steering wheel, ready to drive off but not actually moving. Eventually, she turned off the engine.

'Is everything all right?' Rory asked.

'What did you think about Jonathan and his story?'

Rory let out a loud sigh. 'I've no idea. He's had a bloody rotten life, hasn't he?'

'You could say that. What do you think of his brother?'

'Apart from the fact that he's a complete bastard? Did you notice how Jonathan referred to him as "my brother"? He never used his name and when you did he physically recoiled.'

'I know. His parents were complete shits too by the sound of it.'

'They shouldn't have been allowed to keep him.'

'But if nobody knew what was going on, who was there to take him away? It looks like they wanted to come across as a family unit rather than just a power couple. When Jonathan came along, Matthew had been palmed off on a nanny and they could concentrate on their careers. Jonathan really was a spanner in the works.'

'So they just left him to bring himself up.' Rory completed Matilda's thought.

'Or maybe they expected Matthew to look after him, which is why he bullied him so much. He could have resented having to be the permanent babysitter when he should have been out with friends.'

'That's true. I hated having to look after my little brother sometimes during the school holidays.'

'As most kids do, but what has to happen to go from a teenage tantrum into a double murderer?' Matilda asked, more or less thinking aloud.

'I suppose it depends on how often Matthew was made to look after Jonathan. If it was literally every single day then maybe he started to hate his parents for making him look after Jonathan all the time and one night he just snaps and goes berserk with a carving knife.'

'That's one possibility,' Matilda mused.

'Any others?'

'Not off the top of my head.'

Without warning, tears started to flow down Matilda's face. She cursed under her breath and dug into her jacket pockets for a tissue, eventually finding a crumpled up one.

This is not what Matilda wanted. She knew she was an emotional mess but thought she had a handle on it at work. With the exercises from Dr Warminster and her medication, surely she should be able to control her tears. Obviously not. She hoped Rory wouldn't repeat this episode back at the station. The last thing she needed were rumours circulating of her instability.

'Are you OK?' Rory asked.

'I'm really sorry Rory,' she said between sobs, wiping her eyes. 'I'm not crying for anything specific. Well I suppose I am. I'm just thinking of Jonathan aged five being in bed fast asleep, all tucked up without a care in the world, then he opens his eyes and his brother, his protector, is pissing all over him. I just find that incredibly sad.'

'I can't believe someone would do that. My younger brother was a real shit growing up at times but it never entered my head to do anything like that. I mean, what was wrong inside his head that made him want to torture his brother so much?'

'That's what we're going to have to find out.' Matilda wiped her eyes, the worst of her emotional outburst was over. 'Come on, let's go and have a stiff drink. I think we've earned it.'

Chapter 13

DC Faith Easter was panicking. She had spent the last hour trying to obtain CCTV footage from the City Hall, the nightclub, and the car park, all of which overlooked Holly Lane. Unfortunately, the range from the camera at the City Hall didn't go that far, the ones from the nightclub only covered the entrances, and the cameras on all four corners of the car park were dummies.

'Shit.' She slammed down the phone and ran her fingers through her long hair.

'Problem?' Sian asked without looking up from her computer. She had no idea why, but Sian couldn't seem to get on with Faith. It had nothing to do with her unblemished coffee-coloured skin, her shiny, long, dark hair or natural pout, nor was it her ridiculously long legs and size eight figure.

'Holly Lane is a complete no man's land.'

'No footage?'

'None whatsoever. Hales is going to kill me.'

'It's not your fault. You didn't install the cameras.'

Hales entered the room with a spring in his step. An active murder case had elevated his mood. He took a swig of coffee from his chipped mug and reluctantly swallowed the cold beverage.

'Are you making a fresh coffee Sian?'

'I wasn't planning to.' Again Sian didn't look up. *Since when was I the office junior?*

'Would you like to?'

'Not particularly.'

'Sir, I've got some bad news,' Faith began. She took a deep breath and let the words trip over themselves as they fell out. 'There's no CCTV footage from anywhere looking onto Holly Lane.'

'What?' He raised his voice and slammed his mug down. 'How is that possible? It's the city centre. It leads on to West Street. We live in a nation where cameras are on every corner, Big Brother is watching and all that bollocks.'

'I've spoken to the manager of the nightclub,' Faith said. She picked up her notebook and flicked back a few pages. 'He said they had a problem with drugs about a year or so ago and he did look into putting up a camera looking onto the alleyway but he couldn't afford it. He's got dummy ones up instead and that seems to do the trick.'

'Jesus Christ.' He cursed through gritted teeth. 'Are you seriously telling me that not one camera has Holly Lane in its sights?'

'That's right sir.' She looked at Sian who was watching the proceedings out of the corner of her eye. Sian raised her eyebrows and gave a sympathetic smile.

Hales was just about to scream more abuse at the young DC when his phone rang. He snatched up the receiver and shouted an angry greeting before lowering his voice and sitting down. 'Oh, sorry about that ma'am.' It was ACC Masterson. 'Yes, of course. I'll come right away.' He hung up, cleared his throat, took a couple of deep breaths then stood up. 'The ACC wants to see me.' He almost sounded pleased.

'I thought you were going to the PM?' Sian asked.

'You go on ahead. Take Connolly with you,' he said over his shoulder as he bounded out of the room.

'Dickhead,' Sian said quietly under her breath.

*

Sian Mills and DS Aaron Connolly arrived ten minutes late for the post-mortem, something which Adele Kean chastised them for. She was a punctual person and found it the height of bad manners for others to be late, especially when it came to attending a PM. The dead deserved respect. Adele was also none too happy about Acting DCI Hales's absence either. Hales didn't have a professional obligation to be there, but he had stated he would be.

The body of the dead man lay naked on the stainless-steel table. His face was swollen with bruises, as were his chest and stomach. Adele's Anatomical Pathology Technologist was photographing the body from different angles and Adele was indicating particular points of interest where she wanted close-up pictures taken.

The hands of the dead man were wrapped in paper bags to avoid the loss of any fibres or skin samples from underneath his fingernails.

'How's the investigation going?' Adele asked.

'Slowly,' Aaron was not good with post-mortems. He had attended many in his time but it didn't get any easier. He found it an unnatural act to desecrate another human being in such a way. He understood the purpose of it and the usefulness in making his job easier but he could not bring himself to look down on a cold dead person and watch them being cut open. He always kept his eyeline a few inches from where he was supposed to be looking.

'Have you identified him yet?'

'Not yet. He had no wallet on him. Let's hope his fingerprints are in the database when you give us a set.'

'I don't think identification should be too much of an issue,' Adele said.

Sian and Aaron exchanged curious glances. 'What makes you say that?' Sian asked.

'He's missing two toes from his left foot.'

She stood back from the body and revealed her find. The two smallest toes on his left foot were missing.

'Bloody hell. How did that happen?' Aaron asked.

'Well it's not recent. It's also a very neat cut. I'm guessing it's from surgery from when he was younger. There'll be a record of it somewhere.'

'Why do people have toes removed?'

'Any number of reasons; he could have been involved in an accident and they were beyond repair, maybe they were infected, or he could have lost them due to hypothermia.'

'I'm all done here, Adele, if you want to get started,' the young technologist said stepping away from the table.

'Right then, are we all ready to take a look inside and see what killed this poor young man?'

'Hang on.'

All eyes turned to Aaron whose skin had gone so pale he was almost an X-ray of himself. 'I think I'm going to have to sit down for a bit.'

Chapter 14

The temperature seemed to keep dropping on an hourly basis. During the demolition this morning it was cold, but nothing a brisk walk couldn't chase away. By the time Jonathan arrived at Waterstones in Orchard Square he was shaking with cold. He was wrapped in a thick winter coat, hat, leather gloves, and a knitted scarf long enough to go around his neck twice, yet he was still shivering.

The day before he had told his boss Stephen Egan that he would only be an hour late for work at the most; as he looked at his watch he saw that it was almost lunchtime.

Stephen was busy serving a customer so Jonathan just mouthed 'sorry' then went upstairs to the staffroom to store his bag and coat before returning to the shop floor. He was warming himself up on the radiator when Stephen entered.

'How did it go? Are you all right?'

'It went . . . well, it went as well as could be expected, I suppose.'

'Are you all right?'

'Yes, I'm fine.'

'Come here.' Stephen stepped closer to Jonathan and folded down the collar on his polo shirt, which was creased due to the heaviness of his coat. As he wrapped his hands around his neck to straighten the shirt he looked Jonathan in the eye and gave him a smile. 'There you go, all neat and tidy.'

'Thank you.'

'Now, are you sure you're OK? You didn't have to come back into work.'

'I'm sure. Thanks. I didn't stay long; just long enough to see it get started. I had no idea how easy it was. The thing almost fell apart as soon as the digger broke into it.'

'Were there many sightseers?'

'The usual ghouls and a journalist from *The Star*.'

'Jonathan, if you want to talk . . . '

'Well I can't stand around here for much longer,' he interrupted, eager to miss another conversation about how was he feeling and if he needed a shoulder to cry on. 'I'll work through my lunch seeing I was so late.' He strode towards the door. Stephen had to quickly sidestep to allow him to pass.

Stephen sighed and rubbed his hands over his face. The large bookshop had many staff, all of them polite and friendly in their own way, but Jonathan was different.

There was something about him that Stephen couldn't quite put his finger on. He was very intelligent and well read but he gave off an aura of sadness. He knew his parents had been killed, and he had read the book by Charlie Johnson, but he felt there was something else beneath the surface that was bothering Jonathan; another tragedy he was allowing to eat away at him instead of releasing the burden.

Stephen left the overheated staffroom and went in pursuit of Jonathan. He found him at the downstairs tills. He was serving an elderly lady who was buying four paperbacks. He couldn't hear what their conversation was about, but Jonathan looked relaxed and had a genuine smile on his face. He guessed Jonathan had read a couple of the books she was buying and was telling her how much he'd enjoyed them. Jonathan really was the perfect member of staff. When the customer left, Stephen approached the counter.

'Are you sure you're all right?' he asked with a frown.

'Yes I'm fine,' Jonathan almost snapped. 'Why?'

'You look very pale.'

'Well it is cold out.'

'And you have a red mark around your neck.'

'I do?' Jonathan felt at his neck.

'Yes. It looks sore.'

'I probably had my scarf too tight. It'll be a friction burn, bloody wool. Like I said, it's very cold out there.' He walked away from the tills leaving Stephen alone.

When Stephen looked up he saw another member of staff at the next till looking at him; she looked smug.

'What?' he asked.

'Never going to happen.'

'Just get on with your work, Claire.' He walked away, his face reddening with embarrassment.

It was almost lunchtime and Lloyds Bar at Barker's Pool was filling up nicely. Sitting in the front window, Matilda glanced out onto the cold city centre. People were moving around in their own little world, wrapped up against the elements, carrying bags of Christmas gifts. The automatic doors of John Lewis kept yawning open and closed, open and closed as festive shoppers went in empty-handed and came out with heavy bags and a lighter wallet.

'Can you believe people are still having their picture taken next to the post box even after all this time?' she asked Rory.

He turned to look out of the window and saw a trio of Japanese tourists taking it in turns to stand next to the gold-painted post box in honour of Jessica Ennis-Hill's triumphant gold medal at the London 2012 Olympics.

'Me and Amelia have a picture of us standing next to it. It's in a frame above the fireplace,' he beamed.

Matilda rolled her eyes. 'Did you attend her victory parade here too?'

'Of course. It's not very often Sheffield has something to celebrate. Our football teams certainly don't give us much to cheer about.'

A barmaid arrived with their food: a shepherd's pie for Rory with a side dish of mixed vegetables, and a cheese toastie for Matilda, not that she was hungry. She smiled her thanks then looked down at the limp brown sandwich and pushed the plate away.

'Not hungry?' Rory asked as he shovelled a laden forkful of minced beef and potato into his mouth.

'Not really.'

'I was thinking about Jonathan,' he said between chewing. 'Do you think he's got that illness . . . ?'

'OCD?' Matilda interrupted.

'No, the one where they can't make friends, what's it called?'

'Asperger syndrome.'

'That's the one.'

'I'm not sure,' she said with a frown.

It would certainly explain a lot. Maybe he did have some kind of mental health issue. It would hardly be surprising given his tragic past. She looked through Rory and out of the window into the distance. She hadn't even thought about Christmas and the nightmare of gift buying, food shopping, and the organization that went with it. She supposed it wouldn't be necessary this year. There was no husband to buy for, no elaborate Christmas meal to cook; it would just be her. It would be a complete waste of money buying a tree, a turkey, a pudding, and all the trimmings.

The thought of her mother popped into her head. How long would it be before the phone would ring and her mother's throaty voice tried to placate her youngest daughter? *'Matilda, sweetheart, it's Christmas. You shouldn't spend your first Christmas without James alone. Come and see me and your father. Your sister's coming with her husband and she's bringing the kids. We're having a goose and your father's made his famous pudding. You wouldn't want to miss that would you?'* The thought of having to fake enjoyment among people she loved but didn't really know was enough to lobby Parliament and ask for a ban on anything festive.

'Or is it autism?' Rory asked, a puzzled expression on his face and a blob of mashed potato on his chin.

'What?' Matilda asked, snapping out of her daydream.

'Autism and Asperger's; are they the same?'

'I've no idea Rory. Look, I don't think we should speculate too much on Jonathan's mental health until we know more about him. Let's not label him just yet. When you've finished that, and you've washed your face,' she said, pointing to his chin, 'I want us to go and have a word with Pat Campbell.'

'Who's she?'

'She was the DS working on the original Harkness killings. I'd like her to have . . . '

Matilda stopped talking as her gaze picked up on a man selling copies of *The Star* at a small kiosk. The headline on one of the posters he was fighting to attach to the stand against the fierce breeze had caught her attention. Rory followed her line of sight and understood why she had gone so deathly pale.

'Jesus Christ,' he said, almost choking on his mouthful of shepherd's pie.

'COLD' RETURN FOR DISGRACED DETECTIVE
By Jonas Hamilton

Shamed detective, Matilda Darke, is back on the case – nine months after her lack of judgement led to the botched rescue of missing Carl Meagan.

Detective Chief Inspector Darke, 41, is no longer fronting the prestigious Murder Investigation Team and has been reassigned to working on cold cases.

She was seen in Whirlow earlier today at the demolition of the five bedroom house in which Stefan and Miranda Harkness were murdered in 1994.

As we reported last week, the Harkness case is being reviewed as the flattening of the murder house has brought the case back into the headlines. According to an unnamed police source there is no new evidence to warrant the case being fully reopened.

DCI Darke looked a shadow of her former self as she chatted with material witness Jonathan Harkness, 31, at the scene.

When asked if the review was a publicity stunt and merely a project for DCI Darke to work on while the force decided what to do with her, Assistant Chief Constable Valerie Masterson said in a statement 'We never use criminal cases as a publicity stunt. The Harkness case is a major event in Sheffield's history. The fact it has never been solved is a shadow hanging over us and I for one would like to see the brutal killer brought to justice.

'DCI Matilda Darke is a well-respected member of South Yorkshire Police and I would like to welcome her back after such a difficult time. Matilda feels this case needs to be solved and is dedicating her time to doing so and I give her my full support.'

Seven-year-old Carl Meagan was kidnapped from his home ten months ago. He was being looked after by his grandmother while his parents were away for the night. His grandmother, Annabel Meagan, 72, was killed on the night he was taken. He has never been found.

ACC Masterson refused to comment on whether DCI Darke would review the Meagan case in the coming months.

Chapter 15

It took longer than usual for Matilda to regain her composure. She worked her way through the entire list of British Prime Ministers and still she was breathing heavily. She was hot and could feel her shirt sticking to her back with sweat yet when she took her jacket off the freezing temperatures made her shake with cold. She looked down at the copy of *The Star* on the front passenger seat next to her and read the headline '"COLD" RETURN FOR DISGRACED DETECTIVE'. Those five words were like five daggers sticking in her chest.

After seeing the newspaper she decided to give the rest of the day a miss. Pat Campbell could wait for another day. She left Rory in the pub, told him to read through Charlie Johnson's book and she would see him tomorrow. She wanted to be alone.

The drive home was a blur. She wondered how many red lights she'd driven through or if she'd driven the wrong way down a one-way street. Her mind was elsewhere. It was bad enough her superiors were questioning her abilities, now the entire population of Sheffield would be talking about the competency of Detective Chief Inspector Matilda Darke.

'I don't deserve that title any more,' she said to herself. It was the only sentence she'd said with any confidence all day.

Matilda opened the front door, kicked the mail from the doormat, and slammed the door behind her. The house was cold;

she didn't notice. The answering machine on the hall table was flashing three messages at her. Could this be the dreaded Christmas invitation from her mother? She headed straight for the kitchen, threw the local newspaper down on the counter, and went to the fridge where she knew a half-bottle of wine was waiting for her. The paper was calling to her and she couldn't resist reading it again. And again.

A cold shiver brought Matilda back to reality. She looked around to find herself encased in darkness. How long had she been sitting at the kitchen table staring into space, her mind elsewhere? She turned on the lights and squinted under the brilliance of the neon. Once more her eyes fell onto the cruel headline.

'Fuck,' she said to herself in frustration. She popped two Venlafaxine from the blister pack, washed them down with the wine, and left the house, taking the newspaper with her.

Sitting behind the wheel of her car outside the apartment block where Jonathan Harkness lived, she was shaking and her head was pounding. The rage and tension building up inside her was agony.

Inside, Jonathan had eaten quickly; a cheese sandwich and a packet of ready salted crisps, and had taken a large black coffee into his library. In less than an hour he had finished *On Beulah Height* and was back in the living room choosing another book.

He picked up Ian Rankin's latest hardback and was just about to close the door to his sanctuary behind him when the sharp sound of the intercom buzzer tore through the heavy silence of his home.

He stood stock-still for a moment. Nobody ever visited him from the outside world. Only Maun came to see him, and she lived directly upstairs. Her three little taps on his front door was her signature. This was an unexpected visitor.

He decided against answering and walked slowly into his reading room. No sooner had he sat down on the wing chair than the buzzer sounded again. It sounded louder this time even though he knew that was impossible. He would have to answer it.

'Hello?' he asked, his mouth too close to the speaker. His voice was quiet and there was a nervous shake to it. He was not used to receiving guests and, if he was truthful, he didn't want to receive them.

'Mr Harkness? It's DCI Darke from South Yorkshire Police. I was wondering if I could have a word.'

Jonathan noticeably relaxed when he knew who his caller was. It was not a complete stranger. Although he hadn't enjoyed talking about his past to DCI Darke earlier, it wasn't the traumatic ordeal he had been expecting. She had a plain face and there was sadness in her eyes that he was drawn to. Since their chat, he had spent most of the afternoon wondering if she had a similar tragedy in her past to cause such a faraway look of loneliness.

'Yes, OK. Push the door.'

He pressed the buzzer and waited for the click before he released his fingers. He took the Ian Rankin novel into the reading room and placed it on the small table next to his chair and closed the door behind him. He had a brief look in the living room to make sure it was neat and tidy; it was never anything but, and then looked at his cold reflection in the mirror. His eyes were wide and starry. He looked at his neck and the red marks. Were they ever going to fade?

He opened the front door before Matilda had a chance to knock and let her into his flat. In the hallway he offered her a coffee, which she accepted, and he ushered her, once again, into the living room while he disappeared into the kitchen.

She headed straight for the wall of bookshelves. 'Your collection certainly is impressive Mr Harkness,' she called out.

Jonathan smiled to himself as he prepared the drinks. He was proud of his collection and it warmed him when others were impressed.

'I wish I had the time to read more,' she continued, 'unfortunately this job doesn't give you much free time for anything.'

Jonathan entered carrying two large black mugs. He handed her one and invited her to sit.

'Is it just mysteries that you read?' Matilda smiled and nodded at the bookcases.

'Yes.'

He looked at his collection as if he were seeing it for the first time. It was a collection he had spent years building and he was incredibly proud of his library. Jonathan had every published novel by the likes of Minette Walters, Val McDermid, Peter Robinson, Mark Billingham, Reginald Hill, Ian Rankin, M. R. Hall, Stuart MacBride – the list was endless.

'I'm afraid I don't know most of those authors.' Matilda scanned each shelf from left to right and stopped when she found someone she recognized. 'Simon Kernick. My husband used to read him. Once he picked one of his books up I wouldn't get a word out of him until he finished it.'

The conversation dried up. Jonathan smiled and turned towards his books. He felt comfortable among them. Just reading the titles and the name of the author gave him a relaxed feeling. It was as if he was among friends. All he had to do was look at the books and he felt a warm glow grow inside him and a sweet smile spread across his face. He slowly reached out a hand and his fingertips lightly touched the spines. They felt warm and comforting. They didn't judge him or hate him. They offered him a release from his agonies and he loved every single one of them for it.

'I wanted to come and see you because of the local newspaper. Have you seen tonight's edition?' Matilda asked.

'I saw it in the staffroom at work.'

'Ah. Well, I wanted to explain. I didn't want you thinking your parents' murder was being used as a way to ease me back into work.'

'I didn't think that. I thought the article was very unfair.'

'Thank you,' she said.

'I remember the Carl Meagan case. You mustn't blame yourself for what happened. People who kidnap for money are always thwarted in their task. They will have turned up at the exchange, I'm sure of it. They will have seen how they couldn't possibly have gotten away from there without being caught and simply bolted. No amount of ransom money was going to save them from capture, and if they had got away, they would have been looking over their shoulder for the rest of their lives. It was much easier for them to run empty-handed.'

'They were hardly empty-handed. They had Carl. They still have Carl.'

'I think it's a safe assumption to say that Carl Meagan is dead,' Jonathan said matter-of-factly. He showed no emotion for Carl.

'You sound like you know what you're talking about.'

'Probably too much crime fiction,' he said.

'Well I just wanted to allay any fears you may have that the reopening of your parents' case was a publicity stunt.'

'Thank you. I appreciate you coming here to tell me that.'

There was a long and awkward silence while they drank their coffee and gazed around the room. Apart from the books there was very little else to focus on.

'May I ask you a personal question?'

Jonathan looked across at her from the top of his coffee mug. He didn't like the sound of this. 'Of course,' he said through gritted teeth. He braced himself.

'After your parents were murdered and you moved away, did you ever have counselling or see a therapist?'

'I saw one straight away. While I was in the hospital here a counsellor was sent to my bed. She kept telling me that it wasn't my fault and wanted me to open up and tell her what I saw but I didn't trust her.'

'Why?'

'I'm not sure. There was just something about her I didn't like. She told me that whatever I told her would remain between the two of us but I knew she was going to run straight to the police and tell them. She had a devious look about her.'

'What about when you went to live with your aunt, did you have any counselling then?'

'My aunt was always taking me to the doctor. She was petrified that I would never speak again. I was sent to a quack who charged about a hundred pounds per hour. He saw me alone; my aunt was in the waiting room. He closed the blinds and turned the lights off and told me to close my eyes and hold my hands out. He put something in my hands that was cold and slimy. He asked me what I was feeling.'

Jonathan had no idea why he was opening up so much to Matilda. He had never told anyone about his visits to the many therapists before, not even Maun, and she had asked on several occasions. Talking to Matilda seemed easier. He didn't feel he was being judged.

'What did you say?'

'I didn't. He asked if it brought back any memories. He took whatever it was out of my hands then told me to open my eyes. I looked down at my hands and they were covered in blood. I just screamed and screamed. That's when my aunt came rushing in.'

'What was it he put in your hands?'

'It was meat. Cold raw meat that was all bloody and sticky. I could smell the flesh.' He took a deep breath to control his anxiety at the memory.

'That must have been horrible.'

'It was. My aunt was livid. She ranted at him for ages. I think she even hit him with her handbag.' He smiled at the memory. 'Strangely, I've not been able to eat meat since.'

'Are you on any kind of medication?'

'No,' he lied quickly. He didn't know why he suddenly decided to lie. He didn't like people thinking he wasn't able to get through life without prescription drugs. 'I used to be when I was a teenager but I read something once about being dependent on them and it put me off. I didn't like the idea of drugs controlling my thought patterns.' Jonathan genuinely believed that, but it still didn't stop him popping a few pills when he felt particularly anxious.

'Were they controlling your thought patterns?'

97

'I think they were.' He looked up at her and, for the first time, they made eye contact. He quickly looked away.

'Have you been diagnosed as autistic or having any mental health issue?'

'Why are you asking all these questions?'

'You seem to be extremely nervous and you're finding it difficult to make eye contact. You don't look relaxed at all even though this is your home. I just want to know a bit more about how you're coping.'

Jonathan took a deep breath. 'If you want to know how I'm coping then I'll tell you. I'm not. It doesn't take a psychologist to know that I lose myself in fiction because I'm frightened of facing my own reality. I read far too much but I do it because if I stop, if I sit down and allow myself to think for one minute, I'll be back in that house at the age of eleven wondering why my parents are covered in blood and not moving.'

Matilda put down her coffee and clamped a hand over her mouth. 'You really should seek professional help,' she said with a quivering voice.

'No thank you,' he said stoically. 'I'd rather continue the way I am. I know I'm not really living or using my life to its full potential but I'm coping with this situation in the best way that I can.'

'How have you coped, over the years, with the attention from the press and the fact that the case has often been referred to whenever a murder isn't solved?'

'I don't bother with newspapers so I don't know what's getting said about it. The only reminder I get is when Charlie Johnson contacts me.'

'If he contacts you again and it upsets you, let me know. I can have a word with him or you can apply for an injunction to stop him from contacting you.'

'That's taking it a bit far isn't it?'

'Not if he's upsetting you.'

Jonathan gave a weak smile and a slight nod of appreciation.

'I'd like to talk to Matthew at some point,' Matilda said. 'I know you don't know where he's living now, but do you know anyone who might?'

'No I don't. I'm sorry but like I said earlier, we're complete opposites. I don't know anything about him.' He thought for a second and his eyes widened at a flash of a memory. 'You could go through the medical archives. When he disappeared he was living in a den he made in the woods for a few days. When he was found he was freezing and had to have a couple of toes removed due to frostbite. That will be on his medical records. I'm sure there aren't many people in the country who are missing two toes.'

Chapter 16

In the last days of her husband's illness, Matilda gave a key to Adele Kean so she could check on James whenever Matilda was held up at work. She knew her husband was going to die; what she didn't want was for him to die alone.

Whenever Matilda had to work late Adele would go around and sit with James until she returned. When he died and Matilda fell into a deep depression of grief, Adele hung on to the key and used it more and more. Now, she used it whenever she visited.

It was just gone eight o'clock in the morning and Adele opened the front door of Matilda's house only to be hit in the face by a wall of heat. The central heating was turned up high and even though it was well below freezing outdoors it was far too hot inside.

In the living room, Adele found Matilda asleep on the sofa wearing the same clothes she wore yesterday. The coffee table was a mess of paperwork. On the floor was an empty bottle of vodka, and in her right hand, Matilda held tightly onto a glass half filled with the clear alcohol.

Adele rolled her eyes at the scene of self-destruction laid out before her. This could not go on, not if she wanted to keep her job.

'Matilda, come on, wake up.'

Matilda didn't even stir. Adele took the glass from her hand and picked up the empty bottle from the floor along with a few sheets of paper that had spilled out of the Harkness files.

'Matilda, it's morning, you have to get up now,' she said loudly. Matilda gave a grunt in reply as she adjusted herself into a more comfortable position.

Adele leaned over her friend, she was almost unrecognizable. Her hair was tangled, her skin dry and flaking, and the dark lines under her eyes were deep and cavernous. She looked down on her with sadness. It was upsetting to see the once confident and stable woman turn into a ruin, but there was nothing Adele could do. Only Matilda could decide to change.

She grabbed her by the shoulders and shook her hard. 'Matilda, wake up. It's time to go to work. Come on.' She continued shaking vigorously until Matilda's bloodshot eyes opened.

'My God, you look like a basset hound.'

Matilda tried to talk but her mouth was dry. She coughed a few times and leaned down to the vodka bottle that wasn't there. 'What time is it?'

'It's just gone eight.'

'Is it?' She struggled to get up from the sofa, wincing with each muscle that ached. 'I should get ready for work.'

'I don't think so.'

'What? Why not? Is it Sunday?'

'You're not going anywhere until you've showered, had something to eat, and you and I have had a good chat.'

'I don't have time for this.'

'I don't care. You're going to make time.'

'Adele, not now.'

Adele left the room and came straight back in carrying the mirror from the hallway. She held it up for Matilda to see her reflection.

She blinked hard a few times to clear her blurred vision and sighed at the tired face staring back at her. 'So?'

'This is not you Matilda.'

'It looks like me.'

'No it doesn't.' She put the mirror down and took the silver-framed picture of Matilda and James on their wedding day from the mantelpiece. 'This is you. This is Matilda Darke; neat hair, well turned out, confident and smiling.'

'That Matilda's dead.'

'No she isn't, she's just in hiding. She's feeling low because of what's happened this past year but she's still with us. You just have to make the effort.'

'I don't have the energy for this.'

'Then what do you have the energy for?'

'Going back to sleep.' She tried to lie back down on the sofa but Adele grabbed her by the shoulders again and hoisted her up.

'Do you honestly think I'm going to let you stay here in this mess? What kind of friend would I be if I just allowed this to continue; drinking every night so heavily that you pass out on the sofa, not eating, and wallowing in your own self-pity?' She waited for a reply but didn't receive one. 'What do you think James would say if he could see you now?'

'Well he's not here is he? If he was I wouldn't be like this,' she snapped.

'Do you think he'd want you grieving for him like this? This is not the Matilda he married.'

Matilda's bottom lip quivered in emotion and a single tear fell from her left eye. 'I just miss him so much.'

Adele sat down and put her arm around Matilda. Adele could feel her best friend sink into her. It wasn't long before she could feel Matilda's body begin to relax and the tears began to flow freely. 'I know you do, sweetheart. He was a good man; one of the best, but you're still here and you can't allow yourself to suffer in this way.'

'I know but I don't know how else to cope.'

'Yes you do. You go out there fighting like you've always done. You hold your head up high and you don't take shit from anyone.'

'I don't think I have the energy for that.'

'Yes you do. You have a hot shower; you have a good breakfast, take a deep breath of toxic air out there, and stick two fingers up to the world. We're two of a kind you and I; we get kicked in the teeth but we keep getting up and showing the big man upstairs that he can throw anything he likes at us and we're going to carry on regardless.'

There was a long silence while Matilda took in Adele's words.

'I went to see Jonathan Harkness last night. He's not living either, he just exists. You should see his flat Adele; it's just full of books. He spends every waking hour reading, throwing himself into fiction to get away from his own life. There's not a single photo of any friends or family, hardly any furniture, just books. He's just waiting to die.'

'And you don't want to end up like that.'

'I am like that,' she shrugged.

'No you're not. Not yet. It's not too late to save you.'

'And what about Jonathan?'

'Not to sound heartless but he's not your problem. It's sad what happened to him, tragic even, but he's just a case you're working on. He'd have been offered counselling and therapy all those years ago after his parents were killed. Even as an adult he could have gone to see a professional and talked through his problems, but he's obviously decided the way he's living is the best way he can cope with it.'

'But he's not living.'

Adele shrugged. 'Then maybe he's punishing himself for what happened. Maybe he thinks he should have died along with his mother and father, and by living in a self-induced exile he's denying himself the life he believes should have been taken from him.'

Matilda looked at Adele with wet eyes and a deep frown. 'Where do you get all this crap?'

'It just comes to me,' she said with a smile.

'It's lucky you work with the dead and they can't hear you,' she chuckled.

103

'Look, go upstairs and have a hot shower. I'll tidy this mess up and make a start on breakfast. It won't matter if you're a bit late for work. Go on.'

She nudged Matilda with her elbow until she eventually stood up. Adele watched as Matilda had to hold on to the wall to steady herself. It was only when she was out of the room and slowly plodding up the stairs that Adele turned to the mess in the living room and began tidying up.

Following DCI Darke's visit last night, Jonathan didn't return to his reading room; he went straight to bed. He spent several hours wide awake as his mind took him on a journey through his past. He remembered the many therapists he saw and how useless they were in trying to unlock his sealed memory. He was suspicious of their motives for wanting him to open up. He didn't trust a single one of them not to sell his story to a newspaper the second he left their office.

That was part of Jonathan's problem; he didn't trust anyone. Even when his parents were alive he didn't accept their love as true. He saw the way they allowed Matthew to get away with murder and how they continued to lavish gifts upon him even though he defied their rules. To their faces Matthew had the smile of an angel, behind their backs his halo slipped and the smile changed to a lethal sneer.

On the sidelines, Jonathan watched this behaviour unfold. If Matthew's love for his parents was false then was the reverse true? Did Stefan and Miranda really love their children or were they just there to be used as props to show the world they had the perfect family life? Either way, Jonathan didn't trust anyone and that wariness continued into adulthood.

The only person he came close to trusting was his Aunt Clara. It took him a while to see she had no ulterior motive for taking him into her home. She made sure the press stayed away and stopped the police from pressuring him into answering the same questions over and over again, even to the point of giving a false statement saying Jonathan had told her everything that had happened on the night in question, when in fact he still hadn't uttered a single word to her. She wanted him to have a normal childhood, as normal as possible under the circumstances, but when she saw Jonathan isolate himself from the other children she decided to allow him to live his life the way he wanted. It was this freedom that earned her his trust.

During the darkest hours when he struggled to sleep, Jonathan examined his life. It wasn't a life, merely an existence, but he was content with his lot. He just wished people would leave him alone to get on with it and stop trying to rake up the past.

Despite having only an hour's sleep, he was dressed and ready to leave the flat for work at eight o'clock. As usual he was smartly turned out in his black trousers and shoes and a freshly laundered Waterstones' shirt. His hair was bland but neatly trimmed and brushed forward; he didn't use any fancy products. He spent time putting on his coat, scarf, and gloves, making sure the buttons were fastened and he was well protected against the bitter wind outside.

Before leaving he went on a tour of every room. He made sure all the windows were closed and securely locked, all the plugs were pulled out and a good distance away from the sockets, the fire was turned off and the central heating was timed to come on one hour before he returned home. Satisfied, he left the apartment.

He just stepped out of the foyer into the cold light of day when a car pulled up in front of the building.

'Jonathan,' called the driver to get his attention. 'Jonathan,' he called again when he was ignored the first time.

Who was calling his name? There wasn't anyone who knew Jonathan by name, to call out to him and have a chat in the street. He stood stock still and surveyed his surroundings. He was too far away from his apartment block to dash back inside and there was no side road or alleyway he could run down. He could feel a cold sweat flow down his back. He took a deep breath to compose himself and tried to slow down his rapid heartbeat. With trepidation Jonathan turned around. He bent down to look through the window and saw the smiling face of his boss Stephen Egan.

'Get in,' Stephen said with a smile on his face.

'What are you doing here?' Jonathan asked, not moving closer to the car. Despite knowing the driver he was still reluctant to relax. Seeing Stephen out of context was worrying.

'I'm offering you a lift to work.'

'But you don't live anywhere near here.'

'I had to drop something off for a friend. She only lives a couple of streets away. I thought I'd come and give you a lift.'

'That's very nice of you, thank you. I have my weekly bus pass though.'

'You're not telling me you'd rather sit on a bus full of moaning people than get driven there in my car with heated seats?' He smiled and leaned forward to open the passenger door. 'Get in.'

Jonathan thought for a while. He assessed the situation in his mind before deciding it was safe to proceed. He found himself smiling as he lowered himself into the car. Stephen was right; the seats were heated and very comfortable too.

'I almost bought a house around here a few years ago,' Stephen said after a couple of minutes of silence.

'Really? Why didn't you?'

'After the viewings and putting mine on the market and all the fuss with redecorating the deal fell through and I just couldn't be bothered searching again. Shame really, I could have given you a lift to work every day.'

'I think I would have got used to that, especially with these seats.'

'I told you they were comfortable. How come you don't drive?'

'I'm not sure. It's just something I've never really thought about. Besides, there's nothing wrong with public transport.'

'There's a lot wrong with public transport,' Stephen scoffed. 'For a start the buses never run to time, the drivers are surly, the other passengers always seem to fit into one of two categories; the

106

ones who have a body odour problem or the ones who wear far too much perfume. Either way they're all an assault on the senses.'

Jonathan laughed. 'That sounds like everyone who's ever sat next to me on a bus.'

From inside the apartment block, Maun was looking out of her window as Jonathan, with what looked like a genuine smile on his face, eased himself into his boss's car. She watched until it turned the corner and was out of sight before turning away from the window. She was still in her dressing gown, with no reason to get dressed and leave the flat, until now.

Chapter 17

Acting DCI Ben Hales looked harassed. He was alone in the Murder Room and hunched over his laptop. Yesterday he had sent Charlie Johnson twenty-three emails and not one had been replied to. He wondered if there was any way you could tell if an email had been read. He guessed the officers who worked in computer fraud would know, but then it would get out that he's contacting Charlie Johnson when he shouldn't be. He opened his email once again and composed another message.

> **FROM:** "Ben Hales"
> (BHales@SYPolice.gov.uk)
> **TO:** "Charlie Johnson"
> (CJohnson37@hotmail.com)
> **SUBJECT:** URGENT!!!!!!!
> **Message:** Charlie, I need you to email me, text me or call me immediately. You're leaving me hanging here and I need information from you. How can I help you if you won't help me? Please get in touch with me today. It really is bloody urgent now Charlie. Ben

The door to the office opened and he quickly snapped shut his laptop. It was Sian. She was wrapped tightly in her winter finery.

'Blimey it's cold in here, has the sodding heating not come on again?' she asked, removing a glove and placing her hand on a lukewarm radiator. 'I bled them only a couple of weeks ago. Aren't you cold?'

'I've not noticed it.' He was looking into the distance, the weight of the world on his shoulders.

'I'll make us a coffee. You want one?'

'Please.'

'So what's the plan of action for today then?' Sian asked as she filled up the kettle and flicked the switch. As it started to boil she tentatively placed her hands around it to warm them up.

'I want to know who our dead man is and who killed him,' Ben replied, almost spitting his words out in frustration. 'Not a single person has called to say they're missing a relative, friend, or colleague. Not one person saw him get beaten to death. It's like he just fell out of the sky.'

'Maybe he did. People are busy; they don't want to get involved in things that don't directly involve them any more.'

'Well that's a reassuring sentiment. Since when did you become so cynical Sian?'

'It's working in this job that's done it.' She smiled, handing him his coffee mug. She took a packet of Bourbon biscuits out of her bottom drawer and placed them on his desk for him to help himself. The caffeine and the chocolate seemed to perk him up – a little. 'We'll get him identified today. There'll be a record of him somewhere and he shouldn't be too hard to track down with his missing toes. Once we've got an ID we'll soon find out who killed him.'

Ben didn't look convinced. He started to say something then changed his mind, sighing instead.

'Is something wrong?' Sian asked.

'What?'

'You look like you're sat on a knife-edge. What's the matter?'

'Nothing.'

'Well I know that's not true. Come on Ben, there's only us two here, spit it out. It's because Matilda's back isn't it?'

He flinched at the mere mention of her name. 'I can't help it. I know I shouldn't be so angry towards her but it's like she can do no wrong. I don't care what that review panel concluded, she ballsed up the Carl Meagan case and she should have been fired, at the very least demoted. What happens? She's still heading MIT and I'm still a fucking DI arresting scummy drug dealers and abusive husbands.'

Sian stared deep into her coffee cup. Ben looked up and remembered how close Sian and Matilda were. Would she tell her what he had just said?

'Did you talk to her yesterday?' Sian asked.

'No. I didn't even see her.'

'What? Why not? Look, make the first move. Go and see her, welcome her back. Whether you mean it or not it will help.'

He shrugged. He wasn't convinced. 'I need some air. Thanks for the biscuits,' he muttered, leaving the room before she could stop him.

Matilda came down the stairs feeling like she had undergone a make-over. Her hair was still damp from the shower but neatly combed. Her face was red from the heat but it was clean and her eyes were bright.

She entered the kitchen and Adele looked up at her. Matilda held her arms out to show the new and improved Matilda Darke. She was dressed in black trousers and a white shirt, crisp, clean and professional.

'How do I look?'

'Like a poorly poured pint of Guinness with a load of froth.'

'Excellent. That's the look I'm going for.'

Adele pushed the plunger down on a cafetière. Under the grill were two bagels slowly toasting. 'Right, the bagels are a couple of days past their sell-by date but they'll be fine toasted. You really need to do a shop.'

'I know. I can't remember the last time I did one.'

'I tell you what; I'll order you some stuff from the Internet, just the basics and I'll have Chris come round and sit in when it's due to arrive.'

'You don't need to do that. I'll go to Tesco this weekend.'

'No you won't. Besides, Chris won't mind. He's very easily bribed.'

'Thank you,' Matilda said, bowing her head, embarrassed about needing to be looked after like this.

'Now, what do you want on your bagels? I've thrown the cream cheese away. For some reason, grey cheese didn't look appealing. All you've got is apricot jam and butter.'

'Butter's fine.'

'Good, because apricots shouldn't smell like feet; I think I'll chuck this out too.'

Adele set about finishing off the breakfast while Matilda sat down at the table in the corner of the kitchen. She looked out of the window for the first time this morning and saw her abandoned back garden. The trees needed pruning; the bushes were wild and the grass almost knee-high. It was a mess but under a thick layer of frost from a night of freezing temperatures it looked lovely.

'This winter seems to be dragging on.'

'It's only December,' Adele said, bringing the coffee and bagels to the table. She sat opposite her and took a lingering sniff from her own mug of coffee. 'We've got a few more months of this to come.'

'I thought we'd have had snow by now. It's cold enough.'

'I love this time of year. I spent a fortune on my winter coat so I don't mind a long cold winter. Eat your breakfast.'

Matilda began to eat slowly. With each tiny bite she took she spent time chewing before swallowing. She looked straight ahead, straight through Adele, and seemingly into another dimension.

'What are you thinking about?'

'Nothing,' Matilda said.

'You're thinking about Jonathan Harkness aren't you?'

'Are you telepathic?'

'I am. Why do you think Chris stays out of my way?' She smiled. 'So go on, why has Jonathan Harkness got under your skin?'

'I don't know. He's just so sad. You can actually see it on his face.'

'I can see it on your face too sometimes. You get a look. It's like you're here but you're not here.'

'He has the same look.'

'That's why you're thinking about him a lot. He's been like this for twenty years. You've been like this for almost one. You think you're going to end up like him.'

'Maybe.'

'You're not though. You have me and you have Chris, and your parents and your sister, when she remembers to call.'

'Jonathan's in his early thirties, right, and I don't think he's been happy for one single day in his life.'

'That can't be true,' she scoffed. 'He'll have had some happy times as a child. He's lived through a traumatic experience; he's just blocked it out.'

They fell silent while Matilda took small bites of the stale bagel and struggled to swallow them. Adele drank her coffee, analysing her friend from the top of the mug. 'You can't save him, you know.'

'Sorry?'

'Jonathan Harkness. You can't save him.'

'I don't know what you mean.'

'I knew this would happen. You blame yourself for Carl Meagan so you're latching on to Jonathan Harkness as some form of redemption.'

'That's ridiculous.'

'Is it?'

She relented. 'Well can you blame me? Everywhere I look I see Carl Meagan. I killed him.'

'Carl Meagan is not dead. He's just missing.'

'I should have found him.'

'And Scotland Yard should have found Jack the Ripper but they didn't. You cannot blame yourself for what happened. He was kidnapped, the ransom didn't go to plan, and they fled with the child. Until a body is found he is still alive and could turn up at any time.' She paused, allowing Matilda to take it all in. 'Jonathan Harkness is a completely different person. This is a different case. So stop trying to save a lost cause.'

'Jonathan's brother used to abuse him. I get the feeling his parents knew and were too busy or just couldn't be bothered to stop it.'

'That is sad but it's just a case you're working on,' Adele said, looking down. 'What happened to the brother after they were split up?'

'I've no idea. Jonathan seems to think he went to university in Manchester, after that he doesn't know.'

'So they lost contact?'

'I think Jonathan would have been happy to get away from Matthew after everything he put him through. There's nothing in the files that says where he is now.'

'Maybe he's left the country.'

'Maybe. Listen, can you track people down through the medical archives?'

'How do you mean?'

'Well, if you've had an operation or whatever, it stays on your medical records doesn't it, for future reference?'

'Yes.'

'So we could track Matthew down through his medical history?'

'It's possible I suppose. Though if you're talking about a guy who's had his appendix out, that's going to be a bloody long list.'

'It's more than that. When their parents died, Matthew went missing for a few days. It turned out he'd been hiding in the local woods in a den he'd built. By the time he turned up he was suffering from severe frostbite. He had to have a couple of toes removed.'

'You're joking?'

'No. Why?'

'Yesterday, a body was found in the city centre, on Holly Lane. I went to the scene and you're Acting DCI Hales was there. It was a man in his mid-thirties who had been beaten to death. He was unrecognizable. His liver had actually exploded inside him. He was also missing a couple of toes from his left foot.'

'Matthew Harkness?'

'As of yesterday afternoon they hadn't yet identified him.'

'It's got to be him. Surely.'

'I don't know.'

'Oh come on Adele, how many people do you know have toes missing?'

'It certainly is a coincidence.'

'The police don't believe in the c-word. It's got to be him.'

Suddenly Matilda came alive. The tiredness left her eyes and she was filled with the energy needed to get through another day. If Matthew was dead, murdered, then whoever killed him could be linked to the cold case of the Harkness killings.

Chapter 18

Matilda was happy to be stuck in traffic. For the first time since her return to work she had an energy that could see her pick up Ben Hales's sodding Audi and throw it to the other side of the car park leaving her space free.

The news from Adele that her latest lodger in the mortuary was missing toes, just like Jonathan's brother, gave her a smile on her face, and an eagerness to get to work. If it was the same person, could it be that the reopening of the Harkness case had brought the original murderer out of hiding? If so, why kill Matthew? He wasn't even at home on the night his parents were killed. However, did he know something about who was responsible?

She drummed her fingers on the steering wheel. It had been five minutes since she'd moved. Chesterfield Road's traffic problems seemed to be getting worse by the day. The council had spent thousands of pounds putting in parking bays and new traffic light systems, but the flow of traffic had not eased.

She bit her lower lip in anticipation of a productive day's work ahead. She could feel the prickly heat of anxiety rising up her back but it wasn't a worrying feeling; she was anxious because she wanted to get to work. She was almost excited.

By the time she kicked open the door to her claustrophobic office-cum-cupboard, DC Rory Fleming was already waiting for her. He was dressed in a light grey suit, white shirt, and grey tie. He looked smart, fresh, and raring to go. Matilda was hot, flushed, and sweating.

'How long have you been here?' she asked, trying to get her breath back.

'About half an hour or so.'

'You come the same way as I do. Didn't you hit the traffic on Chesterfield Road?'

'No,' he shrugged, turning in his seat and getting back to the sports section in *The Sun*.

'You can put that away. There's been a development.' She sat down and looked at him with wide eyes. She couldn't wait to get started. 'Have you heard about the case the murder team are working on?'

Rory rolled his eyes. 'No. I've been left out of all the excitement. It's like I've been ostracized since working this cold case. I said hello to Sian this morning and she looked at me as if she was trying to remember who I was.'

Matilda couldn't help but smile. 'Well, you may be back in the Murder Room sooner than you think.'

'Really?'

'Yesterday morning a body was found in Holly Lane, in the city centre, next to an 80s themed nightclub.'

'I know it,' Rory said, interrupting. 'It's just off West Street. I've had some great nights out around there.'

'Anyway,' she continued, ignoring him, 'the body was missing a couple of toes on his left foot. Last night when I went to visit Jonathan Harkness . . . '

'You visited Jonathan Harkness last night? I thought you had a curfew?'

Matilda sighed. 'Do you want to hear this or not?'

'Go on.'

'I was talking to Jonathan about his brother. Just after their parents were killed Matthew went missing for a few days. Now, it was December and freezing cold and he was hiding out in a den he'd made in the woods. When he was found he was suffering from mild hypothermia, and, get this, he had to have a couple of toes removed from his left foot.'

'Seriously?'

'Yep,' she said, sitting back in her chair and smiling.

'So the dead body is Matthew Harkness?'

'He'll have to be identified, but it's a bit of a coincidence don't you think? How many people do you know have missing toes?'

'Have you shared this with the Acting DCI?'

Matilda's smile suddenly dropped and she felt her blood run cold. Just because the man had nicked her parking space did not make him evil. Why was she feeling such animosity towards him?

'Not yet. I just wanted to sound it out, make sure I'm not jumping the gun or anything.'

'Well, like you said, it's a mighty coincidence, and, as you know, rule number one of the police handbook: there is no such thing as coincidences.'

'I should probably go and see him then.'

'Probably.'

They both remained motionless in their seats.

'Did Sheffield United win last night?' She nodded at his open newspaper.

The walk from her small office to the Murder Room felt endless. Every tap her shoes made on the plastic tiled flooring seemed to get louder as if announcing her journey. As she turned the corner and saw the double doors up ahead she felt a heavy weight upon her. She felt as if she didn't belong here.

At the glass doors to the Murder Room Matilda stood looking in. This was no longer her domain. Standing on the threshold she felt like a stranger. As she opened the doors everyone stopped in their task to look at their visitor. Suddenly the ticking clock was the loudest noise. If there had been a man in the corner playing

117

the piano he would have stopped and headed for the safety of his seat by the bar.

Sian moved first and gave her a little wave. The smile on her face was beaming. Ben looked up from his laptop and their eyes met. Who would blink first? Matilda was frozen to the spot. Her hand was gripped firmly on the door handle and the whiteness of her knuckles suggested she was not going to let go. The silence lengthened.

The two cowboys were at a stalemate, both waiting for the other to make the first move.

Walpole, Compton, Pelham, Pelham-Holles, Cavendish.

From out of nowhere, Rory Fleming squeezed past Matilda and entered the room. 'Aaron, you owe me a fiver you loser.'

His outburst broke the silence and the mannequins of detectives felt they were able to move again and return to their duties.

'Don't think so,' DS Aaron Connolly said. 'It was a draw. The goal was disallowed.'

'The ball was way over the line. It was obvious.'

'That's not what the referee said,' Aaron said.

'The ref and the linesmen were tossers. The ball was definitely over the line, everyone says so. You owe me a fiver.'

'Officially, the ball didn't make it into the goal. Therefore the fiver stays in my pocket. Better luck next time,' he said. His grin was wide and cheeky.

Matilda made her way gingerly over to Ben's desk.

'Hello Ben,' she said in a quiet, pathetic, voice.

'Matilda. Good to see you back.' His lie was obvious.

She tried to remember if Hales had used her Christian name before, but her mind was a thick mist. It felt strange hearing him drop rank.

'It's good to be back. How's everything going in here?' she asked, looking around the room and seeing nothing had changed. The room did look smaller for some reason.

'It's going well.'

118

'Good. I hear you've got a dead man who is missing a few toes,' she began, eager to drive the conversation forward so she could get out of here. She suddenly had the urge to vomit and she didn't know why.

'That's right.' He looked over at Sian and his frown deepened.

Matilda wondered whether he thought Sian was feeding her information. Even if Hales did accuse her, Sian could take care of herself. 'Have you managed to identify him yet?'

'Not yet, no, but it's early days.'

'I'm sure you know that I'm working on the Harkness cold case.' Ben nodded and his lips moved as if to smile. Matilda pushed on. 'I was talking to Jonathan Harkness yesterday and he happened to mention that his brother's left foot is minus a couple of toes.'

'Really?' He folded his arms in defence.

'Yes. I'm wondering if I could get Jonathan Harkness to have a look at the body; see if he can ID him.'

Ben bit his bottom lip. 'I think perhaps we should go and have a chat with the ACC.'

'Surely we don't need to involve the ACC. If it turns out not to be Matthew then we've wasted everyone's time.'

'This is my case Matilda. I want the ACC to know everything that is going on.'

Chapter 19

Maun Barrington was wrapped up against the elements. It was the sixth day in a row that daytime temperatures had barely scraped zero degrees and forecasters were not optimistic of a respite in the cold weather. Snow was on its way, apparently. When, the forecasters couldn't say, but Sheffield was in a prime position as it was sheltered by the Pennines that bore the brunt of any heavy snowfall coming in from the west.

Maun, however, was not taking any risks. The heavy snowfall of 2010 had caused her to be housebound for several days, unable to get out and restock her cupboards of the most basic provisions.

Her Morrison's trolley was stocked with everyday needs. Reluctantly, she added several tubs of powdered milk. She hated the taste of the stuff and it didn't matter how many times she stirred her coffee, little flakes of powder floated to the top, but needs must when the devil drives.

As she made her way to the cashier to pay, she stopped at the newspaper stand and added several dailies to her shopping along with the locals; the *Sheffield Star*, the *Sheffield Telegraph*, and the *Yorkshire Post*.

It took three trips from her car to her flat to unload her provisions. On the final leg she came across two of her neighbours in the foyer. They both turned their back to her as she came through the door. They lowered their voices and waited until Maun had disappeared up the stairs and around the corner before they returned to their normal speaking voices.

It no longer bothered Maun that she was being shunned in such a way by her childish neighbours. She had been ostracized for the best part of twenty-five years, she was used to it. She had Jonathan to chat to and keep her company, which was enough for her. Things seemed to be changing though. Jonathan was reluctant to engage Maun in conversation. He didn't want her with him when his childhood home was being demolished, and she guessed he wouldn't want to talk about events in the newspaper. He had also been dropping Stephen Egan's name into conversation. She guessed he was someone from work, but who, and why did he seem to have such an effect on Jonathan?

From a bag she removed the ingredients for making moussaka, Jonathan's favourite meal, onto the kitchen counter. By the time he arrived home from work it would be fully prepared and the smell floating down the stairs would be irresistible to him.

Before the arduous task of cooking, she decided to have half an hour with the newspapers. She made herself a large mug of coffee and sat in front of the fire, which was blasting out the maximum heat possible.

The national newspapers didn't carry much of the story of the demolition of the Harkness house, just a photograph of the building mid-collapse and a few lines of text underneath. They didn't seem too interested in the case being reviewed either. The three local papers were though. They had colour pictures of a bulldozer tearing through the roof, small black and white images of the house in its heyday, and passport size shots of Stefan and Miranda Harkness. There was a brief history of the case followed by a paragraph on the Detective Chief Inspector who was heading the review. On the basis of her tired-looking photo, Maun didn't think there was any chance of the case being solved. The DCI lacked the professional grace of a serious detective.

The three local papers all sounded the same. Maun wondered if just one person had written the story then syndicated it out to the other locals. The odd descriptive word had been changed but the body of the text was uniform.

Carefully she cut out all three stories and went over to the sideboard in the corner of the large living room. In the cupboard was a thick red leather-covered photo album. There were very few blank pages left. The first five pages were full of pictures from her wedding day. She used to look at these photographs and smile; not any more. The further on in the book she went the fewer photographs there were; they were replaced by newspaper and magazine cuttings. Her eyes glanced at the headlines: LOCAL BUSINESSMAN KILLED ON NOTORIOUS COUNTRY ROAD; EYE WITNESS: BARRINGTON CAR WAS SPEEDING; BARRINGTON PASSENGER WAS NOT WEARING SEATBELT.

She turned the pages quickly. She was in no mood to relive the events of more than two decades ago when her husband and his young secretary, Dawn Edwards, were tragically killed while on their way to Manchester for a meeting. She didn't even think about it when she saw pictures of the wrecked car, or his smiling face looking out at her. She no longer felt anything for the man she had been married to for thirteen years.

The headlines continued to scream out at her: FULL DETAILS OF BARRINGTON RELATIONSHIP WITH SECRETARY REVEALED; WAS DAWN EDWARDS PREGNANT?; MAUN BARRINGTON BRANDED A LIAR BY EDWARDS MOTHER.

Maun closed her eyes as she flicked through the book. Although she felt nothing for her cheating husband she did not enjoy seeing her name in print. Eventually the events of her husband's death stopped making the headlines and the cuttings of stories changed from being about her life to that of Jonathan Harkness. The original stories from when Jonathan's parents were murdered adorned the dark pages: HUSBAND AND WIFE BUTCHERED; 11-YR-OLD SON WITNESSED PARENTS SLAYING; TEEN SON MISSING;

JONATHAN MAY NEVER SPEAK AGAIN; MATTHEW FOUND! They went on and on through the book, detailing every event of the police investigation, from the false sightings of Matthew to the interviews with animal rights activists. She had it all in pristine condition; a macabre collection of the Harkness horror.

It had been many years since she had entered a new clipping. The final one: THREE YEARS ON: WILL HARKNESS KILLERS EVER BE FOUND? read like a fitting conclusion. Since then, nothing, the case was cold after all, but now it was warming up, the hunt was on for the killer. She wondered if she would need to purchase a thicker book.

Chapter 20

Matilda had to trot to keep up with Ben as he stormed down the corridor; his strides long, his footfalls heavy and determined. She shook her head then rolled her eyes. This was an exercise in futility; it did not need the approval of the ACC. She had information that could lead to the identification of his dead body. It was as simple as that. Why involve a higher rank? What was his game?

Luckily for Matilda there was a sizable gap between Ben knocking on Masterson's door and being called to enter. She managed to catch up and regain her breath.

Valerie Masterson sat behind her large desk. She had an iPhone in one hand and was frantically smashing a cordless mouse onto the pad next to the wireless keyboard. When she saw who her visitors were she put down the phone.

'Have you ever noticed how computers seem to freeze when you need them the most? Bloody thing!'

'You know,' Ben Hales began before Matilda could chime in, 'there is something to be said for turning it off and back on again. That seems to work for me almost every time. Shall I get someone from IT to come and take a look at it?'

'Don't bother I've already called. They're sending someone up. So,' she said, giving up on the computer and pushing the keyboard to one side, 'to what do I owe the pleasure?'

Matilda quickly jumped in before Ben, and gave Masterson a brief rundown of recent events; how Matthew Harkness was missing toes due to frostbite when he disappeared and how a dead body recently discovered also had toes missing.

'It sounds like the past meets the present,' Masterson said. 'How do you want to play this?'

'I want to bring this Jonathan in,' Hales jumped in.

'Hang on a minute,' Matilda called out, eager to protect Jonathan from Hales and his bully-boy tactics. 'You've not met him, I have. Jonathan is extremely fragile. I think we need to take the softly-softly approach.' She couldn't see him, as they were standing side by side, but Matilda was sure Ben was rolling his eyes. 'I suggest I go and see him again. I'll take Rory. We'll mention that a body has been found and get Jonathan to ID him. If it's Matthew then we bring Jonathan back here and question him.'

Masterson shrugged. 'Sounds good to me.'

'If the body is Matthew, I want in on the interview,' Ben said.

'Of course. It's your case Ben. This Jonathan Harkness, Matilda, is he depressive? Does he have a mental health problem?'

'I'm not sure. I did ask but he wasn't very forthcoming. I wouldn't be surprised if he was depressed or had some kind of mental impairment. He is taking medication for depression though.'

Their eyes locked. They seemed to be reading each other's minds. If anybody could recognize the signs of severe depression it was someone who had been through it.

'OK, here's what you're going to do; Matilda, go and see Jonathan, get him to ID and bring him back here if the body is that of his brother. However, we need to tread carefully. If he ends up being a material witness it's not going to look good in court if he's been mistreated here. Matilda, you'll act as a go-between. Ben, anything you need from Jonathan, you go through Matilda. Understand?'

The sudden change in Ben's appearance was palpable. He clenched his fists, his face turned red and, if possible, steam would have come out of his ears. He agreed through gritted teeth and left the room, taking long strides once again. Matilda waited where she was in front of Masterson's desk, her hands behind her back; they were clammy and itching. She blinked when the door slammed.

'I don't think he's too keen on me being back at work.'

Masterson smiled. 'He's a man, they're not very adaptable. He'll get used to it. How are things anyway?'

'They're good. I'm getting there.' She smiled an awkward smile; it was bitter and cold.

'Good. Anything you need, you know where to find me.'

'Thanks.' *How about getting that tosser to move his prick-mobile from my parking space?*

Matilda eventually caught up with Ben back in the Murder Room. This time, she didn't hesitate; she pulled open the door with force and marched in.

'I want a word with you,' she called out. 'In private,' she added when she realized everyone in the room was staring at her.

'Of course. Let's go into *my* office,' he said, over-emphasizing 'my' to let her know he'd taken over her old office.

She took a deep breath and followed him, taking heavy strides. She slammed the door behind her with her foot. 'What the hell is wrong with you?' She tried to keep her voice down but it didn't work, she was fuming. This was hardly going to be a private conversation either; they could still be heard by the others in the main part of the large open-plan office.

'There's absolutely nothing wrong with me.'

His demeanour was quieter and more relaxed. He had a slight smile on his lips that infuriated Matilda. He was doing this on purpose, trying to get a rise out of her, make her snap and lash out, maybe even slap him.

'You stormed out of the ACC's office like a child. Do you have a problem with me?'

'No.' He lowered his head. Clearly he did have a problem.

126

'Why don't I believe you? Look, I know you've been Acting DCI while I've been away, and while I'm working on the Harkness case this department is all yours. If you think I'm stepping on your toes you're completely wrong.'

'I don't know what you're talking about.'

'I think you do. I know you resent me coming back. You think the MIT should have been yours in the first place. When I left you couldn't wait to get your feet under the table. Well I'm sorry to tell you this Acting DCI Hales,' she over-pronounced the acting, 'but I'm back and I'll be having that desk very soon.'

She quickly turned on her heels and made to leave the room.

'Hang on a minute.' Ben lifted himself up to his full height. 'Your return to this department is not a forgone conclusion. I have a one hundred per cent success rate while I've been in charge. Can you say that?'

There was a noticeable gasp from the rest of the Murder Room. Both Matilda and Ben suddenly realized they were being overheard. The walls of the partitioned office were very thin and they were hardly whispering. She couldn't think of anything to say. Suddenly an image of Carl Meagan came into her head; his fluffy blond hair, his bright blue eyes, his smooth pale skin. She had failed him and his entire family.

'You can't can you? You fucked up, DCI Darke, and I don't care what happens when you've finished with the Harkness case, but you're not coming back here. Not if I have anything to do with it.'

Matilda bit her bottom lip. She had plenty to say to Hales but was afraid of opening her mouth in case it released a flood of emotion. She tried to keep her stare cold and icy before turning and leaving the room. She wanted to slam the door, but didn't want to give him the satisfaction of knowing he'd managed to get under her skin.

The silence was tense. Nobody uttered a single word. In the end it was Aaron Connolly who broke the silence with a sneeze. Sian blessed him and the room continued to go about its business.

*

'Sian,' Faith called out, her voice an octave above a whisper. 'Were they talking about Matthew Harkness?'

'No, Jonathan. Why?'

'Shit.'

'What's wrong?'

'The car park next to the nightclub where the body was found, there were five cars parked in it. I ran the registration numbers through the computer and one of them belonged to a Matthew Harkness. Do you think he could be a relation?'

Sian rolled her eyes. 'Matthew is the name of Jonathan's brother.'

Sian went over to the office and lightly tapped on the glass. She opened the door a crack and stuck her head inside. Faith leaned back in her chair as far as she could to try and hear what was being said but couldn't.

'What?' Ben shouted, slamming his hands on the table. He practically jumped up out of his seat and barged past Sian to get to Faith. 'How long have you been sitting on this?'

'I . . . well. I didn't know the name Harkness was important.'

'How can you not know? Don't they teach you anything at school any more? Twenty years ago the whole country was looking to Sheffield to find out who murdered Stefan and Miranda Harkness.'

'Twenty years ago I was only four.'

Sian sniggered and received a dirty looked from Hales.

With shaking fingers, Faith rummaged through the mountain of paperwork on her desk. She had witness statements from workers in the nightclub and the City Hall. She had names and addresses of people who worked in the area who she had yet to contact. She couldn't find the computer printout at all. She pulled it out from under her laptop and flicked through a couple of pages.

'What am I looking at?' Hales asked impatiently.

'Silver Audi TT. It's registered to a Matthew Harkness. He lives in Manchester.'

'Have you contacted him yet?'

128

'Not yet, I've been busy. He's probably staying in one of the hotels, probably here on business.'

'Or probably in the morgue. You should have given me this sooner.'

'I'm sorry. I didn't know,' she said, her head bowed.

'And get your bloody desk sorted out. It's a tip,' he called over his shoulder as he left the room.

Feeling like she had been told off by a strict teacher, Faith sat down in her chair and slowly began pulling the paperwork together, trying to neaten things up in an organized fashion.

Sitting at the desks behind her, Aaron and Sian exchanged glances. Sian wanted to smile. Hales's blue-eyed girl was no longer flavour of the month. She couldn't help feeling sorry for her though. She'd give her a few minutes to compose herself then offer her a cup of tea and one of her own Tunnock's Teacakes she kept in her bottom drawer.

Chapter 21

It took Matilda a matter of minutes to reach her broom cupboard of an office but the news of her public outburst with Hales had already reached Fleming.

'I heard you've just torn a strip off our beloved Acting DCI,' he said with a smirk on his face.

'Were you eavesdropping?'

He waved his iPhone at her. 'It's called instant messaging. Aaron was telling me all about it.'

'There's no wonder cases go unsolved if people are more interested in office gossip. We may as well be working in a call centre.'

'Nah, this is much more fun. Are you going to give me all the gory details?'

'Why don't you log on to YouTube? Maybe Aaron filmed the whole argument and posted it online. Come on,' she grabbed her coat from the back of her chair and walked out of the room with Rory hot on her heels.

It would have been easier and quicker to walk from the station to Waterstones in Orchard Square but they needed the car to take Jonathan to identify the dead body. The traffic was slow and, adding in the array of one-way systems, road works, and pedestrian crossings, the simple five-minute journey turned into a twenty-minute headache.

However, Matilda used the time to indulge Rory in her argument with Ben, which he lapped up like a secretary at a water cooler. She lost count of the number of times he said 'I wish I'd been there'. As she was coming to the end of her story her phone beeped with a text message from Sian: I DOUBT HALES WILL TELL U BUT AN AUDI TT IN CAR PARK NEAR DEAD BODY BELONGS TO MATTHEW HARKNESS OF MANCHESTER. Matilda sent a quick reply before relaying the information to Rory.

'So it looks likely the dead body is Jonathan's brother.'

'It would appear so.'

'It can't be just a coincidence can it? I mean, Matthew's a common enough name, but is Harkness?' Matilda asked.

'I'm not sure. I had a teacher at school called Mrs Harkness. She was a real bitch.'

'Did she have a son called Matthew?'

'I don't think so.'

'Jonathan says he didn't know where his brother was living. I'm guessing he didn't know he was back in Sheffield either.'

'Maybe he'd come back for the demolition.'

'If it was you, wouldn't you have visited your brother too?'

'Well I would, yes.'

'So then what happened to get himself murdered in the few hours he was here?' She suddenly became restless. 'Oh this is taking forever,' she moaned at the lack of progress in the journey. She unbuckled her seatbelt. 'You park up and join me. I'm going to walk the rest of the way. I can practically see the sodding shop from here.'

The blast of hot air from inside the shop was like a warm hug and made Matilda smile. The smell of freshly ground coffee from the upstairs café was inviting too. What could be more inviting on a freezing cold day than a hot coffee and a good book? Maybe even throw in a double chocolate muffin too.

Classic Christmas carols were quietly played throughout the store and customers talked to each other in hushed tones as they went about their book-buying business. The biography section seemed to be busy as did the crime-fiction corner. Last year she bought her husband a couple of sporting biographies and the latest John Grisham as part of their huge Christmas extravaganza. This year she didn't have anybody special to buy for. She decided to make a point of buying Adele and Chris something expensive to thank them for all the help they'd given her this year. She'd send a card to her sister and one to her parents but that was all.

Matilda could understand Jonathan and Matthew being separated. Like them, she and her sister Harriet were completely different people. Despite there being only two years between them they had very little in common. Matilda had been career driven since leaving school with good exam grades and from an early age knew she wanted to join the police force. Harriet, on the other hand, just wanted to fall in love with a tall handsome rich man and have children. She eventually married at the age of twenty-five, but her husband wasn't overly tall, he certainly wasn't handsome, and he probably would have been rich had he not married her sister. Harriet now lived in a bland suburban street in Grimsby close to the coast where she worked for three days a week in a boutique and looked after her family. Very conservative.

Matilda's parents were constantly trying to compare the two daughters, and until she met James, she was often bombarded with calls from her mother asking her why she hadn't met a man yet. With the amount of work being piled up on her in her aim for a top job and the constant nagging from her parents, something had to give. Eventually Matilda started to screen her calls and only phoned her mother once a month. Contact with her sister was now reduced to birthday and Christmas cards. They literally had nothing in common, like Matthew and Jonathan Harkness.

'Is there anything I can help you with?'

A member of staff wearing a Santa hat broke Matilda's contemplation. 'I'm sorry?'

'You look a little lost. Is there anything specific you're after?'

132

'No. I mean, could you tell me where Jonathan Harkness is please?'

'Jonathan?' Stephen Egan overheard and came over to join the conversation. 'Is there anything I can help with?' he asked.

'You are?'

'I'm Stephen Egan, the manager. And you are?'

'I'm Detective Chief Inspector Matilda Darke, South Yorkshire Police. I'd like to have a word with Jonathan if I may.'

'I think he's in the storeroom. Wendy, would you go and get him for me please?'

The assistant looked from her boss to the detective and back again with a quizzical look before heading off in the direction of the storeroom.

'Is there something wrong?' Stephen asked after looking around to make sure they weren't being overheard.

'Not really. Well, yes and no. May I ask you about Jonathan?'

'What do you want to know?'

'Is he all right?'

Stephen frowned. 'All right? Yes he's fine. Why?'

'I don't mean if he's unwell or anything but is there something troubling him? Well, not troubling as such.' She was floundering. 'Does he have any kind of illness?'

'I'm not sure I know what you're getting at.'

'I'm sorry. Is there anywhere more private we can chat?'

Stephen led the way up the stairs to his office. As they reached the top of the stairs Rory entered the shop and quickly followed them. Stephen's office wasn't very large, no bigger than the one Matilda was being forced to use, but it was bright and well decorated. There was a window which was clean, and the venetian blind seemed to work. Stephen took a pile of books off a couple of chairs and asked his guests to be seated. He took his usual seat behind the desk. With three of them in the room it gave a slight claustrophobic feel. Matilda wondered how Jonathan would cope when he entered.

'What's this all about?'

'I don't want to say too much at the moment but do you know much about Jonathan, about his past?'

'You mean his parents being murdered?'

'Yes.'

'I know the basics. I know what Jonathan's told me and, unfortunately, curiosity got the better of me and I read Charlie Johnson's book.'

'Do you know about the case being reviewed?'

'Yes. I read about that in the paper last night.'

'How's Jonathan taking it?'

Stephen thought for a moment. 'He's no different. In a way I think he expected it.'

'What do you mean?'

'Well he's known about the house being demolished for a while now. I think he knew interest was going to be raised once again.'

'And he's OK with it?'

'He seems to be.'

'I've spoken to Jonathan on a couple of occasions, he seems a bit ... I don't know how to put this without sounding indelicate ... '

Stephen gave a half smile. 'You want to know if he has any mental illness.'

'Yes,' she said with a slight tilt of the head.

'As far as I know he's not. I'm sure he's depressed, but he's never sought medical advice that I know of. Jonathan's a bit of a loner. He just wants to come to work, do his job, and go home again.'

'Do you know anything about him personally?'

'What do you mean?'

'Relationships.'

'I've known Jonathan for about five years or so. In all of that time I've never known him mention a relationship or any friends, apart from his neighbour, Maun Barrington.'

'Does he have Asperger's?' Rory asked, speaking for the first time.

'Sorry?' Stephen asked almost shocked by the question.

'People with Asperger's Syndrome find it difficult to make friends and develop relationships.'

'I think you may be reading too much into this,' Stephen began. 'There is nothing wrong with Jonathan. What happened to him as a child has had a deep effect on him. We all handle situations differently and the way Jonathan is dealing with this is by playing a background role in his own life.'

'That's not a very healthy way to live though, is it?'

'No it isn't, but it seems to suit Jonathan. Surely it's up to him how he lives his own life, or doesn't live it.'

'Who knows Jonathan most of all?'

'That would be me I suppose.'

'I don't just mean at work, I meant in general. Is there anyone he is particularly close to?'

'No. Like I said he has a neighbour, but she is in her sixties, I believe, so I can't think they'd have a great deal in common.'

'I have some delicate information for Jonathan and I'm not sure how he'll take it. Would it be better if you stayed?'

'Is this about the body that was found in Holly Lane?'

'How do you know about that?' Matilda asked almost accusingly.

'It's only a stone's throw away from here. People talk.'

Matilda sighed. Bloody gossips. 'We think it may be his brother.'

'Oh my God,' Stephen brought his hand up to his mouth. 'Are you sure?'

'Not one hundred per cent, no. That's why we're here. We need him to identify it.'

'Oh God,' he said.

'How do you think Jonathan will react when we tell him?'

'To be perfectly honest I don't think you'll get a reaction out of him. I have never seen him display any signs of emotion. Whether he goes home at night and cries himself to sleep I'm not sure, but he's never shown his emotions at work.'

'Is there anyone who could accompany Jonathan to identify the body?'

'I could come,' he answered rather quickly. 'I mean, if he didn't mind that is.'

135

Matilda wondered how Stephen could proclaim to be close enough to Jonathan to want to assist in the identifying of a dead body, yet know so little about the man. Jonathan really must play his cards close to his chest. And Matilda thought she was being guarded with her feelings!

In the bowels of the shop Jonathan Harkness was going about his business in his usual professional manner. He loved everything about books, the feel, the smell, the weight. He opened a plastic crate from a recent delivery and took out a handful of cookery books by a celebrity chef he had never heard of. He wasn't a fan of cooking. He knew the basics so he would never starve, but he didn't go in for messing around with herbs, spices, and he wouldn't know what to do with a pestle and mortar. The subject of cookery may not interest him but it didn't matter, it was still a book and it deserved his respect.

He cast his book-lover's eye over each copy, making sure there were no tears in the cover, no dents, no creases or marks. This batch passed his test and he placed them on the trolley to take up to the cookery section.

'Jonathan, you've got a visitor.'

He heard Wendy's voice coming from somewhere but he couldn't see her. He felt unsettled. He didn't receive visitors at home, why should he have one at work?

'Who is it?'

'The police,' she replied in a sinister voice, as if he should be guilty of something.

He closed his eyes and pictured his reading room, his happy place. Sitting alone in his leather wing chair, his feet up on the footstool, and reading a hardback crime novel. Why couldn't that be his life? Why did he have to be a part of the real world?

'I'll be right up,' he said with a broken voice.

Chapter 22

As he marched down the corridor Ben looked at the display on his Blackberry. He had four missed calls from his wife. He pulled a crumpled packet of cigarettes out of his inside jacket pocket; only three left. He had given up smoking years ago but there was always a stray packet of fags laying around the office somewhere. This was a very stressful job; even the non-smokers sometimes gave into their urges. Everybody needed a release at some point.

He lit up as soon as he left the building and sucked hard on the filter tip. He could feel the smoke enter his lungs and his body giving in to the addictive power of the drug. He sucked again, harder this time, and felt himself become light-headed. It was a good feeling.

'You called,' he said into his phone when his wife answered on the second ring. He could picture her curled up on the sofa watching mindless daytime crap on the television.

'Yes about half a dozen times.'

'Four, actually. What's up?'

'Nothing. I just wanted to see what you were up to.'

'It's called work.' *You should try it some time.* He took another long drag on the cigarette and felt his nerves begin to settle once again. Sometimes he really loathed his wife.

'There's no need to snap; I was only asking.'

'Sorry,' he apologized, without meaning it. 'I was in with the ACC this morning. She asked me to start preparing to hand back over to Matilda.'

'You're joking, surely?'

'Nope.'

'She's not even considering you taking her place permanently?'

'Nope,' he said through gritted teeth.

'The bitch. Do you want me to have a word with Daddy?'

He closed his eyes and counted to ten. He came very close to screaming down the phone YOU'RE FORTY-SIX YEARS OLD FOR FUCK'S SAKE. STOP CALLING HIM DADDY.

'Ben, are you still there?'

'Yes I'm still here and no I don't want you calling your daddy,' he said with as much sarcasm as he could muster.

'You're not just going to roll over and take it are you?'

'I have no choice.'

'You have every choice. She practically signed Carl Meagan's death warrant and she's getting away with it. What about this case you've got on at the moment, how's that going? Surely you'll get some brownie points for solving that.'

'Well it would appear my case is connected to Matilda's case. It's not confirmed yet but it looks like our victim could be Matthew Harkness.'

'Who's he?'

He gripped the phone tightly in his left hand and sucked even harder on his cigarette, inhaling as many toxins as he could in one breath. He leaned against the cold stone of the building to steady himself. How could she not know who Matthew Harkness was? He supposed that if he'd never been a guest on *Loose Women* she wouldn't know.

'He's Jonathan's brother. Remember, twenty years ago when his parents were butchered, he's the kid who disappeared?'

'And his body's just been found now?'

He sighed audibly at her ignorance. 'I'm going now, I've got things to do. I'll be late home.' He hung up without waiting for her to say goodbye. Why hadn't being married to the daughter of a Chief Constable opened any doors for him? What did he have to do to get promoted? He was a good detective, a brilliant one in his own opinion. He kept his nose clean, obtained results and had given his father-in-law two selfish bitches for granddaughters. He could not do anything else, yet once again, he was being overlooked.

He looked at his tired reflection in the dirty window. He was fifty years old and he was beginning to lose his grip on reality. What was the point in being the good guy if it didn't get him anywhere?

He searched through his mobile for a number he had been using a lot lately and pressed the green button to call. After three rings the voicemail kicked in. Frustrated, he sighed. He could really have done with talking to someone with intelligence right now, someone who knew the case and could tell him where to go next. He left a message.

'It's me. Where the bloody hell are you? Matthew Harkness has been found murdered in Sheffield. Ring me as soon as you can. I need your help.'

'Where is everybody?' Faith entered the room and was surprised to see only Sian in there. She was standing at the drinks station waiting for the kettle to boil.

'You don't want to know,' she replied without looking up. She could smell the strong perfume before she even came in. Unconsciously she looked at the young DC and saw her eyes were red, she had obviously been crying. 'Would you like me to make you a cup of tea?' Sian asked in her soothing, motherly tone.

'I'd rather have a coffee if you don't mind? Strong, dash of milk.'

Sian smiled to herself. She wondered how long it would be before the flavoured teas went out of the window and the lure of caffeine brought her over to the dark side. Consciously, and with a hint of malice, Sian made the coffee in a generic mug reserved for visitors rather than using Faith's own china mug with butter-flies on it.

Faith took the coffee from her without saying anything and took a sip. The caffeine seemed to work immediately and she visibly relaxed. It was like a syringe full of heroin shooting up her veins.

'Is everything all right?'

'You don't have to ask Sian. I know I'm not well liked in here.'

'I wouldn't have asked if I wasn't interested.'

Neither of them acknowledged whether Faith was liked or not.

'I think I just let everything get on top of me. DCI Hales having a go at me in front of everyone didn't help. I'm trying my best here.' She flicked her head back, which caused her ponytail to swish.

Sian wondered if this was just something she did to get people to sympathize with her; put on the little girl act.

'I so want to do the right thing but there were a lot of people at the murder site to go through and it took forever to get someone at the City Hall to get back to me about the CCTV.'

'Look,' Sian went over to Faith's desk and perched on the end. 'Ignore Hales; his nose is all out of joint because Matilda's back and he's worried she'll take over.'

'Will she?'

'That's for the ACC to decide.'

'What's Matilda like to work for?'

'A lot better than Hales,' she scoffed, then suddenly remembered it was his protégée she was talking to. 'Don't get me wrong, Hales is a very good detective, but Matilda is a people person; she knows how to get the best out of her officers, well, she used to,' she added, almost to herself.

Faith took another sip of coffee, a heavy frown on her face. 'Sian, do you think I'm cut out for MIT?'

It was at this point Sian saw Faith for who she really was; not the brainless bimbo who had seen one too many episodes of *CSI: New York* and wanted to be a part of the glamorous lifestyle of ridding the world of crime, but an almost frightened young woman eager to please, impress, and work her fingers to the bone.

'That's not my place to say,' Sian replied as magnanimously as possible. She headed back to her own desk.

'I know, but I would really appreciate your opinion.'

'To be honest Faith, you haven't been here long enough to decide for yourself whether MIT is for you or not, let alone anyone else.'

'You don't, do you?'

'I'm not saying that. Look, wait until this case is over with, then evaluate your own input. If you're happy with the contribution you've made then so be it. Then, in the next case, go one step further and do more.'

'I'm so green; I had no idea of the amount of repetitive work involved. It's all, question this witness, question another witness, get everyone's details, run a check on every single car in the car park. Before you know it a whole day has gone by and you've just been checking the PNC.'

'I know. I've been there myself. Look, there are only so many hours in a day and you can't solve a murder case on your own, despite what Columbo thinks.' She wondered if Faith had even heard of Columbo. 'Now drink your coffee and we'll take a look at what you've got left to do, OK?'

Faith smiled and seemed to relax a bit more. 'Thanks Sian.'

'That's OK. Now, I've contacted Manchester police and they're sending a couple of uniforms around to Matthew Harkness's apartment to see if he is our dead body. In the meantime Matilda and Rory have taken Jonathan to ID the body; Aaron is around here somewhere; I'm going to have to have a chat with him at some point today too; he seems a bit moody, but then what man isn't? And I've no idea where Hales is.' She rolled her eyes. She didn't care where Hales was.

The door was kicked open and DC Scott Andrews entered. His face was red with anger and his blue eyes were steely and wide. He was tall and muscular, throwing the heavy door open was no problem for him and it bounced back on its hinges. 'Two days in that fucking courtroom waiting to give evidence and the prick changes his plea at the last minute.'

'What?' Sian asked.

'Daniel bloody Bishop. He's spent two days watching the evidence mount up and realized he's screwed so decided to plead guilty. I could have killed the little prick.'

Sian smiled; again, she had been in his position many times too. Faith was pleased Scott had returned, she would be able to team up with him and share the humiliating dressing-downs Hales gave her in front of everybody. She suddenly felt better about being in the MIT.

Chapter 23

Jonathan's reaction wasn't what Matilda had expected. She had been dreading informing him of the brutal death of his brother but he just nodded his head and said, 'I see', dispassionately. He listened intently as she asked him to ID the body and allowed himself to be led out of the shop as if going for a pleasant Sunday afternoon drive.

Standing in front of the double doors to the mortuary, Matilda once again checked Jonathan out of the corner of her eye; he looked calm, but he had been immersing himself in the gruesome world of crime fiction for the past decade, if not longer. He should know everything about what went on behind the doors.

Inside the morgue Adele's assistant was scrubbing vigorously at a stainless-steel tabletop. She had finished cleaning it of its latest occupant and was buffing the steel to a shine.

From her corner office Adele Kean saw her visitors arrive. She leapt up from her seat, quickly swallowing her bite of tuna salad sandwich, and went out to greet them. Her usual friendly smile was replaced with one of sympathy and regret. She nodded a welcome to Matilda and Rory and offered her sympathies to Jonathan. She led them through to an anteroom where the fridges were kept. In the middle of a single table was a body covered with a plain white sheet.

'I want you to take a good long look,' Matilda said. 'Take your time. There is absolutely no rush. I'll need you to tell me clearly if this is your brother or not. Do you understand?'

'Yes,' replied Jonathan, his voice firm and emotionless.

He took a long deep breath and braced himself. His hands were by his side and once again he was tapping his fingers against his thumb.

Matilda took a step back from him and gave the nod to Adele, who unfurled the white sheet to reveal the head and shoulders of the dead man.

His hair was neat and clean, dark brown and combed, not a strand out of place. One eye was covered with a small surgical pad held in place by tape. He had a purple bruise on his lower lip and another pad on his neck. His skin was pale and cold and his mouth was almost smiling. He looked at peace, as if he was in a deep sleep.

Jonathan looked at the dead man. Slowly, he stepped forward and leaned over him to get a better look.

From their positions, only Adele could see his face and noticed that his expression didn't change.

Seconds passed by, then a whole minute and still the heavy silence entombed them.

'Jonathan,' Matilda prompted, her quiet voice resounded off the stainless steel of the fridge doors.

'Yes. Yes it's Matthew.' His voice was broken.

'Are you sure?'

'Yes. I'd know that face anywhere.'

Jonathan was transfixed on the body of his brother.

Matilda nodded to Adele once again, who covered the body with the white sheet, but still Jonathan refused to look away.

Staring widely, he could not take his eyes from the mound on the trolley.

'We will, of course, need to ask you a few more questions Jonathan; this time back at the station. It's just routine. Stephen can come with you if you wish.'

144

He didn't hear her. He was locked inside his own mind and fixed on his dead brother. There was a blank expression on his pale face. His eyes darted left and right in quick succession as his brain processed what it was seeing.

Matilda looked at him, into him, to try and read what he was thinking, but she couldn't. Had he worked so hard on alienating people that even his subconscious refused to give anything away?

'We don't have to do this now. Perhaps you'd like to come down to the station tomorrow.'

Again, silence. She looked up at Adele and across at Rory but they were as dumbfounded by Jonathan's silence as she was.

Stephen stepped forward and gently placed a hand on Jonathan's shoulder.

'I'll make sure he comes to see you tomorrow. I think this has been a bit too much for him.'

'I understand.'

'Jonathan, come on, let's go and get some fresh air.'

It was a while before Jonathan moved, and eventually Stephen had to apply a little pressure and coax him out of the mortuary.

'Bloody hell, he was mesmerized wasn't he?' Rory said when the doors had closed behind them.

'Can you blame him? He was abused by Matthew for years and the next time he sees him, he is a corpse. I was waiting for Jonathan to jump onto the trolley and start pummelling him.'

'That thought crossed my mind too.' Rory smiled. 'I don't think I would have been in a rush to stop him either.'

'Jonathan's very fragile isn't he?' Adele asked. 'He looks like a strong gust of wind would snap him in half.'

'What did you get from the PM, Adele?' Matilda asked after a few long seconds of deep thought.

'What I expected to really, judging by his injuries. I did get a wee bit excited about some skin samples under his fingernails but it turned out they were his own.'

'How does that work?' Rory asked.

'Well imagine you're on the ground being kicked black and blue, you lift your arms up to protect the most delicate part of your body, your head. It's instinctive. He's had his hands wrapped around his head so firmly that he's actually broken the skin on his scalp. You can see the nail indentations.'

Adele pulled back the white sheet once again and messed up Matthew's neat hair with her fingers. She showed the detectives the several small crescent marks made by the deceased's own fingers.

'He suffered many blows to the head, chest, and trunk of the body. His liver was almost double the size it should be; it practically exploded. Every rib is broken, his head has been pierced twice, as has his right lung, and his stomach wall is ruptured.'

'Bloody hell.'

'A professional beating maybe?' Rory asked.

'Or a very enthusiastic amateur.'

'Anything from toxicology?'

'It's a bit early for that. I'm hoping it will show he was pissed out of his brain so he didn't feel much. Oh, his last meal was a KFC, if you're interested.'

'Not a very appetizing choice,' Rory said.

'How's the investigation going? Have you got a suspect yet?' Adele asked. She moved away from the body and Rory followed.

'Not yet. We've got Manchester police searching his flat, going door to door. As soon as we find out what kind of a person he was and what he was doing here in Sheffield we should start putting things together. I wouldn't mind betting Jonathan knows more than a thing or two.'

'What?' Matilda snapped out of her musings and joined them in the main part of the mortuary.

'I'm just saying they were brothers; how can Jonathan not know anything about his own brother?'

'Have you actually read any of the statements and reports? They were split up. They haven't seen each other for the best part of twenty years . . .'

'We only have his word for that,' Rory interrupted.

'Jonathan is tortured, he's frightened, he lives on his nerves. He doesn't have the energy to inflict such violence on another person. Look at the facts before you start making assumptions. James is not a killer.'

'James? Who's James?'

The Freudian slip caused the blood to rush from Matilda's face and she was suddenly as pale as Matthew. She quickly looked at Adele, whose expression spoke a thousand words. Matilda was missing her husband; that much was obvious. He had been torn from her and she would give anything to have him back. As that was not possible she was transferring her emotions, her protecting, loving nature, and putting them on Jonathan. She couldn't be a loyal and protective wife to James any more, so she would be a loyal and protective mother figure to Jonathan.

Adele took hold of Rory's arm and led him back into the anteroom. 'Let me show you something.'

She quickly threw back the sheet. The extent of the injuries to Matthew Harkness was palpable. He was covered in various shades of purple bruises depending on the density and velocity of their making. His body was a textbook for every size, shape, and mass of contusion.

Rory took an intake of breath at the condition of the body. The amount of trauma on one body was difficult to comprehend. This truly was a beating designed to kill rather than a chance mugging by a stranger.

'Do you know what causes a contusion?' Adele asked.

'A good kicking?'

'It's damage to the capillaries by trauma, allowing the blood to seep into the surrounding tissue. A bruise is named depending on its size. As you can see here he was beaten so severely that it's very difficult to tell where one bruise ends and another begins.'

'Jesus! What kind of person could inflict such violence?'

147

'Well you're the detective, that's a question only you can answer. Though, of course, it does depend on the circumstances; was he drunk, was he attacked from behind, was there more than one attacker? Though looking at him, he's over six-feet tall and obviously worked out. If he knew what was happening then you're looking for someone much bigger and stronger than him. If he was unaware of his attack then it could be anyone.'

'Including his brother,' Rory said with a sense of drama in his voice.

'Rory, listen to Matilda on this. She knows what she's talking about. Jonathan is probably scared of his own shadow and I can't see him going out after dark let alone beating someone up.'

'I think we can all agree that the balance of his mind is greatly disturbed. I personally think anybody is capable of anything if they put their mind to it.'

'So cynical so young,' Adele smiled, tapping him slightly on the side of his face.

148

Chapter 24

Maun's apartment was the mirror image of Jonathan's, but the style of decoration was completely different. Where Jonathan had opted for a minimalistic approach to furniture, and filled the rest of his home with books, Maun cluttered her flat with sofas, armchairs, antique furniture and ornaments. It was in urgent need of a clearout and, as Jonathan was her only visitor, she could stand to lose a couple of chairs and open up the floor space. The flat was always hot, too, to the point of causing drowsiness.

By three o'clock, darkness was falling. She guessed Jonathan would be working late as Christmas drew ever near, but she decided to make a start on the moussaka anyway.

Maun's kitchen was much like her lounge; cluttered, with very little space on the work surfaces to prepare a meal. She had an old-fashioned, handwritten recipe book given to her by her mother. The pages were yellowed and the handwriting fading but it was still useful and one of the few keepsakes she had left.

Tears streamed down her face as she chopped the onions. She stuck out her tongue, as her mother taught her, but it didn't work, the tears still came. She added the minced lamb and the garlic, maybe too much, as the fumes made her choke. Then she tipped in the tin of tomatoes and the spices and waited for it to simmer.

Moussaka, when made correctly and using an old-fashioned recipe like this one, took a long time to prepare and even longer to cook in the oven. However, she knew it was one of Jonathan's favourite meals and she knew he didn't eat very well. She had never been able to smell anything cooking when she'd passed his flat. On a cold night like this he would appreciate the gesture. There was bound to be plenty left over too. He could take it home and warm up the leftovers for the following evening's meal.

Even if Jonathan was working late he should have been home by now. Maun looked at the clock on the ornament-strewn fireplace. It was 7 p.m. The bookshop had closed more than an hour ago. The weather was awful outside; the roads icy, a low hanging mist, so drivers would be more cautious, but still, he shouldn't be this late.

She opened the oven door and looked at the moussaka. It had been ready to eat an hour ago but was keeping warm on a very low heat. The once bubbling cheese had dried into a thick brown crust. She slammed the oven door closed, picked up the bowl of curling lettuce and practically threw it into the fridge. Maun didn't know if she was angry at the wasted meal, the fact Jonathan was late home, or that she didn't have a clue what was going on in his life any more. Since the news of his childhood home being demolished hit the press he had been more withdrawn and secretive than usual. He didn't want to visit her and wasn't interested in her coming to his flat. It was as if the rest of the residents in the block had won Jonathan over to their side and he was purposely blanking her like they did. Was that it? Had the stories of her relationship with her husband finally sunk in and he believed her to be the twisted, cold-hearted bitch everyone claimed her to be? 'They have no idea who I am,' she said to her tired reflection in the mirror above the fireplace. Her voice was full of venom and she spat out each word as if it had a bitter taste.

People are far too quick to judge others, especially when they don't have the full facts. Just because she hadn't shown any emotion over the death of her husband or given her side of the story to the newspapers when revelation after revelation was revealed, everybody made up their own version of events. Did privacy mean nothing any more? Why must people know every detail about each other?

The stories: Maun resenting her husband's success; her inability to have children; the humiliation over his many affairs; the refusal to give him a divorce; the mind games she played to drive him, literally, to his death. They weren't all untrue, but it was the fact people jumped to conclusions that annoyed her the most, and if her two-faced neighbours had broken Jonathan then it would be the final straw. Drastic action was needed.

Chapter 25

It wasn't until Jonathan and Stephen had left the hospital that it dawned on them they had no transport to get back to the book-shop. They set off tentatively on foot. Luckily, they were both wearing layers to keep out the freezing cold air. Jonathan walked at a brisk pace; his steps were heavy and erratic and matched the miasma of thoughts running through his brain.

'Jonathan, will you please slow down? I'm not as tall as you. I can't keep up,' Stephen called out.

Jonathan didn't hear him. He was in a world of his own. It wasn't just the torment of seeing a dead body; it was the sudden realization that he was the last surviving Harkness. He had never been bothered by the family unit before, knowing his brother was out there somewhere often filled him with dread and horror, especially knowing he could turn up at any time, but now that thought was gone, he suddenly felt all alone in the world. He wondered who would come to his funeral, who would arrange it?

'Jonathan, stop!' Stephen shouted.

Jonathan halted and spun on his heels. 'What?'

'I'm cold and I need a drink. Let's find a pub.'

'I don't drink.'

'Well I do. Come on, I'll show you how, it's easy.' He smiled and had a twinkle in his eye as he crossed the road without waiting for Jonathan.

Technically, Stephen and Jonathan were still working and were needed back at the bookshop, but that didn't stop Stephen ordering a pint of Guinness for him and a mango and passion fruit J2O for Jonathan. Stephen told Jonathan to find a table while he fetched the drinks.

Naturally he chose a table in the darkest corner furthest away from the other early-evening drinkers.

'How are you feeling?' Stephen waited until he had sat down, made himself comfortable, and had a good long swig of his drink before beginning the conversation.

'I'm fine,' he lied, giving his staple response to every question he had been asked in his life that involved discussing his feelings. A simple 'I'm fine' didn't usually lead to any follow-up questions.

'It's OK not to be fine.'

'Is it OK to be just fine?'

'Yes but you've just identified a dead body who, as it turned out, belongs to your brother . . . '

'Estranged brother,' Jonathan interrupted.

'But your brother nonetheless.'

'I haven't seen him for years. I can't even remember the last time I did see him.'

'But he is still your brother; your last surviving relative.'

'I'm aware of that.'

'How does that make you feel?'

He thought for a while before answering. 'I don't know. I honestly do not know. I feel kind of . . . empty.'

'Empty?'

'Look, Stephen, I know you want me to be sad, upset, or angry and shout and burst into tears but I can't do that. He was my brother in name only. He was a horrible man and his death means absolutely nothing to me. I know that sounds bad and makes me

153

out to be cold and hard but I'm sorry. How am I supposed to feel? I know the same about him as you do.'

It was the first time Stephen had heard Jonathan talk so confidently and passionately about something other than books, and he was taken aback by the harsh reality of Jonathan's feelings of animosity towards his brother.

'I'm sorry.'

'No, don't be. I'm sorry. I shouldn't involve you in all this. Thank you for coming with me though. I really appreciate it.'

'You're welcome and why shouldn't you involve me? Everybody needs someone, a friend, or someone to confide in.'

Stephen leaned forward and placed a comforting hand on top of Jonathan's. When he recoiled, he quickly removed it.

'I'm fine on my own,' he said, once again lying. He turned away and took a sip of his ice-cold drink.

'You can't go through life on your own.'

'Why not? I don't do anyone any harm. I keep myself to myself. I work, I pay my taxes, I'm doing everything right. Why can't I just be left alone? Who am I hurting?'

'Yourself.'

'What?'

'It's not natural to be alone, to spend your entire life trapped inside your own mind.'

'What makes you think surrounding yourself with people makes life better? You read the newspapers; the majority of crimes committed against the person are performed by someone the victim knows; rape, abuse, assault, murder, the victim nearly always knows who is harming them.'

'What about love, friendship, happiness, and relationships?'

'Love and happiness do not last forever. You can't live an entire life with a permanent smile on your face. Whenever there's a positive item leading the news the first thing people think is that it must be a slow news day. We're used to the horrors, the wars, the murders and the corruption. It's all part of our everyday life.'

'Well it shouldn't be.'

'But it is and it doesn't matter how in love with somebody you are, how many friends you have, one day something will happen that will destroy your way of life and turn it all upside down. Why risk the pain?'

'All of that's a part of life. The downsides and the upsides shape us. They make us who we are.'

'I was made who I am by the age of eleven. My entire world collapsed. Why repair it just for it to get broken again?'

'Who says it will get broken again?'

'It's the natural order of things. We're born alone and we die alone.'

Jonathan's defeatist attitude to life was often infectious. Stephen had gone from listening intently to looking despondent. 'Life is not that black and white, Jonathan. You can't think like that, you really can't. People need each other to survive. Allow somebody in to help you. Allow me in.' He took another large swig from his Guinness. If he ever doubted the use of alcohol as a confidence booster, he didn't now.

'You?'

'Why not?'

'Look at me; I'm a car crash on legs. My mind is poison. Why would you want to help me?'

'Because I like you,' he said. He smiled.

'What's to like?'

'You're intelligent, well read, passionate about the things you believe in. You're neat, polite, you don't conform to society by grabbing the latest technology the minute it's created. You're an individual, not one of the flock who has a Facebook page or a Twitter account. There's something refreshing about a person who doesn't own a mobile phone.' Stephen laughed. He took another drink of Guinness and a deep breath. 'You also have an incredible smile, on the odd occasions you use it, and you're very good-looking.'

155

'What?'

'You're good-looking.'

'Why would you say that?'

'Because it's true.'

'Stephen, I . . . '

'Jonathan, I've worked alongside you for years. You're a kind, generous person and as each day has gone by I've liked you more and more. You're hurting, I can see that, and I want to help. I want to take care of you. I want to hold you in my arms and protect you from your demons.'

'Stephen . . . '

'I love you Jonathan.'

With each minute that ticked by, the stronger Maun's anger grew. It had been a long time since she had actually created a meal from scratch and here she was having her kindness thrown back in her face. She didn't warrant this behaviour. All she wanted was to sit opposite Jonathan and enjoy a home-cooked meal on a cold winter's night and chat; was that too much to ask? Evidently it was.

She stormed into the kitchen and pulled open the oven door. Using a tea towel so as not to burn her fingers she pulled the ruined moussaka out and kicked the door closed. The meal had dried up; it was inedible. She pressed the pedal on the bin in the corner of the room and threw the whole thing into it with a heavy thud, including the ceramic dish she had cooked it in.

Her nostrils flared as she took deep breaths of exasperation. Jonathan's treatment of her was intolerable. She was angry, frustrated, a seething mass of rage. She had the urge to throw something, to smash something, to completely destroy something.

Stephen's bombshell had come completely out of the blue for Jonathan. He had no idea his boss felt this way about him. They had worked together for years, how had he not known? But then, how could Jonathan even begin to recognize love when he had never known it before. Did the staff at Waterstones know how Stephen felt? If so, why didn't they say anything? Jonathan hoped they hadn't all been talking about him behind his back. He didn't want to be the centre of gossip. He tried hard to fade into the background; why couldn't people just leave him alone?

Nobody had ever said they loved him before. As much as his Aunt Clara took care of him and welcomed him into her home, he'd always believed, deep down, she had done so out of duty.

Now here he was sitting opposite someone who had just declared their love for him. How was he supposed to react? Was this genuine or was Stephen playing a cruel joke to lure Jonathan into a false sense of security, before finishing him off completely and destroying him?

The silence grew.

Stephen looked into his almost empty Guinness glass.

Jonathan could see that he kept trying to look up, but nerves got the better of him. It was up to him to take the lead.

'Shall we go for a walk?' he asked Stephen.

157

Chapter 26

Not for the first time today DS Sian Mills found herself alone in the Murder Room. Acting DCI Hales had been missing in action for several hours, and Faith Easter had disappeared to the toilet more than half an hour ago. She was blaming an upset stomach for her sudden and frequent departures, but Sian heard the catch in her throat as she tried to swallow the tears from her previous run-in with Hales.

She was about to make a private call to her husband when her extension sang its usual irritating tinny ring. She sighed, and picked up the phone, identifying herself.

Earlier in the day she had contacted Manchester police and given them the address of Matthew Harkness to which his Audi TT was registered. Now, three hours later, they were calling back with their findings.

'Your dead man had some really expensive stuff. I thought my young PC was going to set up home there.' DS Richard Bellamy had a gruff Manchester accent.

Sian liked it. His fast pace of talking and his jokey attitude made her smile.

'Stylish then?'

'I believe it's called minimalistic. Everything was very clean and tidy, put away in drawers and cupboards; magazines neatly stacked on the coffee table. I don't know who his cleaner is but they deserve an OBE.'

'Do you get awarded an OBE for services to cleaning?'

'Probably. They hand them out for anything these days.'

Sian could sense a rant coming on so asked how he and his team entered the flat.

'His next-door neighbour had a key; lovely woman, blonde hair, blue eyes, nice . . . '

'I don't need her particulars, thanks. Did you find anything?'

'The usual. He had a neatly arranged concertina file in his spare bedroom that gave us plenty of information so we didn't have to do much snooping: gym membership, rugby club membership, casino, bars, et cetera. Contract of employment with all the details on it too, which was useful. I had a couple of uniformed lads go round to the gym and clubs to have a chat and find out what he was like. Oh and I found his car insurance details, which match the reg. number you gave me, and his passport was in his bedside cabinet. I'm scanning it as we speak; it will be with you shortly.'

'Anything more personal?'

'Not really. There were no photos on the walls, just very nice, expensive furniture, and a TV and entertainment unit that I would kill for.'

'Is that a confession?'

'Bugger. You've got me bang to rights,' he said with the throaty laugh of a heavy smoker. 'He had all the mod cons in the kitchen too, my wife would love a kitchen like his, not that it would stay clean for long with our kids, pair of monsters.'

'Did you find an address book or anything?'

'There was a small black book in his bedside cabinet that had a few numbers in it. I'll scan those too.'

'Anything for a Jonathan Harkness?'

'Hang on.'

Sian could hear the rattling of pages.

159

'No. Nothing under H or J. There's a newspaper clipping though, which was tucked into the back. It's from a national about a house being demolished in Sheffield. That'll be the infamous Harkness haunted house will it?'

'It certainly will. Can you email me the cutting too?'

'No problem.'

'Did you find anything out from the neighbour, the one with the key?'

'Yes, she's married and her husband's in the armed forces.'

Sian laughed. She wondered what it would be like to work alongside DS Bellamy. He could be fun around the office, brighten up a dull or difficult day. Though his constant joking would probably wear a little thin after a while.

'The neighbour with the key said she hardly ever saw him, and a few other neighbours backed her up. Apparently he's always away with work. She only had the key in case of emergencies and she picked up his mail too from time to time.'

'What work does he do?'

'His contract says he's a Technical Financial . . . I've got it here somewhere. His neighbours said it was something to do with accountancy but he's not an accountant. My eyes glazed over after a while. I've no idea how money works, just that my wife likes spending it. Head office is in London so he spends a lot of his time there.'

'I wonder if he had a place in London too,' Sian said, mostly to herself.

'No, I asked and the company puts him up in hotels.'

'Were there any photo albums, scrapbooks?'

'Yes there was. He had an album in his wardrobe and it had all the newspaper clippings of the case about his parents.'

'Interesting,' Sian said thoughtfully. 'Was there anything there that you thought a bit odd?'

'Yes. He's got eight copies of *A Christmas Killing* by Charlie Johnson.'

'Eight?'

'Yes.'

'Why would he have eight copies?'

'No idea. Maybe he liked to hand them out to girlfriends and play the poor wounded victim to get some action,' he said with a belly laugh.

'That's what you'd do is it?'

'Why not? Might as well use your personal tragedy for something.'

Sian laughed. 'Thanks for everything Richard. You've been a big help.'

'No problem. Anything else, just give us a call.'

'Will do and the next time I'm in Manchester I'll buy you a pint.'

'You certainly know the way to my heart; straight through my liver.'

As Sian hung up Rory breezed into the room with all the social grace of a hungry elephant. Sian wondered if she would ever get around to making her private phone call.

'Where is everyone?'

'Your guess is as good as mine. Hales is probably sulking somewhere, Aaron's going through statements, and Faith's in the toilets. Again.'

'Again? Is she not well?'

'I think she's allergic to being shouted at.'

'Oh. I was hoping for a full room when I burst in with my super fantastic news.'

'Well I'm sorry to disappoint you, you're going to have to settle for just me. So what's this fantastic news; you've solved the murders and we can all go home early?'

'Early?' He looked at his watch and saw it was just passed half-past eight. 'You call this early?'

'Actually I do. Come on then, tell me your news and if it's worth it I'll give you a chocolate teacake.'

'Jonathan ID'd the body as Matthew Harkness so we have one hundred per cent confirmation that our dead body is the oldest child of Stefan and Miranda Harkness. He was killed the night before his childhood home was being demolished. It's all fitting together rather nicely,' he said, rubbing his hands together.

'Well, I've just been on the phone to Manchester; they've searched his flat and I'm being emailed all the personal stuff, contract of employment, passport. It's definitely him.'

'Where does he work?'

'For some accountancy company in London.'

'Not short of a few quid then. Do I get my teacake?'

Sian smiled, opened her bottom drawer, and tossed a small foil-covered teacake across to him. Sometimes work in this office was like being at home with her kids.

'Oh, before I forget, DCI Darke asked me to ask you if you'll track down Charlie Johnson. She wants to talk to him, find out who his sources were when he was writing his book, that sort of thing.'

'OK. Have you read the book yet?'

'I'm about halfway through; bit of a slow reader.'

'According to the police in Manchester, Matthew Harkness had eight copies.'

'Eight? It's not that good. So what happens now that your case is linked with Darke's cold case?'

'I'm not sure. I'm guessing Matilda is going to want to be in on this. It's looking like a safe assumption to say that whoever killed Matthew has some connection to the Harkness killings twenty years ago.'

They sat in silence for a few seconds while they thought about what Sian had said.

'Maybe Matthew knew who killed his parents and now the case is back in the spotlight the killer is afraid of being caught so killed Matthew to silence him,' Rory guessed.

'But if Matthew knew who the killer was, surely he would have mentioned it years ago. You'd want the person who murdered your parents locked up wouldn't you?'

162

'OK. Well, maybe the killer thought Matthew would put two and two together now the case is reopened so had to be silenced before he could do anything about it.'

'What about Jonathan putting two and two together?'

'The killer could have been keeping an eye on Matthew and Jonathan over the years. He knows Jonathan's a bit of a paranoid wreck, but Matthew, who is a sane and strong individual, is more of a threat.'

'That's possible, I suppose,' Sian said.

'Or maybe the killer arranged to meet Matthew here in Sheffield to talk things over, see the house get demolished together as a sort of therapy thing, and the killer lured him into a trap and killed him.'

'If that's the case and the killer of Stefan and Miranda Harkness also killed Matthew, then Jonathan could be in very serious danger.'

Chapter 27

Jonathan and Stephen had been walking for half an hour in complete silence. There was no particular destination; they just ambled, following the road. Jonathan was going over the conversation from the pub in his mind, wondering what he should do and say and then questioning himself for taking everything so seriously. Stephen kept stealing glances at Jonathan, trying to read his expression, but, as usual, his face was blank.

They crossed over the road at the traffic lights outside Sheffield Children's Hospital and Jonathan headed straight for the open gates of Weston Park.

To their left was the large building of Weston Park Museum; a place Jonathan had been to many times in the past, always alone. The park was beautiful, with tennis courts, a band stand, and benches for workers from the nearby hospital to sit with their packed lunches during the day. At night it had a different feel. The sky was clear and a full bright moon cast long shadows from the trees. It wasn't late but the park was mostly empty. Who would want to walk through an open park in freezing-cold temperatures in the pitch-dark?

'Nobody has ever told me they love me before,' Jonathan eventually said as they passed the museum.

'I find that hard to believe,' Stephen commented.

164

'Well, my Aunt Clara always wrote it on my birthday cards and I think she did say it to me once on the anniversary of the deaths of my parents, but that's different isn't it, from what you mean?'

'Yes it is.' He smiled, wondering how a man in his thirties can lack the concept of emotions. 'Look, Jonathan, I know you haven't had the easiest of lives so far; I can't even begin to imagine how difficult things have been, I don't think anyone can unless they've been through it, but I can understand why you are like this.'

'What do you mean?'

'You close yourself up; you don't let anyone get close to you at all. You've spoken of your neighbour Maun and said how she has helped, but I doubt you've even fully opened up to her. You shouldn't keep everything bottled up. It's not healthy.'

The tennis courts were empty and a cold wind caused the nets to sway. It was eerie. If Jonathan had been alone, he would have been petrified, even of his own shadow. They left Weston Park and crossed over Winter Street and entered Crookes Valley Park. To get to the path there was a winding rugged track through some trees. Even though it was the middle of winter and the trees had shed their leaves, the thick branches covered the moon causing the darkness to close in. The silence was intense.

'Stephen, everyone I have come into contact with has died. My parents, the two people you should be able to depend on and love unconditionally were snatched away from me. My Aunt Clara died, Matthew went to live elsewhere, and now he's dead too.'

'I honestly have no idea what to say to make you feel better.'

'Why is it happening to me?' Jonathan looked over to his boss as if seeking an actual answer to an impossible question.

'I have no idea Jonathan. Why does anything happen to anyone? It's one of those "what's the meaning of life?" questions.'

'So you're saying I just got dealt an unlucky hand?'

'It would appear so, yes. I wish I had the answer you're looking for.'

'I don't even know what the question is.'

They came to the end of the wooded area of the park and it opened out onto a clearing. The lightness from the moon returned and they could see each other's faces once again.

'Jonathan, you have had an awful time of things and you shouldn't go through them alone. I know you're very guarded when it comes to opening up and that is perfectly understandable, but I think you're pretty great and I want to be there for you. I want to help you, to look after you, to make you smile once in a while. Please Jonathan, let me in.'

Jonathan was overwhelmed. Throughout the whole of this corrupt and diseased world there was another human being who wanted him in their life for no other reason than simply wanting to make sure he was happy.

Even Maun, the only other person he ever told his life story to, he suspected of having ulterior motives for befriending him. He knew about her past, her marriage, her husband's death and the way the rest of the neighbours in the building ostracized her, but he suspected she only had him in her life because she had nobody else left.

Jonathan had never thought of Stephen as anything other than a boss. If he thought about it, which is what he was being asked to do, he would look upon Stephen as representing something more. Jonathan did like him. He was a good man, a kind man, a generous man, intelligent, funny and warm, with a soft southern Irish accent, deep, dark brown eyes, smooth complexion, full lips . . . what did this mean? How long had he thought of his boss like this?

'Do you mind if I sleep on it?' Jonathan asked.

'What? No, no, of course not. Take all the time you need.'

'It's been a long day. I just want to go home and have a think.'

'Yes sure. No problem. Do you want me to give you a lift?'

'No that's OK. Look, Stephen, thank you for everything today; coming to the hospital and for what you've said to me tonight. I really appreciate it, honestly. Can we talk about it tomorrow morning, before work?'

'Sure. I'll pick you up if you want?'

'I'd like that, thank you.'

Jonathan smiled. He didn't do it very often but when he did, it lit up his face. The smile reached up to his eyes; they sparkled.

'Well, I'll see you in the morning then.'

They said their goodbyes and went their separate ways. Jonathan turned away first and headed for the bright lights of Albion Street while Stephen turned and walked up the narrow and dimly lit Oxford Street.

Jonathan had barely walked ten paces when he realized he felt different. He held his head high instead of permanently looking at the ground. His shoulders were no longer hunched and he felt relaxed. Someone in his life cared for him, loved him, and that made him happy.

As his mind raced to tomorrow morning and what he was going to say to Stephen when he called to pick him up, he barely registered the sound of car brakes squealing, but on hearing the angry thud he turned around: Stephen was lying ahead, in a crumpled heap on the cold road.

Jonathan opened his mouth to say something, to scream, to call out, anything, but no sounds came. Not for the first time in his life, he was struck dumb.

Jonathan's heart stopped. This could not be happening. Not again. Not to Stephen. He was one of the good guys. Jonathan ran to his fallen boss and dropped to his knees. He felt sick as he looked down on another life being snatched from him far too soon.

There wasn't a single mark on Stephen. His complexion was still smooth, his hair still neat, yet his limbs were in a painful position. His eyes were closed. He looked as if he had just lain down to take a nap in the middle of the road.

Jonathan picked up Stephen's cold left hand and held it tight. It was unresponsive. The world around him suddenly fell silent and there was just the two of them, alone yet together, for one last time.

'Stephen,' Jonathan's voice was a whimper; the smallest sound left his lips and drifted away on the cold breeze unheard. 'Stephen . . . please . . .'

The rough, angry sound of an engine revving caused Jonathan to look up through tear-stained eyes. The car ahead that had knocked down the only person ever to make him smile and feel a modicum of happiness had its reversing lights on and it was slowly gaining speed.

Chapter 28

To the untrained eye, the unconscious passer-by, the large, double-fronted detached Victorian house on Manchester Road looked like any other family home. It was only when you opened the front door and saw one of the front rooms had been turned into an open-plan waiting room that the true purpose of the building was revealed.

As soon as Matilda looked up at the large imposing façade she felt her heart sink. She had hoped returning to work would signal an end to her biweekly meetings with the patronizing and plain Dr Warminster. When the ACC told her the return to work was on the proviso the meetings continued she could have screamed. Was she ever going to be free of this woman with her ugly floor-length skirts and pastel cardigans?

The petite blonde twenty-something at the reception desk looked up when Matilda entered. Did she wonder about the mental capacity of the people who came here, or was this just a job to her? As she gazed around the room, taking in her fellow patrons with their anxieties on display, she pondered whether the receptionist pigeon-holed her with the man with the facial tics, the woman who gently rocked from side to side, and the elderly gent who looked as if he was about to burst into tears at any moment.

It had been six months since Matilda's first appointment. Why was she still coming here? Despite Dr Warminster's diagnosis, she wasn't depressed. Yes, she missed her husband. Yes, she questioned her ability to perform her duties at work. At a push she would admit to using alcohol to mask the pain of her loss, but depressed? Absolutely not.

Matilda looked at her watch. Her appointment should have begun five minutes ago. She was always late going in; something she believed all therapists did on purpose to render their patients into a sense of anxiety so they could witness them at their worst. Eventually the door opened and she was asked to enter. She took a deep breath and did as she was told.

Dr Sheila Warminster was indeed wearing a pleated floor-length skirt, a cheap white blouse, and a pale blue cardigan. She was a tall and wiry woman with an uncontrollable shock of dyed red hair. Her complexion was rough, as if she'd just had a vigorous wash with a scouring pad. Her perfume was strong and French; her accent south-western and very deep.

Matilda disliked therapists. She considered them to be nosy and expected them to get together once a week and have a good laugh at their patients' expense. Sometimes, paranoia got the better of Matilda.

Upon meeting Dr Warminster, Matilda had tried, literally forced herself, to like her, but it wasn't possible. It wasn't the woman she took a dislike to, it was her profession. If Sheila had been a shop assistant or a bank clerk she could have been lovely to chat to. Once the sessions began, Matilda realized Sheila wasn't as bad as she first thought, but the shocking dress sense and sickly smile were difficult to warm to. She was tolerable, but for a whole hour?

Matilda sat down on the leather sofa while Sheila took her usual place in a large leather office chair. Between them was a low coffee table, which had the obligatory box of tissues, and a small digital clock facing Sheila.

'So, you've been back at work a few days now. How are things?' Sheila crossed her legs and balanced an A4 pad on her knee. With a silver ballpoint pen in her right hand she was poised for Matilda to pour her heart out. She would have a long wait.

'Very well thanks,' Matilda said. She smiled. Her reply came out louder than expected. Who was she trying to convince; Sheila or herself? It had been her plan to come across as happy and cheerful; she was back at work and loving it and had no reason to come here any more. Unfortunately it wasn't coming across that way.

'And the four o'clock finishing time; are you OK with that?'

'Not really, but those are the conditions I must abide by. Besides, it won't be for long.' Now Matilda was the one sporting a fake sickly smile.

'How have your colleagues taken to your return?'

'Very well.'

'Good. So, no animosity?'

'Of course not. Why would there be?' she asked with a frown. She had promised herself to just answer Sheila's questions with ease and the most basic of information and not ask any in return. She had barely been in the room five minutes and she had broken her promise to herself.

'You have been away for a very long time; things change, people change, attitudes change.'

'I have a very loyal team.' She tilted her head and smiled.

'So they've all welcomed you back with open arms?'

'Yes.'

'That's good then.'

Matilda looked around the room, which was decorated in soothing tones. It was supposed to resemble a living room and have a relaxed atmosphere, but she wasn't convinced. The smell from the air fresheners was overpowering, the soft furnishings were trying too hard to be comforting, and the framed prints on the walls were lifeless and boring.

'How are you coping with the job?'

'Very well.'

'Not getting tired or too bogged down with things?'

'Of course not. I've been doing this job for years.'

'But you've been through a great trauma, it takes time to readjust.'

'A trauma? You make it sound like I'm the only survivor in a plane crash.'

'Your career is very important to you Matilda. Your position is something you have been working towards your whole life. Almost a year ago something happened to destroy that. That is a trauma. Your husband, the man you loved more than anything in the world was cruelly snatched from you in the most horrific of ways. That is a trauma.'

Would smashing you in the face be a trauma?

'It's life.' She shrugged, trying to hold back the tears. 'These things happen to people all over the world every single day. We get knocked down but we get back up again and move on. It's all manageable.'

'Has Carl Meagan been mentioned at work?'

Matilda's heart skipped a beat. 'Yes.'

'Who brought it up?'

'I did.' *You big fat liar, Matilda.*

'Really?'

'Yes.' For a brief second she wondered if the ACC would hear about this conversation and confront her with her lies. She shrugged the thought away. She didn't care.

'And how were you?'

'I didn't break down in a flood of tears if that's what you're hoping.'

'You don't like coming here do you?' Like a dog pining for a treat, Sheila tilted her head to one side. The raising of an eyebrow indicated she expected an answer. If one didn't come, she'd tilt her head to the other side.

Give me a paw and I'll answer your questions.

'No.' The pretence was too much for Matilda to keep up. Despite what she told herself she couldn't fake in front of Dr Warminster and her smug self-righteousness. She could feel the pretend cheerfulness slipping away.

'Why not?'

172

'Because I think it's a waste of time. I'll admit I had difficulty when James first died and when the Carl Meagan case collapsed, but I've managed to work my way through it all and out the other side. I'm fine now.'

'You're sure?'

'Yes.' She honestly meant it this time too. Well, until the next breakdown.

'How is the work/home-life balance?'

'What do you mean?'

'You've said in previous sessions that you don't allow your colleagues into your private life. I was just wondering how you're able to keep your work and home life completely separate.'

'My colleagues are my colleagues. I work with them. I see the grim side of society with them, the evils people do to each other. I don't want to be reminded of that in my social life.'

'What about your best friend, Adele Kean?'

Matilda adjusted herself on the sofa. She was uncomfortable, or was it irritability? 'What about her?'

'Would you describe her as a colleague?'

'Yes I would. She is a very good colleague. She is also a very loyal friend.'

'What is so special about Adele that has allowed her to cross the divide between colleague and friend?'

'Adele is a warm and caring person. I have known her for many years and I know that whatever I tell her will not go any further. She's been through her share of heartache too. She knows what it's like to have to bring yourself back from the brink and start again.'

'So she's been using her life experiences to help you through yours?'

'Yes.'

'You're very lucky to have Adele in your life.'

'I know.'

'It's important not to rely on just one person though. You need to open yourself up to allow other people into your circle. Would you allow any of your other colleagues in?'

173

Why do you want me to be best friends with my colleagues?

'I'm not sure. It's difficult. I work with them every day. They chat, things get passed around and, like Chinese whispers, they get altered.'

'Is that what you think; that they'll gossip about you and talk about you when you're not there?'

'Just because we're detectives it doesn't mean the usual laws of an open-plan office don't apply. People gossip; they slag each other off, make fun of a new haircut. It's what people do to get through the day. I don't want to be a part of that.'

'But you've just described your team as being loyal. Surely they wouldn't do that to you?'

Matilda took a deep breath. She could feel her hackles rising. Everything she said was being twisted, misinterpreted. She loathed coming here so much.

'I'm their DCI,' Matilda said with a forced calm tone. 'Their boss. It wouldn't be good for a boss to socialize with their employees. I don't socialize with the ACC so why should I with my DS and DCs?'

'But you do go to the pub with them at times?'

'Yes of course. After a hard day or in celebration at solving a case, I like to share a congratulatory drink with them; a thank you for their hard work. I'm not a complete robot. I wouldn't expect you to invite me round to your house for a meal. Professional relationships are completely different things.'

Again Sheila paused and did the head-tilting thing. 'Are you still taking your medication Matilda?'

'Yes.'

'Have you missed a dose?'

'No. Why do you ask?'

'You seem a tad irritable. You're jittery.'

'I'm fine.'

'You're sure?'

'Yes.'

174

'I'm getting the impression you're not telling me the whole truth. You're placating me aren't you? You're giving me the answers I want to hear so you can go.'

'I am very busy and have a twenty-year-old murder case to solve.'

'But it's after four o'clock. You wouldn't be working now even if you weren't here with me.'

It was Matilda's turn to pause the conversation. She took another deep breath, crossed her legs the other way and tried, but failed, to relax. Her shoulders were aching with all the tension she was holding on to. 'Just because I'm not in the office it doesn't stop me thinking about the case.'

'Do you have difficulty turning your mind off at the end of the day?'

'You're reading far too much into this. If you have a client who talks about how they were abused as a child do you stop thinking about it when you leave the office?'

'Of course not.'

'There you go then. I'm trying to solve the double murder of a married couple who were stabbed to death in front of their eleven-year-old child. That kind of case stays with you.'

'Do you want to talk about it?'

'No.'

'Can it be solved?'

'Every case can be solved.' *No it can't.*

'Will you solve it?'

'Yes,' Matilda said doubtfully. *Your pants should be on fire right now.*

Sheila turned a page in her notepad. It was the first time Matilda had noticed she had filled a whole side of A4 with notes. She wondered what she had been writing and whether she would be able to read her own file at some point.

'I'd like to see you again. Maybe next week rather than in a fortnight.'

'Why?'

'Your return to work and its progress needs to be closely monitored.'

'ACC Masterson is monitoring me very closely. I am having regular meetings with her.'

'I need to assess your mental well-being.'

'There is nothing wrong with my mental health,' she almost shouted. 'I'm fine. I just want to return to doing my job. Why won't people allow me to get on with it?'

'Because you've been through . . . '

'A great trauma, I know,' she interrupted. She needed to get out of this room. The overbearing heat from the single radiator was causing her to feel sick. She could feel beads of sweat running down her back. She also needed a drink. 'How's next Wednesday for you?' Matilda asked standing up, ready to make a mad dash for the door.

'That's fine. Same time?'

'I have nothing else to do with my evenings.'

Usually when a client leaves a therapist's office they feel lighter; as if a great weight has been lifted from their shoulders. They have shared their deepest, darkest thoughts and talked through what problems and obstacles they are having difficulty overcoming. Solutions may have been offered, talked through, and the client would be able to see the world not as a place to fear, but as a manageable place to live.

When Matilda left Dr Warminster's office she was a seething mass of pent-up frustration. She didn't like therapy. She didn't like talking about herself, and she hated going over old ground every single session.

As she climbed into her car behind the wheel she wondered if she had any vodka left at home. Surely a visit to a therapist shouldn't leave you aching for alcohol?

Chapter 29

By the time the ambulance had arrived at the scene of the hit-and-run, Jonathan was sitting at the edge of the road hugging his knees. His eyes were staring and he was visibly shaking. He was cold and his chattering teeth echoed along the silent highway. His vision was fixed firmly on the still, broken body of Stephen Egan not three feet away, yet his mind had placed him back in time to the night his parents were murdered.

He was sitting at the top of the stairs, his thin pale arms wrapped tightly around the bannister. He was cold, and his breathing was rapid and shallow. His white shirt was forever stained with the flecks of drying blood from his mother and father in the next room. He felt sick but he couldn't move; he was frozen to the spot. The rest of the house was silent. He could hear the distant ticking of a carriage clock in the living room; the whirring of the fridge from the kitchen, and the rasping painful breaths as his mother died.

When the initial shock had worn off, and Jonathan emerged from his trance, the junior doctor at the Northern General Hospital let him leave the emergency room. He immediately went in search of Stephen.

At first the receptionist was unwilling to tell Jonathan about Stephen's condition or even which department he was in. It was only when Jonathan told her he was the closest person to a next of kin he had outside of the Republic of Ireland that she relented.

The impact of the car resulted in a broken left leg, but it was hitting the tarmac with such force that had caused his greatest trauma: a subdural haematoma. The impact created tears in the bridging veins that crossed the subdural space in his head. An increase of intracranial pressure was squeezing his brain and urgently needed to be released. By the time Jonathan had located Stephen's whereabouts, he was already in the operating theatre.

There was nothing for him to do now but wait. He found an uncomfortable plastic chair close to the theatre and settled in. It was happening again. Someone had tried to get close to him and now their life was in danger.

Matilda was driving through the dark streets of Sheffield, her mind going over the conversation with Dr Warminster. It was strange that, although she didn't want to go and she found her therapist to be patronizing, she did have good ideas; the reciting of British Prime Ministers definitely helped with her anxiety and panic attacks. Maybe it wouldn't hurt to let more people into her social life. She had a sort-of relationship with Sian out of work; surely it wouldn't be the end of the world to meet Aaron Connolly or even Rory Fleming out of working hours? Well, maybe not Rory.

She was waiting at a red traffic light when her phone lit up with a text message from DS Sian Mills. Matilda read the message while putting the car into first gear as soon as the amber light shone. STEPHEN EGAN IN NGH. HIT&RUN. DOESNT LOOK GOOD. At the next available opportunity Matilda performed an illegal U-turn and headed for the Northern General Hospital.

Matilda flashed her warrant card and demanded information from the same receptionist that Jonathan had had difficulty with. Within seconds she was storming down a corridor, and stopped dead in her tracks when she saw the lonely sight of a despondent

178

Jonathan Harkness sitting on the edge of a seat, gazing out into a world of his own.

'Jonathan.'

At first he didn't look up. She could guess the thoughts racing through his mind: the murder of his parents, the lifeless body of his Aunt Clara, the battered form of his estranged brother, and now the image of his boss, Stephen Egan. This was not a fragile young man living on his nerves; this was a broken young man.

Matilda called his name again and this time he looked up. His face seemed paler, if that was possible, his eyes wide and hollow: utter terror was etched on his face.

'What happened?'

His voice was barely above a whisper. 'A car came out of nowhere.'

'Are you hurt?' She pulled a chair up next to him and sat down.

'No. I was walking in the opposite direction. We'd just said goodbye and I was going home. It was the noise that made me turn back. The sound he made when he hit the ground.'

'Did you get a good look at the car?'

'Yes.'

'Did you get the registration number?'

Jonathan was on his knees looking down at the man who had declared his love for him. For a brief second, for the first time in his life, he had known happiness, and now it had been snatched away from him. Something caught his eye and he looked up. The bright red of the reversing lights caused him to squint. A few seconds later and the car started moving, heading straight for Jonathan. The fight or flight tendency did not enter his head. He was trying to make sense of what had just happened. He looked down at Stephen, who was still unconscious. He didn't have the strength to pull him out of the way and he didn't have the time either; the car was gaining momentum. He had two options; run and allow the car to run over Stephen again, finishing him off, or stay and become a victim of the hit-and-run too. In the space of a blink of an eye he made up his mind. Running away was not an option. He held Stephen's cold hand firmly in his and closed his eyes tight, waiting for the impact. The wheels crunched over loose stones as it reversed. Ten seconds went by, then twenty. Jonathan could smell the exhaust fumes and feel the heat coming from the car. It was almost upon him. Eventually he opened his eyes. The car had stopped in front of him, less than a yard away. He was staring straight at the number plate: YS08 DPT.

'Jonathan,' Matilda repeated his name, 'I know you've been through a lot tonight but I need to ask you these questions now while the events are still fresh in your mind so we have a chance to catch the person who did this. Did you see the registration number?'

'No I didn't. It happened too quickly. One minute he was standing there just walking away and the next he was . . . I told him this would happen.'

'What?'

'I told him that if anyone tries to get close then this would happen. People don't last very long when they know me; my parents, my Aunt Clara, my brother, and now Stephen. I'm jinxed.'

'That is ridiculous. You're not jinxed. It's just one of those things.'

'No. One of those things happens just the one time. My entire family has been killed. All of this does not happen to just one person.' He looked up at Matilda with wet eyes.

'Look, Jonathan, there is nothing I can say to make you feel better and I'm not going to even try to placate you, but you mustn't dwell on everything. You've been through hell I understand that, but you can't stop that from living your life. You can't live in the past.'

Jonathan was silent for more than a minute. He sniffled a few times then looked up. 'Are you saying that to me or yourself?'

'Sorry?' she asked, taken aback.

'I've read up on what happened to you. I know you went through some personal crisis while you were investigating the Carl

Meagan case. That's why you blame yourself for it going wrong. Your mind wasn't one hundred per cent on the case. I bet you feel as jinxed as I do right now.'

'But I'm getting on with my life. I'm back at work. I have friends around me. I'm getting there. It's a slow process, but it's something we have to do.'

'Do you drive?'

'I'm sorry?' She was shocked by the sudden change of subject. She sat back in her chair, distancing herself from Jonathan.

'Do you drive?'

'Yes I do.'

'Did you pass on the first attempt?'

'No. Third actually,' she replied with a frown, wondering where this was leading.

'What caused you to fail on the previous two occasions?'

She smiled at the memory. 'Reversing around a corner always stymied me.'

'What would you have done if you'd never mastered it? Would you have continued learning to drive, taking test after test after test?'

'Probably not. I would have given up if I'm honest. I'm not a very patient person.'

'There you go then. I've tried living. I've tried life and I can't do it. That's why I don't allow people to get close.'

'Why did you allow Stephen in?'

'He told me he loved me.' Jonathan smiled at the memory. 'Nobody has ever said that to me before. It felt . . . nice. I believed him too. He actually made me feel happy.' He paused. 'And I think I made him happy too.'

'So there's still life out there for you.'

'No. Look at what happened. The first hint of happiness and it's snatched away.'

'You can't give up, Jonathan.'

'Why not?'

181

She had no answer for him. 'You just can't,' she said quietly, not believing it herself.

A harassed-looking doctor came through the doors. She had a sheen of sweat on her forehead. She gave a weak smile and asked Jonathan if he was the next of kin. He told her Stephen's family was in Ireland and he was the closest to a relative he had. The doctor didn't seem convinced and was reluctant to continue until Matilda pulled rank and flashed her warrant card.

'Mr Egan suffered a subdural haematoma. We had to perform a craniotomy to release a build-up of blood and control the bleeding. Unfortunately the bleeding was too heavy and the site of the tear was difficult to find. He lost a lot of blood before we could locate the trauma site. Mr Egan developed a brain oedema, which is when the brain swells up due to the trauma. I'm afraid there was nothing we could do for him.'

'So what does that all mean?' Jonathan asked.

Matilda placed her hand on his arm and turned him towards her. 'Jonathan, Stephen died.'

Chapter 30

Jonathan had lost all sense of time. If asked, he would have difficulty recalling what day it was. He declined Matilda's offer to
drive him home saying that he wanted to walk, to clear his head
and think things through. He had been walking for half an hour
before he stopped in his tracks and looked around him. It was
dark and he had no idea where he was.

As he walked the streets of Sheffield, Jonathan's mind went
over everything in his past; that was one of his problems, he was
never able to relax, his mind was always ticking over, remembering
mindless conversations and bus journeys, people he met during
his working day he'd never see again. Why did they all occupy a
space in his head?

His mind went to his Aunt Clara, the one person in his life he
had loved and trusted. Her death was sudden and a shock, just
like Stephen's had been. She was a wonderful woman, strong,
determined, funny and full of love and kindness.

At first, Clara tried to engage Jonathan in interaction with
the neighbourhood children. She invited them round to her
large house and played games, but Jonathan was reluctant and
eventually the other children stopped visiting. In the end, she
left Jonathan to his own devices. He spent the majority of his
childhood in his room reading Dickens. The only way to expel

the horrifying memories of life in Sheffield and to silence the seemingly endless screams in his head was to immerse himself in Victorian fiction.

Eighteen months after arriving in Newcastle, Jonathan eventually spoke. It was a Sunday evening in mid-June and, not surprisingly, summer had yet to arrive in the north-east. Heavy rain was falling and a strong wind battered tree branches against the living-room window. The television was turned up louder than usual to block out the sound of the intense weather.

'Can you turn the volume down please?' Jonathan asked.

Did Jonathan just speak? Surely not. It was probably the television, or maybe she had fallen into a light sleep and had dreamt it. She looked over at Jonathan, who, in his usual armchair, was reading her battered paperback copy of *Bleak House*.

'Did you just say something?'

'I just wondered if you could turn the volume down a bit.' His voice was quiet and fragile, not much louder than a whisper. 'It's a bit loud.'

'You're talking. My God, you're actually talking,' Clara said, sitting up from her slouched position and quickly muting the television.

Jonathan smiled. The look on his aunt's face; wide eyes and beaming grin, was infectious.

Clara jumped up, grabbed Jonathan into a tight embrace and held him against her breast. 'My darling boy, you're actually talking,' her voice quivered and tears began to fall.

After that evening, Jonathan began talking like a regular teenager and they would spend their time together talking about the family. Clara would tell stories about her long-dead husband and his experience as a fire fighter. She'd tell him about her brother, his father, and what the two of them were like as children. She became more animated; she had someone to share her life with. She never pressed him on what happened in the house. Not once did she initiate the conversation. She waited for Jonathan to broach

184

the subject; but it would be another six years before he brought it up again.

As Jonathan grew older, he became more awkward – with himself, society, and life in general. He often joked that he was born one hundred years too late and yearned for a lifestyle not so dependent on modern technology. He refused to invest in a mobile phone and, although he was computer literate, he never wanted one in his home.

He was relaxed around Clara and joined her on weekends away to her static caravan in Whitley Bay, but apart from that, human relationships eluded and baffled him. From Jonathan's point of view, he could function perfectly well alone. Following the horror of what he had witnessed in Sheffield he thought it unfair to inflict his dark, depressive personality on another individual. Providing things stayed how they were he would be fine in his own self-induced cocoon.

Things didn't stay the same. Four days after her sixtieth birthday, Clara died peacefully in her sleep from a massive heart attack. It was not a surprise. Where her brother Stefan was trim and athletic, Clara was obese. Her diet comprised fried foods, packets of crisps, and bars of chocolate. She spooned sugar in her tea and coffee by the tablespoon and smoked forty cigarettes a day.

Jonathan had lost the only person in his life he had loved. There was nobody else left. He had been hurt for the final time. He was truly alone.

Clara had left everything she owned to Jonathan in her will, hoping he would continue to live in the stable environment she had created for him. However, after a short period of mourning, Jonathan sold Clara's house in Blaydon-on-Tyne, and the static caravan, and found himself heading back to Sheffield. To him, Newcastle belonged to Clara and that life was now gone forever. Sheffield was calling him home.

*

Jonathan was standing in the middle of a generic street with semi-detached houses on both sides of the road. He could be anywhere in the country. The pavements were dotted with leafless trees. Most of the families had one, two and sometimes three cars; all fighting for a parking space. In the dead of night with all occupants at home, traffic was restricted to single file only.

Most of the houses' downstairs lights were off with just a few of the upstairs ones lit; people reading before going to sleep presumably. Jonathan envied their lives; coming home from work, sitting down to eat a meal with the family, talking through the events of the day, watching a few hours of television before retiring to bed to recharge. The next morning they would wake up and begin another day in their mundane lives. Mundane they may be, but in these large Victorian houses, at least they had someone to live them with.

It had been Jonathan's choice to live a solitary lifestyle. What he had told Matilda was true; he remained alone so he couldn't ruin anyone else's life. What was he going to have to do to make sure people stayed away? Was he going to have to move?

He turned a corner onto yet another street, which could be in any city throughout the country. Ahead was a brightly-lit corner shop he recognized. He had been here before. He knew where he was and he wasn't far from home.

Home. His lonely flat in a concrete block of eight apartments. Apparently, home was where the heart is, but what if you had no heart? What if your heart was so cold and damaged that it didn't know a place of comfort? He didn't consider his flat to be his home; it was somewhere to close himself off from the rest of the world. He didn't feel comfortable there, just safe.

As he headed for home a car pulled up just ahead of him. Jonathan should have been more alert of strange cars after what had just happened, but he continued walking in his own little world.

'Jonathan Harkness.' The driver had stepped out of the car and was now standing in the middle of the pavement.

Jonathan turned. The stranger was tall and solidly built. He was wearing dark clothing and his face was hidden by the shadow of a nearby tree. Usually, when confronted with the unknown, Jonathan would be a mass of fear, but the events of the past few days had dulled his emotions. If this man was to be his killer then so be it; just please let it be quick and as pain-free as possible.

'Are you Jonathan Harkness?'

'Yes,' he replied with confidence as if in a stance of defiance. His last stand.

The stranger reached into his inside coat pocket slowly. What was in there, a gun, a knife? He pulled out his warrant card and held it aloft.

'I'm DCI Ben Hales, South Yorkshire Police. Jonathan Harkness, I'm arresting you for the murder of your brother, Matthew Harkness. You do not have to say anything but it may harm your defence if you do not mention when questioned something which you later rely on in court. Anything you do say may be given in evidence. Do you understand?'

Chapter 31

Acting DCI Ben Hales was doing everything wrong. He was about to conduct an interview alone and he had told the custody sergeant to look the other way while he led Jonathan Harkness to interview room two. Should anything go wrong, Ben promised to take the blame. For the benefit of the station's CCTV cameras, the custody sergeant went to the toilet giving Ben the opportunity to escort his prisoner unseen.

Hales left Jonathan in the interview room for over an hour. He was watching him for the majority of the time from the observation room next door; Jonathan would say more with his body language than in actual conversation. Hales knew this type of criminal; he'd clam up during questioning, but left alone, his unconscious mind would give him away.

Jonathan was unaware he was being watched. At the height of his anxiety, when the urge to release tension was at its most prevalent, he rolled up the sleeve on his shirt and bit down hard on his arm. Ben Hales winced at the sight.

Jonathan's right arm was covered in healed bite marks. The sudden pain caused his mind to concentrate on what was causing it. A rush of adrenaline shot through his entire body and as he slowly exhaled, he began to relax. Hales could only compare it to a drug addict taking their next hit; the immediate effects were the same. Jonathan visibly relaxed.

The detective entered the interview room with a folder in his hands. He informed Jonathan that his interview was going to be recorded and videoed and once again read him his rights.

'I've been very busy over the past couple of days,' Hales said sitting back in his chair. 'And I'm not the only one am I?'

'I don't know what you're talking about,' Jonathan said.

Ben Hales looked harassed; he had the weight of the world's problems on his shoulders. His face was drawn and his eyes drooped like sleep had eluded him for weeks.

'Where were you on Monday night?'

'I was at home.'

'All night?'

'Yes.'

'Can anyone vouch for that?'

'No. I live alone.'

'Did you have any visitors?'

'No.'

'So you came home from work and didn't see another soul until you went into work the following morning?'

'I didn't go straight to work the following morning. My child-hood home was being demolished. I went to see it come down.'

'Did you know your brother was in Sheffield?'

'No.'

'He didn't contact you beforehand, or even on the day itself, telling you he was planning to come back to Sheffield?'

'No.'

'I find that very hard to believe.'

'I'm sorry. I don't know what to tell you. I honestly cannot remember the last time I heard from my brother. I had no idea he was back in Sheffield.'

Ben leaned back in his seat and folded his arms. He looked at Jonathan for a while in complete silence, studying him.

'What I don't understand is how two brothers could be so estranged following such a horrific event. Your parents had been murdered, brutally so, yet you didn't forge a bond. There was no brotherly love. You just went your separate ways. Why did you do that?'

'I don't know,' Jonathan answered.

'Surely you must agree that it was strange; the final two members of the Harkness family being split up rather than uniting in your shared grief.'

Jonathan didn't reply. He bowed his head. He really didn't want to have to think about any form of relationship with his brother.

'Does the name Aoife Quinn mean anything to you?' Ben asked suddenly.

Jonathan frowned. 'No. Should it?'

'How about Andrea Bickerstaff?'

'No.'

'I am surprised. Surely you remember the name of the women who rescued you from your home on the night your parents were murdered.'

'Oh.'

Jonathan looked down at the scratched table in front of him. He wondered how many people had sat here under interrogation and how many of those were innocent, like himself. The table was covered in a pattern of coffee rings, some relatively fresh, some faded long ago.

'Oh indeed. Do you remember them now?'

'Yes,' he said to the table.

Their faces came back to the front of his memory. He remembered being picked up by a friendly smiling face, though the eyes looked terrified. He remembered the strong smell of a cheap perfume as he was held tightly to someone's chest and carefully led down the stairs. He remembered clinging to his saviour as a red blanket was wrapped around him and the same woman carried him into the back of an ambulance.

'Would it interest you to know that they both remember every single detail of that night? I've tracked them down. I've interviewed them. I've talked to other people who were in your life around that time too; your head teacher, your babysitter. They all remember you in glorious technicolour.'

He opened a brown folder and lifted out its typed contents. 'Aoife Quinn calls you a strange boy. She said you'd just stare straight through people. You used to play with her son but she had to put a stop to that after you bit him on the arm and drew blood.' He looked up at Jonathan, as though searching for a reaction.

'Andrea Bickerstaff says there was an incident with you at school where you held a young boy's head under water. Do you remember that?'

Jonathan didn't reply. He continued to look straight ahead of him. He wished Matilda Darke was here. He didn't like this man with his frightening eyes and his constant fidgeting. He was like a caged animal waiting to pounce. Jonathan started scratching his hand again.

Ben continued. 'Your head teacher was even making preparations to have you removed from school as you were disruptive to other children, some of them were afraid around you.'

'What does this have to do with my brother?' Jonathan asked.

'You never got on with him did you? He resented you and you hated him. I suppose it's just pure luck I'm talking to you and not your brother. I think you killed him before he had the chance to kill you.'

'What?' Jonathan seemed genuinely shocked to be accused of murder. 'This is ridiculous. I had no idea my brother was even in Sheffield. I didn't know where he was living.'

'Do you know Holly Lane?'

'Of course I do. It's close to where I work.'

'Exactly.'

'It's close to where a lot of people work. Look, I did not kill my brother.'

191

'Really? I have a report here that says otherwise.' He moved the witness statements to one side and pushed the report across the table to Jonathan to read.

PERSONALITY REPORT ON JONATHAN HARKNESS

BY CHARLIE JOHNSON

I have written extensively about Jonathan Harkness over the years and believe he is suffering from a number of mental and personality disorders which I have detailed below. It is my own personal view that Jonathan has been storing up his emotions and feelings rather than finding an outlet for them. He lives in his own world, content and safe, yet highly unstable. He is on the brink of self-destruction. Left alone, he could function to a degree of normalcy. However, if he was crossed, upset, confronted in any way, he would have the potential to be highly dangerous.

PERSONALITY DISORDER

A personality disorder refers to a class of personality type and enduring behaviour associated with significant distress or disability, which appear to deviate from social expectations particularly in relating to other people.

Behavioural patterns in personality disorders are typically associated with substantial disturbances in some of the behavioural tendencies of a person, usually involving several areas of the personality. They are nearly always associated with considerable personal and social disruption.

A person is classified as having a personality disorder if their abnormalities of behaviour impair their social functioning. Their behaviour may result in maladaptive coping skills, which may lead to personal problems that induce extreme anxiety, distress or depression. The onset of these patterns of behaviour can typically be traced back to child-hood, early adolescence, and the beginning of adulthood. It is no secret that what Jonathan went through as a child would be the basis for the shaping of his future character. The fact he has refused to be interviewed and had no significant therapy could reveal his coping mechanisms are seriously impaired. This is abnormal in the everyday function of an individual.

SELF-DEFEATING PERSONALITY DISORDER

The person affected may often avoid or undermine pleasur-able experiences, be drawn to situations or relationships in which he or she will suffer, and prevent others from helping him as indicated below:

- Choose people and situations that lead to disappointment, failure, or mistreatment even when better options are available;
- Rejects or renders ineffective the attempts of others to help;
- Following positive personal events, responds with depres-sion, guilt, or a type of behaviour that produces pain;
- Incites angry or rejecting responses from others and then feels hurt, defeated, or humiliated;
- Rejects opportunities for pleasure or is reluctant to acknowledge enjoying himself despite having the capacity for pleasure;
- Fails to accomplish tasks crucial to his personal objectives despite demonstrating the ability in which to do so;
- Uninterested in or rejects people who consistently treat him well.

I am unaware if Jonathan is currently taking any medication for depression or anxiety and I doubt, after all this time, if he has suddenly decided to seek therapy. If this is the case then his personality disorders will be prevalent in the make-up of his character. What Jonathan witnessed as a child will still be with him and he has yet to come to terms with it. He is still trapped as a frightened child. He has not yet made the transition to a well-adjusted adult.

DCI Hales waited until Jonathan had finished reading the report before he continued with the interview. He looked at his watch; it was incredibly late. The station was quiet and a skeleton staff was operating during the night-time hours. He hadn't called his wife since yesterday lunchtime, he didn't even text to say he wouldn't be home, not that she would have noticed.

'Well?' Hales asked. He leaned back in his seat and folded his arms.

'This is just . . . it's . . . how can you take the word of a man who has never even met me? I have never even spoken to Charlie Johnson. My aunt refused to allow him to meet me when I was a child and I've refused all interviews with him since. What he has written is baseless and untrue. He's not even a qualified psychologist; this is just the ramblings of a hack.'

'You weren't well behaved at school though, were you?' Hales asked, moving the psychological report out of the way and placing the witness statements on top.

'Taken out of context anything can be made to look worse than it is. Yes I bit Joseph Quinn on the arm, but that was because he had me on the ground; he was trying to choke me. The only thing I could do to get free was to grab his arm and bite him. I don't have any memory of holding a boy's head under water.'

'What about the statements from your neighbours calling you a loner and weird?'

'I was a loner, so what?' He shrugged. 'My parents didn't have any time for me, Matthew was out living his own life, so who did I have to hang around with? Nobody. I had to look after myself. Your so-called evidence carries no weight whatsoever.'

Hales was defeated. He was sure he could prove Charlie Johnson's report if he had a psychologist talk to Jonathan. He would have to speak to the ACC in the morning for permission.

'Tell me about the night your parents died.'

'I thought you arrested me for killing my brother? What, you're now accusing me of killing my parents too? I was eleven years old.'

'Answer my question,' Ben said with deep determination in his voice. He was beginning to lose patience with Jonathan. His hands were flat on the table, his arms tense as if in a position to pounce.

'You know it all. There is nothing I can say that will add anything new. I can't do this any more.' His voice broke and he was almost crying.

'Why not?'

'Because it hurts,' he yelled. 'I have to live with this every single day. How can I move on with my life when I'm being constantly asked to go over it again and again and again? You have files, you have statements, you have Charlie Johnson's bloody book. You know everything I do.'

'Oh come on. Do you honestly expect me to believe everything that went on in that house is in the public domain?'

'I'm sorry but it's true.' Jonathan leaned on the table and put his head in his hands. He appeared to be shattered – both mentally and physically.

'Tell me again about your brother.'

'What do you want to know?'

'When was the last time you saw him?'

'I don't remember.'

'Oh come on, he's your last surviving relative, or was, surely you remember the last time you met.'

'I don't. It was years ago.'

'How many?'

'I don't know.'

195

'So you didn't see him on Monday night, the night he was killed?' He was asking the question for a second time, hoping for a different answer than before.

Jonathan paused. 'No.'

'Are you sure?'

'Yes.'

'Tell me who Dawn Marwood is.'

Jonathan's face looked blank. He was too tired to think properly yet he knew the name from somewhere. 'She's a woman who lives in my building.'

'Which apartment number?'

'Number one.'

'That would be the first apartment on the ground floor?'

'Yes,' Jonathan sighed.

'On Monday night, Dawn Marwood was in a lot of pain and couldn't sleep. She suffers with arthritis and the cold weather leaves her joints stiff. She was awake until the small hours of Tuesday morning. She was in her living room reading a book when the sound of shouting distracted her from her book. Do you know where the shouting was coming from?'

Jonathan didn't reply. He continued to look straight ahead. He could see the enjoyment on Hales's face.

'The shouting was coming from your apartment, Jonathan. At first Ms Marwood thought it might have been the television but then remembered you don't have one. When she heard the sound of breaking glass she decided to investigate. As luck would have it, Ms Marwood isn't a fast walker and she took some time getting to her front door, when she did and she looked through her spy hole, do you know what she saw?'

Hales's smile was almost smug. Jonathan saw the light dancing in his eyes. He was enjoying himself.

'She saw a man leaving your apartment and exiting the building. She gave quite a good description too. He was your brother wasn't he?'

History was beginning to repeat itself. Jonathan was back in a room in a police station made to look like an ordinary living room. He was on the floor with a large drawing pad and a bucket of wax crayons. While creating a picture a woman was chatting to him, asking him how he was feeling, what he had seen in his house, was there anybody in the house who shouldn't have been? Now, twenty years later he was reliving the horror. This time, however, there would be no kid gloves.

'This isn't happening,' Jonathan said, barely above a whisper.

'What isn't?'

'I don't think I can go through with this. Can I go? I want to go home.'

'I think it'll be a while before you see your home again. Now, why did you lie when I asked you about your brother, and what was he doing at your apartment on Monday night?'

'I have a headache.' He felt like his head was going to explode.

'Answer my questions.'

'I can't.'

'Why not?'

'I don't want anyone to know.' His bottom lip began to quiver.

'Know what?'

There was a lengthy silence. Jonathan curled up on his seat, cradling his head. He sniffed back the tears and looked up.

'All right, Matthew did come to see me on Monday night. It was the first time I'd seen him in years. I recognized him straightaway though. God only knows how he knew where to find me.'

'What was his reason for visiting?'

'The demolition. He'd come to see the house get knocked down.'

'What did you talk about?'

'Our parents, mostly. He kept asking me to go over that night again and again, all the details. It was like he enjoyed it. He kept smiling at me.'

'Did you tell him?'

'I had no choice. He scared me. He always scared me.' Jonathan hugged himself, protected himself.

197

'In what way did he scare you?'

'He was angry, volatile. I thought he was going to hit me.'

'Did he?'

Jonathan suddenly lost it. It was as if his spine had been torn out of his body and he just slumped on the table. His grip on his emotions went too, and out came a torrent of tears and wailing that resounded around the cold room.

Hales took a cotton handkerchief out of his inside pocket and handed it to him. 'Here, take this. It's crumpled but it's clean.'

He took the proffered handkerchief and began wiping his eyes and his nose. The tears still came.

'What happened?' Hales asked when there was a brief gap in the sobbing.

'Matthew kept staring at me, staring through me really. I knew something was going to happen, something horrible, but I had no idea . . . ' He couldn't finish his sentence; the tears were overwhelming him.

'Take your time Jonathan. Take deep breaths.'

'He lunged at me and grabbed me by the throat. He squeezed hard and I couldn't breathe. I tried to scramble free, but he was too strong. I thought I was going to pass out, but just before I did he released his grip, he pushed me and I fell into my coffee table. My head broke the glass and I hit my head on the floor. That didn't stop him though. I honestly thought he was going to kill me. I looked up at him and he was smiling. He was just standing there and had this huge smile on his face. He was enjoying himself. He said that if he knew how fragile and fucked up I was he would have come round to see me much sooner.'

'What did you say?'

'There was nothing I could say. I was having difficulty breathing. I just wanted him to go. I thought that if he was going to beat me up then just let him do it and go.'

'Why was he doing this to you?'

198

'Because he could. He always hated me, right from birth. I thought I was free from him when I moved to Newcastle and when I came back I had no idea he'd find me and do this to me.'

'What did he do?'

'He picked me up from the floor. He held out his hand for me to take and helped me up. He dusted the broken glass out of my hair and pulled me towards him in a hug. He had a powerful grip. He whispered in my ear that we'd never hugged before and that brothers should always hug. He said that we'd had a lousy childhood and lousy parents who had never shown us love and attention. He released me and I looked into his eyes and I just saw pure evil. I knew what was coming . . . '

Chapter 32

Sian Mills was having difficulty sleeping. Next to her, hogging most of the duvet, was her husband whose latest device for helping him to stop snoring wasn't working. She tried to roll him over onto his side but it was no use, he was far too heavy for her. The sound of her mobile ringing was music to her ears. She didn't mind if it was someone from India wanting to talk to her about her broadband supply; she'd happily have the conversation.

'Hello?' she asked, not lowering her voice. She didn't care if she woke her husband. It would make a change from it being the other way round.

'DS Mills?'

'Speaking.'

'It's PC Murphy. I'm sorry to wake you at this hour but I thought you should know what's going on.'

'PC Murphy? What's happened?'

'I'm on night duty and I heard screaming and shouting coming from one of the interview rooms. I went and had a look and Acting DCI Hales is interviewing Jonathan Harkness. I probably shouldn't be calling you but I know DCI Darke is working on the case and thought she should know about it. I couldn't find her mobile number so thought I should call you. Is that OK?'

He was talking to a broken connection. As soon as she heard who Hales was interviewing she hung up the phone and scrambled around in the dark for her trousers. She was dressed and out of the house in record time.

The green digits on the dashboard told her it was almost 2 a.m. Why was he interviewing Jonathan Harkness in the dead of night? In fact, why was he interviewing him at all?

The temperature was minus four degrees on the gauge, and her car took several attempts to start. The sodium lights from the street lighting danced on the frost. There was no other traffic about and Sian was soon on the main road heading into the city centre. While waiting at a red light she searched for Matilda's number in her phone.

'Hello?' Matilda's voice was croaky and she sounded groggy. Sian had wondered how she was coping with everything that had befallen her over the past nine months, now she knew: alcohol.

'Matilda, it's me, Sian. Are you lucid?' She didn't mean to ask that but it came out before she had time to think.

'Lucid? Of course I am. What makes you ask that?'

'Look, I've just had a call from a PC on night duty; Hales is interviewing Jonathan Harkness.'

'What?' Now Matilda really was lucid. Alcohol had helped calm her down after her disastrous meeting with Dr Warminster and the horror of Stephen Egan's hit-and-run. Add to that Jonathan being constantly on her mind and worrying she was going to turn into him, an isolated recluse, and of course she needed a bottle or two of something to help her relax.

She had fallen asleep shortly after midnight. Once again she had been on the sofa and just passed out from exhaustion and drunkenness. The phone call hadn't woken her though, her bladder had done that. She had been on her way back to the sofa when her mobile burst into life.

'What the fuck is he doing?' she screamed down the phone.

'I've no idea. Are you coming in?'

'Of course I am.'

'Are you OK to drive?'

'Just get Jonathan away from Hales and wait until I get there.'

Matilda hung up and went into the hallway to look at herself in the mirror. Would she pass for a respected member of the police force? Not with a stained shirt, knotted hair, and bags under her eyes big enough to hold a weekly shop. She ran up the stairs two at a time and turned on the cold water tap in the bathroom. She gave a sharp cry each time she splashed the icy water onto her face. It physically hurt but it did the job. She looked at her reflection once again and appeared to be better for it.

She was frantically running a brush through her tangled hair when her mobile started ringing again. She wasn't going to answer, but saw Adele's name as the caller. What was everyone doing awake at this time of the morning?

'Adele?' Matilda answered.

Adele was whispering into the phone. 'I can't talk for long but I really think you should get to the station right now.'

'What's going on?'

'I was on call. I was here to see to a bloke in custody who was having a seizure when Hales found me. He's asked me to conduct a rape exam on Jonathan Harkness.'

Chapter 33

Matilda pulled up in the car park of South Yorkshire Police HQ and slammed her car door closed. The noise resounded around the empty space, bouncing off the walls of the building. Not caring whether she slipped on the frost, she stormed to the back entrance and almost pulled the door off its hinges.

The station was silent. Office doors were locked, windows had closed venetian blinds, and just the strip lighting in the corridor lit up the station. It was eerie. The only sound was footsteps and the distance buzz of the lighting.

Matilda made her way straight to the MIT room. It was empty. She hit her palm down hard on the table; the sound resounded around the room.

'Sian?' she called out.

Matilda left the room and stormed down the corridor in search of DS Mills. She eventually found her coming out of the toilets.

'What the hell is going on?' Matilda yelled. Her eyes were wide with anger, she was physically shaking.

'OK, calm down.'

'Calm down? What the fuck has Hales got to do with Jonathan Harkness? What right does he have to bring him in for questioning without running it by me first?'

'Come with me.' Sian tried to lead Matilda away from the middle of the corridor and into a private room where they could chat, but Matilda was seething.

'He's really going to pay for this,' she continued her rant. 'Masterson said to him . . . '

'Look, Matilda just calm down all right? Come in here, now. Come on.'

Sian opened the door to the closest office she could find and turned on the lights. She had no idea who this room belonged to but they kept it very neat and tidy. She waited until Matilda sat down on a chair and showed visible signs of relaxing before she continued.

'Here's the situation as I understand it; I had a phone call from PC Murphy . . . '

'Which one's he?' Matilda interrupted.

'Er, tall, lanky, Beatles haircut, got run over by that transit on Queens Road trying to stop a robbery.'

'Oh yes, I remember him. Go on.'

'Well Murphy called and told me he heard shouting from one of the interview rooms. He went into the observation room and saw Hales interviewing Jonathan Harkness. He had a word with the duty sergeant who said Hales had arrested Jonathan for the murder of his brother.'

'What?' Matilda shouted, jumping up. Sian held out her hands to try and stop her running out of the room and hunting down Hales.

'Wait a minute, Matilda. Sit down and let me finish.' She waited, again, until Matilda had sat. 'Before he rang me, Murphy was told by Hales to fetch a doctor as Jonathan needed an examination. Luckily, good old Adele Kean was downstairs tending to a man in custody who had had some form of seizure. Anyway, Hales told Adele that Jonathan said that on the night his brother was murdered Matthew was in his flat and he sexually assaulted him.'

'What?' Matilda shouted again, though this time not out of anger but out of horror. 'Why didn't Jonathan bring any of this up before?'

'I've no idea.'

'Didn't Hales ask him that?'

'I don't know. I haven't spoken to him.'

'Where are they all now?'

'As far as I'm aware Adele is still in with Jonathan. Hales is around here somewhere.'

'I'm going to tear that bastard limb from limb.'

This time Sian didn't try to stop Matilda from leaving the room. She took a step to one side and followed her down the corridor. Unfortunately being a few inches taller than Sian and fuelled by rage-induced adrenaline Matilda was soon around the corner and out of sight. Sian broke into a jog. She had a feeling she was going to have to act as referee.

'How long does a rape examination take?'

Hales was sitting in the lonely canteen with a tired-looking desk sergeant opposite him. The hours of darkness were slowly ticking away and with each minute that passed Hales knew it was getting closer to Matilda coming in and finding out he had usurped her case. He hoped he could get a confession or a new development out of Jonathan to rub in her smug self-righteous face.

'You know how long a rape exam takes,' the reply came.

Hales looked at his watch, again. 'I'm not sure whether to believe this or not. Why would a man rape his own brother?'

'That's a question for a psychologist. I'm just a semi-retired desk sergeant with Type 2 diabetes running out the clock.' He looked up and saw Matilda storming towards the double doors of the canteen. 'I think I'll be heading for the bomb shelter now.'

Hales looked at him with a frown, wondering what he was talking about until he heard his name being called.

'Hales, what the fuck is going on?'

He smiled to himself. As soon as he heard Matilda's bark his mood lifted. He wasn't dreading this at all. He would delight in bringing her down a peg or two.

'Ah, Detective Chief Inspector Darke, what brings you here at such an early hour; on your way to the off-licence and thought you'd drop in to say hello?'

Matilda stopped in her tracks – she looked as though she'd been slapped in the face. 'What's going on?' she asked. Her voice was quieter and shook slightly.

'I'm sure you've been filled in by whoever it was who called you. I've arrested Jonathan Harkness.'

'On what grounds?'

'I'll admit it's circumstantial at the moment, but I'm sure once we get him fully questioned he'll confess.'

'You're wrong.'

'I don't think I am. I have witness statements and psychiatric reports saying he's completely crazy and a very clever psychopath.'

The double doors to the canteen creaked open and Sian squeezed herself through the small gap she had made.

'Oh, that's who called you. I might have known. Thanks for your loyalty Sian.'

Sian looked at the stained floor. She hated having to take sides.

'Why are you doing this?' Matilda asked.

'My job is to make sure that people are brought to book for the crimes they have committed and see that justice is served.' He stood tall with his hands behind his back and a sense of smugness on his face.

'You're a bastard, do you know that? Why didn't you bring any of this to me?'

'You? You are joking, surely? Have you looked in the mirror lately? You're a wreck. I don't even know what you're doing back here. There's no way you can lead a team of detectives in a murder case any more. You're finished.'

Matilda swallowed hard. 'What's this about a sexual assault?' she eventually asked, her voice was brittle and quiet.

'A complete fabrication. It's a ploy to buy time.'

'There could be something in it.'

206

'Why would his brother rape him? What possible motive could there be? He's lying.'

'Jonathan Harkness is a victim in all this. Why are you treating him like a number one suspect?'

'Because he is a number one suspect.'

'You're wrong.'

A PC pushed open the canteen doors, which bumped into Sian, pushing her out of the way. 'Dr Kean has finished,' he said before disappearing.

As Hales headed for the doors he stopped by Matilda and leaned in to whisper in her ear. 'You reek of alcohol.' He sniffed harder. 'In fact, you stink of failure too. You may as well pack your desk up now.'

Adele Kean was in the incident room helping herself to a coffee. She was shattered. She spooned three heaped teaspoons of espresso instant coffee into a mug and gave a loud and wide yawn while she waited for the kettle to boil.

'Let's hear it then.' Hales entered the room and didn't hold the door open for Matilda who followed. A few seconds later Sian came in.

'Good morning to you too. Anyone want a coffee?'

'Nobody wants a coffee. Just tell me what you found.'

Adele could almost feel the tension radiating from Hales. She looked at Matilda, whose face was expressionless. 'What's going on?'

Matilda shook her head as if telling Adele not to push anything and she'd fill her in later.

'Nothing's going on. Come on Adele, out with it.'

'Well, since you've asked so politely, Jonathan has undergone a series of tests and I've taken samples from him, which will have to be sent away, but there is evidence of severe anal bruising consistent with a sexual assault.'

'Fuck!' Hales screamed, kicking a dent into a filing cabinet. 'You're sure?'

207

'Definitely. I also found fragments of glass in the back of his head, which, he says, came from a glass-top coffee table in his living room that his brother pushed him into.'

'He could have done that himself,' Hales said. 'Have you seen *Scream 4*? At the end the killer . . .'

Matilda jumped to Jonathan's defence. 'I doubt he's getting ideas from films. He doesn't even own a TV for Christ's sake.'

'Freak!'

'Did he say anything to you?' Matilda asked Adele.

Adele frowned when she looked at her friend. Matilda's timid voice and red eyes were worrying her. 'He said that his brother sexually assaulted him on Monday night and that it wasn't the first time. Matthew raped him twice when they were boys before their parents were killed.'

Chapter 34

Assistant Chief Constable Valerie Masterson did not enjoy being woken up at 7 a.m. but DS Sian Mills felt she didn't have much choice in the matter.

As soon as it was established Jonathan wasn't lying about his allegation an argument had erupted between Matilda and Ben. Eventually, Sian stepped in, literally, to stop them coming to blows. She told them both to calm down and move to other parts of the station, that she was going to phone the ACC and inform her of the latest developments and they were to do nothing until she arrived.

It was the first time she had raised her voice to her bosses, but this was an exceptional circumstance. The investigation was at risk of being compromised and it needed to get back on track. Also, if any uniformed officers saw what was happening and the gossip mongering began who knew where it would lead; suspensions, reports, dismissals. Sian did not want that to happen, not to Matilda, even Ben Hales didn't deserve that.

Masterson laid down the law as soon as she arrived. She wanted a briefing of the whole team and bringing up to speed on the cases. She made it clear she was not happy with the situation and she wanted to see Ben and Matilda in her office when the briefing was over.

The Murder Room was full. The entire team was assembled, as were several uniformed officers, scene of crime officers, and the crime-scene manager. The atmosphere, like the sky outside, was grim and heavy.

'Due to recent developments it has come to my attention that the investigation into the death of Matthew Harkness, and the cold case surrounding his brother and the murder of his parents, is in danger of getting out of control. I am sure all of you are aware how high profile the Harkness case is. The press watch us constantly due to the events in Rotherham and at the Hillsborough Inquiry, but add the Harkness case into the mix and they've practically moved into the area. We have to do this right. I want South Yorkshire Police to be shown in a positive light for once, and inform criminals in this county that no matter how long it takes you will not get away with your crimes. Now, DS Sian Mills is going to bring us all up to speed on the investigations and we will go from there. Sian.'

Masterson stepped to one side while Sian moved up to the front of the room. She looked ahead to her colleagues, and her bosses, and suddenly felt under intense scrutiny. She had never led a briefing before and had only conversed about an investigation on an informal level. Now here she was being made head girl and watched by two DCIs and an ACC.

'Right, well, I've been speaking to Manchester police and they have given Matthew Harkness's apartment the once-over and spoken to his colleagues and neighbours. Matthew was an accountant of some description and, although based in Manchester, went several times a month to head office in London. He was a hard worker and dedicated to his career, by all accounts. Obviously the brass at head office didn't know him on a personal level, but they describe him as professional and diligent.

'His colleagues in Manchester, however, have a different view on things altogether.' Sian looked down at her large notepad and skipped a few pages to find the place she needed. She stumbled over her words. 'The, er, the female members of his team refer to him as a tosser, while the male members call him a player. He was a friendly, chatty person in the office, often the loudest in the room, oozing confidence and never missed a day's work. He was flirty and dated many members of staff. One member of staff said he had a narcissistic personality.

'There was one male member of staff, a Timothy Lightfoot, who knew Matthew more than the others. They went to the gym together most evenings after work and often went on mountain bike holidays together. According to Tim, Matthew was bisexual and wasn't shy about coming forward. He had plenty of money in the bank and enjoyed spending it on designer clothes, the latest in modern technology, and taking out women, or, indeed, men.'

'Did Matthew ever talk about his parents' murder or his brother?' Masterson asked from the sidelines.

It was her interruption and questioning that caused Sian to falter. She stuttered a few times before getting back on track. 'Well his colleagues all knew of his background. They knew who his parents were, and according to Tim he played on it quite often.'

'In what way?'

'Well Harkness isn't a very common name and often when he introduced himself the obvious question came up; "any relation to the famous Harkness murders?" which Matthew answered with a yes and painted himself as a victim to gain sympathy and to get himself . . . well, you know . . . '

'Laid.' DC Rory Fleming completed her sentence for her.

'Well quite. His neighbours have said he kept to himself and rarely chatted to any of them. He hardly stopped to speak to them though he did contribute heavily to the upkeep of the building and maintenance of the communal garden. He was the perfect neighbour. The only complaint was the loud noises coming from his apartment from time to time.' She coughed and consulted her pad to avoid eye contact with anyone.

'Loud noises?'

'Shagging.' DC Fleming called out to the merriment of the rest of the room.

'Thank you DC Fleming.' Masterson said above the murmur of giggles. 'Your grasp on the English language is a joy to behold. Carry on DS Mills.'

'I've tracked down the couple that Matthew went to live with after his parents were killed and Jonathan moved up to Newcastle.'

This piqued the interest of both Matilda and Ben, who were sitting at opposite sides of the room.

'Matthew moved in with Robert and Judith Clayton and their son Philip. The family moved away from Sheffield when both Philip and Matthew grew up and left home. They now live in Skegness. Philip died in a car crash on the M1 three years ago. They had contact with Matthew but sometimes it was many months between phone calls. They were both shocked to hear of his death.

'They described him, as a child, as being quiet and timid and he took a long time to come out of his shell once he'd moved in with them. They gave him a stable and supportive atmosphere to live in and he reacted positively to their warmth. Judith said that he was often left out at home. He was an only child until Jonathan came along and then he was left on the sidelines, so to speak. Judith believes Matthew resented Jonathan and agreed with their Aunt Clara that splitting them up was the best for both boys.

'The Clayton's gave him the stable upbringing and home life he desired and he thrived. All he wanted was a set of parents to take care of him, love him, and help him with his future, and they provided that. They helped him through exams, college, and even paid for his first year at Manchester University.'

'I don't think it takes Freud to tell us his lack of a stable parental authority figure in his formative years led to his life-style of casual sexual relationships and his rather narcissistic personality. Stefan and Miranda Harkness have a lot to answer for,' Masterson said. 'What about this Jonathan character; is it possible he killed his brother?'

'Possible?' Hales almost jumped out of his chair. 'I think it's a bloody certainty. Why aren't we interrogating him?'

Masterson gave him an icy glare. 'I think we can all agree that Jonathan is a rather fragile individual, which is why all contact *was* to go through DCI Darke. You, however, Acting DCI Hales, took it upon yourself to conduct an unlawful interview. I will admit that if you hadn't done so we may not have found out about his sexual assault, but that does not mean I will condone your behaviour.

'This is a team. I thought this team worked well together and got results by including all its members; obviously I was wrong. Now Jonathan Harkness will be interviewed again when I give permission. Where is he right now anyway?' she asked Sian rather than anyone else in the room.

'He's in the family room. He witnessed his boss getting killed by a hit-and-run. Then he was dragged in here late last night. I've had Sergeant Taylor de-arrest him. Not that he should have been arrested in the first place.' She said as an aside. 'He hasn't been to sleep yet so he's getting some rest until we can take him back to his flat. We're going to need a forensics team to go over it.'

'Does Jonathan have anywhere to stay?'

'I'm not sure. I'll ask.'

Hales rolled his eyes at the soft treatment Jonathan seemed to be receiving. Under his breath he mumbled, 'Fucking kid gloves.'

'Is this hit-and-run linked, do we know?'

'I don't think so. Traffic are appealing for witnesses and there's a team of uniforms going door to door in the area. They're going to keep me informed.'

'Good job Sian. Right we need to interview Jonathan's neighbours; I want to know whether they heard or saw anything on the night he was attacked. Let's give Jonathan a bit of time to calm down and get some rest, but we will need to interview him again in the next day or so. Sian, you're in charge until I say otherwise and I'll leave you to deal with duties. Ben, Matilda, I want you both in my office in five minutes.'

With that she marched out of the room. Everyone was silent until the door had fully closed. Matilda sat staring into space, her mind elsewhere. In five minutes her future within the police force would be decided.

Chapter 35

Jonathan was curled up in the corner of a light green three-seat sofa. He was wearing a white paper forensic suit, as his clothes were taken from him during the examination. They weren't the clothes he was wearing on the night of the attack but they did have blood on them from Stephen's hit-and-run.

The room was stifling; the windows were sealed shut, and the single radiator beneath a large smeared mirror was giving out heat of nuclear proportions. Jonathan had barely been on the sofa a minute before his eyelids grew too heavy and he was enveloped by sleep.

Quietly, Sian entered the room and carefully roused him by shaking his shoulder. When he opened his eyes he thought he was in his own bed until his mind woke and he looked at his surroundings. The pale yellow wallpaper, the cream carpet, the fake pine coffee table; these did not belong to him. This was not his décor. Where the hell was he?

'Jonathan, how are you feeling?' Sian asked in the relaxed motherly tone she usually used when her children were ill.

'What time is it?'

'It's coming up to nine o'clock.'

'A.m. or p.m.?'

'A.m.' She smiled. She sat on the sofa next to him, taking care not to get too close. 'Jonathan, we need to have a forensic team look around your flat, see if there is any trace evidence from the night you were attacked. We'll also need the clothes that you were wearing on the night too. Is that all right?'

'Yes. Fine,' he said, almost incoherent. He was feeling groggy from the short amount of sleep he'd had. 'Am I allowed to go home?'

'Not at the moment. Do you have a place you can go?'

'I'm not sure. I could ask Maun I suppose. I just want to have a shower and go to sleep.'

'OK. Well, I'm going to drive you home to collect a few things and for you to give me your clothes, then I'll take you to Maun's. I'll let you know when you're able to go back into your flat. Do you understand?'

'Yes I think so.'

'Do you have any questions?'

'I'm not sure.' He seemed confused.

'That's fine, don't worry about it. Any time you think of anything just give me a call. I'll give you my number before I leave you.'

'Do I have to go home in this?' he asked, pulling at the extra-large paper suit.

'No.' She smiled. 'I'll find you something to wear.'

Jonathan took time standing up. He was shattered and he ached all over, even his hair hurt when he ran his fingers through it.

Sian led him out of the room by the elbow.

'Who do you reckon is for the chop; Hales or Darke?' Rory asked sitting back and spinning on his office chair.

'Hales, definitely,' Aaron chipped in straight away. 'The ACC has never liked him and she's always had Darke earmarked for her job when she retires. There's no way she'll send Matilda packing.'

'I don't know,' Rory teased. 'She seemed pretty pissed at the briefing.'

'Of course she was pissed; Sian called her up at 7 a.m. Wouldn't you be pissed?'

'I think Matilda'll be for the chop,' DC Scott Andrews chimed in from the drinks station where he was making everyone a cup of tea. 'Hales will call his father-in-law who'll call Masterson and he'll come out of this with Matilda's job and a wage increase. Mark my words.'

'The oracle has spoken,' Aaron joked, which received a two-fingered reply from Scott.

Sitting quietly at her desk, Faith Easter was familiarizing herself, once again, with the Harkness case. She was fascinated by it. It took her back to her police training when she was given an imaginary cold case to go through and work on a series of questions to ask a new witness who had come forward.

'When you've finished with your bets, can I ask a question?' Faith asked, looking up from her notepad.

'Shoot,' Rory replied.

'The murder weapon, the one used to stab Miranda and Stefan to death; where is it?'

'What?'

'According to this report, a large kitchen knife was used to kill them and there was one missing from a block in the kitchen, but there's no mention of the knife anywhere else. What happened to it?'

Aaron frowned. 'I've no idea. Rory, you were working on this with Matilda, did you come up with anything?'

'No. According to a report by the DI, can't remember his name, the weapon was never recovered.'

'So let's run through it then,' Faith began. 'There are two entrances to the Harkness house; the front and back door. Both of these are locked from the inside. Whoever killed them was obviously let in, which means they were known to the family . . . '

'So how did they get out?' Aaron interrupted. 'If the doors are locked from the inside how does the killer escape?'

'Logic dictates that he was still in the house or he escaped through a window.'

'Were any of the windows open?'

They both looked to Rory who had been designated unofficial authority on the Harkness cold case having read the files several times.

'Look, the files are very basic; there's no mention of anything to do with the house, windows, doors, locks, nothing. There are no sketches and layouts, no photographs, apart from in the main bedroom where they were found. It's like a huge chunk has been stolen or it was a half-arsed investigation in the first place.'

'Probably why it was never solved,' Scott muttered.

'What kind of windows were there on the ground floor?' Faith asked.

'Now that I do know.' Rory dug around in a folder and pulled out a copy of the local newspaper from a few days ago. 'There's a picture in the paper of the house in its glory days and sash windows are clearly shown throughout the house.'

'Bugger. Sash windows are piss easy to open from the inside and outside.'

'Unless they had locks on them,' Faith said.

'This was the 90s. I doubt they had locks on them. We didn't start being scared until after 9/11,' Scott said, handing out the teas. 'So we know how they were killed but still not why and how the killer entered and left the scene.'

'Another thing,' Rory said, rummaging through Sian's snack drawer and helping himself to a KitKat, 'say the killer broke in, he didn't obviously intend to kill them because he came unprepared. He used one of their knives. How did he know they'd have a block of knives in the first place?'

'Everybody has knives in their kitchen. What we're looking for is someone who knew how to gain entry to the house and how to leave without it being known,' Faith said, thinking aloud.

'My money is on Matthew Harkness.'

'Mine too,' Aaron agreed.

'I'll go with that as well,' Scott added.

'What is it with you three and betting on everything?'

'Got to do something to pass the time. At the end of the day we're still no further on than when the crimes were committed all those years ago. Stefan and Miranda Harkness were stabbed to death in their bedrooms; killer or killers unknown.'

'The killer was obviously known to the Harkness family though,' said Scott.

'Why obviously?'

'Because the second the news is released that the case is being reviewed, and the house demolition hits the papers, Matthew is bumped off too. The killer is still out there and wants to remain free, so he's taking out those who can identify him.'

Scott was well known within the team for not saying much, but when he did, he often came up with something thought-provoking. The others looked at him with perplexed frowns.

219

Chapter 36

'What the hell are you two playing at?' ACC Masterson was fuming. For a tiny woman with a slight build she certainly knew how to command fear in those beneath her. Her eyes were wide and starry; her face was puce, and the veins in her neck were throbbing. In front of her desk, Hales and Matilda stood side-by-side, grim-faced. 'Look, Ben, I know you have a hard time with Matilda being back at work and I know you think you should be in charge of the MIT. I also know you think you should have been promoted to DCI years ago, but the fact of the matter is none of those things happened. You're a DI in CID. Presently, you're Acting DCI of the MIT, so deal with it. Do you understand?'

'Yes ma'am,' he said. He had his hands behind his back which were clenched tightly into fists. His face may have looked calm, but inside he was screaming. 'I just do not understand why I'm being vilified for doing my job. Jonathan Harkness knows far more than he's letting on and we're treating him like he's made of glass.'

'I have made my feelings very clear on this Ben. God only knows what is going through Jonathan's head. I don't even think he knows. What we need to do is make sure we have all the facts before we question him further. Dragging him in off the streets in the early hours of the morning and accusing him of murder is not the right way to go about it.'

'But I thought . . . '

'No. No, you didn't think. That's your problem. You're so keen to get one over on Matilda that you didn't think about Jonathan at all. You knew the score; any questions for Jonathan go through Matilda and you ignored that. That order came directly from me and you disobeyed it. Take the rest of the day off. Go home, get some sleep, and tomorrow morning I want you in my office at 9 a.m. Do you understand?'

Hales was silent. Was this the beginning of the end of his career within the police force? He thought of what his wife would say, what his father-in-law would say. He'd be a disgrace if he lost his job. All his married life his wife has been comparing him to the great Superintendent and now he would end his career in the gutter, or worse, back in uniform. He swallowed hard and quietly he said, 'Yes. I understand.'

He closed the door carefully behind him and headed for his car. He shook his head when he thought of his car; even that belonged to his bloody father-in-law.

Masterson waited until Hales was out of earshot. 'You promised me you were well enough to return to work,' she began, her voice low but rising with each word. 'I had a phone call last night from Dr Warminster. She told me you were rude, insolent, and unstable.'

Although Matilda was hearing what her superior was saying she wasn't registering any of the words. She didn't care any more what happened to her. Surprisingly, she was thinking about Jonathan Harkness and how she missed the signs of his attack. Why hadn't she seen that his narcissistic brother could inflict such horror on his younger, more fragile sibling?

'I like you Matilda, I really do. You've been through so much this past year, but you've managed to come through it and I respect you for that. I don't think I'd have been able to remain so strong. But over the last couple of days you've really not been fair, not to me, your team, the force, or to Jonathan Harkness.'

Matilda was on the verge of tears. The emotion in her voice was obvious. 'I know I haven't performed at my best lately, but Hales has not been playing fair either. I'll admit I'm questioning everything at the moment and I'm scared of screwing up again, but I'm getting there, slowly. It doesn't help that Hales is using every opportunity possible to have a dig at me.'

'Hales isn't the easiest person to work with I know that. He's got his own demons too, one of them being his father-in-law . . . '

'That is not my problem,' Matilda interrupted.

Masterson raised a hand to silence her. 'However, you need to find a way to work together or the investigation will suffer and I will not allow that to happen again in my station. Now, I've sent Hales home for the day and I'm sending you home too.'

The look of horror on Matilda's face was palpable. She needed to keep busy in order to survive. If she went home and sat and wallowed in her own self-pity she would not be alive by the end of the day. She needed to keep working. She tried to protest, but Masterson put her hand up again.

'There is no room for compromise here. I want you to go home, get some sleep, have a hot meal, and come back tomorrow. No arguments. Just go.'

Masterson stared her out. Matilda turned on her heels and headed for the door. She had one foot out of the office when Masterson stopped her.

'And Matilda, I do not want to smell alcohol on you ever again.'

Matilda couldn't remember the journey home. It all seemed to have happened in a blur. She was sitting in the driveway for almost ten minutes before she realized she was home.

She looked at herself in the rear-view mirror and didn't recognize her reflection. Masterson was right; she was a mess. She was worse than a mess; she was about to self-destruct.

She opened the door and kicked it closed behind her and headed for the kitchen. There was a bottle of vodka in the freezer. She didn't care what Masterson said, she was going to let the alcohol put her to sleep and by the next morning she'd be fine. She hoped.

When she got into the kitchen she saw a note leaning against the kettle. She didn't recognize the handwriting:

'Tesco order arrived on time. I've put most of it away but not sure where you keep some items so I've left them on the kitchen table. Hope that's OK. Mum says to remind you to come to ours on Sunday for lunch. See you later, Chris.'

It was from Adele's son. As promised she had ordered a supply of groceries and had her son wait in for it. She opened the fridge door and saw it stocked with cheese, milk, salad, yogurt, butter, meat, bottled water, fish, and eggs. The generosity and kind spirit was overwhelming. The tears flowed in a torrent and she collapsed on the floor in a glass-shattering wail of emotion.

Ben arrived home to a house of calm. His two daughters were upstairs in their rooms. He could hear the dull thudding of music. His hackles rose immediately. What happened to respect? What happened to the £100 headphones he'd bought them both? He wondered if he was to blame for the way they were turning out; had he spent too much time at work when they were growing up? No, that wasn't it. Besides, their mother didn't work so they always had some parental figure at home. He scoffed. Parental figure? That was a joke. She didn't care what anybody did as long as she didn't have to get up off the sofa.

'I've had enough of this,' Hales said under his breath. It was time to put his foot down. Sara and the girls took advantage of him, treating him like a cash machine and a taxi service. It was time to stop. 'Turn that bloody music down right now!' he shouted up the stairs. He waited a few seconds for his request to be adhered to but nothing happened.

He kicked off his shoes and hung up his coat in the hallway. He listened intently for any sign of where his wife was. He could hear the sound of the television from the living room. What a shock! The bloody thing was never off.

His wife, Sara, was five years his junior. She was yet to understand the pressure of approaching a fiftieth birthday, the questioning of life and position that went with the half-century. She was curled up on the large cream leather sofa, her feet tucked under her. A loud and bright game show was blaring from the screen. She was engrossed and didn't turn to her husband to say hello.

Ben knew he wouldn't get a word out of her until the programme finished. He went over to the drinks cabinet and poured himself a large measure of whisky and downed half in one gulp. It was still only early in the day, not even lunchtime, but what did it matter now?

The awful music, a mess of a tune, signalled the programme was over. Sara picked up the remote and muted the television.

'What are you doing home?' Her voice was soft and accentless. She used to be an attractive woman, but since passing forty she had failed to keep up with her eyebrow plucking, exfoliating, and expensive haircuts. She used to offer a touch of glamour. Now she could easily mingle into the harassed-looking mothers waiting outside a school gate at 3.30. Her hair needed a trim and the dark roots were showing.

'Nothing. There's not much to do at present so I thought I'd take some time away from the office.'

'Is that wise? I mean, if Matilda's back and doing a wonderful job she may regain control of MIT much sooner than you thought.'

'To be honest, I couldn't give a fuck.' He tried to control the bitter rage building up from within but it wasn't working.

'Well that's a nice attitude to take,' his wife said. She picked up the remote and turned on the on-screen guide, flicking down through the menu of channels to see what she could watch next.

'And what have you been up to this morning, light of my life?' The sarcasm was not lost on his wife.

'Are you sure you're all right?'

'I'm fine. So, what *have* you been up to? Done a weekly shop, been jogging, attended a board meeting, found a cure for the common cold?'

'What's got into you? You know I don't go out during the week.'

'No you don't do you?' He made his way to the living-room door.

'Are you off back to work?' she asked in a cheery voice, as if the awkward and stilted conversation hadn't taken place.

'No. I'm going for a shower; providing I can get into my own fucking bathroom.'

'Flick the kettle on for me will you?'

Ben could feel the rage building up inside him. There was a tension in the back of his neck and his skin itched with the prickly sensation of anxiety. If he didn't find a way to release it soon then he would end up exploding and God forbid anyone on the receiving end of it.

Chapter 37

DC Scott Andrews pulled up outside the apartment block where Jonathan Harkness lived. Sian was in the front passenger seat, and Jonathan was in the back trying to keep his eyes open. The smooth ride in the Peugeot and the monotonous sound of the engine and the warmth of the heater had made him even more tired. He longed for his bed.

As he entered his flat, with the detectives following a few paces behind, he looked around the living room. It seemed like an age since he was last here. Everything was how he had left it, neat and tidy, yet he knew a whole team of scene of crime officers would soon be trampling through his life. They would be opening drawers and cupboards, going through his books, and under the cushions on his sofa, and under his bed. This would no longer feel like his home.

'Where was the coffee table Jonathan?' Sian asked.

'Just there. In front of the sofa. I bagged the glass up in a black bin liner and it's in the bins around the back. There was a metal frame. That should still be at the side of the bins.'

'OK. I'll need your clothes from the night you were attacked.'

'They're in the laundry basket in the bathroom. I can't remember if I had changed out of my uniform or not. It's a bit of a blur.' He rubbed his tired eyes and ran his bony fingers through his tangled hair.

'That's OK. I'll take a look. If you just want to get a few essentials, and I'll take you up to your neighbour,' Sian said.

He went into his bedroom, Scott following, and collected the basics; shirt, trousers, underwear, T-shirt, jacket, and placed them carefully in a small rucksack. Before leaving the room he picked up his hardback copy of the latest Ian Rankin from his bedside table and nodded to Scott, telling him he'd finished.

'Anything else?'

'I don't think so.'

'Nothing from the bathroom?'

'Oh. Yes of course. Sorry.'

From the bathroom Jonathan collected a washbag and put in a toothbrush, toothpaste, face wash, and a can of deodorant. He didn't look back at his flat as he left his home. He doubted he would call it a home the next time he came here.

Maun was already waiting in the doorway of her apartment when Jonathan eventually climbed to the floor above. She offered a weak smile and stood to one side to let him in.

'How's he doing?' Maun asked Sian in a hushed tone.

'He's extremely tired. I think he's going to be sleeping for a very long time.'

'What's happening now?'

'Well we need to go over his flat, just to make sure the evidence corroborates his story and then we'll go from there.'

'Right. Will you let me know when he can go back home?'

'Yes of course.'

Jonathan stood in the hallway to Maun's flat listening to the conversation between the two women, talking as if he was too fragile to hear what was going on.

'Jonathan, if you need anything, you know where to contact me,' Sian said before turning away and heading back down the stairs.

By the time she reached the bottom Jonathan heard her mention 'forensic team' to someone. They would be rummaging around his flat shortly. It was too horrible to contemplate.

'Would you like a shower?' Maun asked Jonathan in a tone more suited to a nursery teacher. 'You'll need to get out of those clothes,' she said, looking at the oversized grey tracksuit he'd been given at the police station.

'I just want to go to sleep.'

'That's fine. The spare room is ready for you.'

The spare room was always ready in case somebody, Jonathan hopefully, needed it.

She led him into the room. The curtains were already drawn; the room was cool and in complete darkness. The duvet had been turned down.

The deep mattress and plump pillows were almost calling to Jonathan.

As Maun closed the door on him she heard him say, 'I just want to go to sleep and never wake up again.'

Matilda

Chapter 38

By the time she woke, Matilda had been asleep for over fourteen hours. She had slumped onto the sofa and was in a deep sleep within minutes. As she stirred, she stretched her limbs and gave a wide yawn. She looked up and saw Adele sitting in James's armchair, reading one of James's hardback novels.

'Adele?' she asked, confused at her presence.

Adele reacted with a start and looked across at her friend. 'Good morning. How are you feeling?'

'Like I've been on a weekend bender. What are you doing here?'

'I came as soon as I finished work. Chris has been looking after you most of the day.'

'Where is he now?' she asked, looking around her as if unaware of her surroundings.

'He's gone back home.'

'What time is it?'

Adele looked at her watch. 'Just coming up to one o'clock.'

'It's dark already?'

'One o'clock in the morning.'

'What? How long have I been asleep?'

'I'm not sure; about thirteen, fourteen hours maybe.'

'Oh my God. No,' she exclaimed, sitting up quickly.

'You obviously needed it.'

229

'I can't have been asleep for fourteen hours. Why didn't you wake me?'

'Well I've only been here since ten. You looked peaceful so I thought I'd leave you. Your sister rang. She said your mother has been on to her as you were supposed to keep her updated on your return to work but haven't. Don't worry, I was very sanguine and said you were busy chasing a suspected Lord Lucan around Europe. I also had a call from Sian. She's worried about you. Everyone's worried about you.'

'There's no need to be. I'm fine.'

'Is that just something you're used to saying now? You're not fine. You're as far away from fine as you can possibly get. Now I want you to go upstairs, have a shower, and when you've freshened up I'll be here with coffee and a sandwich and we're going to have a serious conversation.'

As she struggled off the sofa, Matilda said, 'I'm having a strange sense of déjà vu here.'

'Well this is where the déjà vu ends. You've reached the end of the line. If you don't change right now there really is no way back for you. You'll be finished. When was the last time you ate?'

'I can't remember.' She ran her fingers through her knotted hair. It felt greasy. 'What's happening to me?'

'Well fortunately it's nothing that can't be fixed. At the moment you're on a one-way trip to oblivion. However, I'm not going to allow you to get there. Now, stop dwelling, get upstairs, get showered, and then we'll work something out.'

Matilda was in the shower so long Adele was beginning to worry. She was contemplating going upstairs to check on her. She stood at the bottom of the stairs, hand on the bannister, when she heard the toilet flush; there was life up there. She ran into the kitchen and flicked on the kettle.

'So, are you going to tell me what's going on?'

Matilda and Adele were sitting at the kitchen table. Matilda had changed into her dressing gown. She looked fresh and clean from her shower; the heat and pressure from the water had cleansed her and put a glow in her cheeks.

'It's work. I can't cope.'

'That's bollocks for a start,' Adele said, almost flippantly. 'We both know you can cope.'

'I can't. I feel like an outsider among my own team. And fucking Ben Hales doesn't help,' she said, putting as much bitterness and rage into his name as she could muster.

'So would life at work be more bearable if Hales wasn't there?'

She thought for a while before answering. 'No. I suppose not.'

'So what is the problem then?'

'It's me. I've just lost all confidence. My mind's all over the place. I keep thinking I'm going to screw it all up again like I did with . . . Carl Meagan.' Just saying the name of the little boy she failed was painful.

'That's perfectly natural. The last major case you worked on didn't go as planned and you're worried you'll repeat your actions, yes?'

'Yes.'

'What are the actual odds on that happening?'

'I'm not sure,' she replied with a frown.

'Personally I don't think you should blame yourself for Carl Meagan, but, for argument's say, let's say it was your fault. How many cases in your career have you screwed up?'

'Just that one.'

'So you have a very high percentage success rate?'

'I guess so.'

'There's no guessing about it. You're an excellent detective. Do you really think Masterson would have given you the MIT if you weren't? You're more than capable of solving any crime you work on. Like you said, you're just lacking a wee bit of confidence at the moment.' Adele picked up her bacon sandwich and tore off a huge bite.

'So how do I get over that?'

'You give yourself a good kick up the backside. You stop dwelling on the past. You say "yes I screwed up; yes I made an error, and I'll make bloody sure I don't do that again".'

'How did you cope, you know, when your life turned to shit?'

'So nicely put,' Adele said with a smile. 'Our situations are totally different Mat. However, I did feel completely helpless when that bastard walked out on me and Chris.' She looked into the distance, shaking her head. 'You know, it still angers me to this day. Don't get me wrong, I love Chris to bits, but he wasn't planned. Who knew a three-minute quickie in the back of a car could change your whole life?'

'And you're supposed to be a doctor?' Matilda asked.

'I wasn't then. I was naive . . .'

'Don't even think about saying virginal,' Matilda scoffed.

'The second I found out I was pregnant with Chris I thought my life was over. Then that bastard, as he's now known, came up with a brilliant plan. He'd go to university, I'd stay at home, then when he'd qualified, he'd get a part-time job and I'd go to university. He'd not been graduated a week before he ran off to Birmingham with that goofy, flat-chested trollop. So there I was, completely alone, trapped in a manky bedsit with a child, and no hope.'

'Did you feel then like I do now?'

'No way out? No future?'

'Yes.'

'I certainly did. I just kept picturing myself being one of those women who work part-time in a supermarket to make ends meet and resent their children. I didn't want to hate Chris.'

'The difference is though; you had your parents to help you.'

'Well, yes, but I didn't ask them for help. Dad came out to Manchester, saw how I was living, and practically dragged me to Sheffield. He and mum took care of Chris during the day while I was at uni and the rest you know about. I'd given up though. It took someone else to save me.'

'I'm not as strong as you.'

'Bullshit. You're stronger. I couldn't run a murder team. You have so much responsibility at work, so many people looking to you for help and advice. I'd hate that.'

Matilda looked away and out of the window. It was pitch-dark outside and the kitchen light was on. All she could see was her own reflection looking back at her. She was sitting slumped in her chair, the look of defeat etched on her red face.

'What are you thinking?' Adele asked after a minute of silence.

'I'm thinking about how much I want to run away.'

'Would that solve anything?'

'No. It would make me feel better though.'

'Really? You think if you left Sheffield, Carl Meagan and Ben Hales would just stay here and not go with you?'

'I just hate Sheffield so much.'

'No you don't.'

'I bloody do.'

'What is it about Sheffield you dislike?'

'Everything. It's in decay. Look around you, the whole city is crumbling. The majority of the shops in the city centre are closed, there are estates littered with troubled families and unemployment. Everywhere you go is just so depressing.'

'I think you'll find a lot of cities are like that. Every city is trying to go through some form of regeneration. You're just seeing Sheffield in a negative light because you're feeling negative. You used to love this city, the Winter Gardens, the Crucible and Lyceum theatres, the botanical gardens, the fact we're on the edge of the Derbyshire countryside, the parks.'

'I only enjoyed those things because I was going to them with James. There's no arguing that I've changed in the last year.'

'Of course you've changed, but you need to adapt.'

'How?'

'You accept help from those around you.'

'I can't expect you and Chris to look after me.'

'I should hope not. My babysitting days are over.' She smiled as she helped herself to a rasher of bacon out of the cooling sandwich in front of Matilda. 'I love the really crispy ones. We're not here to look after you; we're here to help you. Any time you need to cry and scream about Carl Meagan then you come to my house, we open a bottle of wine, or three, and we talk through it. Any time you want to kick off about Ben Hales, you come to my house and we smash some plates. It's fine to think about James and about how much you miss him but give yourself an allotted grieving time.'

'What do you mean?'

'Well, for example, say about six o'clock every night sit on the sofa looking at your wedding album for an hour or so and have a good cry. Think about your honeymoon and the time I came round on your birthday and found you both in an embarrassing position in the back garden.'

Matilda blushed and put her hand over her mouth. 'Oh my God I'd forgotten about that.'

'Unfortunately I haven't.'

'Do you remember the look on James's face? It was weeks before he could make eye contact with you again.'

They both laughed and they remembered the fun they had on the night of Matilda's birthday four years ago; the drinking, the bad dancing, the food, the presents, and the uniformed police officers turning up at three o'clock in the morning following complaints from the neighbours.

'Would that work though; you can't give grief a timetable,' Matilda said, getting back to the topic in hand.

'That's true, you can't. But if you allow yourself time each day to think about these things you won't allow them to disturb your working life, eventually.'

'Where do you get all this stuff from?'

'I'm an extremely intelligent person,' Adele answered. She was smug, smiling. 'You also need to cut out the alcohol too.'

'Oh God.' Matilda put her head down in shame. 'I never used to touch vodka, except as a mixer, now I'm taking it neat straight from the bottle.'

'Not any more. I found your three bottles in the freezer and I've emptied them down the sink.' Nothing needed to be said. Matilda proffered a small smile of thanks. 'You need to take your medication regularly too. According to the packet, from the date you had the prescription filled you should have eight tablets left; you've got twenty-three. Also, try eating too. Having regular healthy meals will help your energy levels.'

'I know. I'm really sorry. I honestly don't know what I'd do without you Adele.'

'Well, as Christmas is just around the corner, keep in mind that I like diamonds.'

235

Chapter 39

Jonathan had slept longer than Matilda. By the time he woke it was daylight. He pushed the duvet back and swung his pale spindly legs out of the bed. His head felt fuzzy; the aftermath of a much-needed deep sleep. He felt as if he'd been in a coma for a week.

In the living room Maun was sitting in an armchair reading the local newspaper. She heard shuffling feet behind her and turned to face him.

'Good morning sleepyhead. How do you feel?' She smiled at him.

He returned her smile. 'I'm not sure yet. I feel a bit light-headed.'

'I'm not surprised. You've been asleep for almost a full day. Do you want something to eat?'

'Not at the moment. I'd love a coffee though.'

'Come and sit down. I'll make you a drink.'

Jonathan was suddenly cold. He had spent the last twenty-four hours wrapped comfortably in a thick feather duvet. Now his arms and legs were exposed to the daytime temperatures and judging by the thick layer of frost outside it was well below freezing. He looked across at the newspaper Maun had left on her chair. It was folded in half so he couldn't see the headline but he recognized the photograph of his childhood home. He wondered what had been happening while he had been sleeping.

Maun brought a black coffee for him in a large mug. He wrapped both hands around it firmly to warm up and took several lingering sniffs of the hot drink. He took a sip and felt the hot liquid race through his body. He was beginning to thaw.

'Stephen's dead,' he said without looking up.

'I know. That detective, DS Mills, told me yesterday. I'm so sorry Jonathan. I know how much you liked him.'

'A hit-and-run. A car just came out of nowhere and killed him. One minute he was walking along and the next he was dead. How does that happen?'

'I don't know. Life is very fragile. We take it for granted sometimes.'

'Oh my God, his family,' he burst out. 'Who's going to tell his family?'

'DS Mills said they've been in contact with the local police in Dublin and they're going to send someone to break the news. Don't worry about anything Jonathan; it's all being taken care of.'

'I can't believe this is happening to me. All my life I've tried to stay in the background; go to work, come home again, and not bother anyone. Why can't I just be left alone? If Stephen hadn't tried to befriend me, he'd still be alive. I told him this would happen. Why did he have to get involved?'

'I wish I knew the answer Jonathan I really do. Unfortunately there are some sick people out there who get their kicks out of harming others.' She looked at him carefully over the top of her coffee mug.

'I'm going to have to move,' he blurted out.

'What?'

'I can't stay here. I should never have come back to Sheffield in the first place. I was foolish to think I could. Now it's all tainted. It's death and destruction wherever you look.'

'You can't move,' her voice had changed. She sounded upset.

'I've got no choice. My home is not going to feel like my home any more. Did the scene of crime people come?'

'Yes. They were here a while and left around early evening.'

'Did they say anything?'

'Not to me, no.'

'Have you been in?'

'No.'

'I bet they've made a mess; fingerprint dust everywhere, drawers left open and things tipped out. I bet they've moved my books too.' The thought of strangers going through his personal possessions made him feel sick. He felt the prickly sensation climb up the back of his neck. Unconsciously, he started rocking slightly, back and forth. 'They've been in my flat with their shoes and touched everything. I can't go back living there. I can't.'

'Jonathan, calm down.'

She leaned forward and placed a comforting hand on his lap but he recoiled from her touch.

'We'll get your flat sorted out. We'll redecorate, get some new furniture. It'll look like a completely different place when we've finished.'

'No. That's not going to work. I need to go. I need to make a fresh start.'

'Where?'

'I've no idea. I don't care. Anywhere. I'll give head office a ring, explain everything and see if they'll transfer me to another store, maybe Scotland.'

'Scotland?'

'Or Wales, I don't know. I just have to leave this place.'

Chapter 40

Before leaving for work Matilda had another shower. Adele had left an hour before, making sure her friend was well enough and giving her a long and tight embrace. She made Matilda promise to call her often and give her a progress report, which she agreed to. While in the shower, Matilda cried, the hot shower washing the tears away. If it wasn't for Adele, she honestly believed she would have taken her own life by now. Everybody deserved to have an Adele in their life.

As she pulled into the car park, she passed Hales's Audi and, for the first time, she didn't want to snap off a wing mirror and throw it through the windscreen.

If it was possible it seemed to be getting colder. Matilda felt the bitter wind cut through her as she climbed out of the car. She pulled her jacket tight around her and realized she didn't have a winter coat that fitted her. She would have to go shopping at the first opportunity, especially if this winter was going to be as harsh as predicted.

Matilda smiled to herself. She must be feeling better if her mind was turning away from the case, Ben Hales, and the plight of Jonathan Harkness, to having a wander around the shops for a winter coat. What would it be next; new furniture for the conservatory, a new car, a walking holiday in Cornwall?

She made her way to the back entrance of the police station with her head held high and an inner smile. The permanent aching in her shoulders from where she held herself rigid with tension and fear was gone. Maybe she had turned a corner. Maybe Matilda Darke was on her way back.

The mobile phone she struggled to get to grips with rang in her pocket. It was Adele.

'You'd better not be checking up on me,' Matilda said with humour in her voice.

'Of course not. I wouldn't do a thing like that. You are at work though aren't you?'

'Yes I am. I've just arrived.'

'Good. I did have a genuine reason for calling; it's not long until Christmas. Now, before you say anything I know you'll probably want to forget all about it this year and work all the way through, and that's fine, however, for Christmas lunch I want you here with me and Chris. No questions, do you understand?'

'How do you know I haven't made plans?' Matilda joked. 'I may have decided to spend the day with my adoring family.'

'And I may find Benedict Cumberbatch under my tree on Christmas morning.'

'Fine. You win.'

'I always do. Have a good day.'

There was no way Matilda would enjoy Christmas to its full potential this year. It didn't matter what she did, she would be comparing it to her last one with James. However, the thought of having Christmas lunch with Adele and Chris cheered her up slightly.

I can do this. I can bloody do this.

Chapter 41

Maun could perfectly understand Jonathan's decision to leave. In his position, she would be saying exactly the same things, but from her point of view, she wanted him to stay. She needed him to stay. She would do everything in her power to keep him here. Jonathan leaving Sheffield was not a possibility.

Maun had convinced Jonathan he should eat something and was in the kitchen rapidly making sandwiches of various fillings. She had been thrilled yesterday when DS Mills had contacted her, asking if Jonathan could stay at her place. She didn't need to think of an answer. He finally needed her. When the call had ended, Maun had dashed about, tidied up, and quickly vacuumed the spare bedroom. Jonathan would feel safe and comfortable here. She'd make sure of it. Now, he was planning to leave Sheffield. Her mind raced with scenarios in which she convinced Jonathan to stay in Sheffield. She couldn't risk him leaving and being on her own. What would she turn into? 'He can't go,' she mumbled to herself. 'He can't. I won't allow it. He's not leaving.' She cut her finger while slicing a cucumber. 'Shit!' The stainless-steel blade had made a perfectly neat cut. Blood began to pour out and she quickly made her way over to the sink. Despite the pain her mind was still on Jonathan's revelation.

241

In the living room, Jonathan was getting comfortable in the armchair. He was warming up nicely and felt himself relax. He thought about Stephen, of what he had said on their last meeting. Why hadn't he suggested they go for something to eat and talk things over? Why had he decided to go home? Yes it had been late but did it matter if he'd been late for work the following morning; Stephen was the manager after all.

Jonathan felt tears roll down his face. He found this feeling strange. He had always been careful about displaying emotions and preferred to keep everything to himself. Since the case of his parents' murder had been reopened he had been feeling more tearful, more fragile, more afraid.

'Maun, do you have any tissues?' he called out to her, hoping his voice didn't give his sadness away.

'On the sideboard. If the box is empty there's another in the cupboard.'

The box on the sideboard was indeed empty. He bent down and opened the cupboard door. This was obviously Maun's knick-knack cupboard; a place where things were put away that didn't have a designated area. He had to hunt for the tissues, moving a shoe box full of odds and ends to one side and lifting out a red leather scrapbook, the front of which had 'Memory Lane' written on it in gold copperplate. The book was full and heavy. He lifted it up and placed it on top of the sideboard. He knew he shouldn't look inside and invade Maun's privacy but he couldn't help himself. He opened it at random.

The first few pages were taken up with old photographs from Maun's wedding. He had never seen these pictures before. She was a very beautiful woman in her youth, in a classical Jane Austen way. Her husband stood proud next to her, head held high, and an almost smug smile on his lips; he had just married the most beautiful woman in the world.

Maun was wearing an elegant, simply designed, floor-length wedding dress, while her husband Peter wore a traditional grey morning suit. They looked happy and in love.

The following pages contained holiday snaps of the happy couple, probably from the honeymoon. It looked hot and exotic. He wondered why Maun had kept these after the marriage had ended so painfully for her. Eventually, the photographs stopped and were replaced with newspaper cuttings. At first these were stories of achievements her husband had made in the business world; land he had acquired, homes he had built, run-down areas of Sheffield he had developed into prime locations for families to live in. He had obviously worked hard to build up a business empire. Maun must have felt immense pride.

Unfortunately, the good news stories didn't last for long and eventually the press started to write about the Barringtons' private life and rumours of his affairs were obviously more interesting that his latest property development.

Jonathan didn't need to read the stories to find out what the trouble was; the headlines alone were bitter and scathing enough to enlighten him in the Barrington problems: BARRINGTON LEAVES BUSINESS AWARDS WITH 18YO; PROPERTY DEVELOPER'S HOMES DON'T REACH BRITISH STANDARD; BARRINGTON HOMES IN CITY COUNCIL BRIBE; DIRTY TRICKS OF BARRINGTON LAND PURCHASING; BARRINGTON MISTRESS IN KISS AND TELL.

Jonathan stopped to read one story. It didn't carry much detail and it was obvious the story had only broken as the newspaper was going to print.

BUSINESSMAN KILLED IN CAR PLUNGE

Property magnate Peter Barrington has been killed in a freak car accident.

Police were called to Snake Pass, the A57, between Glossop and the Ladybower Reservoir early this morning. According to a police source, no other car was involved in the incident. An investigation into the cause of the crash is underway. Mr Barrington's wife, Maun, has been informed and is currently being looked after by neighbours.

In a brief statement from Barrington Homes and Development, chief executive Justine Clement-Hill said, 'It is a complete tragedy that Mr Barrington has been killed and we are all grieving. Our thoughts are with his wife Maun and we offer our sympathies.'

Further stories followed from the local press: speculation as to the cause of the crash, who his mystery passenger was, why there were two overnight bags in the boot when Peter Barrington was only going to Manchester to sign a contract. Then, what must have been agony for Maun, the story of her husband's secretary, travelling with Peter and killed along with him, was three months pregnant with his baby. Jonathan immediately felt sympathy for Maun; hearing the news of her husband's betrayal must have been like a slap in the face.

Maun had never been able to have children and had told him that not becoming a mother was the biggest tragedy in her life. To be faced with news that Peter's secretary, twenty-seven years his junior, was having his child, must have been heart-breaking to say the least.

The following pages of the scrapbook continued with the story of Peter's death, including an interview with the secretary's mother who fed a platter of lies to the press about how her daughter was the only woman ever to make Peter happy and how Maun had constantly ground him down over the years. Jonathan wondered how many times Maun had read these stories; each word must have been like a knife in the heart. People would read it and they would believe it. Suddenly, Maun was the villain of the story.

When there were no more revelations left the press moved on. The final story Maun had saved was about her husband's burial.

Turning another page, Jonathan staggered back as he saw a headline that broke the news of the murder of his own parents twenty years before. As far as he was aware, Maun had no previous connection with his family. He thought they had been total strangers when they first met on his return to Sheffield.

The Harkness murders gained plenty of press attention, mainly because the key witness was an eleven-year-old boy who had seen his parents brutally murdered. The following pages in Maun's scrapbook contained story after story covering the case, from different newspapers, covering the same angle. Jonathan flicked through the pages with wide-eyed horror. It was as if Maun was obsessed with the case, but why? Who was she to the Harkness family?

The sound of a cup being dropped and smashing in the kitchen brought Jonathan back from his reverie. He suddenly remembered where he was. He flicked to the back of the book, to see what the final entry was. At first he couldn't make sense of the carbon-print receipt he was looking at. Why would Maun hang on to a car-hire receipt? His eyes widened and it all fitted into place. Maun had recently hired a car with the registration number YS08 DPT. That registration number was emblazoned on his memory and would be until the day he died. It was the car that had killed Stephen, which had shattered any illusion of a normal life, which had reversed and almost killed him.

Maun pushed the living-room door open and entered backwards. She was carrying a large wooden tray she had spent plenty of time preparing; two side plates full with tiny crustless sandwiches, a large white teapot, steam rising from the spout, and two matching cups and saucers. She had a smile on her face, a smile that stretched her skin and exposed the wrinkles she loathed. She was in her element; here was Jonathan at the height of anxiety and he had come to her for help, he had taken some coaxing, but he was here. That was a start. She just had to make sure he stayed here.

As soon as she saw the red leather scrapbook in Jonathan's hands the smile fell from her face.

The silence was intense. Maun could not take her eyes from the book and Jonathan could not take his eyes off Maun.

Suddenly it was cold and dark. The room seemed smaller and claustrophobic. For Jonathan, the heaviness of the tension enveloped him. His mind was working overtime, trying to make sense of the situation he found himself in.

For Maun, her home felt like a coffin being lowered into the ground and she was still alive inside. She could feel the pressure of the pouring earth trapping her. She wanted to scream, to shout, to kick and plead for mercy, but she knew she wouldn't be heard.

'Who are you?' Jonathan shattered the heavy calm. His words bounced off the wall with all the force of a ball in a game of squash.

'Jonathan, let me explain,' she said as she carefully placed the tray on the coffee table. Her hands were shaking and the cups rattled. 'They're just newspaper cuttings, that's all. I was . . . interested.'

He tore the car-hire receipt from the back of the book and held it up. 'Explain this then.'

'Oh my God. I . . . I can't explain that. I wasn't thinking straight. I . . . He was going to take you away from me.' She said slowly. She was deflated. The wind had been knocked out of her sails.

'What?'

'I'm not daft Jonathan. I could see it coming. Stephen was a very clever man. He was much more subtle than I was. He was a very good shoulder for you to cry on and you took him into your confidence. Eventually he would have convinced you to put Sheffield behind you, draw a line under all this and move on, and you would have listened to him. He would have probably taken you back to Ireland with him. I couldn't have that. I couldn't lose . . .'

'What are you talking about? He wasn't playing a game at all. Stephen was a good guy. There aren't many left in this world. He liked me. Actually he loved me. I've no idea why but he did and he wanted to help me. That's all. He had no ulterior motive and he wasn't taking me anywhere.'

Maun looked up. Her eyes were red and full of tears ready to fall. 'I am so sorry Jonathan.'

'Sorry? How can you say that? You killed him in cold blood and all you can say is sorry? I don't believe you. I don't believe you're sorry at all. You planned this all along. It takes time to

246

hire a car, to find out where he was, and when to strike. It was in your head all that time and you went through with it without a second thought.'

'That's not true Jonathan, I . . . '

'No. You don't get to say anything right now.' He slammed the red leather scrapbook down on the floor. He sat down on the opposing armchair and leaned forward. His eyes were wide and starry, his jaw clenched and determined. 'Why did you reverse?'

'What?'

The bright red of the reversing lights caused him to squint. A few seconds later and the car started moving, heading straight for Jonathan.

The wheels crunched over loose stones as it reversed. Ten seconds went by, then twenty. Jonathan could smell the exhaust fumes and feel the heat coming from the car. It was almost upon him. Eventually he opened his eyes. The car had stopped in front of him, less than a yard away.

'After you ran over Stephen you carried on driving then stopped. A few seconds later the brake lights came on and you reversed. Why?'

She stuttered. 'I . . . I was going to make sure he was dead. I thought you would have jumped out of the way but you didn't. I saw then how much he meant to you. You were willing to die with him weren't you?'

He leaned back in his chair and held eye contact. 'Yes. He was all I had left.' Jonathan didn't even have to think about his reply. Of course he was willing to die with Stephen.

'What about me? I've not meant anything to you all these years have I?'

'That's not true. You're a good friend. Correction, you were a good friend.'

'Don't say that Jonathan. Please. I'm sorry. I really am sorry.'

'You've done this your whole life haven't you? Any time something happens that you're not in control of or that will upset you,

247

you leap in and change it. You destroy it. If you can't be happy then why should anyone else.'

'That's not true.'

'Of course it is. The evidence is right here in your scrapbook. What happened between you and your husband that caused you to do this?'

Jonathan opened the scrapbook, flipped through a few pages, and when he found what he was looking for he turned it towards Maun.

She winced at the headline: 'WAS BARRINGTON'S CAR ROADWORTHY?' She didn't say anything. She just looked into the face of the young man she thought she knew. The rage building up inside him was intense. She could see the veins in his neck throbbing.

'Tell me about your husband,' Jonathan said.

'What do you want to know?' She swallowed hard and fingered the tight collar on her blouse.

'Everything. Everything the press left out.'

'Sit down Jonathan. Come on, sit down and have a cup of coffee. I don't know what you're thinking here but . . .' She trailed off. She couldn't finish that sentence.

'You've always said the neighbours shunned you because you didn't seem particularly upset at your husband's death. However, he was cheating on you with his secretary and she was pregnant with his child, the ultimate kick in the teeth for a woman unable to have children. So why did they shun you? Surely they would have been sympathetic to a wronged woman whose private life was suddenly splashed all over the papers?'

'You'd think so wouldn't you but that's not how it turned out,' she replied with a shrug.

'Why?'

'I don't know.'

'You do. Come on Maun, you're talking to me now. You're a very strong woman. If someone had been ignoring or bad-mouthing you for no reason you would have found out. You knew about the affair didn't you?'

She paused. She waited until she had the courage to allow it all to come out. The strength, the energy, rose up inside her like an erupting volcano. She looked Jonathan in the eye and knew it was time to tell all. 'Of course I knew about the affair,' she said with an angry bitterness. 'Peter was an excellent businessman but as a person, as a hider of secrets, he was terrible.'

'How did you find out?'

'I saw it in his face straightaway. I left it for a while and gathered evidence; the sudden weekend meetings, late nights at the office. He turned into a walking cliché. One night over dinner I just came out with it. He tried to deny it, obviously, but his face gave him away. That's why he was such a terrible poker player. Every lie he tried to feed me I saw through straightaway. Then came the biggest betrayal of all; his young tart was pregnant.'

'He told you?'

'Oh yes. Well, he sat me down and said he had a plan. His exact words were "I have a business proposition for you my dear". He wanted a divorce but he didn't want any scandal, so he wanted me to file for divorce and say I had met somebody else. Can you believe that? He was the bastard yet he wanted me to become the social pariah.'

'What did you say?'

'I said I'd think about it. He'd already given it plenty of thought; he'd put together a very attractive package to sweeten the deal.'

'But you weren't having any of it?'

'Of course not,' she blustered. 'Did he honestly think he could treat me like that after all the years of playing the dutiful wife and attending all those dull meetings, dinner parties, conference weekends in sodding Worthing? I wasn't prepared to be cast aside like a dirty towel. He was going to pay and I wanted more than any amount of money he was prepared to offer.'

Jonathan allowed the silence to build. 'You killed him didn't you?'

'You know, cutting the brake line on a car is more difficult than the films have you believe. I looked under the bonnet of his car and had no idea what to do. It took some researching to figure out how to make it look like wear and tear. I suppose it's much easier these days with the Internet. I got a book from the university library and ended up interfering with the brake pedal, and to make sure it worked, I sabotaged the linkage on the steering too so that, at some point in his journey, he'd lose control of the steering, slam on the brakes, which would also fail, and that would be it. He was on the Snake Pass when it happened. He went over the side and crashed into the countryside.'

'He had a pregnant woman with him. How could you . . . ?'

'Hand on heart I genuinely did not know she was going to be in the car,' she interrupted him. 'I knew he was going to Manchester, but it was just to sign a contract. There was no reason for her to be with him. It was just a happy accident.'

'A happy accident? My God, you're proud of what you did.'

'Of course I am. I was being humiliated.'

'And what about his secretary?'

'What about her?'

'She was innocent in all this . . . '

'Innocent? She was sleeping with a married man. How is that innocent? Since when was being a whore innocent? Whatever happened to her she deserved.'

'I can't believe you've just said that. You killed two people, three if you count the unborn baby, and you're not even bothered about it.'

'I had no choice,' she stated matter-of-factly.

'And what about Stephen. Did you have no choice there either?'

Maun fell into her armchair. There was no way for her to talk herself out of this. Her demeanour changed. She felt no emotion for her husband and his bit on the side. Jonathan, however, was a different story. She loved him.

'Jonathan . . . I'm so sorry.'

'It's far too late for apologies. You're a control freak. You've tried to control everything all your life and when anyone got in the way of what you wanted you killed them. Is there any wonder you're on your own? You're evil. You're an actual psychopath.'

Jonathan calling Maun a psychopath seemed to resonate within her. The pathetic tired look in her eyes had gone and she stood up and loomed over him.

'Well, you'd know all about that wouldn't you?' Her voice was quiet and deep and held a vicious bitterness.

'What do you mean?' Now it was Jonathan's turn to look worried.

'Sometimes it takes a psychopath to find another psychopath.'

'What?'

'Oh don't come the innocent with me Jonathan Harkness. The clues are all there in the newspaper cuttings. I've read them over many, many times and I've spoken to people about you. I know more than you think. I know all about you.'

'You don't know anything,' he said, swallowing the bile that had risen in his throat. A sheen of sweat appeared on his forehead and his hands were visibly shaking.

'Wrong. I know absolutely everything.'

Chapter 42

The Murder Room, the unofficial name for the Murder Investigation Team's briefing room, was a mass of noise; several conversations going on at once between plain-clothed and uniformed officers, telephones were ringing and rapidly answered, and computer keyboards were being heavily beaten with the fast-paced fingers of the stressed-out officers.

Matilda walked to the head of the room and stood in front of the whiteboards covered in crime-scene photographs and a blown up copy of Matthew Harkness's driving licence. By the time she turned around to face the room everyone was silent and awaiting her to begin the briefing. It felt like old times. Where was the anxiety, the fear of failure, the paranoia?

'Good morning everybody. Nice to see you all bright-eyed and raring to go. Now, I have spent the last half an hour with ACC Masterson and we have made some decisions in how these cases are currently run. I think it is safe to say that the killer of Stefan and Miranda Harkness and Matthew Harkness is one and the same person. Also, the hit-and-run, which left Stephen Egan dead, is too much of a coincidence not to be connected, but for now it is being investigated by CID. DS Jackson is leading that case and will keep us informed. We will, however, conduct our own investigation into it and liaise if and when necessary.

'Now, as Matthew Harkness is our more recent victim we will concentrate on his killer. I've been told there is no CCTV of the murder scene, but there aren't many exit points from Holly Lane. Do we have anything at all from the surrounding area?'

Matilda looked around at the faces staring back at her. There was no nervous tension, no prickly sensation crawling up her neck, no sweaty palms, no stuttering with self-doubt, no negative thoughts, and not a single Prime Minister in sight. She could see the usual crowd, her dedicated team she could always rely on, and a few uniformed officers she remembered from before her enforced sabbatical, and plenty of new, fresh faces too. Acting DCI Hales was notable by his absence.

'We have managed to get footage from a number of cameras in the area and there's a team of officers going through it all.'

'Thank you. It's Faith, isn't it?'

'DC Easter, yes ma'am.'

'I'm sorry we haven't had time to chat yet but we will soon. In the meantime, please ignore any rumours you may have heard about me.'

Easter's face was stony until Sian Mills laughed. The rest of the room murmured and Easter smiled, relaxing in the presence of the formidable DCI.

'Who do we have as a suspect for Matthew Harkness?'

Sian put down her cheese salad sandwich and dusted her hands free of flour. 'Current thinking is Jonathan may have killed him out of self-defence after Matthew attacked him. However, if we're saying Matthew was killed by the same person who killed his parents, are we really believing an eleven-year-old could butcher his parents in such a manner?' She pointed to the crime-scene photographs of the Harkness double murder on a separate whiteboard.

'There's no way an eleven-year-old could have committed those crimes,' said DC Scott Andrews. 'Look at the pictures of a young Jonathan; he's a bag of bones. He looks like a good meal would kill him. There's no way he could have overpowered two adults.'

'So if Jonathan didn't kill his brother then who did? Who knew he would be in Sheffield on that night?' Matilda asked nobody in particular. This was an open discussion and she welcomed comments from everyone.

'Maybe it was a random killing,' Rory said taking a final swig of coffee.

'If Matthew had been to Jonathan's flat, beaten him, and sexually assaulted him isn't it a bit of a coincidence that he then just happened to get himself killed in a random attack?' Aaron pointed out. 'This is real life, not *Emmerdale*.'

'I really don't think we can rule Jonathan out as a suspect,' Sian added.

'What is his official statement for the time of Matthew's death?'

'Well obviously he had just been attacked. He says he was in his flat on his own.'

'What do the neighbours say?' Matilda asked.

'A neighbour saw Matthew leave the apartment building but nobody else heard or saw anything,' Aaron said. He had been one of the officers who had spoken to everyone in the building. As the majority of the residents claimed to have heard and seen nothing, he didn't need to consult his notebook.

'His neighbour upstairs, Maun Barrington, bring her in, let's have a full statement from her and get her to dish the dirt on Jonathan,' Matilda said. 'Faith, check to see if there have been any similar attacks recently. We need to cover every angle of this, but I'm with the majority; I don't think this was a random attack. Did the search of Jonathan's apartment reveal anything interesting?' Matilda asked, looking at Sian.

'Apart from the fact that he's not normal,' Rory said, concentrating on opening a Mars Bar. 'I mean, how can you not have a TV?'

'He doesn't have a telly?' Scott Andrews scoffed.

'No. It's just books, books, and more books.'

'Bloody hell! Imagine a house with no background noise. I'd go mad with all that silence.'

Matilda interrupted before the discussion lost its way completely. 'Apart from the fact he doesn't watch *Match of the Day*, did we find anything useful?'

'His story seems to be backed up. There were fragments of glass in the living-room carpet and specks of Jonathan's blood. Matthew's fingerprints are all over the living room too,' Sian said.

'What about his bedroom?'

Sian was just about to put the last bite of her sandwich in her mouth when Matilda asked a follow-up question. She placed it back into the plastic box she had brought it in and picked up her notebook. 'No. Just Jonathan's in there. It looks like the sexual attack took place in the living room.'

'Did we go through his bins?'

'We did. Nothing unusual in there either; empty tins, used tea bags, deodorant can, old razor blades, etc. Nothing out of the ordinary.' She quickly ate the last bite of sandwich.

'So, on the basis of Jonathan's story being true and Matthew sexually assaulting him in his own home, are we going down the route of Jonathan following Matthew and killing him in an act of self-defence?'

'I think we have to, unless Matthew had an enemy in Manchester who followed him to Sheffield.'

'Please don't complicate matters any further Sian,' Aaron said, rubbing his temples.

'Not a bad question though Sian. Get back on to Manchester police and ask them to delve into his life a bit more. Oh, did you get in touch with Charlie Johnson?'

'I called his agent yesterday. She says he's away finishing his next book due out next summer. Apparently she's tried to contact him herself but hasn't been able to locate him.'

'Is this something we should be worried about?'

'His agent isn't worried. She says a lot of writers go off the radar when they're putting the finishing touches to a book.'

'Right. Well keep trying. I want a word with him.'

The atmosphere in the room suddenly darkened. Matilda saw Ben Hales enter before anyone else did, but the look on her face told them something was horribly wrong. Everyone turned to look at the doorway. He perched on the edge of the nearest desk and looked to Matilda with a smirk on his face. He was unshaven and his hair was an unruly mess. His eyes looked dull and the bags underneath were noticeably bigger than they were yesterday. Maybe he hadn't had the much-needed sleep she'd had. She smiled to herself as she considered sending Adele round to help him out.

The silence dragged on and the oppressive tension was felt by everyone. Aaron nudged Sian, prompting her to say something, do something to lighten the mood, move the situation along, but Sian was struck dumb.

'Right, I think we've covered just about everything,' Matilda stuttered. She was just about to recite the names of British Prime Ministers from the beginning of the twentieth century when she stopped herself. Hales was not worth the anxiety. 'So, does anyone have any questions?'

'Are you taking the kid gloves off?' Hales asked. His voice resounded off the walls and everyone held their breath. Hales was covering the only exit to the room. Matilda was at the top, everybody else was in the crossfire.

'I'm sorry?'

'Are you still treating Jonathan Harkness like he's made of glass or are you finally looking at him as the key to this whole affair?'

'In what way is he the key?' Matilda asked, folding her arms so nobody would see her shaking hands.

'Well, we can definitely get him on killing his brother for a start . . .'

Matilda interrupted. 'I will be interviewing Jonathan later today and putting questions to him about his brother's death.'

'What?' Hales's voice rose and he spat his question out like he would a hot chip. 'You'll be putting questions to him? Over tea and scones presumably.'

'Whether Jonathan killed his brother or not we still have to take into consideration his anxiety disorder and treat him accordingly.'

'Jesus Christ!' He rolled his eyes.

'Perhaps we can continue this chat in the office, Acting DCI Hales.' Ben didn't say anything, just walked past her into the small office at the back of the room. 'Don't go anywhere Sian,' Matilda said to her quietly in her ear as she followed him.

Matilda closed the door behind her, and, this time, she pulled the blind halfway down. 'Do you have a problem?'

'Yes I do. I have a problem with you and your so-called leadership. Can't you see behind the fake anxieties? He's using it as an excuse to avoid questioning. Anyone can fake a panic attack for fuck's sake.'

'You have to look at the bigger picture. If he is faking them he has been putting on an act for the majority of his life. He'll be good at it by now and won't just drop it if you go in with all guns blazing.'

'You're going about this completely the wrong way.'

'Do you ever wonder why you haven't gone further than a DI?' Matilda surprised herself by her sudden exclamation. 'It's not just the results; it's how you go about getting them. It's opening your eyes and your mind. Yes, I have considered Jonathan may be faking his anxiety but I cannot risk going in like a wrecking ball and him shutting down completely. If I charge him with murder he'll probably get a bloody good solicitor who'll get a doctor to confirm his illness and the whole thing won't ever see a courtroom. Oh, and while we're on the subject of handling people, you also need to connect with your team too.'

'What?'

'What's Sian's husband called?'

'What?' He looked confused.

'How many children does she have? What's Rory's relationship status? When is Aaron's birthday? What rumours about Scott are going around? You need respect and support from your team and you only get that by talking to them, interacting with them, and getting to know them.'

Hales was speechless. He looked at Matilda with wide eyes, but they weren't the wide steely eyes of an enraged man, they were sad. Matilda's confidence had come from nowhere. He didn't hate her, he was jealous of her. He quickly turned on his heels, pulled open the door, and stormed out.

Matilda wasn't the type of person to ridicule and mock and gloat at the suffering of another person. 'We've all got jobs to do now let's get on with them,' she said quietly to a room of open-mouthed gawkers.

Slowly, the Murder Room returned to normal and the chattering began once more.

Matilda sat down behind the desk and pulled the nearest file to her. She opened it and stared at the top page, not reading the information. She just wanted to look busy while she calmed down. She sat on her hands and took several deep breaths.

'I wasn't sure if you wanted to see these or not,' Sian said, walking up to the desk Matilda was temporarily using.

'What is it?' she asked, not looking up from the file she was pretending to study.

'When Hales was interviewing Jonathan he had a load of paperwork he'd managed to get from somewhere. I've just picked it up off his desk.'

Now she had Matilda's interest. 'What is it?'

'Witness statements.'

Matilda's eyes widened. For a split second she thought they were original witness statements from twenty years ago that Ben had stolen from the files, but as Sian placed them in front of her she saw them as dated just a couple of days ago. She picked them up and quickly skimmed through them.

'He's been running his own investigation,' she said with amazement.

'No wonder he's not been around here much lately. The last couple of pages will interest you.'

Matilda flicked to the back and just read the title. 'A psychiatric report on Jonathan Harkness by Charlie Johnson.' She was visibly shocked. 'What the hell? He's a journalist isn't he? What does he know about psychology?'

'I've no idea. It's basic Wikipedia stuff anyway.'

'And Ben was actually using this as evidence against Jonathan?'

'It would appear so.'

'Bloody hell. What's wrong with him?' The question was rhetorical. Matilda sat back in her seat. 'Right, Sian, find out all you can about Charlie Johnson. Get back on to his agent and really get the full story on him. I want to know what he's playing at and why he's so obsessed with Jonathan Harkness.'

'Not a problem. Oh, by the way, Matthew Harkness had eight copies of Charlie's book in his apartment.'

'What? Eight?'

'Yes.'

'Why would he have eight copies?'

'I've no idea.'

'Give me his agent's number.' Sian passed over the slip of paper with the London number written on it.

It took four rings for the call to be answered, and Matilda was left on hold for almost ten minutes before she was put through to the agent.

'My name is Detective Chief Inspector Matilda Darke from South Yorkshire Police. I'd like some information on a client of yours, Charlie Johnson.'

'A member of my staff spoke to a colleague of yours yesterday . . .'

Matilda cut her off. 'I'm aware that he's away writing at present but I'd like to talk to you about Charlie the person, rather than Charlie the writer.'

'Oh. Well what do you want to know?' The agent had a silly, high-pitched floaty voice.

'What's his background?'

'He's a journalist.'

Matilda waited for the agent to continue and was surprised when she didn't. 'Is that it?'

'Charlie is an extremely private person. I know he grew up in the north-west. According to his CV he worked on a local newspaper straight after leaving school as an apprentice and they put him through further education. He moved around from paper to paper in the north before eventually moving down here. I think he worked freelance for a few nationals.'

'And privately?'

'He's not married and doesn't have any children. I get the impression he's a bit of a loner.'

Matilda was starting to hate the word loner; it was a horrible word to describe someone. 'Why did he get so interested in the Harkness killings?'

'Now that, I've absolutely no idea. He pitched the book to me several times. To be honest the first draft of his book was very poorly written. His second wasn't much better, but it was his enthusiasm and his attention to detail that convinced me to take him on as a client. After two more drafts I eventually got someone to completely rewrite it.'

'Didn't he mind?'

'No. He did all the hard work; it just needed putting into some kind of order. His name still appeared on the front and it's sold very well. It won the non-fiction dagger at the Crime Writers' Association Awards in 1999. I still have the photo of him holding his award on the wall.'

'Can you keep trying to get hold of him for me? It really is important that I speak to him.'

'I will try.'

'Thank you. Oh, by the way, could you email me that photo of Charlie?'

Matilda gave the agent her email address and hung up. She was still in the dark about Charlie and his obsession with the Harkness case and why he felt qualified to write a psychiatric report on him. She suddenly felt very tired and in urgent need of some fresh air. She rose from behind the desk and pulled her jacket from the back of the chair. She called Rory over. 'You and I are going to get this sorted once and for all.'

'Where are we going?'

'To see a real expert.'

Chapter 43

Former Detective Inspector Pat Campbell lived in the leafy suburb of Bradway on the edge of the steel city and on the border with the Derbyshire countryside. One leap over the garden fence and you would actually be in Derbyshire.

She'd taken early retirement due to health reasons, and when her husband retired they moved as close to the countryside as possible without paying countryside house prices.

She opened the front door to Matilda and Rory, red-faced and slightly out of breath. She was a tallish woman, and had filled out since her days as a detective, but was far from overweight. Her grey hair was in a stylish cut. There was a smell of strong coffee in the background.

Matilda had never worked with Pat but she had seen her around the station from time to time and her formidable, no nonsense reputation preceded her, making her a woman to be looked up to. She doubted Pat would remember her.

'You'd better come in. Keep the cold out,' Pat said, her accent broad Sheffield. She stood to one side to allow her visitors to enter.

'Madam, I think you should ask who we are first,' Rory said. 'You shouldn't just let strangers in off the street.'

Pat laughed the rough throaty laugh of a smoker. She looked to Matilda. 'Don't you just love how the young think anyone over fifty needs a nursemaid? Young lad, I can smell a copper at fifty paces in a force nine gale and even if you weren't police and tried anything you'd be flat on your back with my foot on your throat before you could shout for your mummy.'

Pat led them into a very large living room that ran the full length of the house. It was tastefully decorated in creams and very modern furniture. It was minimalist and tidy, apart from a few children's toys and board games on the sofas. She quickly tidied them away.

'You caught me in the middle of cleaning,' she began. 'I've had the grandkids for a few days. My daughter is in hospital giving birth to her fourth, silly cow. My husband drove off with them about half an hour ago. I feel like I've gone deaf. Sit yourselves down; I've got a pot of coffee just made.'

She returned in no time with a tray holding three cups, a full cafetière, and the usual addition of milk and sugar.

'I can't offer you a biscuit or anything; the bloody kids have had the lot. I need to restock.'

Matilda smiled. 'I doubt you'll remember me, Pat. I'm . . . '

'I know who you are. You were DC Darke the last time I had anything to do with you. I've forgotten your first name, sorry. I'm guessing you've been promoted since then.'

'It's Matilda and I'm a DCI now.'

'Good for you. I only made it to DI and then my sodding hip popped.'

'I'm head of the Murder Investigation Unit.'

'They tried setting one of those up in the 80s but nothing came of it.'

'We're looking at a cold case . . . '

'The Harkness killings,' she said, interrupting.

'How do you know?'

'Educated guess. I heard about the demolition. I went along to watch it. I took my oldest grandson, thought he might be interested, but he wasn't.'

'Why did you go?'

'I'm not sure, professional interest or just plain nosiness, you decide. Are you fully reopening the case?'

'It looks like it,' Matilda replied, wrapping her cold hands around the mug of coffee and breathing in the hot vapour. 'Is there anything about it you can tell me that we don't already know?'

'I doubt it. Everything you need to know is in the files, surely.'

'Why wasn't it solved?' Rory seemed to be in awe of Pat.

'Because we didn't know who the killer was,' she said with a heavy hint of sarcasm. 'I'm sorry, son. I shouldn't take the piss. It's just that you look like you're on bloody work experience. Please don't tell me you're anything higher than a DC.'

'No.' He smiled. 'Just a lowly DC.'

'Never underestimate a DC. That's what my old DI used to say.'

'Was your old DI the SIO on the Harkness case?' Matilda asked.

'Yes. DI Ken Blackstock, bless him. He died of a heart attack in 2005. His wife never got over it and died about eighteen months later. Poor thing.' She slipped into a moment of reverie as she pictured her former boss. She hadn't thought about him in years. When she realized four eyes were glaring at her she snapped back to the present. 'Sorry. DI Blackstock, well, he was a good copper and a decent bloke. He was fair to his team, didn't mind cutting corners if necessary but never anything against the law. He went a bit dark after the Harkness case though.'

'What do you mean, dark?'

'He couldn't get over not being able to solve it. He kept reminding us "there's an eleven-year-old boy out there who witnessed his parents get slaughtered. We need justice for him." When that justice didn't come he fell to pieces. He had to take some time off if memory serves me correctly. A lot of people were obsessed with Jonathan Harkness.'

'How so?'

'There was one PC. He was first on the scene and went with Jonathan into the ambulance. Their eyes were just locked on each

264

other. It was surreal. I remember this PC kept coming into the incident room to see how everything was going. He helped out with the search for the brother, Matthew, but didn't have any other involvement. Yet he was constantly asking questions. I think he even visited Jonathan a few times when he was staying in temporary accommodation with his aunt before he moved away.'

'Can you remember his name?'

'Not off the top of my head, sorry. I'll have a think though. I think Ken ended up having to have a word with his sergeant, give him a bit of a friendly warning.'

'What about the investigation itself; any realistic suspects?'

'No. It was a bizarre case from start to finish. No one in that family's lives stood out as a clear favourite. We did think Matthew might have killed his parents for a while but that was soon discounted.'

'What about the link with animal rights groups? Stefan's work involved testing on animals didn't it?'

'It did, yes, but again, that was just a five-minute wonder.' She leaned back on the sofa and sipped her coffee. 'God I wish I had a biscuit; I could just do with something to dunk. No, if it was an animal rights activist they would have just trashed the house, put a pig's head in their rose bushes or something. They don't go around hacking up people.'

'What was your main line of investigation then?'

'It was definitely a personal attack against the family. The only thing we could never work out was why kill the parents and leave an eleven-year-old witness? Surely when you hack a couple to bits you've no qualms about killing a little boy?'

With no more questions for Matilda to ask the conversation turned to the changes in policing. As they made their way to the door Matilda asked Rory to go on to the car while she had a final word with Pat.

'What did you make of Jonathan?' Matilda asked once they were alone.

265

'It was difficult. Witnessing the murders completely messed him up. We got nothing out of him. He went mute didn't he?'

'That's right. But the neighbours and friends said he was a bit of a loner, didn't mix with the other kids; didn't you find that strange?'

'A little I suppose,' she said. 'Whatever happened to him?'

'He's back in Sheffield now, but he's very withdrawn. I think he's scared of his own shadow.'

'I'm surprised he's still alive.'

'What makes you say that?'

'I wouldn't have been surprised to read in a paper that he'd jumped in front of a train or walked into the River Don with a brick in each pocket.'

'It's been suggested that Jonathan may have killed his parents.'

'What?' Pat's eyes almost doubled in size at the question. 'He was eleven years old. If you'd seen that crime scene you wouldn't even consider that possibility.'

Matilda said her goodbyes and returned to the car.

'What are you thinking?' Rory asked after a long silence.

'I find it very hard to believe someone can kill two people and just disappear. The way they were hacked to death suggests someone with real anger towards them. That person was obviously in their lives, but why didn't anybody notice anything?'

'What I don't get is the complete difference in the murders,' Rory began, making his way slowly through the car-strewn streets of south Sheffield. 'You've got Stefan Harkness stabbed once in the back of the neck; bosh, job done. Then you've got Miranda Harkness; stabbed umpteen times front and back, blood splashed all over the place.'

'Well she put up a fight didn't she? We're working on the assumption that the killer sneaked up on Stefan, yet Miranda put up a fight once she'd found her husband. Maybe she struggled, tried to break free or call for help.'

'And there's only one person who can tell us exactly what happened . . . '

'I know what you're going to say Rory,' Matilda cut in.

After a long silence Rory continued. Matilda could see him itching to say something. He had a very expressive face. 'Unless the beef was with Miranda. The killer could have loathed her so much that he wanted to cause her maximum suffering.'

'No,' Matilda was almost thinking aloud. 'We need to look at why they were killed rather than by who. Once we know that, the killer will be easy to identify. There has to be a why. I refuse to believe in a motiveless crime.'

Chapter 44

Hales drove home in record time; ignoring red traffic lights, zebra crossings, and give way signs. He was a man on a mission. He threw open the front door and slammed it closed behind him. He swore under his breath as he was greeted with the tinny sound of daytime television emanating from the living room. He could feel his blood boiling.

His wife didn't raise a question about who had entered; it was unusual for anyone to come home at this time of the day. She just continued with her usual routine of nothingness.

Hales went straight into the kitchen, which was in need of a good clean. He looked around the cluttered surfaces for what he needed but couldn't find it so he frantically opened drawers and searched in the mess of collected junk.

'What are you doing in there?' The eventual question came from Sara in the living room. The endless clattering was disrupting her viewing. She turned up the volume but was still irritated.

'Nothing,' he called out.

'What?'

'Nothing,' he almost shouted in anger.

'I can't hear you.'

Finding what he needed, Hales put it inside his jacket and stormed into the living room. 'For fuck's sake; turn down the television and you may be able to hear,' he shouted.

She jumped in her seat. 'What's wrong with you?' Hales finally had a reaction from his wife. She briefly looked at him with a heavy frown before turning back to the large plasma screen on the wall.

'There's absolutely nothing wrong with me.' There was a sheen of sweat on his forehead and his breathing was erratic. His eyes were wide and he clenched his fists in an attempt to suppress the rage he was feeling. Who the rage was aimed at he wasn't fully aware; Matilda for showing him up in front of his entire team, ACC Masterson for not trusting him enough to give him Matilda's job all those months ago when she first went on leave, or his wife, his bitch of a wife, who just sat there every single day watching mindless crap on television and getting fatter with each passing year.

'What are you doing home so early?'

'No reason.'

Sara Hales hadn't moved since he'd left the house at six o'clock that morning. That was more than eight hours ago. She was still in a baggy grey jogging suit, which was old, bitty, and out of shape.

With every passing year and every passing failure Hales loathed his wife just a little bit more. He had finally reached the point where he hated her. He hated feeling her body next to his in bed at night, the sound of her breathing, the gentle snoring, the lack-lustre attitude for a life of her own; her baseless passion for soap operas, reality TV, and make-over shows; her constant eating and ever-expanding waist line. He more than hated her, he despised her, he resented her; he abhorred her with every fibre of his being.

'Are you doing anything today?' His voice was loud. It had to be. He was in competition with the television.

'Like what?'

'Oh I don't know, clean the house maybe or perhaps you could go outside and get some fresh air.'

'I don't think so.'

'Don't you think you should?'

'Why?'

'Well you're wasting your life just sitting there. You could do something; go out and get a job.'

'Why? You earn enough for us all.'

'How about for some self-respect? How about for some extra money so maybe we could have that conservatory I've always wanted or maybe we could have a holiday abroad instead of a week in Torquay every fucking year?'

'What's wrong with you today?' She finally turned to look at him.

'Can't you see? I work my arse off for this family. I'm out all hours and what do I get in return? When was the last time we all sat down for a meal as a family? In fact, I can't actually remember the last time you cooked. I can't remember the last time I saw the girls, and every night when I come home you're sat there in the same position I left you in with your eyes fixed on the TV like some demented old duffer in a nursing home.'

'Ben, what's brought all this on?' Despite the wild ramblings of her husband, Sara did not raise her voice at all. This all seemed to be going in one ear and out the other.

'I'm tired of being taken for granted around here. You and the girls see pound signs whenever you look at me as if I'm only here to dish out the cash. Well those days are over. From now on everyone has to contribute to the running of this house. Including you.'

'What?' An expression of genuine worry ran across her face.

'You heard. Get off your fat arse, go out, and find a job. You may even lose some weight.'

The sound of raucous applause from the television temporarily distracted Ben from his rant. He turned to look at the forty-two-inch screen. Like everything else in the house he had paid for it, yet he couldn't remember the last time he sat down and watched anything. He went over to the back wall, grabbed the set with both hands, and tore it from its housing. He jumped back as it tumbled to the floor and smashed at his feet. The room suddenly fell silent. Hales felt a weight lift from his shoulders.

'What the hell . . .?' exclaimed his wife.

He slowly walked over to the sofa where Sara was cowering. She was visibly shaking and looked horrified at the transformation of her husband. His face was barely inches from hers, their noses almost touching. He lowered his voice but the bitter hatred was still there. 'Now you've no excuse. Get changed, get out, and get a fucking job.'

With that final outburst he stormed out of the living room and the house, slamming the front door behind him.

Chapter 45

In the space of an hour his whole life had changed, once again. Jonathan left the apartment building and was hit by the cold – it was well below freezing. The sky was clouding over and snow would fall before the end of the day. He wrapped his scarf tightly around his neck, buttoned his coat, and pulled up the collar. He couldn't remember what he'd done with his leather gloves. He plunged his hands deep into his coat pocket, and with his head down, he slowly made his way down the steps.

He felt a strong urge to turn around and look at the building he suspected he would never return to, but he managed to stop himself. He continued to walk to the end of the street and turned the corner.

Jonathan was a man of simple means. All he wanted out of life was to be left alone. His parents, his brother, Maun Barrington, the police and, to an extent, Stephen Egan; they all seemed to want Jonathan's life to alter from the state he was content with. Did it matter if he didn't interact with other people? Who was he harming if he never spoke to another person again?

With his head down and a heavy frown on his face he walked to his own pace while his mind ran at warp speed: the night his parents were killed kept replaying in his head, the visit from his brother, and then having to view his dead body, Stephen being thrown into the air by a bitter Maun Barrington and then landing in a pile of broken bones and internal bleeding, and the police interview he had been subjected to by Acting DCI Hales in the claustrophobic interview room, followed by the internal examination by the kindly Dr Kean. His mind refused to switch off, refused to focus on one thing, refused to allow him a moment's peace. It felt like he was rummaging through a ten-thousand-piece jigsaw searching for just one particular piece, which, when he found it, would bring the whole picture together and make perfect sense.

A car, driven at speed, swerved in front of him, mounting the pavement. The screech of the brakes echoed around the street.

'Jonathan.'

His name was called as the window from the front passenger side lowered. Jonathan ducked down to look at who was driving. It was Acting DCI Hales. He looked angry. His face was flushed and despite the freezing cold, beads of sweat were forming at his hairline.

'Get in the car,' he said, indicating Jonathan should climb into the front passenger seat.

'Why?'

'I want to talk to you.' Hales spoke quietly now, almost in a whisper, but his words were harsh and heavy. He meant business.

'I don't want to.' Jonathan shook his head and slowly backed away, sensing danger.

'I'm not asking you Jonathan. This isn't a social call. Get in the fucking car.'

'No.'

Jonathan turned and walked away, his strides longer than before. He didn't look back and the scenes repeating themselves in his head were too loud to hear what was happening behind him. It was only when he felt a firm grip tighten around his arm and swing him around that he realized Hales had grabbed him.

They looked into each other's eyes. Jonathan saw a determined, angry man on the edge.

'If I have to pick you up and throw you in my boot I will do so but I don't want it to have to come to that. Now, get in the fucking car.'

Gripping his arm, Hales dragged Jonathan to the Audi, opened the front passenger seat, and pushed him inside. He even fastened his seatbelt to avoid him trying to jump out quickly while he ran around to the driver's side. He slammed the door closed, put the car into gear, and drove off at speed down the road.

Hales failed to notice he was being followed and that his encounter with Jonathan Harkness had been witnessed.

DC Rory Fleming had pulled up a safe distance away and watched the scene play out in front of him. As soon as he saw Jonathan being manhandled into the car he pulled his phone out of its charger and called Matilda. She took a while to answer.

'What is it Rory?' she asked. She sounded tired and annoyed.

'Hales has just kidnapped Jonathan.'

'What?' Suddenly Matilda was all ears.

'I'm in the next street to where Jonathan lives. Hales just pulled up, grabbed Jonathan off the pavement, and practically threw him into the car.'

'Follow him,' Matilda shouted down the phone. 'Put your foot down and follow him.'

'What's going on?' Sian Mills saw the look of sheer horror etched on her boss's face.

'I have absolutely no idea,' she replied, struggling to get into her jacket.

DC Scott Andrews burst into the room. His face was red from running up three flights of stairs. 'Ma'am, I think we've had a breakthrough.'

'It's going to have to wait Scott. Aaron, you're with me.'

'Uniform has found the car that knocked down Jonathan's boss, Stephen Egan,' Scott called out.

Matilda stopped in her tracks at the door. She turned on her heel. Sian pointed to her collar, instructing her to straighten out her rumpled jacket.

'Where?'

'Well they think they have. An abandoned car has been found on farmland right on the outskirts of Sheffield. There's evidence it was involved in some kind of collision.'

Matilda thought for a split second before turning to Sian. 'Get forensics at the scene, get it impounded, and brought back. I want every inch of it analysed. Scott, get traffic to check if any cars matching the description have been reported stolen and interview the person who called in; how long has it been there, did they see anything, the usual.'

She left the room with a spring in her step. A thought shot into her mind to make her stop; a thought she didn't really want to contemplate: she wondered if Jonathan Harkness could drive.

Chapter 46

Matilda was halfway down the stairs before realizing she hadn't told anyone where she was going. She fished her mobile out of her jacket pocket, finding a hole in the lining, and called Sian.

'Hello.'

'Hales has taken Jonathan . . . '

'What?' Sian interrupted. 'Taken him where?'

'I've no idea. Just listen. I want you to check his computer, see what he's been working on that he's kept close to his chest. I want to know everything he's been up to. Also, tell the ACC what's going on but don't make out it's anything too serious. I can handle it but not with her breathing down my neck. And I want you to give his wife a call; ask her how he's been lately, if anything has been worrying him. Don't give anything away, just general chatting. You OK with that?'

'Sure.'

Matilda hung up before anything else could be said. If there was one person who could be trusted to get a job done to her specific requirements, it was Sian Mills.

By the time Matilda had finished dishing out her orders she was already strapped into the passenger seat and Aaron was slowly making his way out of the car park.

The weather was starting to turn. The sky was deep grey. Snowfall had been threatened for days and there was plenty stored up to release. If there was ever a good time for a high-speed car chase across the battered and broken roads of Sheffield, during an intense snow storm was not it.

'Do you know if anything has been bothering Hales lately?' Matilda asked. It wasn't the ideal time to question a colleague while he was navigating his way through busy traffic with snow starting to fall but what else was she going to do in the passenger seat, window shop for Christmas gift ideas?

'I'm sure that huge pole he's got rammed up his arse is causing a bit of pain,' he quipped, not taking his eye off the road.

Matilda suppressed a smile. 'Apart from that.'

'Not really. He's not one for talking with the team is he? He's a very private bloke.'

'What about when you're in the pub together? Does he ever let his guard down?'

'Acting DCI Hales have a pint with the minions? You must be joking.'

'What about when you've closed a case? Surely he joins you all for a celebratory drink?'

'God forbid.'

'But he should be buying the first round to congratulate you all on a job well done.'

'Nope.'

'Bloody hell,' she sighed. 'What about his home life, does that ever get brought up?'

'No. I didn't even know he had a home life. I know he's married, but that's about it.'

'What about his kids; any problems with them?'

'I didn't know he had any.'

Matilda left the questioning there. It was obvious Hales kept his home and work life separate but this wasn't a job you could switch off from at the end of the day. Surely he took his cases home with him from time to time? If a murder case was a particularly sensitive one his demeanour would be altered at home and if there

277

was anything worrying in his home life, which is often the case when you work long and unsociable hours, it would tell at work too. Everybody needed someone to talk to, confide in; Matilda had Adele and, to a lesser extent, Sian. Who did Ben Hales have?

Matilda called for Aaron to stop when they reached Jonathan's apartment block. Parked outside was Rory who immediately jumped out from behind the driver's seat when he saw the pool car screech to a halt.

'I thought I told you to follow them?' Matilda called while wrestling with her seatbelt.

'I did but I lost them.'

'How?'

'He's in a bloody big Audi and I'm in a shitty Seat. He went through a red light and was racing down the street like he was driving away from the apocalypse.'

'Where was he heading?'

'I've no idea. I thought it best to circle back and meet you here.'

'OK, don't worry about it. What exactly went down?'

'I don't know. I was too far away to hear anything. Hales looked seriously pissed off though.'

'And how did Jonathan look?'

'Shit scared.'

Matilda turned to Aaron who was standing next to the car with his arms firmly folded across his chest trying to keep warm. 'I want that car found.'

'I'll get on to traffic, get them to put his number plate through the ANPR and I'll get all patrolling uniform to keep an eye out.' He pulled his mobile out of his trouser pocket and turned away from the car to make the call.

'Have you spoken to Maun?'

'No. I thought I'd wait for you. I didn't know if you wanted me to mention Jonathan being taken.'

'No. Just ask her everything she knows about him from his childhood onwards. I want to know what makes him tick, has he ever spoken about his parents being killed, what other people say about him, if she saw anything on the night his brother was killed.'

'Right,' he said, still unmoved from the spot next to his car.

'Would you like it in writing?' she shouted. He apologized then turned away and headed up the steps to the apartment building.

Aaron ended his call just as Matilda's phone started ringing. It was Sian. 'Sian, hold on one second. Go on Aaron,' she prompted, placing the phone to her chest.

'Traffic is keeping an eye out. There are some mobile units with cameras patrolling south Sheffield today so they're going to be rerouted to look out for him.'

'Excellent. Get in the car. We'll have a scout round too. I've got a few ideas.' As she scrambled back into the car she continued her conversation with Sian.

'First of all, the ACC says the minute you hear anything to let her know. Secondly, I've just got off the phone with Hales's wife and she was in bits.'

'What do you mean?'

'Apparently Ben has been very hostile and difficult to live with lately. No offence or anything, but she says it got worse when you returned to work . . . '

'None taken,' Matilda scoffed.

'He went back home earlier this afternoon and just started ranting at her about how lazy she is and how she does nothing for the family. He tore the TV off the wall and smashed it onto the floor. He called her names and threatened her. He stormed out of the house and he's got a knife with him. She saw it in his pocket when he was having a go at her. She's really shaken up.'

'Jesus,' Matilda sighed.

'I'm going to go through his computer now. I've sent for someone from tech to give me a hand.'

'Good idea. Ring me the second you get anything.'

'What's going on?' Aaron asked once Matilda had ended the call.

'Hales is unhinged and he's armed.'

'Shit.'

The stairs in the apartment block were wet with melted snow which had fallen off residents' boots as they'd made their way home to the warmth and comfort of their homes. Rory tentatively took each step one at a time.

He knocked on Maun's door with a hard rap, which resounded around the bare walls in the stairwell. He waited, head leaning to the door for any sound coming from inside. There wasn't any. He knocked again, louder this time. He was just about to bend down to look through the letter box when the front door of the flat opposite opened and an elderly man peered around the smallest gap possible.

'Do you have to knock that bloody loud? I can hear it in my living room.' His voice was gruff and full of throaty phlegm.

'DC Rory Fleming, South Yorkshire Police,' he said, fishing out his warrant card with freezing cold fingers. 'I'm looking for your neighbour, Maun Barrington.'

'Well she's in,' was all he replied. 'That queer young lad from downstairs left her about an hour back.'

'Jonathan? Jonathan Harkness?'

'That's the feller.'

'Did Mrs Barrington go out with him?'

'No.'

'Have you seen her at all today?'

'I don't have nowt to do with her, lad.' He pulled his head out of the small gap he'd made and slammed the door, securing a chain and deadlocks.

'What lovely neighbours,' Rory said to himself. He knocked once again and then bent down to the letter box.

There was a light on in the living room at the end of the long hallway and Rory had to squint while his eyes adjusted from the gloom of the grey stairwell.

'Hello? Mrs Barrington? It's DC Rory Fleming, South Yorkshire Police. Could you answer your door please?'

He listened intently but all he could hear was the distant sound of a couple of clocks ticking and what he guessed to be the faint humming of the fridge from the kitchen. He looked again and could just make out the figure of someone sitting in an armchair just inside the living-room door. Was it Maun? Was she sleeping? He doubted it. His banging on the door had been loud enough to wake the dead.

'Shit!' he said to himself as he stood up.

Chapter 47

Snow was falling at a steady pace now; the flakes getting fatter by the minute and the lying snow getting deeper. It wouldn't be long until roads were closed and travel seriously hampered. In the tense silence, Ben wondered if the Snake Pass, the road leading Sheffield to Manchester, was already closed. It didn't take much to close it; a strong wind, a heavy rain shower, or a few flakes of snow was enough to make it impassable. He made a mental note to give it a miss, just in case.

Public transport in Sheffield wasn't much use either. Buses would already be struggling on the steeper roads, and his Audi wasn't faring much better. Unfortunately, Sheffield was a very hilly city. His choice of route was severely limited.

He was driving at a snail's pace and almost at a stop as he took the corners. Nothing seemed to be going right for him.

He slammed on the brakes and braced himself. The locked wheels continued in the snow. He steered into the skid and the car managed to stop just short of hitting a four-wheel drive in front.

'We're here,' he said.

Jonathan looked up. He had spent the journey with his head bowed and dark thoughts running around his mind. He kept going back to Maun's treachery and murderous actions. He'd no idea he'd been living directly below such a scheming woman all these years. How could he have misunderstood her so badly? Had his own self-pity blinded him to her evil manipulations?

Through the thick flakes of snow Jonathan saw where Hales had brought them. At first it was difficult to make out. The last time he had been here it looked completely different; the house had still been standing. He'd left the demolition team to it after the roof was torn open and the corner of his bedroom had been exposed. The sight of his old wallpaper had plunged him back into his nightmare, and as he'd turned to walk away he'd hoped never to lay eyes on the place again.

When he saw what was left of his home now, he recoiled in horror.

The majority of the house had been razed to the ground. All that remained were the foundations and, for some reason, the staircase at the side of the house and a small section of the landing. Surrounding the site, wooden barriers had been erected with warning signs telling people not to enter as the site was unstable and dangerous.

'Get out!' Ben said. His voice was deep and angry. His face was red and tense; a heavy frown on his wrinkled brow.

Jonathan had to battle with the wind to push open the door. He pushed his feet into the deepening snow.

The snow didn't seem to bother Ben. He marched around to the passenger side of the car, grabbed a handful of Jonathan's collar, and forced him around to the front.

'Nice house. Could do with a lick of paint here and there.'

He kicked hard at the padlock on a makeshift door in the wooden surround and after two blows it eventually opened. The sound of banging and splintering wood echoed around the empty street. It swung open on its broken hinges and Ben pushed Jonathan inside. He swiftly followed, kicking the door closed behind him.

Jonathan stumbled. He looked at his hands, white with cold, his fingertips almost blue, and sharp dashes of red where the jagged broken brickwork had cut into him.

'What are we doing here?' he eventually asked, his voice quivering with the cold.

'Up the stairs.'

'What?'

'Get up the stairs.'

Jonathan stood motionless among the ruins of his former home and looked up at the exposed staircase. The last time he had been on them was twenty years ago; he was shivering with cold then too and he'd blood on his hands. History repeats itself.

Driving through Sheffield wasn't an easy task at the best of times; it didn't seem to make any difference how much money the council spent on improving the roads and redesigning bus lanes, the traffic never seemed to ease. Add to this, late-night Christmas shopping and the heavy fall of snow, and it was almost impossible to find a clear road.

'You're going the wrong way,' Matilda said as she looked up from her phone. She was using Google Maps, trying to find a quicker route to the murder house, but the red dot was travelling in the opposite direction, and so were they.

'No. I'm going the quickest way. There's no way I'm even attempting Chesterfield Road,' he said through gritted teeth as he chicaned through stupidly parked cars.

Matilda held on to the door handle as Aaron took a sharp turn without changing down a gear.

'Did you actually pass the advanced driver's test?'

'Yes. It was a while ago though,' he said with a wicked smile.

Aaron took another corner at speed and was presented with an empty road ahead. He slammed his foot on the accelerator and ignored the twenty miles per hour speed limit signs.

Matilda looked down at her phone and saw the red dot race back up the screen. They were back on track. They were getting closer.

Jonathan was sitting on what was left of the landing. The crazed pattern of the well-worn carpet was covered in a layer of snow, which was soaking through his trousers. He was back at the top of the stairs, in the exact same position he had been when he was rescued by a neighbour two decades ago.

Looming over him with a steely determination in his wide eyes, Ben Hales was shaking, but it wasn't because of the cold weather and the biting northerly wind, but the magnitude of the situation he had created.

'Does this bring back any memories?'

'Of course it does,' his teeth were chattering through fear and cold.

'That's good.' He smiled. 'Which memories?'

'I'm sorry?'

'What are you remembering?'

'Why are you doing this?'

'Answer my fucking questions,' he screamed, his angry face just inches away from Jonathan's. 'You faked it didn't you? The whole shocked into amnesia thing. It was all bollocks wasn't it? You know exactly what happened on the night your parents were killed. You saw everything and it has stayed with you ever since; every single detail. You've relived it over and over again. Tell me what happened.'

A warm tear fell from Jonathan's left eye, leaving a track mark on his face as it travelled down his cheek, thawing his cold skin.

'I can't do this.' He voice cracked with emotion.

'Charlie Johnson was right about you. He said you were a fucking nut job. Why wouldn't you talk to him? Why wouldn't you let him interview you? What are you hiding? He's spent all these years trying to work out what's going on in that fucked-up head of yours; tried to figure out the case, and he had two possibilities: either you were the killer or you saw who the killer was. We've decided to go with the second option, so come on, tell me, who did it?'

'Please . . .' Jonathan whimpered.

Losing his patience, Ben reached into his inside pocket and pulled out the kitchen knife with the seven-inch blade he had taken from home. The yellow sodium light from a lamp post hit the pure cold stainless steel, almost blinding Jonathan.

'You're really starting to fuck me off now, Jonathan. I knew there was something weird about you when I was by your hospital bed all those years ago.'

'You were at the house on the night it happened?'

'I was the uniformed copper who sat with you for over twenty-four fucking hours until your fat aunt came down from Newcastle. I looked deep into your soul that night and all I saw was blackness.'

Ben grabbed Jonathan by the throat and lifted him off his feet. Jonathan fumbled behind him for a wall to gain some balance, but it was no use. There was no wall there.

With the tip of the knife pointing to Jonathan's stomach, Ben said, 'This is your final chance.'

'MIT, DC Easter,' Faith answered her phone, stifling a yawn.

'Faith, it's Rory. Who's there with you?'

'It's just me and Sian. What's up?'

'Put me through will you?'

Rory's voice was urgent and filled with panic. He had been trying to call Matilda but she wasn't answering.

'Good evening Rory, what's troubling you?' Sian asked in her usual cheery manner.

'I'm at Maun Barrington's. I've had to force my way in. She's dead, Sian. She's killed herself. I don't know what to do.'

'Bloody hell. All right Rory, calm down. I'm going to send a team over to process the scene. Seal off the flat and don't let anyone enter . . . '

'Sian,' he interrupted, 'she's left a note. She's confessed to running down Stephen Egan.'

'There. Right there. I recognize that bastard Audi,' Matilda called out.

Aaron quickly pulled over and slammed on the brakes. The car skidded on the snow and almost crashed into Ben's precious car.

They both climbed out at the same time, neither of them caring whether they slipped on the icy snow. Before they could reach the broken door in the fence, a piercing scream broke the night's silence. Matilda and Aaron were both frozen in horror for the briefest of seconds. They made eye contact then burst through the door.

Aaron saw them first. 'Over there. On the stairs.' He pointed, and raced up what was left of the staircase and pulled at Ben by the shoulder, almost throwing him back down the stairs. He grabbed Jonathan, who was slowing falling to the floor. If it hadn't been for his quick reflexes he would have fallen back into nothingness and onto the jagged rubble below.

'He stabbed me. He stabbed me.' Jonathan was in shock. He was hysterically holding onto his stomach where three-quarters of the blade was deeply embedded.

'It's OK, calm down. I've got you. You're going to be all right,' Aaron said.

'He stabbed me. Get this out of me. Get this knife out of me right now.'

With slippery red hands, Jonathan fumbled to get hold of the black handle and pulled.

Aaron, a good three inches taller and two stone heavier than Jonathan managed to quickly subdue him. 'You have to leave it in. We'll get you to hospital and they'll take it out. You're in shock. Just breathe. Calm down; take deep breaths and try to remain calm. Listen to me Jonathan.'

At the bottom of the stairs Ben looked up with wide-eyed bewilderment. Next to him, Matilda tried to get her head around the situation, but what she was witnessing didn't seem to be making any sense.

Was it possible? Had an Acting DCI just tried to kill a number one witness in a double-murder case?

Chapter 48

The atmosphere in the darkened police station had changed dramatically since Matilda had returned with a despondent Ben Hales in tow. News of his arrest quickly spread and it wasn't long before officers on the night shift left their posts to try and catch a glimpse of what was happening. This was an unprecedented evening.

Aaron had waited at the scene for the ambulance to arrive; delayed due to the rapidly falling snow. Once they arrived at the Northern General Hospital Jonathan had been whisked straight into theatre; the knife was deep and had pierced his stomach wall. He had internal bleeding and had been drifting in and out of consciousness during the bumpy journey through Sheffield's streets.

Back at the station Hales had been booked in as a prisoner and placed in an interview room. This was a very surreal experience for the duty sergeant; never in all his twenty-five years on the force had he booked in a colleague. Very little had been said to Hales; there wasn't much anyone could say, and all parties involved found eye contact extremely difficult.

Ben Hales was expressionless. His face was pale and his eyes staring. He was in deep shock.

As much as Matilda wanted to go into the interview room, grab Ben by the lapels, and ask him what the hell was wrong with him, she knew this had to be played by the book, and, as much as she dreaded doing it, she phoned the ACC at home and told her of the situation.

Within minutes, Val Masterson was out of bed, in her uniform, and shivering behind the wheel of her car. Fortunately, living on the outskirts of Sheffield on the border with the Derbyshire countryside she had access to a four-by-four and was ploughing through the snow at speed, not caring about the drifts, or the rapidity at which the thick flakes hit the windscreen, making her feel like she was in a snow globe.

She entered the station and powered through the corridors in search of the DCI. How can it be possible for one woman to return to work and within a matter of days arrest her replacement for attempted murder?

The incident room was lit by a single overhead light and Matilda and Sian Mills were hunched over Ben's laptop. They were scanning through the email conversations between him and Charlie Johnson.

'Do you know what this looks like to me,' Sian began. 'You've got Ben Hales in a position of power, able to ask the right questions, and Charlie Johnson has been more or less grooming him, getting him to find the answers to what he wants to know.'

'He does seem to be fuelling the fire doesn't he?' Matilda agreed. 'It's not like Ben though. He's a determined bloke. He'd never allow anyone to lead him. Have we managed to locate Charlie yet?'

'No. I've made a note to give his agent another ring first thing.'

'I wonder if she emailed over that picture of him.'

While she waited for her computer to boot up Matilda sighed and leaned back in the chair, which squeaked with every movement. 'What is this obsession people have with Jonathan Harkness? Maun, his brother, his boss, Ben, and this Charlie Johnson. You've seen him, Sian, what do you think?'

'I have no idea. The guy is weird, there's no denying that, but people seem to fall under some kind of spell with him.'

'There's nothing special about him. He doesn't have a great presence about him or . . .'

Suddenly the rest of the overhead lights were turned on and a loud, dominating voice filled the room.

'For the time being, let's ignore the fact that it is well past four o'clock and you're still in the station; why don't you tell me what the hell is going on here.'

Matilda and Sian looked up and saw the ACC standing in the doorway, her hands on her hips, and a bitter expression on her tired face.

Matilda slammed the laptop closed and explained what had happened, thankfully without any interruption from the ACC. She may come across as a tyrant at times but she always allowed people to have their say.

'And where is Hales now?'

'He's in interview room one.'

'Cautioned?'

'Yes ma'am.'

'Solicitor?'

'He's declined.'

'Right. I'll interview him. Sian, you can deputize.'

'With respect . . . '

'Go home, Matilda.'

'I'm sorry?'

'You should not be in this station right now. I want you gone. We'll discuss this tomorrow.'

'But . . . '

'Matilda, you have no idea how angry I am right now. Your presence is not required here. Go home right now.'

Sian looked at the floor. She had never felt so uncomfortable before in her life. Masterson had the power to strike fear into anyone when she was determined. There was no point in arguing.

*

291

Ben Hales could hardly believe what was happening to him. He felt like a stranger in the police station he had been working in for years. He tried to go over the events of the previous few hours but he couldn't recall anything. His mind was blank. He sat in the sterile interview room and felt like a foreigner. He knew this room; he'd been in here hundreds, if not thousands, of times, but never this side of the table. It felt wrong. It was wrong.

The door opened, making him jump, and the ACC entered, followed by a nervous-looking Sian Mills. He knew them, but when he looked up into their wide staring eyes they were complete strangers to him.

They took their seats and with a quivering voice, Sian went through the preliminaries for the benefit of the recording and video equipment.

'You've waived your right to a solicitor?' Masterson asked.

'I don't need one,' his voice was slow and sounded tired. 'I don't know what's going on here.'

'I want you to take us through your day. You went home around lunchtime I understand, that's not something you usually do. Why today?'

Ben looked blankly at his boss. 'Did I go home today?'

Sian and the ACC exchanged worried glances.

'Yes. You went home and your wife was there. Apparently you had a bit of a disagreement.'

'I honestly don't remember.'

The blank expression and cold wide eyes told Masterson he was telling the truth. Had the events of the day been so horrific for Ben that he had blocked them out? Sian wondered if he was going through a similar mental shutdown to the one Jonathan Harkness had suffered twenty years ago.

Masterson continued. 'You pulled the television off the wall.'

Masterson had been briefed on the events by Sian before the interview began, but even now, as she recalled them out loud, she had trouble believing them.

Something clicked into place and it all came flooding back. The colour returned to his cheeks and a film of sweat appeared on his brow.

'That's right. I remember. She got me so angry. Do you know what she does all day? She sits on that fat arse of hers watching daytime TV. That's it. Then she has the nerve to tell me to make something of myself.' He clenched his fists hard, his knuckles turning white and his fingernails digging deep into his palms. 'Her saint of a father was a superintendent by the time he was my age and I'm just a lowly Acting DCI. I don't know how she can criticize my career when she has done fuck all with her life except give birth to two ungrateful daughters. She's a selfish bitch. All three of them are selfish bitches.'

His palms had little crescent moon-shaped nail indentations on them. They were shaking with decades of pent-up rage finally released.

'Why did you smash the television?' Masterson asked eventually once the tension in the room has dissipated a little.

'Because the fucking thing is never switched off.' The rage in him was as energetic as a thunderstorm.

'And the knife?'

'The what?'

'You had a knife. You threatened your wife with a kitchen knife.'

'I did nothing of the sort,' he exclaimed, genuinely incensed.

'You didn't actually take it out but she saw it. It was in your inside jacket pocket and it matches the description of the knife you used to stab Jonathan Harkness with.'

'Stab Jonathan Harkness? I didn't do that. I didn't stab anyone.'

Chapter 49

Matilda had no intention of going home. Once Masterson and Sian had left the incident room to interview Ben, she remained seated in the squeaky chair, listening to the sounds of the station around her, the footfalls in the corridors, the ticking clocks, the choking of the radiators struggling to inject some much-needed heat into the room.

She looked at Ben's laptop, tempted to read more in his research into Jonathan Harkness and any number of unsolved murders he had become obsessed with in recent days, but the fight had been knocked out of her.

She went into the toilets to wash her face and compose herself. The water was cold and harsh, just what she needed to kick back the tears. Her reflection was tired and sad. The glimmer in her had long since died. The bodies Adele cut up on a daily basis had more life in them than she had.

As she came out of the toilets she literally bumped into Faith Easter.

'I've been looking for you everywhere ma'am.'

'What's the problem?'

'I've got a photocopy of Maun's suicide note. I thought you'd want to see it sooner rather than later.'

'Thanks Faith. Look, it's late, get off home and we'll try to make sense of all this tomorrow.'

'OK.'

Faith headed down the corridor and turned back a couple of times to see her boss reading the note.

To Jonathan,

I'm guessing it won't be you who finds me but I hope the police will pass this note on to you. I'd be lying if I said I was sorry for what I did to my husband. He deserved everything he had coming to him. He was ruthless in business and thought he could control his personal life in the same way. He surrounded himself with yes men at work and wanted the same at home; you know more than anyone that I'm not that type of woman.

As for his mistress and her baby, yes, I do regret their involvement. I'm sorry she died but at the end of the day, she knew he was married when embarking on the affair. I'm not totally to blame.

I love you Jonathan. I love you like a son. You mean the world to me and I'm sorry I let you down. I'm sorry I couldn't allow you to be happy and I'm sorry I killed Stephen. I know he loved you and I could see it in your face that you felt the same way about him. I just didn't want to spend the rest of my life alone.

I know it won't make up for what I've done but I've left everything to you in my will; the flat, the money, everything, it's all yours. Find yourself another Stephen, someone to love you, and make you realize just how special you are.

I'm so very sorry that it couldn't be me.

Maun

Matilda folded the note in quarters before stuffing it in her pocket. This day could not get any worse. Everything was going wrong. She made her way down the corridor, not knowing where she was going, but not in the mood to go home, or even leave the station.

Before she realized it, she was in the observation room attached to interview room one.

She couldn't believe what Ben was saying. Could he really have no recollection of what had happened to him over the last few hours? She had to believe him, as this was Jonathan's defence with what had happened to his parents. If she ever doubted him before, she didn't now.

The mind was a dangerous instrument. Jonathan blanked out what happened to his parents. Matilda sank into a pit of despair when she lost her husband to a brain tumour. When Adele was faced with a life of being trapped as a single parent with no career prospects she pulled herself up by her boot laces and carried on. We all handle similar events in completely different ways.

She wished Masterson would hurry up. Yes, it was tragic what had happened with Hales's wife, but at the end of the day it was a domestic matter. Nobody had been physically hurt. She should be focusing on what happened with Jonathan, what had led Ben to snatch him from the street and stab him in the stomach.

'Balfour, Campbell-Bannerman, Asquith, Lloyd George, Law, Baldwin, MacDonald, Baldwin,' she said under her breath. She cursed herself; the bloody Prime Ministers were back. Just when she thought she no longer needed them. She could feel pin pricks creeping up her back; a panic attack was imminent. In the small observation room she could smell her own stale sweat. 'MacDonald, Baldwin, Chamberlain, Churchill, Atlee, Churchill,' She felt hot and her breathing intensified; small, rapid breaths. She felt claustrophobic; the room seemed darker and the walls moved ever closer. She needed some fresh air, a wide open space. She needed to feel the cold flakes of snow on her face, see her breath materialize in huge clouds from her lips but she couldn't bring herself to leave the room. She needed to hear Ben's confession. Was her job really so important to her that she was prepared to risk her health? Of course it was; all she had left was her job.

'Eden, Macmillan, Douglas-Home, Wilson, Heath,' she quoted more and more British Prime Ministers and her voice was becoming louder, threatening to be heard from the other side of the glass and expose her to the ACC.

By the time she reached the present incumbent of Number 10 she could feel herself relaxing, yet every time she looked across at Ben, she could feel her hackles rising once again. Maybe she should go home.

The tense atmosphere in the interview room was growing with each question asked. All three knew the situation they were in; the role they were playing was awkward and surreal. It was hard to believe that twelve hours ago they were all colleagues. The two interviewers were growing increasingly uncomfortable at trying to extract a confession from one of their own, while the interviewee was having difficulty grasping the concept of the end of his career and a lengthy prison sentence.

'Tell me about your relationship with Charlie Johnson,' Masterson asked, trying to find another angle to get to the truth.

'He wrote the book on the Harkness killings. He knows the case inside and out.'

'I've seen the emails, Ben.' She hadn't, but she had been given an in-depth summary from Sian. 'You've fed him information from the case notes which should have remained the knowledge of police personnel only. In return, he has given you nothing.'

'That's not true. He's given me an insight into Jonathan Harkness; his character, his frame of mind.'

'The man is a journalist, not a psychologist. He knows nothing of what makes Jonathan tick. He's angry because Jonathan is the only person ever to turn him down for an interview, and without him he has been unable to complete his story. He's a hack, Ben, and he's brainwashed you to get closer to Jonathan. You've shown him witness statements, reports, crime-scene photographs, classified information.'

'I wanted an expert opinion.'

Masterson almost erupted. 'Charlie Johnson is not an expert on anything.'

'He's very well informed.'

'Yes, because you've been feeding him. Why were you even interested in the Harkness case? You know Matilda was working on that.'

'And getting fucking nowhere with it,' Ben answered through gritted teeth.

'How do you know? It's a twenty-year-old case; it can't be solved overnight.'

'She's useless. She's burnt out. You should never have had her back.'

'That is not your decision to make. Why did you take Jonathan Harkness back to the murder scene?'

'To trigger a memory,' he replied flatly.

'Did it work?'

'It would have done if . . . '

'If what?'

'If Matilda hadn't shown up.'

'Why did you stab him?'

'I didn't.'

'You did. You had the knife in your jacket. Your fingerprints are on the handle. You were in a secure area with no one else around. Who else could have stabbed him if it wasn't you?'

Ben didn't reply.

Masterson sighed. She wasn't getting anywhere. Whenever she backtracked and started again they reached the present, to what happened just a few hours ago and slammed into a brick wall. Ben Hales was either highly manipulative, a very good actor, or he genuinely couldn't remember what he had done. Maybe she would have been better off allowing Matilda to have a go at him.

'OK.' She ran her fingers through her tangled hair. 'Tell me about Jonathan Harkness. What's your obsession with him?'

'I'm not obsessed.'

'Sian,' Masterson instructed.

Sian was about to join in the interview for the first time. Usually, the prospect of interviewing a suspect didn't bother her, but when the suspect was her direct superior she wished she was anywhere but here. She would rather be hosing down the cells on a Sunday morning following a busy Saturday night. She cleared her throat and reached for her folder. She cleared her throat again. Why did it have to be so hot in here?

'Within the last week you have sent over one hundred and sixty emails to Charlie Johnson and each email has had Jonathan Harkness as the subject.'

'So? I'm investigating a lead.'

Sian continued. 'Former Detective Inspector Pat Campbell, who worked on the original investigation as a sergeant, has informed us you were present at the scene of the crime. A fact you failed to disclose once you knew the case was being reviewed.'

'An oversight.'

'Pat Campbell told us you were one of the first uniformed officers on the scene, and you led Jonathan Harkness to the ambulance. You accompanied him to the hospital and stayed by his bed throughout the night.'

'It was my job.'

'You also kept making yourself known to the investigating team to the point where DI Ken Blackstock made a formal complaint to your superior. His exact words said you were a pest and a hindrance to the case. You were officially warned to stay away from the incident room.'

Ben's expression remained blank. His eyes were fixed on Sian, but he was looking straight through her.

'So why the obsession with Jonathan Harkness?' Masterson repeated her question.

'The case needs solving,' he snapped.

'It is currently under review as well you know.'

'Yes and look at who you've put in charge. The only case Matilda Darke can get to the bottom of is a case of Scotch. You should never have allowed her to set foot back in this station. After what she did, she should have been sacked on the spot. She might as well have killed Carl Meagan with her own bare hands.'

'Matilda Darke's return was my decision and in my opinion it was the right one. I do not have to justify myself to anyone in this station. DCI Darke is an exemplary detective. I have one hundred per cent faith that she is the best person to solve the Harkness killings.'

'Bollocks,' he exclaimed. He slammed his hands down on the table and jumped up out of his seat. 'I am Detective Chief Inspector Ben Hales of South Yorkshire Police's Murder Investigation Team and I demand some respect around here.'

The atmosphere in the interview room changed. Hales saw the expression on his colleagues change. It wasn't just his actions that were being questioned; now his sanity was in doubt too.

Chapter 50

'I'm sorry to call so late. Can I come in?'

'Oh my God, what's happened?'

'You are not going to believe this.'

Adele saw the look of triumph in Matilda's eyes as she stepped back and let her enter.

'Should I put a pot of coffee on?'

'More like crack open the champagne!'

It was almost midnight and Adele had been in bed when the pounding on the door had disturbed her from her Hilary Mantel. She was reluctant to answer at first; it was never good news when a visitor called in the dead of night, especially during treacherous weather conditions. She had hoped Chris, being the man of the house, would answer the door, but being a typical student he could sleep through an alien invasion.

Matilda headed for the living room with Adele trotting behind like a greedy puppy. She turned on the lights and then looked back at Adele with her mouth open.

'Is that what you wear to bed?'

Adele looked down at her flannel white pyjamas decorated with cartoon penguins. 'What's wrong with them?'

'Nothing if you're an eight-year-old girl.'

'They're comfortable. Besides, it's winter and I sleep alone, who

301

am I trying to impress? Look, forget what I'm wearing, tell me why you look like you've just won the lottery on the same day George Clooney announces his love for you.'

'Jonathan Harkness has been stabbed . . . '

'Oh my God!' Adele held her hands up to her mouth.

'Wait . . . Ben Hales stabbed him.'

'What the hell?!'

Matilda sat down on the sofa and crossed her legs. She visibly relaxed into the leather. Adele sat on the seat next to her but she was perched on the edge, eager for more.

'Hales practically dragged Jonathan off the street, took him to the demolition site of his childhood home, and stabbed him.'

'You're kidding me.'

'No. I was there.'

'Bloody hell. How is he?'

'I don't know. Aaron's with him at the Northern General. I suppose I should go and see how he's doing.'

She rose to leave but Adele stopped her.

'Don't you bloody dare. You don't just wake me up at silly o'clock and expect to leave after only giving me half a story. Let me get us a drink and you can start from the top.' Adele went over to the sideboard where she kept a tray of decanters and glasses. She poured two healthy measures of whisky then returned to the sofa.

'I thought you disapproved of me drinking,' she said, looking up at the elixir.

'I'm a doctor, this is medicinal.'

Matilda took a long swig of the whisky and could feel the burning liquid go down her throat. It was like the central heating had been turned on.

'So, what's going on? Where's Ben now?'

'He's being interviewed by Masterson and Sian. I was listening from the observation room. You should have heard some of the things he was saying, Adele, about me. How can he hate me so much?'

'It's not you personally. It would be anyone who held your position.'

'He just made me so angry listening to him. I could pummel him to death with my bare hands and think I've done nothing wrong.'

'Like Jonathan did to his brother, Matthew?' Adele said, off the cuff.

Matilda looked up, a sudden realization on her face. 'Do you think that's what could've happened? He'd been pushed so hard to the point of no return that he just snapped, beat his brother to death, and because it was so out of character, he wiped the entire incident from his mind.'

'It's possible I suppose. The mind is a very strange object. It can block out anything to protect you from the horror,' Adele agreed. 'What's going on with the Harkness cold case?' she asked, to break the heavy silence and stop Matilda retreating further inside her own mind.

'I've absolutely no idea,' she sighed. 'I think I know who the killer is but I'm afraid of looking stupid if I voice my opinions. Can you believe that? I've never doubted myself before in my life and now look at me.'

'Tell me,' Adele said, leaning forward in her seat.

'I think it's Jonathan,' she said after a beat, not able to look Adele in the eye.

'Jonathan? You think he killed his own parents?'

'Yes.'

'But he was only . . . what . . . eleven years old at the time?'

'That's why I'm afraid of saying anything. I can sort of understand him killing his brother, but his parents? That's taking a great deal of fathoming.'

'Well, what makes you think Jonathan did it?'

'Basic logic. He was alone in the house with his parents. There was no sign of forced entry and the doors were all locked from the inside. It's a classic locked-door mystery, but this is real life, not fiction. There was no phantom or secret passageways involved. The only reasonable person who could have killed them is Jonathan.'

'But what about the murder weapon? Why wasn't it ever found during the search?'

'That's hole number one in my theory.'

'Also, I've seen pictures of Jonathan at the age of eleven. He doesn't look physically capable of killing his parents.'

'Hole number two.'

Adele took a long swig of whisky. 'Mind you,' she mused, 'you hear stories about mothers performing Herculean acts to save their children from a burning building. I suppose it could be the same thing.'

'What are you talking about?'

'If you're filled with so much determination, so much rage and adrenaline, then it's possible you can do anything. Jonathan may have been a weedy eleven-year-old, but if he had such anger and fury at his parents bottled up inside him, then it was bound to snap at some point. Maybe he just exploded.'

'Really?'

'If you seriously suspect Jonathan of killing his parents that's the only way I can think of. You need to ask yourself, do you really, one hundred per cent believe he did it?'

'As far as I can see it is the only possible explanation.'

'And the motive?'

'I have no idea.'

'Bloody hell, Mats. You had me right in your corner then. You need to be more convinced before you go to your boss with this.'

'I know. All I need is one tiny piece of evidence and then I've got him.'

Chapter 51

South Yorkshire Police HQ was reeling from the aftermath of Ben Hales's attack on Jonathan Harkness and the fallout from his subsequent interview. It was obvious he would no longer have a job within the police, but his ending was more difficult to fathom. Was he going to face charges of attempted murder, assaulting his wife, and a very public trial, or would his resignation be enough to draw a line under the entire affair?

ACC Masterson had spent more than an hour on the phone to former Chief Superintendent Monroe, trying to convince him no good would come of his daughter pressing charges against her husband. She hoped, as a former upholder of the law, he would understand her predicament and acquiesce to her request. However, he seemed reluctant to do so.

'At the end of the day Val, he threatened my daughter. She was in fear of her life and the lives of her own daughters.'

'I'm not trying to influence your decision or that of your daughter, but the man will be losing his job.'

Having a serving officer facing a trial for stabbing a victim was one thing, having a domestic element to the case was something Masterson didn't want the public seeing. How would it look for her having a violent and emotionally unstable Acting DCI heading the MIT? The press weren't keen on Matilda Darke returning to active duty, they would slaughter her over the revelations of Ben Hales. 'I see no benefit to your daughter or your grandchildren from dragging him through the court.'

'I just think . . . '

Val cut him off. 'There is also a strong possibility Ben may be deemed unfit to stand trial. He is displaying all the signs of a manic depressive. A court case could send him over the edge and the outcome would not be in anyone's interest.'

It wasn't in Val's interest either. All morning she had been cognisant of the media and their glee over yet another high-ranking officer's downfall. With the Hillsborough Inquiry and the events of child abuse cover-up in Rotherham still making headlines, any more scandal from South Yorkshire Police could result in ACC Valerie Masterson's leadership being called into question. There was always a fall guy in these cases and the Chief Constable may think her resignation would be enough to placate the press.

There was a long silence while Monroe seemed to consider the facts. At the end of the day the decision to press charges was down to his daughter, but Monroe was clearly the driving force in her decision.

'You can consider the charges dropped. You will hear no more from me on the matter.'

Val's relief was apparent. 'And your daughter?'

'I'll smooth everything over at this end.'

With the call ended, Masterson began to relax. It was never easy to have a domestic case turn bitter. Nobody won in those cases. The stabbing of Jonathan Harkness was a different matter entirely, but from a legal point of view, it was more manageable.

In the bowels of the station, in the holding cells, Ben sat on a makeshift bed. His clothes had been removed and he was wearing a blue all-in-one. He hadn't slept and his face showed the sorry signs of fatigue, sadness, and depression. His eyes were heavy as he stared into the distance. His mind was blank, all thoughts had been deleted. His career, his marriage, and his life were all but over.

Chapter 52

It was too early for the Murder Room to be full and Matilda thought she would have the room to herself when she entered. As soon as she closed the door behind her, Sian, at the far side of the room, got to her feet. She was still wearing her coat so had not been in long.

'What are you doing?'

'I'm bleeding these sodding radiators again.'

'Any joy?'

'Well they're gurgling. I've no idea if that's a good thing or not. I thought you were going to see Jonathan Harkness in hospital.'

'I'm going in a while. I thought I'd check on things here first.'

'You mean see what's happening with Ben?'

'Am I that obvious?'

'I've known you a long time. Sit down I'll make you a coffee.'

Sian Mills, mother to the whole team, set about making two coffees while Matilda looked about the room. There wasn't a desk that actually belonged to her in here any more. She didn't feel right going into the office while it was still full of Ben's things. Instead she sat at Sian's desk.

'Do you still have the chocolate drawer?'

'Help yourself.'

307

Matilda opened the bottom drawer, helped herself to a Twix, and pushed the drawer shut with her foot just as Sian was bringing the coffees over.

'What's on your mind?'

'I've been thinking about Maun Barrington's suicide. I mean, the reason behind it is all in that scrapbook she kept, but do you think Jonathan found it, or she confessed?'

'I doubt she would confess, not after all this time. According to her note Stephen was in love with Jonathan. If she confessed to killing Stephen, he wouldn't give her a hug and forgive her would he?'

'I suppose not.'

'Maybe you should ask Jonathan Harkness what happened.'

'I will. I'm just not sure I'm going to get an honest answer out of him.'

'What are you talking about?'

'People seem to die around Jonathan. His parents, his brother, his boss, his neighbour; the people who know the most about him and can help in solving the case seem to get silenced before they can tell us anything.'

'Surely you're not suggesting Jonathan has anything to do with all of this?'

Matilda looked at her trusted colleague over the top of her coffee mug. They made eye contact and her reply was given in silence.

Sian continued. 'So you're saying Jonathan killed his parents, waited twenty years to kill his brother, then killed his boss, which he's blamed on his neighbour, and killed her, but made it look like suicide?'

Matilda scoffed. 'Sure when you say it like that it sounds crazy. Oh I don't know what I'm saying. There's just something about Jonathan that's irritating me. He's not the innocent victim he's making himself out to be. It pains me to say it, but I think Ben Hales may have been on to something by looking into Jonathan's life more thoroughly.'

308

'Go and talk to him. Sit down with him and just tell him to spill all the details on everything that's happened in the past twenty years. Off the record if you like; if you think it will make him open up more.'

'Maybe. Oh, any joy on that abandoned car that was found; was it involved in our hit-and-run? I know Maun's confessed, but it would be nice if we have evidence to back it up.'

'I meant to tell you; that guy with the lisp from forensics called late last night. I told him to email the report over to you.'

'Good. Mind if I use your computer?'

'Go ahead.'

Matilda logged on and opened her email inbox. There were over thirty unread messages. She couldn't remember the last time she had looked at them. She didn't have the time, or the interest, at the moment to go through them all. She sent the forensics report to print then briefly cast her eye over the rest of the emails. There was one from Charlie Johnson's agent with an attachment. She clicked it open, and then jumped up from the seat, sending it crashing to the floor.

'Fuck me!' she exclaimed.

Sian jumped. 'What's the matter?'

'The photo's come through from Charlie Johnson's agent. Now I know why his face wasn't on the book.'

'Why? Is he ugly?'

Matilda didn't reply. Sian put her coffee cup down and walked around to her side of the desk. She looked at the screen and into the eyes of the author of the 'definitive book' about the infamous Harkness killings.

'Bloody hell! Is that who I think it is?'

Chapter 53

'Good morning.'

Matilda had been waiting patiently for Jonathan to open his eyes. She had all the time in the world. She would have waited all day if she had to.

'Good morning,' he replied, croaking. He tried to sit up but the pain in his stomach wouldn't allow it.

He was in a private room in the Northern General Hospital and was slowly recovering from the surgery to remove the stainless-steel blade and repair his stomach wall. At one point it was touch and go whether Jonathan would survive; the internal bleeding was so severe, but the medical team battled hard throughout the night to save his life.

'How are you feeling?'

'Fragile.'

Matilda sat on a chair at the foot of the bed. She had her arms folded and her legs crossed at the ankles. Her hair, freshly washed, was neat and tidy, and her clean clothes gave off the smell of fabric conditioner.

'Will you be out for Christmas?' she asked, knowing the petty small talk would be irking Jonathan.

'I've no idea. I'm not a big Christmas fan anyway.'

'No. Me neither. I think I'll probably be working anyway. What did you do last Christmas?'

'I had lunch with Maun, my neighbour.' He frowned.

'You won't be able to do that this year will you?'

His face remained in a state of confusion.

'Haven't you heard? Maun took her own life last night. DC Fleming found her.'

'She killed herself? Why?' He looked genuinely shocked.

'I think you know the answer to that one.'

'I know she was lonely, but . . . '

'Please don't insult my intelligence, Jonathan. A neighbour saw you leave Maun's flat just minutes before you were picked up by Acting DCI Hales. You slammed the door behind you and charged down the stairs.'

'She wasn't dead when I left her.'

'No, but from what we found in her flat I think it's safe to say you stumbled upon her little secret.'

Jonathan swallowed hard. He frowned; it evidently caused him some discomfort. 'Well, actually, yes, I did.'

'I can't prove any of this, obviously, but I'm guessing an argument broke out in which you told Maun she would be better off taking her own life.'

'That's ridiculous.'

'Not really. Maun was a killer, and even though it happened a long time ago she still would have stood trial for the murder of her husband and his secretary, along with the death of Stephen Egan. I'm guessing it was Mr Egan's death that affected you more than anything else. He was an innocent bystander in all this, wasn't he?'

'Yes.' Jonathan could barely talk.

'Did Maun tell you she'd killed Stephen?'

'No. I found the album she'd kept full of press cuttings. The last entry was the car-hire receipt.'

'Which you left for us to find when we forced our way in?'

Jonathan looked at Matilda briefly before quickly breaking eye contact.

311

'So what happened then? Did you tell her to kill herself, or you'd do it for her?'

'No. It wasn't like that at all. We argued, yes, she'd killed the only person who cared about me.' He raised his voice. 'Stephen had done nothing wrong. I didn't know her any more once I'd found that out. I didn't want to stay in the same building, let alone the same room. I told her I intended moving away but she wouldn't accept that. I stormed out.'

'Was she alive when you left?'

'Of course she was.'

'You didn't give her the alcohol and bottle of pills and tell her to do you a favour?'

'If that's supposed to be a joke then I don't like your sense of humour at all. Yes, I hated Maun for what she did, but I did not kill her.'

'I believe you,' she said, and meant it. 'There is something else you could help me with, however. When we searched your flat, after you reported the attack on you by your brother, we also searched your bins. We found the usual things people throw away; empty coffee jars, empty tins, empty packets, a half empty can of deodorant.'

'So?'

'It's a silly thing to fixate on I know, but I kept wondering why you would throw away a can of deodorant that still had plenty left inside. I did wonder if you had bought a different kind than your usual and didn't like the fragrance, we've all done that, but your bathroom cabinet had three identical cans inside. I then wondered if the can in the bin was faulty, but on closer inspection I found it to be working perfectly. So then I wondered why you would just throw out a usable can of deodorant.'

Jonathan was almost smiling. 'I have no idea. I don't recall throwing it away.'

'I can actually answer the question myself. I sent the can to the lab and had it tested. I had no idea what they were going to find,

312

if anything really, but they did and the results were very surprising. There were traces of faecal matter, blood, and skin cells on it. We matched those to the swabs the doctor took on the night you reported your sexual attack, and guess what – a perfect match.'

'I don't see where you're going with this.'

'I'm sure you do. You're a very smart man and you've read a great deal of crime fiction, so you know what happens during an investigation in a sexual assault case. Unfortunately you need to read a bit more when it comes to hiding evidence. You used the can of deodorant to sodomize yourself in order to try and convince us you had been raped by your own brother.'

'I was attacked,' he said with reduced determination than the last time he'd uttered those words. 'My brother forced himself . . . '

'No he didn't. There is no evidence of your brother having sexual intercourse on the night he died. You inflicted the injuries onto yourself because, after you'd beaten your brother to death and were back in the safety of your own home, reflecting on what you'd done, you would never be able to claim self-defence. Jonathan, you kicked, beat, and stomped on your brother. What you did to him was beyond evil.'

Jonathan looked down at his shaking hands.

'You have no proof of any of this.'

'Not solid proof, no. Tell me, when Matthew came to see you that night, did he happen to reveal anything? A secret maybe that would cause you to fly off the handle?'

'No,' Jonathan replied. He looked confused again.

From her bag Matilda pulled out a dog-eared copy of Charlie Johnson's book and threw it onto his lap. He cried out at the pain to his stomach caused by jumping as the paperback landed.

'What's missing from this book?'

Jonathan looked at it but refused to pick it up. 'I've no idea.'

'I'm guessing you've read it.'

'Yes.'

'I'm guessing you've read it more than once, several times in fact.'

313

'Yes.' He bowed his head.

'You read a great deal of books so you know a lot about what goes in them; an acknowledgements section, a dedication, a biography of the author, but what else?'

Jonathan's thoughtful frown was giving him a headache. 'I don't know.'

'A photograph. A picture of the person who wrote it. You'll have noticed there isn't a snap of Charlie Johnson anywhere in this book.'

'So there isn't,' he said with a slight smile.

'So in the past twenty years when Charlie has written to you and badgered you, you never knew what he looked like, did you?'

'No.'

Matilda went into her bag once more and pulled out a folded sheet of A4 paper. She opened it carefully and placed it on his lap. 'This is Charlie Johnson.'

He laughed. 'No it isn't. That's my brother. That's Matthew.'

'Exactly.'

The world stopped turning and a heavy silence fell. Matilda sat very still in her seat staring at the patient while a wave of emotions swept over his pale and tired face. He looked shocked and confused, angry and frightened.

'You really had no idea did you?'

He shook his head.

'I've spoken to his agent. She had no idea who Charlie really was. She didn't know him as a child so didn't make the connection. She emailed me his CV and it's full of lies; claims of articles he'd written for local and national newspapers. He made himself out to be a very well-respected journalist. Nothing was checked out because the book he'd written about the murders was so incredibly well researched. Now we know why.'

Jonathan eventually spoke. 'Why would he write a book about it?'

'Now that is a question I would love to know the answer to. You really had no idea did you?'

'No.'

'So what's the real reason you killed him?'

Once again they made eye contact. He didn't try to deny it this time. The minutes ticked by without any words being spoken.

'There's nothing I can say,' he said quietly.

'You're trying to think of a lie aren't you? Why don't you just tell me the truth?'

Jonathan reached out to the bedside table and, with a shaking hand, poured himself a glass of room-temperature water. He took a long drink. He lingered over it while he came up with the words to use.

'He knew.'

'I'm sorry?'

Jonathan swallowed hard. Twenty years of keeping everything hidden from the world was about to come out. In one sense it was a relief. In another, he was sealing his fate.

'What did he know?'

'He knew what happened to Mum and Dad.'

'That you killed them?'

Jonathan nodded, refusing to say it out loud.

'How did he know?'

'He worked it out. He said his mind had been returning to events since he found out the house was to be demolished and he just put two and two together.'

'So what happened on that night twenty years ago?'

'There was a Christmas carol concert that we were going to. Mum and Dad didn't really want to go but they were quite important people in the community and it would have looked bad had they not gone. Mum came up to my bedroom and I was sat on the floor playing with my Lego. She wasn't happy as I wasn't fully dressed. I think I was only wearing my underwear and a shirt.

'She was furious as we were running late. She told me to finish getting dressed and then to get Dad to tie my bow tie. I picked the tie up and put it around my collar. Surprisingly I tied it perfectly at the first attempt. I was eleven years old and I could tie a bow tie. Can you believe that? It made me realize that if I could do that for myself what else could I do?

'I knew Mum and Dad never really wanted me. I was a mistake. In an ideal world Mum would have had an abortion. She gave birth to me and that was it. She left me to fend for myself and that's exactly what I did. Matthew was their blue-eyed boy. He got all the love and attention. I got nothing.'

'Did you really have to kill them though?'

'They neglected me. They may as well have left me in a cardboard box on the church doorstep. Don't think they're the victims in all this. They were useless parents who didn't deserve to have children. Everybody thought we were the perfect family; successful parents, two boys, and a nice house. Well, you know what; a hug wouldn't have gone amiss once in a while. That's all I wanted, a hug, to be tucked in at night, but no. I was ignored. I was invisible. Well fuck them.'

His anger exploded as the memories came to the front of his mind. He was no longer the pale, scrawny victim living on his nerves. He was a seething mass of boiling frustration and anger that was erupting from deep within.

'So what happened?' Matilda was mesmerized at his story. It was shocking to see such a timid young man turn into a cold-blooded killer before her eyes.

'I went downstairs to the kitchen. I was going to show Mum how I'd tied my tie by myself but she wasn't interested. I was just about to leave the room and my eyes locked on the block of knives. They stood out as if they were in the spotlight. I was drawn to them. I picked up the largest one and went back upstairs. You know, I didn't even have to hide it from Mum. I could have shouted at the top of my voice that I was going to stab my father and she wouldn't have batted an eyelid. That's how much interest they paid me.

'Dad was sat at his desk in their bedroom. He had some kind of speech he had to give at a dinner before New Year and he'd been fretting over it for weeks. He was hunched over, scribbling away. I didn't even creep into the room. I wasn't on tiptoes or anything,

I just marched right up to him and I slammed the knife right down into the back of his neck. I couldn't believe how easy it was.'

Matilda swallowed hard at the callous way he revealed the truth. 'The attack on your mother was more frenzied, what happened?'

'When I heard her coming up the stairs I hid behind the door. She saw the blood on Dad's white shirt as soon as she entered and ran over to him. That's when I made my move. Unfortunately she looked up and saw me reflected in the mirror. Can you believe that? She noticed me at the one time I didn't want her to. I was midway bringing the knife down when she reacted. She half turned and I stabbed her in the hand. She screamed. I think I screamed too but I just pulled it out and carried on. I couldn't stop. I think I hated her the most.'

'You didn't go mute?'

'Of course I didn't,' he laughed. 'I got the idea from an old Agatha Christie novel. There was an old woman who fell down the stairs, but it wasn't an accident. The only witness was her little dog. It was called *Dumb Witness* and I remember thinking how clever that would be; the only person who saw the crime couldn't actually say what had happened.'

'Why didn't you kill your brother all those years ago?'

'Because I wanted him to suffer. He was a bully. I told you all the things he did to me; they were all true. I wanted him to know what it would have been like to not have any parents.'

Matilda looked blank. Despite the confession she still couldn't get her head around it. 'So your motive was because you could tie a tie?'

'There was no motive. Motive suggests predetermination and I didn't plan it. The opportunity was there and I took it.'

'What happened to the knife?'

Jonathan looked up at Matilda. He looked younger somehow, as if telling his story was releasing a heavy burden he had been carrying around with him ever since it happened.

'Nice try.' He gave a smile that would have made Moriarty proud.

Chapter 54

WATERGATE CHURCH 'DIGGING UP THE DEAD'

Graves are to be dug up and moved in a bid to save a local church from collapsing.

Water main pipes at St James's Church in Watergate, Newcastle had frozen before Christmas as temperatures plunged to below minus 10C. As the thaw set in the pipes cracked and the ground beneath the church and neighbouring graveyard has become saturated, leading to weakening foundations in the eighteenth-century building.

Rev Sebastian Tolbanek said, 'This is a very delicate operation and we have no choice but to move the gravestones and coffins in order to save the site and undertake precise work on the church. We will do our utmost to be considerate to the graves and families of the dead. I have personally written to all the families involved and informed them of our plans.

'We need to dry out the land before work can begin in the early spring. I hope to have the graveyard restored before the end of the summer. In the meantime, family members will still be able to pay their respects to loved ones buried here.'

The Church has been raising funds for the project for the past three years. However, the recent bitter weather has forced work to begin early.

Rev Tolbanek has promised that any coffins which are too damaged to be removed from the ground will be respectfully dealt with and arrangements for reburial made after consultation with surviving relatives.

New Year's Day – Ten days later

Matilda Darke was alone in the incident room. She had worked all through the Christmas and New Year period, despite protestations from Adele and Val Masterson. Her mother had eventually got through to her on Christmas Eve and practically begged her down the phone to join the family. She apologized and said she wanted to ignore Christmas as much as possible this year, but promised she would make the effort next year. She enjoyed a late Christmas lunch with Adele and Chris, and at one point, as they exchanged gifts, Matilda forgot everything in the world and felt a modicum of happiness. It wasn't long before she remembered her reality and was no longer in the mood to celebrate the festive season. If she had stayed with the Keans she would have dragged their mood down to her level and they didn't deserve that. She thanked them, not just for their presents and hospitality, but for everything. Then she left.

This Christmas was a complete contrast to the one before. She'd had four days off work and had spent them all at home with James. They'd cooked a big lunch together, opened gifts together, and watched *Doctor Who* together, completely closed off from the outside world. They loved every minute of it.

James had recently been diagnosed with a brain tumour but had been told it was benign. They knew he would be facing a delicate operation in the coming months, but for the festive season they were not dwelling on that. When he went for a follow-up MRI scan on January 6 he was told the bad news; the tumour had rapidly mutated and there was nothing they could do. Matilda and James would not be celebrating another Christmas together.

The door to the Murder Room opened and DC Scott Andrews entered wearing a new coat and new matching scarf and gloves, obviously a Christmas present.

'What are you doing here?' Matilda asked, looking up.

'I swapped with Rory. Apparently his fiancée's parents were having a New Year's Eve party in Dumfries so I said I'd work today for him.'

'Didn't you have any New Year plans?'

'Not unless you count sitting in the local boozer with your neighbours waiting for the clock to hurry up and get to midnight so you can make an excuse to go home and plan.'

Matilda smirked. 'Put the kettle on Scott and we'll finish off those chocolate biscuits Sian brought in on Boxing Day. Nice coat by the way.'

'Thanks,' he beamed. 'I went to Meadowhall for the sales.'

'You're a brave man. Was it busy?'

'Packed. I got elbowed, shoved, and stepped on. Never again.'

Matilda laughed. She was never a fan of shopping, especially for clothes. Items that she liked always looked better on the mannequins than on her. It didn't help that the mannequins had perfect figures, while she was a misshaped size 12 with chunky thighs.

Scott brought over the box of biscuits, balancing two cups of tea on top, and set it down on Matilda's desk. 'Have you heard any more about DI Hales?' he asked, using his correct title now that Matilda seemed to be back full-time.

'No. The ACC is waiting until we get over the New Year celebra-tions before a decision is made. Same with us really, too.'

'What do you mean?'

'The MIT is up for review. Give it a month and we may all be investigating burglaries and car thefts.'

'Great start to the New Year. Perhaps I should have kept the receipts.' Andrews slumped in his seat and looked despondent. 'Any resolutions?'

'No. I don't bother with that kind of thing,' she lied. She had promised herself to change her life around this coming year, be more positive, and show the world and her boss that she was back to her best. 'How about you?'

'No. I was talking to my sister about it the other day and neither of us have got any vices we'd like to give up. We're a bloody boring family.'

The phone rang; the first time since Matilda arrived four hours ago.

'I'm trying to reach a Detective Chief Inspector Matilda Darke,' said a very strong and deep Newcastle accent.

'You've reached her. How can I help?'

'I'm Detective Sergeant Kevin Schofield from Newcastle CID. I gather you're working on the Harkness double killings.'

Something told Matilda that this was going to be a phone call that would make her day. She sat up and listened.

Andrews could tell from her face that this was an important call. He froze, midway through dunking a chocolate biscuit into his tea, and stared at her with raised eyebrows.

'I am indeed.' Her mouth was dry with anticipation.

'I don't know if you've heard about the problems we've been having with the weather up here, but a church has had a burst water pipe and the whole graveyard is having to be dug up in order to lay new pipes.'

Matilda had no idea where this was going and was starting to lose interest. She looked into the box of biscuits to see which one she would have next.

DS Schofield continued. 'A few of the coffins, naturally, have become very fragile over the years and several disintegrated when they were removed. As I'm sure you can imagine this is not a pleasant sight. As the workmen were clearing up one particular grave they found something and called us in. We think it may be of some use to you.'

Once again Matilda's interest was piqued. 'Go on.'

'The grave belonged to a Clara Ann Harkness. Does the name ring a bell?'

'Yes it does.'

'As the coffin was lifted out of the grave it practically disintegrated. Inside the coffin we found a seven-inch kitchen knife. It was heavily rusted but tests have shown traces of blood around the base of the handle. We're still waiting for DNA results to come back, but I thought you'd be interested.'

'I am very interested,' she said. 'You have no idea how interested I am. DS Schofield you may have just become my new best friend.'

There was no time to lose. DC Andrews followed Matilda out of the room, trotting to keep up with her long strides. She hadn't explained to him what the call was about, that could be done in the car; she just told him to grab his new coat. She had a beaming smile on her face. This was the start to the New Year she was looking for. Fingers crossed it was an omen and her fortunes were about to change for the better.

'So you knew all along that Jonathan killed his family?' Scott asked from the passenger seat.

'Not all along, but I suspected. He did confess from his hospital bed, but there was no way I could have used it and he was hardly likely to give me a signed statement. It was evidence that I needed, and that has been the one thing that's been lacking throughout the whole case.'

'Until now.'

'Until now,' she repeated, and grinned.

They pulled up outside Jonathan's apartment block and Matilda couldn't get her seatbelt off quick enough.

It was a very cold morning. The snow that had fallen just before Christmas was still covering the pavements. It would be a long time before a thaw would set in. Everything was coated in a thick layer of frost and the roads were extremely slippery. Walking was a very difficult task. Matilda didn't care. She took great confident steps while Andrews was more cautious behind her.

Inside, the building wasn't much warmer either, but Matilda wasn't interested in the temperature. She had her mind set on producing her evidence to Jonathan and watching the look on his face drop. His lifetime of manipulation was finally over.

She rang the bell and rang it again barely a couple of seconds later. There was no reply, so she knocked loudly and rang once more.

The front door to the flat opposite opened and a large elderly woman resting all her weight on a walking frame appeared.

'What's going on?' she asked, fighting for breath.

The heat that came out from behind her hit the two detectives in the face. It was no surprise she was struggling for breath living in a sauna.

'We're looking for Jonathan Harkness. Do you know where he is?'

'He went out last night. Are you the police?'

'Yes.'

'Is one of you Matilda Darke?'

Matilda and Scott looked at each other and almost smiled. 'Yes. I am.'

'He left a letter for you. He asked me to give it to you if you came looking for him. Do you want it?'

'Yes please.' She frowned. Of course she wanted it.

The elderly neighbour went back into her flat to get the letter. She took her time and was very wobbly on her feet. They waited and continued to wait until she eventually returned. She apologized for keeping them waiting and made a joke about it not being fun getting old. They said their goodbyes and the neighbour went back to the boiler room she called her flat.

Matilda turned away from Andrews and opened the envelope. Inside was a letter and a newspaper cutting from a couple of days ago which told the story of the cemetery at Watergate being dug up. She read the headline but didn't bother with the story. The letter was more important to her.

Dear Matilda,

The enclosed newspaper article is going to give you the ending to the story you require to solve and close the case. It is the evidence you have been seeking.

I suppose the sensible thing to do would have been to come into the station and confess in person but I'm just so tired of it. I'm tired of telling the story and I don't think I have the energy to say it all one more time.

I thought I had found the perfect hiding place for the knife. If it hadn't been for the burst water pipe it would have remained undetected forever. Unfortunately, I should have realized I'm not that lucky and my Aunt Clara has betrayed my secret. I don't hold it against her though.

History will show me to be a psychopathic murderer but I would hate for my parents to be seen as the eternal victims. They truly were horrible to me. I don't believe people are born evil, I believe they are made evil, and the neglect and hurtful upbringing I had turned me into the person I became.

The only regret I have is that Stephen Egan somehow managed to get embroiled in my life and paid the ultimate price. He is the only victim in all of this and I shall apologize to him in the only way I know how.

I am pleased it is you who handled the case in the end. You have been given a tough time by the press over Carl Meagan and you don't deserve it at all. Any crime writer would be lucky to have you as their heroine.

I hope you will soon have faith restored in your career.
Regards,
Jonathan Stefan Harkness

324

'What is it?' Scott asked, after Matilda had finished reading the letter and looked up.

'It's Jonathan's confession and I think his suicide note too.'

'Suicide? Shall I get on to uniform to come and knock his door down?'

'No. I don't think he'll be in there.'

'Then where is he then?'

Matilda didn't reply. Slowly, she walked past Andrews and out of the building. She didn't say a word to him as she drove them down the street and turned left. She knew exactly where she was going.

She had solved the case, or rather the case had been solved for her, but she didn't feel any euphoria or celebration, she felt empty.

She turned into Abbey Lane Cemetery and pulled up at the side of the road. A large cemetery, it has more than 25,000 graves. Unless you know where to go you could spend days trying to find what you're looking for. Matilda knew exactly where to go.

She walked in silence and at a slow pace over the hard frozen ground through row after row of well-kept graves; white marble headstones with gold lettering, black headstones with a framed picture of a much-missed loved one. The older tombs were grander, with more ornate stonework. Over the years tastes had simplified and less was certainly more.

At the end of a row was the grave she was looking for, and she stopped in her tracks. Scott almost bumped into her. She looked ahead at the sight she had been expecting.

The grave belonged to Stephen Egan, and on the ground just under the headstone, lying in the foetal position, was the frozen body of Jonathan Harkness. He was curled up tight, arms firmly wrapped around his knees. His face was pale and his lips blue; a coating of frost in his hair and his dry eyes wide open.

Acknowledgements

There are many people who have helped me in the publication of this book. Firstly, I would like to thank my brilliant publisher, Kate Stephenson, and the rest of the team at Killer Reads and Harper Collins. Their hard work has turned my dream into a reality and I shall be forever thankful for them.

I have received invaluable support from Margaret Murphy, Danuta Reah, Adele Ward, and Chris Simmons. Their knowledge and words of wisdom were very well received and I hope my constant questions didn't annoy them too much.

A massive thank you must go to my good friends Jonas Alexander for helping me out of plot holes, the coffees and the laughs, and Chris Schofield and Kevin Embleton for the weekends away from reality.

Finally, to my mum – a wonderful and strong woman who has always believed in me from the start, and encouraged me to continue even when I wanted to give in. I will never be able to thank you enough for your support. The homemade cakes helped too.

A special thank you to Woody; the perfect writing companion – always listening, never criticising.